KAREN DUPREE WAS YOUNG, ANGRY, CUNNING . . .

She was just the kind of person Prescott could convert into one of his best assassins.

"Good morning, Karen."

"Good morning, Doctor Prescott."

"How are you feeling?"

"A little tired."

The preliminaries out of the way, the session began.

Karen sitting at a table, empty soda can in front of her. She doesn't move, just sort of casually looks at the can. The can lofts into the air and begins to spin around like a top. Then it begins to ricochet off the walls. And then—a giant, invisible hand seizes the can and proceeds to crush it the way macho teenagers crush their beer cans.

The session presses on, and soon they reach the final part of the test, the fire. This is the most difficult part for Karen. She has more often failed than succeeded. A cardboard box is filled with a number of items. Simple things first. A piece of typing paper.

"Just concentrate on it, Karen. You have the power. All we're trying to show you is how to have the power instantly when you want it and need it."

The right bottom edge of the paper ignites. . . .

Suspense-filled DAW Fiction by ED GORMAN:

DAUGHTER OF DARKNESS
RITUALS

RITUALS

ED GORMAN

DAW BOOKS, INC.
DONALD A. WOLLHEIM, FOUNDER
375 Hudson Street, New York, NY 10014
ELIZABETH R. WOLLHEIM
SHEILA E. GILBERT
PUBLISHERS
www.dawbooks.com

Cover art by Don Brautigam.

DAW Book Collectors No. 1213.

DAW Books are distributed by Penguin Putnam Inc.

All characters and events in this book are fictitious.
Any resemblance to persons living or dead is strictly coincidental.

First Printing, February, 2002
1 2 3 4 5 6 7 8 9

DAW TRADEMARK REGISTERED
U.S. PAT. OFF. AND FOREIGN COUNTRIES
—MARCA REGISTRADA.
HECHO EN U.S.A.

PRINTED IN THE U.S.A.

For Ann and Kelly Laymon,
and in memory of Dick.

I couldn't have finished this novel without the patience and help of Sheila Gilbert, my editor; and Carol, my wife.

PROLOGUE

"There were two types of victims in Salem during that time—those who were genuinely believed to be possessed of satanic powers and those used opportunistically. If one man wanted another's land, what could be more convenient than for the landowner to be called possessed—even though he clearly wasn't? All sorts of very human motives were at play in Salem . . . having nothing to do with satanic powers. What better way to get rid of an enemy than to drag him before a crazed jury?"

—Thomas Finch, *The Real Story of Salem*

DORCAS had the nightmare again, and not even her parents could comfort her there in the small hut on the edge of the village.

She was twelve but small enough to sit comfortably in the lap of her father next to the guttering flame of the fireplace.

"And you were accused again?"

"Yes, Father."

"And it was the Reverend?"

"No, Father. His wife. She followed me around the village and then into the woods and called me the same name over and over again."

She did not have to repeat the name, for it was the most dreaded word in all of the Colonies. The name that had seen thousands burned at the stake in Europe. The name that was now resounding from Puritan pulpits all across this new land.

"I told you, child," her mother said, pulling a shabby blanket around her shoulders, shivering there in the dirt-floor darkness of the hut. "You should never have told the woman what her husband did to you."

Last year, when Dorcas had been working in the rectory, the Reverend had taken her upstairs to his study and taken certain obscene liberties with her. Afraid that he would do those things again, Dorcas foolishly told the Reverend's wife what had happened.

And not long after, the woman began telling everyone in the village of Salem that Dorcas was possessed of Satan. The trials here were already underway. Such was the frantic suspicion of the citizens—signs of Satan seemed to be everywhere; just a fortnight ago an esteemed citizen swore he saw the face of the devil imposed upon the full moon— that no one had trouble believing that Dorcas was a siren of hell.

Her father, hoping to forestall the inevitable, went to the Reverend's wife and said that Dorcas had never told anyone else of her husband's strange passion. And never would. Only their family would know the secret and they would keep it forever.

But the woman only slapped him and spat upon him and said how dare he tell such vile lies. And in the village, in the ensuing days, her accusations only got louder, her demands that the child be put on trial more strident.

"We must send her away," the mother whispered after they finally got their daughter back to sleep this night.

But even before the father could reply, a knock so violent it shook the entire hut fell upon the door and three men with torches pushed themselves inside.

One of the men was the good Reverend himself.

"I am told that the girl Dorcas lives here," said the stoutest of the men, hidden inside his vast cloak on such a frosty night.

And then he saw her in the shadowy corner, on the poor cot.

"Take her," he said to his companions.

The father lunged toward his daughter, hoping to shield her. But the Reverend turned him quickly aside with a club.

Dorcas screamed as she came awake.

Out of a fantasy nightmare and into a real one.

The mother did all she could—knelt next to the husband whose head ran with blood. The good Reverend's club had opened up a wide gash on the back of her man's head.

The sound of massive horses thundered away, the screams of the girl somehow muffled now. The sounds of the father's bitter sobs mixed with his moans of pain.

Gone, she was. Gone unto the prison and the vile judgment and the death that had lately afflicted this small village.

1

THEN

SO one warm afternoon in the autumn of 1975 the two girls walked out the west door of Woodrow Wilson High School and saw a small crowd standing around Laura Caine's car.

There were intimations something was going to happen because of the way Cam Morgan had treated Laura Caine last night. Said he wasn't going to take it anymore. Said not only he but everybody knew what Laura and her friend Abby Stewart were. And said that everybody at the whole school laughed about them behind their backs. And made dirty jokes about them.

One girl in the crowd around Laura's 1965 bronze Mustang hardtop saw them coming and whispered to the other kids. The whole crowd was suddenly watching them. Smirking. The kids in the crowd were kids she'd known since grade school. Friends, she'd thought. But now they wore the harsh masks of enemies.

Laura felt sick. The rumors weren't true, and even if

they had been, nobody deserved to be treated like this. Cam blamed everything on Abby, including the fact that Laura wasn't ready to sleep with him yet. But Laura wanted to make sure he was the right boy for her. She didn't like being a virgin but she wanted to be sure he wouldn't dump her a few weeks after they first made love. Cam had dumped his share of girls.

The crowd parted into neat halves. A few kids sat in their cars watching everything play out. A lot of the kids had obviously been told in advance what was going to happen in the parking lot after school. Somebody should have sold tickets. A Donna Summers disco song on a car radio collided in midair with the strains of the marching band practicing nearby.

And then Laura and Abby saw it. A single word in sloppy whitewash across the trunk: DYKE.

Laura's cheeks were a shade of red; Abby's face seemed to lose all blood.

They could have reacted a number of ways but neither wanted to give the crowd the pleasure of seeing their pain. They walked silently to the car, the crowd moving back.

This was one of the few times the Mustang gave Laura trouble. The motor wouldn't kick over. It took five tries. Neither girl said anything. They didn't even look at each other, as if doing so would just confirm what the crowd was accusing them of.

The Mustang finally fired and lurched out of the parking lot. Some of the boys were yelling now. They tried not to hear the words. Laura leaned forward, snapped on the radio. An Eagles song. She turned it up. Way up.

Laura and Abby had lived on the same moneyed

block since they were little girls. Laura's father was a famous neurologist, Abby's father a prominent investment banker in nearby Boston. They had always been straight A students and were generally considered the two best-looking girls in their class, Laura, the dark-haired one, Abby, with the red hair. Such girls were frequently the social heads of their class, too. But not Laura and Abby. They'd grown up together and they pretty much stayed together. They didn't have many other friends. While Abby had yet to date much, Laura's folks pretty much demanded that she start dating now that she'd turned sixteen. "A nice, normal life, is that too much to ask?" her mother had said in great frustration. So she dated. But she rarely went out with a boy a second time and if Abby asked her to go to a movie or something, even on a Saturday night, Laura always went. So pretty soon the boys she'd dated started bitching about how good old Abby always took precedence. And it didn't take a giant leap of faith—not for the uninformed male high school mind it didn't—to conclude that maybe, just maybe, Laura and Abby were what the *Penthouse* letter column always referred to as lesbos.

And now it had come to this.

Laura paid no attention to where she was driving. Nor did Abby. They still hadn't spoken. They were lost in their separate reactions to the word on the back of the trunk.

Finally, Abby said, "Go over to the car wash. Let's wash it off."

"Good idea."

"And you can turn the radio down. It's killing my ears."

"I was trying to drown them out."

"I know. But they're not calling us dykes anymore."

"Did you see Sara Coburn? God, I made my first communion with her. We shared a locker last year. And she was right there with them today. Laughing at us. I was scared."

"I wasn't. I was mad."

"You're stronger than I am. I wanted to cry."

"Oh, shit, I wanted to cry, too. But mostly I just wanted to tear their faces off. They looked so hateful, like we were some kind of freaks—or aliens. Or something."

The car wash was one of those do-it-yourself deals. The whitewash came off easily. The spraying water made a rainbow. The hot water smelled sort of sour. The big blue brushes slimed the sides of the car, then shimmied the slime away.

Abby said, "Maybe tomorrow I'll come to school with a dildo strapped to my forehead."

Laura laughed. She'd always envied Abby her ability to say outrageous things. "Maybe you'll start a fad."

"Maybe I should sleep with the whole football team."

"Nah. They'd just think you were trying to prove we aren't gay."

"How do you prove you're not gay?"

"God, I don't know."

"Well, I guess there's one thing we could do," Abby said.

"What?"

"Quit making out with each other in study hall."

Laura gave Abby a playful shrug.

Neither of them felt like going home so they stopped by a 7–11 and bought a package of Larks and two big Slurpees. And then they headed out to the country. They loved the country, especially smoky autumn with the pumpkins and the scarecrows in the fields.

Cam Morgan's car showed up in her rearview mirror a little bit after four o'clock. "Guess who?"

Abby turned around. Checked it out. "They've been following us."

"Apparently."

"Pricks."

"I wish I had a gun."

"You? With a gun? Yeah, right."

Laura giggled. "Well, my little brother's squirt gun, maybe."

The Ford Fairlane sped up. Closing the distance. Such a lovely, elegiac day. Wasted now on some dumb game of Cam Morgan's.

"What if they knew our real secret," Abby said.

"No kidding."

Cam swept down on them. Close enough that they could see the other boy in the front seat, the two boys in the back. Cam honking his horn. Flashing his brights.

"Now there's a really mature kid," Abby said. "I can see why you fell in love with him."

"I almost fell in love with him."

"I guess he didn't hear the almost part."

The road here was flat and straight. She sped up. He sped up. She sped up more. He sped up more.

"God, Laura, be careful. No offense but you're a real shitty driver."

"I'm a shitty driver? How about you? You creamed your dad's new Jag."

"Just the fender."

"And the grille."

"Part of the grille. Not the whole grille."

The honking got more insistent. She gave it more gas. She was doing eighty. He was right on top of her.

They went that way for a long stretch. Laura started getting nervous. She actually was a shitty driver (but then so was Abby). She didn't have the confidence other drivers her age seemed to have. She still got confused between second and third gears sometimes. And she still tromped on the brake sometimes when she meant to hit the gas. All of which made for some fun rides.

It happened when the curve came up. One minute you were on a ruler-straight road and the next there were all these signs warning you about this "Dangerous Curve." No shit dangerous.

"God, slow down!" Abby said.

Which was when Laura, Laura-who-meant-to-hit-the-brake-Laura, became Laura-who-instead-hit-the-gas-Laura.

Abby screamed.

The Mustang went into the corner at sixty-seven miles per hour. It went in screeching, lurching left, lurching right, resisting all of Laura's attempts to bring it under control, and heading straight for the deep gully on the east side of the curve.

Cam Morgan's sense—as he watched terrified, horrified, and already blaming himself, as he should have, for what was unfolding before him—was that the Mustang was going to go sailing right off the road and into the gully. Just the way at least six other fatalities occurred in the past ten years. This curve was notorious.

When the rear tires began fishtailing, Laura felt as if she were going to lose her lunch. No matter how much white-knuckled force she applied to the steering wheel, it just wouldn't obey her.

The gully loomed. The fishtailing abated but she couldn't right the car. Abby screamed again.

The rubber tires gripped at last. Not only gripped but took the sharp orders the steering mechanisms had been sending them. The Mustang found the one true path and clung to it. They survived the curve.

Cam Morgan had had time and skill enough to go into the curve at the proper rate of speed. He slowed down to thirty-five to allow the girls plenty of space to resume driving at a normal speed.

"She scared the shit out of herself," Billy Mayhew said from the back seat.

"I thought dykes were fearless," joked Rick Sullivan.

"Shut up," Cam said. "We never should've followed her like this."

"Aw, little Cam's in love," said Mike Hopkins, the kid in the front seat.

Cam grabbed him by the shirtfront so violently that Hopkins' eyeglasses went flying off. "You hear what I said? I said to shut up. And I mean all of you. This was a stupid idea."

"Yeah," Rick Sullivan said, "and it was all yours."

"That's the worst thing of all," Cam said. "That it was my stupid fucking idea."

Laura had never really had the shakes before. Where you can't control the violent twitching of your arms or legs. Her fingers danced on the steering wheel. She couldn't grip it for more than a few seconds.

"Wow, look at your leg."

Abby was right. Laura's right leg was cavorting crazily. So viciously it looked as if she were faking it. Did limbs really do that? This one did.

"You better pull over, Laura."

Same thing Laura was thinking. She forgot all about asshole Cam Morgan behind her. Forgot about the word that had been whitewashed across her trunk.

Just aimed the Mustang, now down to twenty-four miles per hour, to the grassy side of the road. Turned off the engine.

Abby lit cigarettes for both of them. "Here. You need this."

"Thanks."

Set her head against the back of the seat. Closed her eyes. Tried to will her limbs to stop doing this voodoo dance. Spooky, as her little brother would say. Some kind of convulsion.

Cam Morgan pulled his car off the road to the shoulder. Maybe fifty feet behind her.

"What the hell you doin', man?" Mike Hopkins demanded.

"I'm going up there and tell her I'm sorry."

"You're crazy. She'll kill you."

Cam didn't say anything. Just got out of the car, taking his keys with him. These dip shits, you never knew.

"I need to get out and walk around a little," Laura said. "Some air."

"That'll probably help. I'll get out with you."

It was when Laura was getting out of the car that it happened. You took her weakness, her disorientation, her trembling legs and it wasn't all that surprising. Somehow, just as she was setting her second foot down on the ground, one leg became entangled with the other. And when she tried to walk, she stumbled. And when she stumbled, she fell on the ground. Fell in such a way that her left arm, slightly canted inward anyway, hit in just the right way to break. About three inches down from the elbow.

Abby was just coming around the front end of the car and saw it from behind. Laura's cry was not only one of pain but of frustration and anger—all her feelings of the last hour or so contained within the complex animal cry that said I've had enough now. Back off. Leave me alone. And by the way, fuck you.

And when she looked up—Oh, great, just what I need—there was none other than Cam Morgan, sans his usual swagger, walking toward her down the dusty shoulder of the road.

Even from here he could see how angry she was.

Her fall had been right out of a cartoon. And his first impulse had been to laugh. Thank God he didn't. Because now that she was starting to pick herself up, he saw the funny way her arm was bent. And the anguish that carved deep lines of grief into her elegant face.

He hurried toward her. The least he could do—

Abby came around the far end of the car.

This time, he did permit himself the luxury of a quick smile. How fitting that they would both be rushing to Laura, vying for the right to help her. Maybe they really weren't lesbians—deep down he guessed he knew they weren't—but they had one of those relationships that no outsider could penetrate. Not even the boyfriend.

By the time he reached them, Abby had Laura not only on her feet but sitting on the hood of the Mustang. Examining the arm.

"It's broken," Cam said.

"Oh, gosh," Abby said, "thank God medical help has arrived." She couldn't control herself: "Yes, it is broken, you asshole. And it's all because of you."

"Laura, I'm sorry I was such a jerk. God, if I could just go back one hour—"

"Just get out of here, Cam," Abby said.

"How about letting Laura speak for herself?" Cam said and moved closer to the hood of the car. "I don't blame you if you never forgive me, Laura. I love you and I'm sorry I was such a jerk. I just want you to know that." He looked down at her broken arm. Tears gleamed in his eyes. Abby was right. He was the cause of this. The serrated line of bone just beneath the taut flesh of her arm. Her slender, dear arm. *God, why the hell did I ever do anything like that?* This was one of those unreal moments when the mind doesn't want to fully accept what's going on, keeps trying to deny what's going on. But her busted arm, the pain on her face, and Abby's scowl and angry words made denial impossible.

"You need to go, Cam," Laura said quietly. "Please."

"You should go to the emergency room."

"I'll take care of her, Cam. You just go back with your friends and find somebody else to pick on."

Yeah, you'll take care of her. Just the way you always take care of her. So nobody else has a chance of getting to her. They were friends, had been since they were five years old. And he was jealous. It was weird, being jealous of a girl and not a boy. Laura trusted Abby in a way that she'd never trusted Cam—Cam the high school heartbreaker.

"I'm sorry, Laura."

"You've said that several times already, Cam. Now get the hell out of here."

"Just go, Cam," Laura said, still quiet. Holding her arm and grimacing.

So Cam went. What the hell choice did he have?

When they were back on the road—Cam and his friends long gone—Abby said, "Maybe this is the time to try it."

"It only ever worked that one time before."

"Yeah. That sweet little puppy."

"Cam looked so sad."

"God, Laura, listen to yourself. He calls us dykes, he harasses us on the road, and he causes you to break your arm. Who cares how sad he looked?"

"I just meant that he's sort of a jerk but he's sort of not a jerk, either."

"You're in love with him."

Laura looked out the window. They were headed back to town. Late afternoon shadows in the fiery autumn fields and trees. A long freight train, boxcars shimmying, running down a long straight two-mile stretch of track. Town girls prim in their riding attire as they rode their horses at an equestrian academy. "Maybe I am."

Abby said, with an air of reluctance, "I'm jealous."

"Oh, gosh, Abby, just because I love him doesn't mean you and I—"

"No. Not jealous of him. Jealous of you. I want my own boyfriend."

"Well, jeeze, as good-looking as you are—"

"It isn't just looks. Boys scare me. Terrify me. I'm not even sure I'll have a date for the Thanksgiving dance—"

Laura cried out. The pain was less frequent now but when it came, it was like an execution. Her whole body danced to its tune.

"It's worth a try, anyway," Abby said.

She whipped the car off on to a gravel road and drove for a quarter mile to a small parklike area. No cars, no bicycles, no motorcycles, no horses. Perfect. And perfectly empty.

She pulled the car up alongside the small brick building with the sloped roof where you could use the toilet facilities or study maps or join hundreds of others in leaving dirty messages behind.

"Maybe we should just go to the emergency room," Laura said.

"Just give me a sec, all right?"

Abby took Laura's arm. Lightly touched the torn bone beneath the skin. Closed her eyes. That time with the puppy, it had flowed from her sense of the puppy's goodness. She'd made some kind of mindlink with it and had been overwhelmed at the sweet, playful, appreciative nature of the puppy's soul. The puppy got positively rhapsodic about all the things in God's universe—butterflies, Frisbees, Puppy Chow, his master's ample lap, sunlight, the blanket in the cardboard box he slept in. So many, many things he loved in his simple, wonderful way. It was easy for her to meld with this joyousness and goodness and to help—as a conduit for a cosmic power that organized religion with its smugness only dimly perceived—heal the puppy's broken left hind leg.

Even Laura, good as she was, would be more problematic than the puppy. Human beings being much more complex, their goodness could never be as singular as an animal's. Making it, or so Abby thought, a whole hell of a lot tougher to effect a healing. And it didn't always work with animals, either. She'd tried a bird with a broken wing, a lame horse, a raccoon with a savage wound. And nothing. Had the puppy been a fluke? Or maybe even a self-delusion? Maybe she hadn't really healed the puppy at all. Maybe she and Laura had just fooled themselves into thinking the bone was healed.

"I could really use a cigarette," Laura said.

"I don't think you can smoke when I'm doing this."

"Why not?"

"I don't know. It's like farting in church or something."

Laura laughed. "I don't think you should make smart-ass remarks at a time like this, either."

"Just shut up so I can get in the mood, will you?"

"I just keep thinking of Cam's face."

"I just keep thinking of your broken arm. So will you shut the hell up and let me concentrate."

"This isn't going to work."

"One of the things we're s'posed to be able to do is heal."

"Sometimes. That's what my mother says. Very rarely. Upon occasion. And mostly animals. Human beings hardly ever. Oh, shit, it really hurts. Please, Abby, can't we just go to the hospital?"

But Abby was gone. Somewhere. No idea where, if she'd been asked. Just somewhere—not in the car. Not in the town. Not in the county. Not in the state. Not in the country. Some netherworld. That's where she was. Some netherworld.

What she was doing—or trying to do—was plug into that same oneness she'd found with that poor little puppy. The trouble was she had to find the total goodness in the soul/spirit/whatever-you-wanted-to-call-it of her friend Laura. And with Laura there were certain problems. Laura could be—not often but sometimes—crabby, secretive, haughty, selfish, dense and mean. All this was a subjective call on Abby's part, of course, and it might not, in any objective way, even be true. But because she perceived it was true, it hampered her mindmerge.

Which was when she concentrated on all the good things about her friend. Her generosity, her intelligence, her loyalty, her humor, her patience, and her wisdom. Because she really did have wisdom. The same girl who could be so silly—Tampax sticking out of her ears—could also be so freaking wise it was phenomenal. Abby liked/respected/loved her so much. So much.

"Help me!" Abby cried.

And for the first time ever, they joined as one in a mindmerge, Laura, startled, could feel their consciousnesses meld.

Abby didn't see it happen—didn't even hear the stuff Laura said when it started to happen—didn't have the foggiest notion until she started swimming through the dark waters of the netherworld and began to see daylight and shore.

"You did it, Abby! You did it! Look!"

And there was Laura flouncing her arm around. No serrated edge of bone pushing against the soft white skin and the golden down. She was twisting it, turning it, waving it. And no pain. No pain at all.

"You did it, Abby! You did it!"

"Wow, I was really out! But it wasn't just me. It was the two of us. We were stronger together."

"Wait till I tell my mom," Laura said.

"Yeah, wait till I tell my mom!"

On the way home, Laura kept running her fingers over the area of bone that had been broken. She knew enough to thank God. She wasn't sure what God was, only that He/She/It or whatever was up there-out there-in there-over there someplace.

"He saw it."

"Huh?" Abby said.

"Cam. He saw that my arm was broken."

"So?"

"So tomorrow I go to school and I don't have a broken arm."

"It's his word against ours." Abby smiled. "Anyway, they'll be too worried about us being lesbos to worry about a broken arm."

Laura laughed. "Is that supposed to be good news?"

NOW

A while back somebody had made the smart-ass remark that Dr. Abby Stewart was at the cemetery more often than the funeral director was.

With good reason, of course. Her daughter and her best friend were buried here.

This particular sunny autumn day was a special visit. An entire bouquet of yellow roses, not just one or two. And spending an hour, not just fifteen or twenty minutes as she did on her usual twice-weekly visits.

Things're going pretty well, Jenna. I got through your father's wedding much better than I thought I would. You know how I like to pretend that I'm this sophisticated, big-city woman. Even kept my maiden name when I married your dad. So when he invited me I thought, Why not? I'll show him that I've gotten over him. That I can handle it now.

But, oh, honey, I'm such a hick. The governor was there and a couple of the movie stars your dad's ad agency works with on commercials and all kinds of high-powered executives. And the bride. She's so young, your father could get arrested. That was the joke going around anyway. When I saw her, I wanted to run and hide. I looked like his mother compared to her.

The one good thing was we had a nice talk about you. Just your father and I. This is your fifteenth birthday and that's what we talked about. What you'd be doing now; and how you'd be going to Smith soon. You know what a snob your dad is. Smith or nothing for his little girl.

That's the only thing we have in common these days.

You. But that's a very strong bond, kiddo. The strongest bond of all, really.

I did my crying last night. You know, about what happened to you and everything. So I'm going to do us a favor, honey, and spare us both the tears.

Oh, damn. Look what time it is. My practice is my blessing and my curse. It kept me sane after you died, sweetheart; and after your father announced he was leaving. But it sure doesn't give me much time. I always felt so guilty about being so busy all the time. And you spending so much time alone when you were so little.

Oh, shit. I promised no tears, and now look. Sorry. I just had this image of you as a little girl and—

Damn tears anyway.

I've got to get back, sweetie. I'll see you Saturday sometime. I sure love you.

And then the shudder and the stark memories of Jenna's death, the ultimate mindmerge when your consciousness joined with theirs to share the panic and horror of their death. There was no escaping this. Even when you used the drugs that repressed most of your special talents and powers (in the wrong moment, you might reveal yourself and your true nature to a stranger, so it was easier to take drugs which left you no more powerful than your neighbors) . . . even with the drugs, you shared the terrors of those closest to you when they were in trouble or dying. And you never forgot those moments, either. Never.

Some white witches went insane after experiencing the ultimate mindmerge; a few even committed suicide.

Abby had nightmares.

The cemetery was an old one. Some of the oaks and elms went back two hundred years. On the west end you could see the ancient iron gates where the original entrance had been. And the narrow dirt path where the fancy black horse-drawn funeral carriage used to pull up.

On her way down the hill to where her white Volvo waited, she made note of some of the gravestones. Family friends; a few former patients. She'd been practicing in Hastings Corner for the past ten years and in the course of it had lost many of her older patients and even—worst of all—a few young ones.

Near the bottom of the slope was the other grave site she always stopped to visit.

LAURA CAINE MORGAN

1960–2000

The Envy of Angels

Hey, Laura, what a beautiful day, huh? I was just up visiting Jenna. It's her birthday. I know Greer's coming up in a couple weeks. I'll be sure and get her something nice, though I'll have to sneak it to her.

Cam still doesn't like the idea that she comes to see me. For him, nothing's changed. It's still high school, all these years later.

I don't mean the gay thing. He knew better than that. He just always resented our friendship for some reason—he was obviously threatened by it—and now that he's raising Greer alone, he's threatened all over again. She said he's always asking what we talk about and do I ever say anything bad about him. I know you loved him and actually had a great marriage. But Cam and I—I just hope we never get marooned on a desert island together because one of us will never get off it alive.

Got to hurry. Colds, flu, migraines, PMS, acne, etc. await me in my little office. I love you, kiddo. There's not a day goes by I don't think of you. I'm glad our daughters got to grow up together and become friends and—

Shit. And I wasn't going to cry today. I couldn't hold them back with Jenna. And now I can't hold them back with you.

See you soon, kiddo.

There now. She'd seen them both. Daughter and best friend. And she always felt better for doing so. . . .

She rolled the window down on the way back to the clinic she shared with four other young female physicians. Smoky smell of a perfect seventy-six degree autumn afternoon. Handsome men in suits carrying briefcases. Young mothers pushing strollers. Women in smart outfits window-shopping in the business district that was now making a comeback after originally being decimated by the huge mall that had opened up ten years ago. Hastings Corner was a true city now—43,000 population—a small one but a real one. And as a kid who'd grown up here, every once in a while she got a kind of culture shock when she suddenly became aware of just how many changes had taken place here.

She pulled into her parking space. Her ID card slid

into the slot on the side of the rear door. The smell of medicine and antiseptic hit as she stepped inside.

"I saw those flowers you took out to your daughter," one of the nurses said, hurrying past with a patient's file, her white shoes squeaking on the tiled floor: "Beautiful."

Home.

She didn't like to admit it but it was true. She lived in an apartment that was as insolently impersonal as a motel room. This was her true home. And had been since the death of her daughter three years ago, and the desertion of her husband a year after.

A baby wailed in one of the examining rooms. An elderly man said, "Thank you, Doctor." A swaggering pharmaceutical salesman was pouring himself a cup of Mr. Coffee as he waited to pitch one of the doctors.

Home. And the hell of it was, it wasn't a bad home at all.

ELEVEN YEARS EARLIER

Dr. David Prescott of Boston, Massachusetts, was never a suspect in the bloody murders of his wife and two young daughters. While the husband is usually the chief suspect in such cases, at the time his family was being stabbed, disemboweled, and burned, Prescott was a thousand miles away, in Chicago, giving a lecture on the topic that had made him famous, cognitive engineering.

Expanding on the work originally done by neuroscientist Miller Fenton, M.D., and neurosurgeon Raymond Carney, M.D., Prescott took their theories of brain implants—to help stroke and accident victims to overcome (override, really) their paralysis—and learn to use their limbs again. His controversial approach coupled brain implants with what he called "psychological engineering," the use of drugs, hypnosis, autosuggestion and certain techniques associated with brainwashing to insure that the patient's attitude was supportive of the cognitive engineering. In simplest terms, this meant that patients sometimes had reason to remain paralyzed. They luxuriated in the pity of others, they found protection from a world that had never treated them well, they saw their physical limitations as God's punishment for leading bad lives.

Prescott was both a neurosurgeon and a psychiatrist, the two giving him a unique perspective on the human condition he encountered both in and out of the hospital where he was chief of staff.

He appeared in Chicago that night before an audience of four hundred people. Four hundred witnesses.

What the police found troubling was his reluctance to help in the investigation. Oh, he was genuinely bereaved. His grief was expressed in sobbing jags and vomiting. He rushed from his office several times during police visits to throw up in his private bathroom. They could hear him. No doubt he was really puking.

But he seemed to have some secret he wouldn't divulge.

"Anybody you know want to kill your wife, Dr. Prescott?"

"No."

"She never got any threats that you know of?"

"No. None she ever told me about. But if you'd

known her—she was a beautiful, wonderful woman. Nobody would want to kill her."

"Somebody did."

"It had to be random."

"You keep saying that, Dr. Prescott. But there was no sign of forced entry."

"Don't burglars use tools?"

"Yes. But at eight-thirty at night—which is the approximate time of death according to the coroner—no burglar's going to break into a house with all the lights on and everybody inside walking around and talking or watching TV."

"Which is saying what exactly?"

"It's saying exactly that your wife let the killers in."

"I see."

"Which means she either knew them or they presented themselves in a trustworthy way."

"I see."

"You keep saying that—I see—but I'm wondering if you *do* see. I get the sense Dr. Prescott—and I've been a detective for seventeen years now and I've got a pretty good feel for these things—I get the sense that there's something you're not telling us."

"That's not true."

"Dr. Prescott, did you ever suspect that your wife was having an affair?"

"God, I really resent that."

"I don't blame you. I'd resent it, too. But it has to be asked."

"She was faithful to me."

"As far as you know."

"Not as far as I know. I hate that kind of cynical bullshit. I trusted my wife and she trusted me. We loved each other. Our lives revolved around each other and our girls."

"So you never saw anything—"

"God, man, you think I wouldn't notice a change in her attitude? I'm a psychiatrist. I study people for a living. The same as you do. You say you've got a feel for certain things. Well, so do I, and believe me, if Caroline were having an affair—I'd know. And very soon after it started."

And that's how it went for the six weeks when the detectives kept after him for help.

On a windy Tuesday afternoon, rain starting to patter the windows of Prescott's office, the detective said, "You know there's one thing we never considered till now."

"I'm really tired. I haven't had any decent sleep since it happened. I hope we can make this fast."

"You were in Chicago the night they were killed, right?"

Prescott had a tighter grip on his feelings after six weeks. No more weeping. No more vomiting. Not around the detectives anyway.

"You know I was in Chicago."

"In front of four hundred witnesses."

"If you want to put it that way, yes."

"The perfect alibi."

"Again, if you want to put it that way."

"But let's just say you *hired* somebody to kill your wife and daughters."

"I'm surprised it took you this long to come up with that. I didn't hire anybody. I wouldn't even know where to look."

"You're a smart man, Dr. Prescott. You could do anything you put your mind to."

"Well, I never put my mind to that."

"You don't sound insulted the way you usually do when I make little accusations."

"I'm numb. You've been battering away at me for a long time. I don't know what the hell you've been doing, but whatever it is, it hasn't paid off. Because you always keep coming back to me."

"Which just might mean you're our man."

"What it really means is that you haven't been doing a very good job and you can't turn up anybody but me."

The detective who'd been paying him almost daily visits was ultimately reassigned to another high profile homicide investigation. The new detectives had no better luck with Prescott. They, too, felt that Prescott was keeping important information from them. They had no idea what that information might be.

Three hits of notorious Boston mobsters soon filled all the media. Gruesome as the Prescott murders had been, the mob hits ultimately led to a prominent Boston attorney. The Prescotts were forgotten.

On the night of October 4, 1978—six months after the death of his wife and children—David Prescott drove a rented car to an isolated house twenty-three miles west of the city. He wore a theatrical beard, a wig, and had inserted cotton in his cheeks.

The house was dark when he got there. He had spent a week following the couple who lived here. He knew that they had taken their Volvo into the city this evening. To the symphony.

He parked in a wooded area a quarter mile from

the house. Cars traversing the isolated gravel road could not see his rental behind the stand of pine trees.

He had no trouble getting into the house. He'd checked out their security system in advance. The alarm was tripped when a body passed in front of hidden sensors. He had studied the location of the sensors. By hunching down, the sensors were unable to pick him up.

The house was richly decorated and furnished in a style he found oppressively baronial, almost comic in its splendiferous taste. Lost of ersatz Louis the XIV. Lots of love seats. Lots of faux seventeenth-century French paintings and curios. Smells of perfume, some sort of braised meat from dinner, rug shampoo. Sounds of plumbing, heating, lonely wind.

Ethan Allen had been good enough for Caroline and the girls. Nothing fancy or pretentious about Caroline. She'd worked two part-time jobs while he was finishing med school. Only after he was settled in the hospital did she go back and get her masters in psychology. She was frugal and loyal and loving.

But standing here in the darkness of the living room, hidden behind heavy wine-red drapes, he knew that he had to think of something else or he'd start crying. It still came upon him, the grief, like a seizure. A couple of times it had happened in the middle of meetings at the hospital. Fortunately, his staff understood what he was going through. They knew that his grieving was a natural process.

He heard them coming. It could have been someone else, but he knew better. Instinctively. Somehow.

Headlights washed the wall through the large glass

front window. His hand gripped the .38 Smith & Wesson he held. His father's old army pistol. Korea. This was the only gun he'd ever fired. No kind of fancy firearm was required.

The car pulled into the garage.

Voices. Laughter. Key in back door. Voices. Louder.

Sudden light. The kitchen.

"I'm going to turn on the electric blanket. That way it'll be warm when we climb into bed." Her.

"I know another way of getting warm." Him.

"Oh, yeah, and what would that be?"

"That would be for me to know and you to find out."

"Tease," she said.

To reach the bedrooms, Andrea Kent had to pass through the dark living room. Don, the husband, was right behind her. As she bent to click on a table light, he leaned over and pressed himself against her.

"We haven't done it on the couch for a long time," he said.

She laughed. "Then again, we haven't done it in the road for a long time, either."

The moment the light came on, Prescott stepped out from behind the curtains.

"Stay right where you are."

They knew everything instantly. Who he was. Why he was here. What he was going to do to them.

"You sonofabitch," Don Kent said.

"Just be quiet, Don," Andrea said. "I'm sorry for what happened, David. I'm sorry it had to be done."

"All I was trying to do was help you people," Prescott said. He sounded more miserable than angry.

Three centuries his people had been offering their help. Three centuries these people—if such they were—had been spurning it.

"Oh, yes," Don said. "Help us. Turn us into nice little robots that you control."

"You know better than that, Kent," Prescott said.

His dream of this moment had always produced ecstatic rage in him. He would kill them, but before he did so, he would give them a fine immortal speech about the world of good and evil. About how they did not have to do the things they did if only they would listen to him. Let him and others like him help them.

But now, as he faced them here in their living room, the lonely wind cold as it rattled the windows, he felt only emptiness and weariness. No fine words touched his lips; no great hatred touched his heart.

This was a war that had gone on since long before recorded time and protracted war ultimately produced but one emotion—a numbing resolve for vengeance. It didn't matter any longer who had started it—who had committed the latest atrocity—all that mattered was that you performed with full violence when it was your turn.

It was his turn. They had killed his wife and daughters. It was his turn. If they'd had children, he would have to kill them tonight, too. Centuries, it had gone on. Centuries more, it would likely continue.

He could see Andrea straining to unman him in some way. At her best, she could easily have whipped the gun from his hand and flung it across the room. Or melted it down to a searing lump of white-hot metal. Or—this would have taken more time and concentrated effort—she could have started ripping his face apart, blood-leaking fissures that would have filled the living room with his screams.

And done it all standing right where she was now, tall and icy blonde in her dark evening dress and jewelry. She had extraordinary breasts and he felt guilty for noticing them.

The most she was able to do was fling an unlighted table lamp at him. He ducked it easily.

He allowed himself the indulgence of a smile. "We've been experimenting with a new drug. It changes the capabilities of your neurons to affect certain actions. It's not permanent, unfortunately. But the effect lasts for several hours. I put some of it in the milk you used for breakfast this morning. No more magic, I'm afraid, not for another twenty-four hours at least. Throwing that lamp at me was probably the best you can do at the moment. And that's not going to be enough."

He could see her straining again. Concentrating. Focusing. If willpower alone could reinstate her dark witch powers, she would now be sending telepathic commands that would slash his carotid artery—hell, she might even lop off his whole head.

That was how she'd killed his wife and children.

Telepathic commands. Neat and clean. Don, as usual, had been along to offer a strictly human hand if necessary. The warlocks, as history had dubbed them, had no powers of their own. But they certainly could enjoy the rewards of their women's powers.

"Fuck!" she shouted, frustrated with her inability to summon up her full powers. This must be how the light witches felt when they lost their powers at maturity.

She threw herself on the couch and put her face in her

hands. "Just fucking kill us then and get it over with." Her voice was muffled by her long, slender fingers.

He shot Don first. The sound was loud and crude and chilling in the pretentious living room.

A raw red hole in the forehead. Eyes rolling back to whites. A choking gurgling sound deep in the throat as the corpse tried to form a word before the brain shut down entirely.

Don collapsed in sections, accordion-style.

She just watched as he spread out, jack-in-the-box jerky, on the floor, nothing left but reflex and the faint sour odor of his bowels going splat.

Then she looked at Prescott.

"There's nothing I can offer you, is there?"

"No."

"Sex. Money. I'd even give you the names of some dark witches you don't know about. They have a lot greater powers than I do. They'd be a much bigger coup for your little group."

"I was afraid you wouldn't be scared. I'm glad to see you are."

"I'm not lying about giving you names. I will. Really."

"I don't want names. I just want you to be dead. All these years I've wasted believing you people could be changed—I know better now."

Mocking smile. "You should've been a priest, David. You always were sanctimonious. So was that cunt wife of yours."

He emptied the gun into her.

She'd intentionally provoked him. Done them both a favor.

He went over and spat on her dead sensual face.

Ever since it became known in his community that he was going to try and help—convert, as it were—all the people who shared the dark powers—even those who chose not to use them except in self-defense—he had become a figure of scorn.

They'll turn on you someday, David. They always do. Sometimes they're dormant for long periods of their lives, but they always revert, David. It's their nature and there's nothing you can do about it.

His pride had always been that he was smarter and more compassionate than the people who had said these things to him.

He would end the centuries-long war.

Science—and reason and goodwill—would help these lost souls become the normal, caring people he knew they could be.

And for his trouble, for his hope and faith, for all his selfless work . . .

For all that—he buried his loved ones.

He knew, standing in this living room, the stench of blood and feces filling his nostrils, that the war—his personal war—was just starting.

No more reason. No more compassion. No more great goodwill. . . .

He clipped off the table lamp and slipped out the way he'd come in.

TODAY

The young woman was at Level 4 of Recon (Reconstruction). The physical part had been easiest. Six extensive plastic surgeries in seventeen months. Physically, she was a new person. Even her birthmarks had been removed. Even the shape of her earlobes (which had been somewhat distinctive before) had been changed.

Psychologically, the battle had been much more difficult. It always was. The first thing that had to be done was to inflict on her massive numbers of electroshock treatments and drug therapies. Combined, these erased all conscious memory. She was a blank slate. She would always be dangerous until they brought her to Level 4. At any given moment, a dark witch who had been reconstructed through the first three levels could reconnect through some fluke failing in the process and remember just enough to summon her most formidable powers. In his twelve years at this new location outside Boston, Prescott had lost two doctors and three workers to dark witches suddenly in control of their powers once again. Three of the witches had escaped. They had never been recaptured.

The young woman's name was Karen Dupree. That was her name these days, anyway. When Prescott's people had kidnapped her, her name had been Louise Knowles. She'd attended a small college in New Hampshire. There had been a great deal of press interest in the disappearance of the young woman. Her parents were people of means. The reward reached $150,000. But her parents could not push too hard. They did not want the press looking into their own backgrounds. Her mother was a dark witch descended from centuries of dark witches. Her husband was a carrier of the witch gene. These males were not that common. Prescott had observed Karen aka Louise for three years before taking her. Not all dark witches grew into predators. But she had used her powers to drown a romantic rival of hers and to have another classmate break her neck in a football game and be paralyzed for life.

She was young. Angry. Cunning. Just the kind of person Prescott could convert into one of his best assassins.

Dr. Maria Gomez reviewed all these things as she seated herself in front of the one-way window that looked on Room D, where the Level 4 experiments were conducted.

Karen Dupree, thin, pretty in a somewhat pinched way (the plastic surgeons had cared more about disguise than beauty), dark of hair, blue of eye, sat in a blue sweater, white blouse, and jeans at a small table in an otherwise empty room.

Maria was waiting for Prescott. She'd been working with him eight years now, ever since finishing her residency in New Mexico, where she'd been born and raised. She came from many generations of witch-hunters and was thrilled to work for the legendary David Prescott. The young woman this morning was one of their best creations yet. They had great hopes for her. There was talk of needing to create a Level 5 for those who had similar skills.

Prescott was late. In the old days, she had been told—the days before his family had been murdered—Prescott had been an imperiously handsome, fastidious man whose punctuality bordered on the neurotic. This was not the Prescott she knew. Her Prescott had aged quickly and not well since the deaths of his wife and daughters. He'd put on seventy pounds, lost most of his hair, wore trifocals and frequently wore traces of his most recent meal on his white medical smock.

All he cared about was his work. His second wife, Diana, called many times each night to beg him to come home and have a decent meal and some decent sleep. He was more absentminded professor than mad scientist, though at those times when he spoke of dark witches you could see and hear the fanatical hatred he bore them. Even Maria, who loathed witches of all kinds, feared him then. That kind of rage always gives sane people pause.

Prescott appeared a few minutes later.

"Sorry I'm late," he said, out of breath. He had no time—at least, he never *made* time—for exercise. "Damned phone. I'm tempted to tear it out."

She smiled. "Now there's a practical solution."

He laughed. "I admit I get a little extreme sometimes."

"Yes," she said, "sometimes."

He took the chair next to her in the small, bare observation room. "We're all ready to go?"

"All ready. She's just waiting to hear you."

"Did you start the videotape?"

"Of course."

All the sessions were taped.

He spoke to Karen Dupree.

"Good morning, Karen."

"Good morning, Doctor."

"How're you feeling?"

"A little tired."

Finding the proper drug dosage for the hunters was always difficult. The usual symptom of overstimulation was chronic tiredness. Prescott made a note on his clipboard to cut back on four of the five drugs she was receiving. The right balance was critical. He was afraid of "leaking." Fragments of the previous identity occasionally leaked into the new one. Images, fragments of complete memories, sensory data—smells, sounds, skin sensations. This was frightening for both hunter and doctors.

The session began.

Even though she knew what they were about to do, Karen felt anxious. So ingrained was her desire to please Prescott that she worried she would do something to displease him. He was able to give off a sense of disappointment that was almost as strong as an odor. He rarely needed to speak his unhappiness.

Telekinesis came first.

"Do you see that Pepsi can on the table in front of you, Karen?"

"Yes."

"Why don't you do something spectacular with it?"

His voice was pleasant, even courtly. It always was until the hunter failed to perform the way he wanted her to.

"Like what, Dr. Prescott?"

"Oh, give it a little thought and you'll come up with something."

"I'm not very creative."

"Sure you are. You just have to think about it for a minute."

"Is Maria there?"

"Right beside me."

"Hi, Karen."

Maria had given her permission to call her by her first name. They spent a lot of time together.

"Hi, Maria. I sure hope I can do this."

"You're just a little nervous is all. Just take some deep breaths and relax. You know, the way we practiced."

"I'm glad you're here."

"I'm glad I'm here, too, Karen."

So Karen thought.

She spent longer than a minute. She spent five minutes.

Both Prescott and Maria moved around nervously on the surface of their chair seats. Prescott even bit at a fingernail a couple of times. Some of the hunters came right up to it—their practice sessions with Maria having been perfect—but when the moment was here, they couldn't perform. And so they were useless. He couldn't take the chance on them choking this way when they were out in the field.

Would Karen wash out in similar fashion? Had all of Maria's excitement—it had been Maria who'd brought up the possibility of creating a Level 5—been for nothing?

Karen sitting at a table.

Empty Diet Pepsi can sitting in front of her.

She doesn't move. No dramatics whatsoever. Not even a squint. Just sort of casually looks at the can.

And then a sequence of things happens.

The can lofts into the air and begins to spin around like a top. Then it begins to ricochet off the walls.

Maria laughing exuberantly.

Prescott shouting, "Great! Great!" Rising up out of

his chair the way he would at a basketball game when the excitement got to be too much.

Then the can angles down slowly toward the table, like an aircraft executing a perfect landing.

Where it sits for approximately thirty seconds.

Both Prescott and Maria sense that Karen is not finished with this particular part of the demonstration. Oh, no, not quite yet.

And then—

A giant, invisible hand seizes the can and proceeds to crush it the way macho teenagers crush their beer cans.

Folding and folding and folding in upon itself until it is the size of a cigarette package.

"You're doing excellent work, Karen. Excellent."

He is clearly excited. So is Karen.

The session presses on. He is trying to train the ultimate witch killer. He feels he is in the process of finding her right here and right now.

She identifies fifteen numbers correctly—numbers in the head of Dr. Prescott. She identifies the contents of a small box that is taped shut. She identifies the suits of twenty pinochle cards whose backs are held up to her.

And then, the final part of the test, the fire.

This is the most difficult part for Karen. She has more often failed than succeeded.

Maria has explained over and over that Karen panics, which causes her natural gifts to disconnect.

It's no different from crushing cans or guessing numbers, Maria has told her. *Do you remember the chart I showed you of the brain? The motor cortex and the implant and how the cortical tissue grows into the electrode and the implant? All your powers come from the same source. If you have one power, you have them all. All you need to do is relax. Just relax . . .*

The fire test begins.

A cardboard box on the floor is filled with a number of things.

Simple things first.

A piece of typing paper.

"Just concentrate on it, Karen," Maria says gently.

Karen can feel sweat begin to collect on her face and in her armpits.

She feels sick, queasy, the way she always does when she is afraid.

I don't want to see that disappointed look on Dr. Prescott's face.

Holds the piece of typing paper out in front of her.

"Concentrate. Remember what Maria said. Relax and you can do it. You have the power. All we're trying to show you is how to have the power instantly when you want it and need it. That's why you're here at the clinic."

The right bottom edge of the paper ignites.

"Record time," Maria notes proudly, the way a doting mother would remark on her child. "Record time."

A sequence of objects now as Karen reaches down into the cardboard box and brings up one item at a time.

Prescott pretended to be impressed with Karen's time igniting the sheet of paper. He didn't show his stopwatch to Maria. Let her exult. She works hard. And she's—

So he goes along with her excitement over the typing paper. But, in fact, ignition takes two-and-a-half minutes. Fine for laboratory conditions. But in real world application, terrible. What if Karen needs to set a fire to escape an enemy? Unlikely that she'll have two-and-a-half minutes.

They know Karen can set the fire eventually.

Now, the trick is to hone the time so that fire can be a weapon, not merely a carnival trick.

The next object is a roll of toilet paper—2.3 minutes. Slight improvement.

A paperback—2.1.

"Just relax," Maria says. "You're doing better and better."

"How's my time?"

"Don't worry about your time, Karen. You just relax and your time will take care of itself."

But despite Maria's words, Karen keeps glancing at Prescott's face.

Please don't look disappointed. I have nightmares about your face sinking into disappointment because I do something stupid. I'll do better, Dr. Prescott. I promise I will.

The Sunday edition of *The New York Times*—1.9 minutes.

And finally a softball.

This is the most difficult object Karen has ever been presented with. Paper was one thing but a ball as dense as this, with a leather covering yet, poses many problems.

Karen looks frantically at Dr. Prescott for some sort of recognition that this is a difficult task indeed.

He gives her no such recognition.

She glances at Maria. A sweet, almost saintly smile

on Maria's small, heart-shaped face. Giving Karen support, permission to do the best job she's ever done.

Prescott raises his stopwatch to stare at it.

Karen stares at the softball on the table before her.

Maria tenses, crossing her fingers little-girl style.

And the softball ignites.

A beautiful blue-white-red flame that encompasses the entire ball.

Burning blue flame bright.

Burning true.

"Thirty-two seconds," Dr. Prescott says, some of Maria's excitement in his own voice now.

"I'd say she's ready," Maria says. "All she needs is an assignment."

And Prescott says the magic words—magic to both Maria and Karen alike—"Oh, she'll get an assignment all right."

"When?"

"Right away."

"Did you hear that, Karen?"

"Oh, yes," Karen says. "Yes, I sure did."

Not only is Dr. Prescott not looking disappointed. He is smiling and looking almost ridiculously happy.

But Maria is about to change his mood. She clicks off the microphone so that Karen can't hear.

Prescott has started to leave the room but her voice stops him. "I want to talk to you about Kylie, Dr. Prescott."

He is frowning when he turns around. His mood has changed instantly. "There's nothing to talk about, Dr. Gomez. The matter's settled."

"She's eight years old."

"And that makes her perfect as an assassin. Nobody's going to suspect a child until it's too late. She can get into places nobody else could."

"We shouldn't be using children. We need to draw the line somewhere."

"And where do *they* draw it, Dr. Gomez? You think they haven't used children before? Dark witches killed your father, doesn't that mean anything to you?"

"That doesn't give me the right to destroy a little girl's life."

He checks his watch.

"If it disturbs you so much I'll assign Tom Fletcher to Kylie. You won't have to worry about her anymore."

She starts to say more, but he opens the door and says, "The subject's closed, Dr. Gomez."

And then he's gone.

There were only a couple of them but they occasionally ruined it for everybody. Loudmouths. Hotheads. Parents of a few of the girls on the tenth grade Woodrow Wilson girls' soccer team.

You had your elegiac late autumn afternoon competition—so much fun to try and keep your eyes on your daughter who was running all over the field—you didn't want some overly competitive jerk screaming at the coach and the referee.

Greer Morgan of the five-ten body, the elegant, freckled face. Greer Morgan the forward halfback was having herself one hell of a day. Two goals.

What made the day even sweeter was that none of the clown dads happened to be here. They probably got arrested on the way here for road rage.

Attorney Cam Morgan was in the bleachers with a lot of his friends. Mostly couples he and his wife had hung around with. They'd made sure to take extra good care of him since the inexplicable and devastating drowning accident of his wife Laura, mother of Greer, a little over two years ago.

It was funny seeing how people responded differently to the shadowy heat of day's end. Some of the parents and the students wore nothing more than T-shirts and jeans or trousers. Some of the parents wore heavy jackets and drank steaming coffee from thermoses and covered their lower bodies with bright red blankets. Girls' soccer wasn't an important sport at the school. You could tell that by the two cheerleaders Wilson had dispatched. Overweight, pimply, male.

The game was just finishing up. Some of the parents from Roosevelt were heading for their vans, SUVs and station wagons, getting ready to haul their team forty miles west of here. Highly unlikely the score was going to change.

Cam was happy. He knew how much soccer meant to Greer. Soccer and drama club. She was in most of the school plays. Never the lead, not yet anyway. But important roles.

Cam had learned how to be her father and she'd learned how to be his daughter. She'd been Laura's daughter for thirteen years. Cam was too busy at the law firm. Now he worked three-quarters time and tried to be home at least three days a week when Greer got there after school. She made breakfast, he made dinner. They'd learned to conquer the kitchen together. They hadn't had a grease fire in months.

Yelling, screaming, chanting. Roosevelt had managed

to pack in a goal as the game was concluding. They'd lose but 2–1 was no disgrace, especially when your opponent was as good as Wilson.

The whistle sounded. Game ended. The teams shook hands, hugged. Good sportsmanship.

Cam stood up and as he did so he saw her standing down at the far corner of the bleachers. She'd only gotten better looking as she'd gotten older. At least from a distance. Up close you saw the melancholy. He didn't resent her as he once had—he'd never been able to forget the terrible and terribly stupid white-washing of the world "Dyke" on the trunk of Laura's Mustang all those years ago—but he was still uncomfortable around her. And he wasn't all that keen on Greer's visits with her. He didn't blame Abby for wanting to see her daughter's best friend now that her daughter was dead. He just hoped she didn't somehow alienate Greer from him. He knew that Abby wasn't any keener on him than he was on her.

A tall, blond man slid his arm through hers. Smiled. Gave her a kiss on the cheek. This was the first time Cam realized that Abby was seeing anybody.

Cam couldn't believe his reaction to what he saw. Jealousy. God, what was that all about? His whole dismal history with Abby, and now he felt in some way possessive about her? He'd have to stop drinking rubbing alcohol and go a little easier on the cocaine, speedballs, and acid he fed himself three times a day. The stuff was obviously affecting his sanity.

Jealous that somebody was dating Abby?

His friends drifted toward their kids. Hugging, laughing, angling toward the family vehicles.

He found Greer. Abby and her friend had been talking to her and were just now walking away.

Greer managed to be sweaty and cold at the same time. He hugged her with almost brutal tenderness. She was his whole life. He'd been such a pisspoor father in her early years. He hoped it wasn't too late to make it up to her.

On the way to the sensible, hopelessly square royal blue Buick he drove, she slid her hand into his and said, "It's so great to look up and see you in the bleachers."

"I tried to make you proud of me. That's why I mooned the Roosevelt bench."

"That was my proudest moment, Dad." She laughed. Hugged him. "You think we could just get a pizza tonight? Pizza Hut's right on the way."

"Take out or eat there?"

"Eat there."

"I suppose I could see my way clear to do that."

Pizza Hut at suppertime in the suburbs—at least it's democratic. Dusty pickups are parked next to gleaming Lexuses, the occasional Harley next to the Cadillac (yes, they actually make them) SUV. Same inside: the tots of the yuppies are just as badly behaved and noisy as the tots of the man who delivers furniture. And everybody gets the same gum-chewing, high school girl kind of service. And thank God for that sneeze-guard now that flu season is upon us. And at least there aren't any real rap records on the jukebox.

Cam's half was just cheese; Greer's was everything, so much of everything that if Cam even looked at it for very long he'd have acid reflux for a week.

As night came on, stars clear, the quarter-moon bright, the shadows in the place softened the homeliness of the decor. It was kinda nice sitting here, actually. His daughter was what made it that way, of course. But it was nice sitting here with all these people and their kids and young lovers all gaga over each other. It gave him the sense of belonging to the rest of his species, a feeling he'd rarely had, even when he was a popular high school boy. He'd been playing a role, one that ended abruptly in college. Kids from hick schools rarely compete well in major state universities. He'd just been one more student, nobody special in any way. And that had been good for him, damned good. He'd become the same kind of kid he'd snubbed when he was in high school.

"You're watching them, aren't you?" Greer said.

"Watching who?"

"Whom."

"Whom."

"Abby and that guy."

"No, I'm not."

"Yes, you are. And his name's Jason by the way."

"Where'd she get him?"

"He's a doctor, too."

"Oh."

"Specialist. Eyes, ears, nose, throat."

"Oh."

"He's really handsome, too."

"If you say so."

"Divorced. A son at Princeton. Democrat. Six figure income. Owns half the clinic he works at. Most of his mortgage paid off. A home designed by an avant-garde architect named Richard Wohlman. Built back in the thirties. Classical music nut. Fanatical Red Sox fan."

"What'd she do, hire a private eye?"

"She told me, quote unquote, 'He's not like most men. Ask him a question and he'll give you a straight answer.' "

"How nice for her."

"You know what, Dad?"

"What?"

"If I didn't know better, I'd say you were jealous."

"Right."

"You're so sarcastic about this."

"I just wish you didn't hang around her place so much."

"My mother was her best friend. Her daughter was my best friend. Duh, Dad. Isn't it kind of logical that I'd go see her once in a while?"

"It's more than once in a while. And anyway, doesn't it make you uncomfortable, being friends with somebody who hates your old man?"

"She doesn't hate you."

"She doesn't?"

"She said that you weren't half as obnoxious as you used to be." She gave him her best kid-grin as she said it.

"Sounds like she's falling in love with me."

"You know, I've thought of that."

"What?"

"You and Abby falling in love. She's smart, nice, and very sexy for an older woman."

"Be sure and tell her you referred to her as an

'older woman.' And by the way, the chances of Abby and me falling in love are about as remote as me being appointed to the Supreme Court."

The kid-grin again. "When are we leaving for Washington?"

"She still hates me for that stupid gay thing I said. God, and then Lucy turns out to be gay and I love her like my daughter." Lucy was his niece. She'd come out last year after graduating college, and introduced Cam to her friend. He loved them both. And one of his favorite lawyers at work was gay. Every time he thought of what he'd done back there in high school, he felt ashamed and embarrassed. Gay people didn't have enough people on picking them already. They'd really needed Cam Morgan joining in.

"Oh, she's forgiven you for that, Dad. She just thinks you're cold to her." She sipped through her straw until the glass started making that marvelous empty gurgling sound. "And you are."

Upstairs, Greer was doing her homework. Downstairs, sitting in front of the fireplace in his grandfather's rocking chair—one of the few so-called family heirlooms he was actually sentimental about—Cam was reading the new Grisham novel. For all his moral reservations about the legal profession, John Grisham romanticized the profession and that's why so many lawyers bought his books. He turned everything into white hats and black hats. The Gunfight at the OK Corral. And what the hell, he was fun to read.

In the Old Days, as he'd come to think of them, Laura would have been stretched out on the leather couch across from him, reading a novel of her own. Toni Morrison or Saul Bellow or, for relaxation, Anne

Rice. She'd always been smarter and more reflective than Cam, and Cam had never had any trouble admitting that. Indeed, he'd been proud of it. Here was this lovely, gentle, truly intelligent woman who had agreed—for whatever inexplicable reason was in that pretty head—to spend her life with somebody like him. He didn't deserve her and was constantly looking at her and wondering why she just didn't walk out the door. She could have done so much better. And if the early passion had waned some, as it did in most marriages, the love only deepened. He'd always found himself tearing up just thinking of her and how precious she was to him. And this was long before her death.

He glanced up from the book. Imagined her stretched out on the couch. An old sweater and jeans on. Long but well-shaped bare feet except in midwinter when she wore those dorky green socks with the tassels on them. A long-stemmed wineglass on the floor next to her. Chablis. Neither of them had any suburban pretensions as far as wine, serious music, art, or films went. They liked what they liked and were comfortable with that.

The phone rang. Answered on the first ring. Upstairs. Greer no doubt grateful for any interruption in her studies. And it was most likely for Greer. This time of night.

He went back to his reading, startled a few minutes later when Winston, named after Churchill, landed all seventeen pounds of his tomcat hide on Cam's lap. Winston's lap of first choice had always been Laura's lap. He'd learned to make do with those of Cam and Greer.

After turning out the downstairs lights at ten, he went up and got ready for bed, Winston padding after him. They divided the queen-sized bed that Laura had bought with some extra money she'd earned from a garage sale. They'd trysted on it like teenagers.

Pajamas, toothbrush, face cloth. Nightly ritual. And the final stop, Greer's room.

"Night, hon."

No answer. Unusual.

"Night, hon."

Headphones. He knocked, opened the door.

The room was dark. She sat very straight on her desk chair next to the window, traced in silver silhouette by the moonlight. She appeared to be staring out into the backyard at the small white gazebo her mother had loved so much.

"Hon."

Busy signal. Phone. Receiver on her bed. Didn't she hear it? Had it been ringing since the last call? That was more than an hour ago.

He went over, hung the phone up.

She didn't seem to hear him. Didn't seem to be aware of him at all.

"Hon."

He walked around in front of her. Her eyes gleamed in the moonlight. Her mouth was open, slack. Worry stirred in him. The weight of all parental dreads crushed him. Brain aneurysms. Blood clots in the lungs. Heart attacks. Those inexplicable killers of young people. Never mind drowning-car accidents-fires.

Her hands lay upon each other in her lap.

He touched her palm. Cold.

But his touch stirred her, and she came alive all at once, like a marionette whose puppet master had jerked it into life. Eyes focused. Voice clear and bright. Hand taking his.

"Are you all right?"

"Sure, Dad. Why?"

"The way you were sitting there just now—"

"Oh, I'm just tired. I was almost asleep, actually."

"Who was on the phone?"

She had rarely lied to him, and so the way her eyes quickly evaded his was obvious and troubling. "Oh, just this kid. He wants me to go out with him." She nodded at the window, changing the subject. "Isn't the gazebo beautiful in the moonlight?"

"So what's this kid's name?"

"What kid?"

"That marionette sense again. As if she were not in control of her faculties.

"The one you said who called and asked you out."

"Oh. Uh, Sam."

"You don't sound sure."

She smiled, but it was artifice. "Of course I'm sure, Dad. Sam. Sam Pryor. What's wrong with you? You act like I did something wrong."

His artificial smile wasn't any more convincing than hers had been. "I just worry about you, honey. All your activities. You really can burn out, even at your age. When I saw you sitting there at first—"

"What, Dad?"

"Oh, nothing. I guess. Nothing important, anyway." He leaned down and kissed her on the forehead.

"I'm fine, Dad. Honest."

"I know."

But did he? He took the image of her sitting there at her window right to bed with him. Brooded. Worried.

The chill autumn rain started just after midnight, long after Cam fell asleep, and continued on until nearly dawn.

Cam always took the channel surfer with him to the basement so he could go through the entire span of cable stations while he worked out on his Stairmaster. Until a year ago, he'd jogged two miles a day. But he'd slipped on ice one overcast wintry morn and his left knee had never been quite the same since.

Bugs Bunny; stock reports; several religious channels; innumerable chirpy "good morning" shows; old bad movies; new bad movies; where the hell was some good hard-core porno when you needed it?

He was just finishing up his forty-five minutes on the machine when he caught his first glimpse of Greer for the day. She usually had something sarcastic to say—"Nice gams, Pops," or, "With buns like those you should have women calling you twenty-four hours a day." Accompanied, of course, by that heartbreaking daddy-pleasing little-kid grin of hers.

No smart remarks, no little-kid grin this morning. His first impression—she was so pale—was that she was sick. She stood at the bottom of the stairs and said, "Breakfast's ready, Dad."

"You all right, sweetheart?"

"I guess I didn't sleep well."

He remembered her sitting by her window. Staring out.

He was going to see if she felt feverish, but she'd

already turned and begun trudging back upstairs. She usually bounded up them two at a time.

"Why don't I get the thermometer?"

"Your Egg-Beaters'll get cold."

"Maybe you have the flu."

"I just didn't sleep is all, Dad. I'm fine."

But she didn't look or sound fine. Almost haggard. By now, normally, her shower would be done with, her sparing makeup applied, her gorgeous red hair combed. She was still in her pj's.

"Maybe I'll stay home today."

Something she rarely said. Rarely.

"Maybe that's a good idea."

"Maybe it is the flu."

"I'm taking your temperature."

Her first smile, her first smart-ass remark of the day. "The Adventures of Cam Morgan, Male Nurse."

"You just sit there. I'll be right back."

He had her all set up in the recliner. She had her robe and slippers on and claimed to be nice and warm. He'd fixed her a cup of tea. The channel surfer sat in her lap.

"I'll call you as soon as I get to work."

"Gosh, Dad, I'll be fine."

"Humor me."

She gave him her best put-upon sigh. "All right, Dad. I'll get the cell phone so I can answer you when you call every ten minutes."

"Hey, I'm a liberal. I'll only call you every fifteen minutes."

She even had a sweet little giggle for that one. "I

believe it." She paused. "This is like when I was getting grounded all the time." Soon after her mother's death, Greer went through a bad girl phase, smoking marijuana, staying out late, visiting the school counselor twice a week because of detention, even—she'd explained to Cam one night—coming close to losing her virginity. But together they'd pulled her back from the edge of the pit. And just in time.

"At least you don't have a fever," he said.

He kissed her on the forehead. "Well, I'm off to the unjust world of justice."

Boston winds being what they were, he grabbed his topcoat from the hall closet, his hand groping around in the darkness. And that was when he brushed against the blue windbreaker she wore to jog around the neighborhood. Damp. In fact, more than damp. Soaked through. Odd. The rain hadn't started until after she'd gone to bed.

Again he thought of her sitting by her window. Staring out. And of his initial response—the inexplicable, the profound sense that something was wrong.

He walked back to the living room. "You didn't go anywhere last night, did you, hon?"

She was watching Katie Couric. Didn't look up at him. "Just to bed. Why?"

"Your windbreaker's wet."

"That's weird." Still not looking up. "Oh. Wait a minute. Must've been when I went out to get the paper. Ronnie missed the porch as usual. It was out on the grass. That's when I must've gotten wet."

There were a number of things wrong with that. For one thing, it had been, at most, sprinkling about the time she went for the paper. For another, the paper itself hadn't been even damp. And for yet another—

Who was he, The Grand Inquisitor? Maybe he should get a rubber hose and beat her until she came up with some satisfactory answers.

She wasn't feeling well, so he wouldn't keep shoving questions at her. And who knew—maybe she really had gotten soaked going for the paper. Maybe there'd been a mini-squall or something.

He kissed her on the forehead for a second time. "I love you."

"Love you, too, Dad." Still fixed on Katie Couric.

At the back door, he found her penny loafers sitting on the worn pink throw rug. Soaked. Mud-covered, outside and inside, as if they'd fallen off while she was hurrying and she'd shoved muddy feet back into them.

It was clear she'd gone somewhere last night. And without asking his permission. Or telling him about it. Which wasn't like her at all. Not at all.

Something about the early days of Hastings Corner. She wasn't sure what.

After her father left, Greer had drifted off to sleep in the living room. The dream she'd had somehow related to—last night? That was the funny thing when her father said that her jacket was wet. She remembered going somewhere last night, but it had been more like a dream. That's why she'd told him she hadn't gone anywhere. Because—she hadn't, had she?

Something in this morning's dream . . . something in the history of Hastings Corner . . . something about last night?

Before she quite realized it, she was getting herself ready. Bathroom. Closet. Changing clothes. Back porch where she kept her ten-speed. She knew she'd get in trouble if a high school staff person saw her on the street when she was supposed to be home sick. But she didn't care.

She just had this need to know—but know what?

The rain had scrubbed the air and the sky. The soft wind was fresh and cool and refreshing. The library, a new two-story red brick building, had a bike rack out front. She locked her bicycle and went inside.

Her usual path led straight to the science fiction section. She loved high fantasy. Mercedes Lackey and Robert Jordan and Stephen Donaldson especially.

Today she went to the information desk. A slender, pretty black woman in a feminine pink blouse with a big bow waited on her.

"Is there a section on town history?"

"How far back would you like to go?"

"Uh, as far as I can go, I guess."

"The reason I ask is that up here we have two books on the town today with some historical sections. But if you want history in more depth—"

"Yes, please, history in more depth."

"Then here's where you'll go. And while you're back there, you may see an attractive, very tiny woman with big glasses. That's Sara Crawford. She's the head librarian. And sort of the unofficial expert on town history around here. If you have any specific questions, I'm sure Sara would be glad to help you." Then she wrote out some decimal numbers to look for in the stacks. "This is where to look."

"Thanks very much."

Greer loved libraries. The sense of literally being lost in aisle upon aisle of books. There was something safe about a library. Safe and fun. She'd always been a reader.

She found the section on town history. She also found Sara Crawford, who was sitting at a reader table looking through a small stack of books.

The woman was just as the information lady had described her—attractive, probably fortyish, dressed in a sweater that emphasized her well-formed breasts, a woman who'd obviously once been a babe and still clung to her vanity. The gray eyes that peered through the round glasses were somber. She'd seen the woman around for years but had never really spoken to her.

"Yes. May I help you?"

"You're Mrs. Crawford?"

"Yes, I am."

Greer smiled. "You used to read stories to kids every Saturday morning. I loved coming here."

"Thanks. I'm glad you have good memories of it."

"The lady at the information desk—"

"Charlotte."

"Charlotte—she said you could help me find some history on our town here."

Sara Crawford's smile was enthusiastic, almost grateful. She had been asked to do that which gave her the greatest pleasure—talk about Hastings Corner. She had gone back—despite her husband's protestations—to get her Ph.D. in library science. Last year she was named one of the three outstanding librarians in the state. Three years earlier she been cited as a leader in a national magazine. But despite all her accolades—which was why Yancy hadn't wanted her to go back to college, doing something with her life while he did nothing with his—she still loved reading stories to the kids on Saturday mornings and discussing local history more than anything else. "Just last year, I spent three months interviewing our oldest citizens. Their memories of growing up here and everything. We have the tapes right over there on the shelf. You can't check them out, but you're certainly welcome to listen to them here."

"I'm sure those are great. But I'm actually looking for something farther back."

"Oh? Isn't that nice! A young person like yourself taking an interest in the history of our town. Usually people your age want to know something about early Boston. They seem to think that we're this really boring little burg. But I'll tell you something. We're every bit as interesting as Boston ever was—just on a smaller scale is all."

How the town came to be founded. And when. And information about its first citizens. Particularly where they came from.

These thoughts, these questions, where were they coming from? They'd been in her head—as if the history fairy had placed them there while she slept—when she woke up this morning.

She'd never had the slightest interest in town history. Why now? What did this sudden interest have to do with last night? With the wet jacket her father had discovered this morning?

"Are you looking for anything special, dear?"

"Just, you know, kind of the origins of the town."

"Why don't I take you over to the right section and

walk you through the books we have." Sara Crawford smiled at her. "You're the Morgan girl, aren't you?"

"Yes."

"I used to help your father back when we were in high school. That was in the old library, of course. He was always intense, too—just the way you seem to be."

So her agitated state was that obvious. She laughed. "I come from a long line of overwrought people, as my mother used to say."

"Oh, yes, your mother," Sara Crawford said. "I knew her very well." She didn't elaborate on her last thought at all. And yet Greer sensed something odd in her words. She couldn't remember her mom ever mentioning Mrs. Crawford. Had she known Mom as a young girl? A married woman?

But Sara Crawford was standing up—all five foot two of her—taking Greer gently by the elbow and leading her to the town history section.

There were days when Cam agreed with ol' Bill Shakespeare: First kill all the lawyers. Herb Shay—of Shay, Shay, Fallan, and Stephens—had been reading an article in *The Wall Street Journal* about how efficiency experts were saving all these giant law firms so much money on the bottom line.

Thus Herb Shay, first Shay of all the Shays, hired a group of such experts and turned them loose, termite-style, upon his reluctant minions.

This was their second week here. Armed with teeny-tiny tape recorders and clipboards, they worked their way through the alphabet, interviewing every single employee. They were now working on people whose name began with M.

Morgan, Cam, said, "I keep a fifteen-minute breakdown of my day and I've never billed less than six hours a day."

"We're pushing for seven. Maybe even eight."

"But that's unrealistic."

"That's what the folks at Darcy, Darcy, and Darcy said. Until they implemented the PH system."

"PH?"

"Stands for Push Harder."

"Ah." Cam leaned back in his chair. She was blonde, bright, appealing, well-dressed (Armani, if Cam wasn't mistaken), had a pair of long, killer legs and appeared to be utterly humorless. "May I ask you a question?"

"That's why I'm here."

"Do you enjoy what you do?"

"I love what I do. I help companies make their employees more efficient. Who wouldn't enjoy that?"

"They could've used you when they were building the pyramids."

"Funny."

"Or running plantations."

Even her sigh was efficient. "I've heard all the insults, Mr. Morgan. I'm sure I'd resent me if I were in your position. Very few people take constructive suggestions well. Because inherent in any suggestion is a criticism that you could be doing better."

"PH."

"You make fun of it, but it works. And we have the proof of it."

He smiled. "I'm being a jerk, aren't I?"

She smiled right back at him. "Not a big one."

"But maybe a little one?"

"All right. Maybe a little one."

"I got off to a bad start this morning at home. Guess I brought it with me to the office." He always said that he disliked people who closed themselves off to new approaches, new ideas. But here he was doing exactly that. The woman was here to help him. He should at lest give her a fair chance. She was smart and pleasant and deserved at least that. "Tell me your name again."

"Beth Smythe."

"Beth. Nice name."

"Thanks."

"What say we start again?"

"Good. Let's start by looking at your daily patterns. Our computer analyzed the last six months of your daily hours. Patterns are very important."

He did his best to pay attention. He was a big picture sort. This small picture approach couldn't—didn't—keep him interested for long.

Inevitably, he found his thoughts drifting back to Greer's wet jacket and muddy shoes. Where had she gone in the middle of the night?

The image of her sitting by the window was with him, too. It was almost as if her soul had left her body. Or she'd been in the throes of some form of astral projection, if such a thing were really possible. But her clothes wouldn't get wet with astral projection. . . .

And then he thought of his strange, almost shocking feelings of jealousy when he saw Abby with her new man. All these years he'd considered them to be at the least unfriendly. Even when she'd been around the house during his years with Laura they'd been cool to each other. The "dyke" thing had alienated her forever. And as he got older, he didn't blame her. He'd had no reason to resent her high school friendship with Laura. He'd just been spoiled, self-centered, selfish. But there had never been any way to express this to Abby, not even at Laura's funeral where, for the first and only time, they'd held each other. For two desperate weeks, they'd needed each other. But that ended soon enough and then they went back to being distant and proper but never warm.

He wondered about calling her. She'd become Greer's stand-in mother, however anxious the relationship made him. Greer probably confided things to her she didn't to her father. Greer always said they had "girl talks" about "stuff." Meaning, most likely, stuff girls couldn't talk to fathers about, no matter how well-meaning those fathers might be.

"There now," Beth said. "Now that we've gone through your morning patterns, how about dealing with the afternoon?"

He smiled again. "Gee, you mean it? That sounds like a lot of fun."

"Yeah," she said, "I'll just bet it does." And crossed her killer legs.

Cam had always been vulnerable to dusk the way some people were vulnerable to rain. Maybe because his father had died just at brilliant wintry sunset, the sky radiant gold and red and salmon pink as night painted stars and full moon across the sky. In memory, he always heard his father cry out. But his mother had assured him that this was only the active imagination of a twelve-year-old boy who loved his father very much. That his father, overwhelmed by his liver cancer and medications, had been in a deep coma and had not cried out at all. His father had begged for the chance to die at home, upstairs in his own bed, and Kate Morgan had said of course. She died ten years later herself, a freak accident on an icy road. The death of his parents made him turn to Laura for a comfort even she could not give—though God bless her, she'd certainly tried.

The bleat of the cell phone cut through this familiar reverie.

"Hello?"

"Mr. Morgan?"

"Yes."

"This is Dr. Stewart's office."

"Abby's office?"

"Yes, Abby. She just wanted you to know that your daughter is here and everything is all right now."

Panic. A stunning jolt of panic. "All right now? What was wrong? And how did she get there?"

"Dr. Stewart wondered if you could come straight here to her office instead of your home."

"Of course. But—"

"Everything's fine, Mr. Morgan. She'll explain when you get here."

The connection was broken.

"So what're we going to tell my father?" Greer asked.

Abby had been examining her for the past twenty minutes. No fever. Heart rate normal. No dilation of the pupils. Breathing, swallowing, movement of limbs all what they should be for a healthy girl Greer's age.

They were in Abby's office now. They'd left the exam room.

Abby, pretty as a soap opera femme fatale in her white medical jacket, sat behind her desk.

Abby was the mother Greer didn't have and Greer was the daughter Abby didn't have. When Greer was inconsolable over the loss of Laura, it had been Abby—much more than Cam, hard as he'd tried—who'd helped the girl to find a decent life again, despite the terrible nightmares that resulted from the mindmerge Greer had experienced at the time of her mother's death. She had died right along with her mother—frantically, hysterically crying out to keep her mother alive. And when Jenna had died? Greer had consoled Abby. This was about the time the repression drug Angil was first produced. White witches everywhere found their lives more tolerable.

"I'll tell him the truth. That you've had an acute anxiety attack. They're not uncommon in girls your age."

Greer frowned. "I wish we could tell him the real truth."

"So do I. But—I want to think a while about how we approach him with it."

"He's not going to believe it."

"I know."

"Mom never told him."

"She came close one time."

"She did? She never mentioned it to me."

Abby nodded. "Same kind of problem you're having. A lot of evidence that she was going somewhere at night, but in the morning she couldn't remember where."

"It must've gotten bad."

"Very, very bad. She went into a deep depression."

"I guess I've been lucky where that's concerned."

"Sometime I'll tell you about the suicide rate."

"It's high?"

"Very high."

"Poor Mom."

"She almost told him one night, but then a certain infant who shall remain nameless started running a terrible fever and her whole plan got sidetracked." She smiled. "You were about four months old at the time as I remember. They hauled me out of a warm bed about three in the morning to see if you were going to make it. This was before what they call psychoactive drugs—Prozac and Paxil and antidepressants like that—so I had to hurry up and find something that would settle her down so she wouldn't tell your father."

"You didn't think Dad could handle it?"

"No," Abby said. She paused. "And I'm still not sure he can."

Sara Crawford left the library just after six o'clock that evening. The smell of snow was in the air. They were predicting an early winter. She just hoped it wouldn't be this early.

She drove her rusting white Toyota to a strip mall on the east edge of town. Four stores. A chicken place. A video rental place. An Allstate Insurance place. And "Read 'Em Again Books."

The used bookstore was long and narrow. Overhead fluorescents—whose buzz made them sound like summer-night mosquitoes—provided the light. Best sellers and romances up front. Genre stuff—mysteries, science fiction, westerns—toward the back. The checkout counter and a storage room were at the back.

Her husband Yancy was running cash register totals for the day. He'd come into a small inheritance when he was thirty. It paid him about what he'd make working nine-to-five in a corporation. Anything he made here was extra. Lights, heat, lunches—that's what the store yielded most months. This was as close as he would ever get to his dream of being a writer. The store—and the rakish black eye patch—were compensation for failed dreams. He'd had an eye infection years ago and had to wear the patch for a time. He'd never stopped wearing it. Who would? Even to fifty-eight-year-old failed writers—maybe especially to them—eye patches were cool.

While he finished up with the cash register, she scanned the romances. She didn't dare take them home from the library. She was head of the monthly Great Books Round Table. Saul Bellow, Toni Morrison, John Updike. Writers like that. Books with titles like *Texas Lust* and *My Place Or Yours* had to be snuck about like contraband.

She grabbed a couple of Harlequins and walked up to the cash register. Her stomach clenched. Still. Even after nineteen months. She'd look at him as now and the fury would beat within her chest like a vast dark angry bird surging to fly free. She still had dreams of plunging a butcher knife into his chest in the middle of the night. And she still had dreams of having her own affair to pay him back. But her sense of morality kept them just that—dreams. In her thirties and even now in her forties any number of staffers and patrons had come on to her. At a library Christmas party she'd even French-kissed the Bookmobile man and let him feel her breasts. When he guided her hand to his crotch, she'd come drunkenly to her senses.

Yancy had not come to his senses.

A grad student home from college for the summer—this being the summer before last—had been giving him blow jobs for a two-month span. And one night, after closing up the store and killing the lights, he'd gone all the way with her. That was his version of it anyway. "Only once, I swear, only once did I, you know, actually fuck her. The other times she just blew me. And I don't blame you for being hurt and I don't blame you for being pissed. But getting a blow job isn't technically having real sex. It's sex but not real sex." Or so insisted Yancy with the eye patch.

But then Yancy—never wanting for opinions—insisted on a lot of things.

Cut his cock off in his sleep is what she should do. Just cleave it right off and throw it in the garbage.

She had no real need for it anymore. He hadn't had a decent erection in ten years and was too vain to try Viagra.

All these thoughts in less than ten seconds elapsed brain time as she approached the counter where he was just closing up the register.

"Hey, babe." The "babe" thing signified his Vegas lounge act side. He had three distinct personalities. The other two were his bookish, intense artiste ("If the publishing world wasn't devoted to publishing trash, I would've finished those novels I started. But what was the point when all they want is John Grisham junk?"); and the button-down Brooks Brothers man who went to town council meetings and berated council members to the delight of a certain never-satisfied faction.

"Guess who came to see me today?" she said.

"Who?"

"Greer Morgan."

His interest was instant and obvious. "You're kidding."

"No, I'm not."

"What did she want?"

"Seems she's developed this interest in the town's history."

"You don't think she knows anything, do you? Or remembers the little trips she's been taking at night, do you?"

"I don't think so. Nothing specific, anyway."

"My God. I don't believe it."

"I didn't either. And it made me very nervous till I realized that she didn't know what she was looking for."

"You think maybe we'd better call Dr. Cooper?"

"I don't think it would be a bad idea."

"I'll do it while you're making dinner."

"Gosh, you're going to let me have the honor of making dinner again after a full day of working at the library?"

"I work, too, remember?"

"Yes," she said, touching her hair with delicate fingers. She knew she was still a good-looking woman. The number of middle-aged males who had hit on her proved that. Unlike Yancy, she was faithful. "I know you do. Especially when you're in the back room getting blow jobs."

She wished she could just let go of it—not for his sake but for hers—but it wasn't easy. It wasn't easy at all.

Abby's medical clinic was closed when Cam reached it. He knocked on the double-glass front doors. Both Greer and Abby soon appeared, shadow shapes within the darkness of the reception area.

He hugged Greer greedily. So much worry, fear. My God, if anything happened to her—

"I'm fine, Dad. Really."

"What happened?"

"Would you like a cup of coffee, Cam?" Abby asked. "Let's go back to the little lunchroom."

"What about Greer?" he said, not wanting to let his daughter out of his sight.

"I thought I'd catch up on some phone calls, Dad," Greer said. "Abby said I could use her office. I need to find out what the homework assignments are so I can do my work tonight."

Sounded reasonable. Too reasonable. Too preplanned. This had all been set up in advance. But what was the harm? Doctors frequently wanted to talk to parents alone.

"All right, honey. Just don't leave Abby's office."

Greer looked at Abby and rolled her eyes. "I'm sure glad he isn't an overprotective parent, aren't you?"

He followed Abby back through the offices. Doors stood open on empty examination rooms. He had a morbid thought: had any patient been told he had a terminal illness today?

The lunchroom was an oasis of light and warmth. A

Mr. Coffee scented the refrigerator-lunch table-double sink rocm with the pleasant aroma of coffee beans. She got them each a cup of coffee before they sat down.

"Your office scared the hell out of me when they called."

"I'm sorry, Cam. I had to let you know what was going on."

"I know. I appreciate it. But say, what about Dr. Cooper. He's her regular physician. Why didn't she go to him?"

"I think she was embarrassed."

"Is she having trouble with her period or something?"

"No. She—she wonders if she's losing her mind." Abby looked crisp and fetching in her medical whites. The first hint of lines traced her eyes and mouth. But it just made her all the more appealing to him. He'd begun to have a deep appreciation for women who looked a little bit lived-in. He'd finally left his MTV days behind him.

"Is she serious?"

"She told me about last night. I think that's what brought on the anxiety attack that made her call me."

"I'm not following you. What about last night?"

"You found her wet coat."

"Right. And I also found a pair of her muddy shoes just as I was leaving for work."

"Last night scared her. She doesn't have any specific memory of leaving the house, but she knows she must have, with her coat wet and everything. She said she tried to convince you it had gotten wet when she went to get the paper this morning. But she said you knew better."

"What's going on with her? Why doesn't she remember leaving the house?"

"A lot of things are going on, Cam. She still mourns her mother. The prospect of going to college scares her. She's really a homebody, as you know. And as much as she likes soccer, she feels burdened by it. She's the team's high scorer. And she doesn't want to let anybody down. And she worries about you."

"Me?"

"Feels you're just sort of drifting. Not facing how lonely you are."

"I'm fine. I'm so damned busy—"

"That's the other thing. She thinks you hide in your work. That it keeps you from facing how much you're just drifting. She thinks you need a woman."

"Did she mention the woman she had in mind?"

Abby laughed. He saw the girl in her when she laughed. Suddenly they were back in school and she was walking down the hall with Laura. And they were laughing their secret laugh. And he was watching them. And marveling at how much fun the two of them were to hang out with—even if Abby did seem to hate him.

"I believe she has me in mind."

"Right," he said. "Now there would be a pair, wouldn't it? You and me? After all the years we've—been uncomfortable about each other."

"Hated each other, you mean." She smiled.

"You really hated me?"

"Yes. I was jealous because you were taking my protection from me."

"Your protection?"

"Sure, my best friend Laura. As long as she was around, I didn't have to face how insecure I was around boys. I always thought of myself as gangly and homely. And when you and Laura started dating, that left me all alone. I started dating, and the first boy I went out with I fell in love with instantly. And slept with. And he dumped me. And then the same thing happened all over again a year later. Seduced and abandoned. And I sort of blamed you. You'd forced me to become vulnerable to boys."

"That's amazing."

"What is?"

"That you considered yourself gangly and homely."

"Well, I did. Even today when people tell me I'm pretty, I just assume they're being polite. You forget that I grew up in a household where my two oldest sisters went on to become runway models in New York. They weren't only pretty, they were glamorous. Even when they were young girls, they were glamorous. I was always a little bit of a tomboy."

"Well, you're sure not a tomboy anymore."

She laughed. "You know, I think that's the first time you've ever complimented me. I'd better go write that down on my calendar." She finished her coffee. "I'm going to try Greer on Paxil for a couple of weeks. It should help take the edge off. She wants to focus on her studies and school activities, and that'll be hard to do if she's having terrible nightmares and worried about everything."

"So that's what we're dealing with here? She just hit a bumpy patch in the road?"

"Well, it's certainly not uncommon for teenagers to hit bumpy patches."

Now it was his turn to feel—what? Suspicious? No, too strong. But her explanation was so simple. Well, maybe it was simple. Maybe this was the teenage syndrome she described. But every once in a while you talk to somebody whom you sense is withholding something. And he had that sense now.

"I don't want you to hold anything back, Abby."

And for the first time, she averted her eyes. And a small brief tic appeared in her right cheek, almost dimplelike. Or was he imagining this? Seeing what he wanted to see? You had to be careful of that once you started down the long, unending road of suspicion.

She swallowed. Swallowed hard. Wasn't that significant, too? But now he was starting to feel ridiculous. Pretty soon, every single move she made would take on sinister significance. Maybe he needed some Paxil himself.

"What else would there be, Cam?"

"I don't know? Sometimes, doctors want to spare your feelings. You know, don't want you to worry or anything. And—"

"She's a perfectly healthy girl. Being a teenager—especially today—is hard enough. But she's also lost her mother and she's overloaded herself with studies and extracurricular activities. And leaving home for college scares her."

"I guess I don't understand that. Most kids look forward to getting away from the nest."

"I didn't."

"You didn't?"

There it was again, that series of tiny signs: the eyes averted, the tic in the cheek, the hard swallow.

"I was like Greer. I said I wasn't comfortable around boys. I wasn't all that comfortable around other girls, either. I always felt different. And I was. I didn't fit in. I hated having a roommate. I didn't want that kind of intimacy with anybody. Laura was the same way, if you remember, when she went to Smith. Managed to have a room of her own in the dorm and then moved off campus as soon as possible. I was miserable at college."

"I hope you don't say that to Greer. She respects you so much she might decide you're right and not go."

"I've already told her that she needs to go. That there's nothing to fear. And that she'll meet a lot of nice people and have a great time."

Again the feeling she wasn't being entirely forthright. As if there needed to be one more thing added for all this to make emotional sense to him. "I've heard of being homesick but that usually passes after a while. There were boys in my dorm who had some adjustment problems at first, but—"

"But people like Greer and me—and Laura—I guess it's just this feeling of being . . . different. Unfortunately, that doesn't pass after a while. It stays with you. For life."

She'd used that expression a few times now—being different—and he was beginning to feel that this was the whole underpinning of not only her own problem but Greer's as well. And Laura's, too. Laura, in fact, had said that many times over the years, that she didn't really fit in anywhere because she was so different from other people. She'd stuck to her home and family. Had few friends outside the home. Had joined exactly zero clubs, organizations, etc.

But what did "being different" mean exactly? Didn't everybody feel that way to a certain extent? He certainly did. Sometimes, he had the sense that he was an alien sent here to spy on a species he didn't care much for—and certainly didn't belong to. Wasn't that within the normal range of emotions from time to time?

"But what makes you—and Greer—feel so different from other people?" he asked. And was about to say more when Greer appeared in the door behind him. He turned to see her yawning.

"Anybody here want to take a tired kid home?" she questioned.

It should've been a "Leave It to Beaver" moment. He'd get up and put his arm around his daughter and off they'd go to the home front.

But he felt she'd deliberately interrupted him to stop the conversation. And now Greer was watching Abby closely. As if waiting to be instructed on her next move.

Suddenly, Abby was in a rush. "Good idea. Warm food. Going to bed early. That's what you need here. You've got your meds, honey. I told you how to use them."

She walked Cam to the door. "I now leave her in your capable hands."

"I appreciate all this, Abby," he said, knowing that such a remark was expected. And well deserved. It was just that he had this nagging doubt that he hadn't been told everything.

Once again, shadow shapes moved through the shadows of the closed clinic. Abby stood on the inside of the glass doors, watching as the headlights of Cam's car ignited, silver rain slanting down in front of them, windshield wipers slapping away rain beads immediately. She waved until they were out of sight.

"Dr. Cooper, please."

"Who's calling, please?"

"Yancy."

"Oh, hi. It's Linda. Sorry I didn't recognize you."

Linda was Tom Cooper's nurse.

Tom came on.

"Hi, Yancy. How's it going?"

"Just a piece of information."

Cooper chortled. "You do love a good drama, don't you?"

"I'm glad you find this amusing."

"It's not that, Yancy. It's just that you always get so excited about things."

"Well, maybe there's something to get excited about."

"Such as?"

"Such as guess who came to the library today looking for books about the founding of our town?"

"I'm not good at guessing, Yancy. You'll have to tell me."

"Greer Morgan."

Yancy took great pleasure in the pause on the other end of the telephone.

"You think she knows anything?" Cooper asked.

"That," said Yancy, who did indeed love a fuss, "is what I was wondering."

2

ABBY didn't get home until after nine. She had two patients at the hospital she needed to look in on. Both were doing well, though one, who'd just had her gall bladder removed, was suffering from an uncomfortable skin rash.

The misty night slowed her usual quick drive home. She'd been stopped three times for speeding in the past year. She'd been able to convince the officers she was only breaking the speed limit because she had to get to a patient. She wasn't against using both her medical degree and her womanly wiles in such circumstances. She needed a car.

The town was a moody watercolor, a New England Renoir, everything seen through the rain-pebbled windshield—living-room lights glowing warm and private; gray smoke rising from chimneys; streets gleaming clean and wet; stoplights flashing red and sometimes yellow in empty intersections, the emptiness somehow reflective of her own soul at this moment.

She still felt guilty about lying to Cam Morgan. True, hers had been a sin of omission rather than commission, but that didn't matter. He deserved to know the truth about his daughter. He was a good parent and a concerned one. And her vague talk about an "anxiety attack" couldn't have been very comforting.

She'd found herself feeling sorry for Cam, something almost unimaginable. Cocky Cam, the high school show-off and resident ass-bandit. She still automatically thought of him that way. She had to correct herself whenever Greer brought his name up. He'd changed and not just recently. He'd probably changed long ago—maybe starting with that "dyke" incident at school—but she'd refused to see it. But she certainly saw it tonight. His concern for Greer was deep and abiding. He was a first-rate father. And he'd been a first-rate husband for Laura. Cam was one of the males who carried the witch gene. Female witches had to have such carriers father their children.

As for Greer? Abby had drawn some blood and dropped it off at the lab on her way from the clinic tonight. Though Cam didn't know it, Greer was under the impression that she'd left the house in the middle of the night two or three times before last night. And she had absolutely no memory of where she'd gone or what she'd done.

Abby had to be careful. Greer couldn't afford to have her secret become public. That was the problem of all the women—Abby herself, Laura—who had the same secret.

Tomorrow, she planned to call a psychiatrist friend of hers in Boston. Maybe she could explain Greer's behavior. And maybe that behavior had nothing to do with her secret. Maybe it really was simply a manifestation of anxiety, as Abby had told Cam tonight, some form of sleepwalking?

But somehow Abby doubted it, especially given the so-called accidental deaths of three people over the past five years—a woman named Dana Winslow, Laura, and Abby's daughter, Jenna. They'd shared the secret, too. And had manifested strong anxiety right before their deaths. She knew that Laura and Jenna had experienced the same kind of sleepwalking that Greer had. She'd have to come up with some pretext to call Dana's family and ask if there'd been any nocturnal wanderings right before her accident.

A drowning. A car accident on an icy road. A fall down basement stairs. Abby hadn't been suspicious until Jenna's death. An insurance actuarial chart could explain two out of the three dying at or before age forty. But three in a five-year span and with the same secret? That, it seemed to Abby, was defying the odds.

Five women and girls, including Abby herself, had been sisters of a very special kind—and now there were only two of them left. Was somebody killing them off?

(There were other "sisters," too. The bad ones. Two strains of witches. Neither of them were as benign as good old sweet Elizabeth Montgomery had been as Samantha. But there was a drug you could take—made from an herb found only in eastern Europe—and it controlled the predatory impulses among the witch population, which numbered, white and black witches alike, at most twenty-five hundred in the world. But some refused to take it. The predators. Too much fun—the wanton carnality, the even more wanton violence—fuck the meek or however that biblical passage went. The darkness would consume the light. As Abby's friends began to die in the small town here, she was contacted by a coven of dark witches who offered their help in finding the killer or killers. But Abby had thought they were trying to convince her that "accidents" were "murders" just to lure her into their circle, and she knew that once she let them into her life, they would always be there, hovering at the edges of the campfire, waiting to make her their own as they made so many, many unwitting and unwilling ones their own. The good witches had limited powers and used them to defend themselves. But the drug they took inhibited the range of those powers. The dark witches were far more powerful.)

Going to the local police was out of the question. Chief Trueblood would want to know what the women had in common. A logical enough question if somebody was killing a "type" of woman. And what would Abby say then? There were no other real commonalities. One had been poor; two, relatively well-off. Two had been Presbyterian, one Catholic. One had been married, one single and one a young girl. And on and on. No similarities except for the secret one.

Was Abby being set up for an accident? Had a fake accident killed her daughter?

She'd inherited her uncle's Victorian house. In the rain, it resembled a friendly version of an Edward Gorey drawing. The spires and turrets were especially imposing on such a dark and stormy night.

Her cats, Anthony and Cleopatra—Siamese and endlessly mysterious—waited for her just inside the back door. Other breeds pissed and moaned when it was long past their dinnertime. Not Siamese. They simply visited imperious and scornful looks upon the slacker. And that did the job. She felt dutifully guilty and rushed around getting them their food.

They were her great good friends and, damnit, she should feel guilty.

She put Greer and Cam out of her head for the moment and set about making herself a salad and a breast of turkey sandwich.

Time to collapse. Stretch out on the recliner in front of the tube and wait for the headlights of the Domino's car to splash across the front window. Greer across from him on the couch under a blanket. Nick at Night is the channel of choice. Silly sitcoms of the seventies. Even "The Brady Bunch" had a certain panache tonight. Great Gawd A'mighty was Emmy worthy, in fact. How could thick ol' Cam have ever misunderstood the true wit that lay just below the surface of what seemed to be just another ho-hum cornball sitcom? My God, it was a comically eloquent look at modern (well, modern circa 1970) family life in America. He was relaxed and having a mindless ball.

"Didn't one of them become a junkie, Dad?" Greer said during the commercial break.

"I think so, honey. I mean, I think somebody on every sitcom became a junkie."

"And wasn't one of them gay?"

"Yeah. Same thing, though. I think somebody on every sitcom is gay."

"Wasn't there a sitcom once where one of the actors shot somebody?"

"Probably."

"But I don't think he killed him."

"Huh?"

"He shot him, but he didn't kill him. I think the other guy survived."

"Oh. Where do you get all this stuff, anyway?"

"That show 'The Dark Side of Hollywood.' I never miss it."

"You don't?" he said.

"No. They have interesting stuff. Fatty Arbuckle—you know, that big silent screen star—he didn't really rape that girl they accused him of."

"Well, I'll sleep a little better tonight knowing that."

"And that one starlet they always thought the studio president killed? He didn't. She choked while she was giving him oral sex."

"Maybe 'The Brady Bunch' could use that for an episode sometime."

"I love shocking you. You're such a prude."

"I sure wish that pizza would get here."

"And then there was that pretty girl who committed suicide. Dana something."

"Oh, yeah, right."

"Sitcoms today are kind of boring. I mean, the actors don't get in trouble the way they used to."

"Yeah," he said, "what the hell's wrong with them, anyway? They owe us a good show on and off the tube."

And then, thank God, he saw the headlights sweep across the front window as the Domino's car pulled up to the house.

"In fact, I think 'The Dark Side of Hollywood' is on in half an hour."

"I can't wait."

"It's about this Hollywood serial killer who was also a cannibal."

He laughed. "That's right. Make fun of the old guy. Make up these stories so he'll get sick and you'll get his half of the pizza."

"But I'm not making it up, Dad," she said, the kid-grin in full force. "He killed starlets and then he ate them."

Abby didn't remember what the name was. She just remembered her mother telling her that if things ever got very, very bad, there was a woman about thirty miles from here who could help her out.

All through her meal, all through her shower, all through her hour of reading an article on a possible new medical breakthrough for arthritis sufferers—sitting up in bed in her pink jammies and feeling a little of her own arthritis—Abby kept trying to remember the woman's name. She even stared at Anthony and Cleopatra a couple of times next to her on the bed, as if they might not only know the name but tell her the name.

Thirty miles due south, in an Airstream house trailer that had been new about the time Elvis was doing the last of his "fat" tours, Candy Archer, age sixty-eight, was playing footsie—literally—with a nervous young man named Stuff Perringham.

The sign on the door to the trailer read:

CANDY ARCHER, FUTURIST

In times past, the sign had read fortune-teller. But this was the new century and futurist—at least to Cynthia Maureen Archer—sounded much better.

In times past, Candy had also used a crystal ball

and gotten herself up in a vaguely gypsy-style costume ("gypsy" as defined by the great Universal horror films of the forties starring Boris Karloff, Bela Lugosi and her favorite, the sweet-sad-faced Lon Chaney, Jr.).

In keeping with being a futurist, Candy had changed her attire as well. She'd gone punk. Spiky hair. Bustier. Leather miniskirt. Three-inch heels. The trailer was the same, though; all the curtains had swirls of stars and other "mystic" symbols. And the bookcase was packed with faded paperbacks discussing occult matters. Candy had slept with several of the authors represented on her shelves. One of them had given her the clap and another had given her a real pain in the ass.

"Is that your foot, Candy?" Stuff asked.

"I'm just trying to be nice, Stuff."

"I know, Candy. But you're, well, you're a little old for me." Stuff, who worked at a salvage yard, was twenty-four. God only knew where his nickname had come from. He wore a blue-and-white Woodrow Wilson High School jacket, a white T-shirt with some kind of stain up near the top of it, and jeans. He had bad teeth, packed an extra fifty pounds and was constantly inserting the tip of a finger into his left nostril. But Candy hadn't had a man in two months. "And anyway, I couldn't do nothin' anyway."

"Why not?"

"Because of Pammie."

"Maybe that's why she broke up with you."

"Why?"

"Because you call her Pammie."

"Nah, she likes it when I call her Pammie."

"If you say so."

"The reason she broke up with me is because her old boyfriend came back to town and he wears a tie."

"You kind of lost me there, Stuff."

"She says if I had any gumption, I'd have a job where I wear a tie."

"Got ya."

"This guy sells beauty supplies."

"And he wears a tie."

"Yeah. And a sports coat."

"And you wear—"

"I throw scrap metal around all day, Candy. I wear greasy jeans and a shirt in the summer and add a sweatshirt and long johns in the winter."

"And Pammie doesn't like that."

"She hates it. She won't even let me come over to her place and see her unless I go home first and take a shower and put on a shirt and tie. I've got these two clip-on ties. She don't like the idea that they're clip-ons, even. She says clip-ons are for hicks. She says Tyler—that's her old boyfriend—she says Tyler wouldn't be caught dead in a clip-on tie. She says he rides around in a company car all day and has expense account lunches and always brings her a little something when he picks her up."

"She break up with you before or after she started seeing him again?"

"After. How I found out was I saw this red Trojan dealie—you know, one of those little packages they come in that're so hard to open?—I seen one of them in her bathroom wastebasket. I don't use them. I use the store brand—the generic kind, you know—they're just as good and they're a lot cheaper. Anyway, so I lifted this red Trojan wrapper out of her wastebasket and I went into the living room and I held it right up to her face and she could see I was really pissed off and she said, 'Oh, yeah, I was gonna tell you about that.' Just like that. She wasn't embarrassed or ashamed or nothing. Just 'Oh, yeah, I was gonna tell you about that.' And then I did something I never thought I'd do."

"You hit her?"

"No."

"You kicked her?"

"Jeeze, no, Candy, I seen all the trouble my old man got in for punchin' my stepmother those times. I don't want to spend all my time on probation like that. No, what I done was, I cried."

"In front of her?"

"Yeah. I just went across and sat down on the couch and I started blubbering."

"Oh, boy."

"What? Was that the wrong thing to do?"

"That was exactly the wrong thing to do."

"How come?"

"How come? Damn, Stuff. You gotta start usin' that brain of yours. You start blubberin' like that, you know what she's thinking?"

"What?"

"That she can have you any time she wants. That you don't even have gumption enough to stand up to her and tell her where she can put that little red Trojan dealie you found in her wastebasket. She knows she's got you and got you good. So: A) she isn't interested in you anymore because who wants somebody they can have any time they wiggle their little finger and, B) who wants a man who don't have no self-respect for himself?"

"I really fucked up, didn't I, Candy?"

"You sure did, Stuff. You sure did."

"Is there anything I can do?"

"You got to leave her alone for awhile."

"That's hard."

"You still calling her?"

"Six, seven times a day."

"Cold turkey, Stuff. Cold turkey."

"Aw, Candy."

"You still drivin' by her place?"

"Yeah. Every night. Sometimes that's all I do. Get a six pack and turn the radio up good and loud and cruise by her place. I see his car over there I want to go in and kill the sonofabitch."

"Cold turkey on that, too."

"You seein' any pictures?"

"I'm startin' to." That's how she did it these days. Like she was having some kind of minor fit. Her whole body jerking and twisting and twitching. And then covering her eyes and telling her customers what she was seeing. Twenty dollars per picture.

And then it was upon her. Her moment.

Stuff just watched her. He'd been coming here ever since his gal friend problems had started.

First time he saw her go into her psychic mode it scared him. He'd seen a kid on a fourth grade playground have an epileptic fit. He'd turned away and run. Let the other kids handle it. He'd felt not only freaked out but helpless. And a kid his size didn't like to feel helpless.

"You seein' anything?"

"A wedding chapel."

"Really, Candy? Really?"

"Really."

"Aw, shit, that's great."

She writhed. "She looks beautiful in her wedding gown."

"How do I look, Candy? Am I wearing a tuxedo?"

"That's the funny thing."

"What is?"

"She's standing at the back of the church. Just sliding her arm through her dad's."

"Where am I?"

"That's what so funny. I see a groom way, way up the aisle, almost at the altar."

"And that's me, right?"

A little more writhing. Work it, babe. Work it. "I can't tell."

"You can't tell?"

"The groom's too far away. I can't see the face."

"Then, hell, it could be her old boyfriend."

"I guess it could."

His big fist slammed the table. "C'mon, Candy. I got to know. I got to know. Is that me up at the altar?"

She slumped forward, seemingly drained.

"What's wrong?"

"The picture faded."

"And you still didn't get a good look at the groom?"

"Afraid I didn't, Stuff. But we can try again next week." Another twenty dollars next week.

Now it was Stuff who slumped. Put his head down and sort of fell forward in his chair.

She hated seeing him like this. He was just a big

overgrown boy and he really loved this girl, but he was never going to have her and he either wouldn't or couldn't come to terms with that. He appeared to be staring across a vast desert, that kind of bleakness in his gaze. And so, without quite knowing it, she was up and standing behind him and massaging his neck and shoulders. And a few minutes later, also without quite knowing it, she was leading him back to her dark bedroom and easing him onto her queen-sized waterbed and unzipping his pants and groping for his cock.

"I'm too depressed to do anything, Candy. It ain't nothing against you."

"I know."

"I loved her since second grade."

"I know."

"I don't think I can ever stop lovin' her, Candy."

"I know."

"Maybe the picture'll be clearer next week."

"Yeah."

"And you'll see that the groom is me."

"I sure hope that's how that picture turns out, Stuff."

"I sure do, too, Candy."

He started crying. Big man that he was, the whole waterbed shook when he cried. She just held him. The way she used to hold her baby girl before the state people took her away because Candy got arrested for prostitution. Held him and rocked him and let him cry.

"You're sure a good woman, Candy," he said a couple of times there in the darkness.

"And you're sure a good man, Stuff," she said right back.

A stray compliment or two like that, she never charged for. They just came free as part of her feel-better psychic services in the futurist business.

Yancy's cell phone cried out. He punched in. He was watching MTV. These teenage girls on the beach. His dick was weeping.

"Very soon now," Dr. Cooper said.

"Do you ever say hello?"

Cooper sighed. "Very soon. I went through my charts and compared the previous ones with Greer's."

When they'd spoken earlier in the evening, Yancy had asked Cooper to narrow down the date when she would appear. Cooper was like most doctors. He'd been trained to avoid exact answers. It was a litigious society. But what was Yancy going to do, sue him?

"I just hope she'll know where to go."

"Oh, she'll know, Yancy."

"I don't know why we have to try and duplicate what Prescott's doing. He's set up for this stuff. We're not." Implicit in this was a criticism of Cooper. He was, Yancy was saying, a country doc compared to the flashy Prescott. Prescott wanted to take over all the hunting and exterminating. Just let the small cells like this one around the world report their data to the central computer bank and let Prescott and his people take it from there. This was one of few remaining cells that hadn't gone over to Prescott. Cooper was too proud to do it. "She wasn't any particular trouble when you were prepping her?"

"No. We already discussed that. She was one of the easier ones, in fact. If she responds to the clues I gave her with hypnosis, that means the drugs are working. So when we have her trial, the drugs will have brought her along to the point where she'll be receptive to the sodium Amytal."

Yancy was tired of talking to Cooper already. They'd never gotten along.

"Give my best to your wife," Yancy said.

"Call me as soon as she gets there."

"I will, Doctor. And, Doctor?"

"Yes."

"She has a very nice young body. You must enjoy examining her."

"That's not funny, Yancy."

"Good-bye, Doctor."

He hung up. Still smiling. Was there anything more pleasurable than irritating a prissy old fart like Cooper?

After her shower, Greer came downstairs in her pajamas and fuzzy slippers and gave her father a good night kiss on the cheek. He was watching a political talk show.

"Boy, don't you ever get tired of that stuff?"

"I suppose I should. They say the same old crap over and over. Maybe tomorrow night I'll try pro wrestling."

"Oh, yeah. I can see you watching pro wrestling, all right."

She sat on the arm of the recliner. "I remember how you and Mom used to take turns reading to me."

"Your mom always read you Mother Goose and I always read you adventure stories."

"So that's why I'm so warped."

"I never thought of it that way before, but I'll bet it just could be."

"You coming up?"

"In a while. Thought I'd watch a little bit of Letterman."

"He's too mean."

"Sometimes he is."

She kissed him on the top of his head. "Night."

"Night."

He heard her on the stairs. And then her bedroom door opening and closing. He yawned, stretched. Maybe things had settled down again. There had been a time when he'd craved stimulation, excitement. No longer. Nothing was more appealing to him these days than a long, uninterrupted spell of peace and tranquillity.

He stayed up to watch Letterman but gave up midway through the first interview. Letterman was being mean again and it always made Cam uncomfortable. Letterman's stock-in-trade was violating the social contract, i.e., belittling or ridiculing his guests. Sometimes he was funny at it. Sometimes, as tonight, he just seemed nasty, his own apparent spiritual sourness boiling up and taking over.

Cam locked up, went upstairs, got ready for bed, picked up his Grisham, and read much later than he should have. He went to sleep thinking that things were all right again. It was a wonderful feeling.

Cynthia Maureen Archer.

That was the name.

Abby hadn't been able to sleep trying to remember

the name, so she climbed the dusty stairs to the dusty attic and sat in her grandmother's dusty rocking chair and read her mother's diary.

Cynthia Maureen Archer.

The diminutive beauty of her mother's college class. Mom and Cynthia had gone to Europe together for a summer. Mom had to have an abortion before coming back home. She'd never told her parents. Cynthia had been luckier. A true blue-blooded count had fallen in love with her and pursued her all over Paris. There was a photograph of Cynthia standing in front of the Louvre that summer. A beauty. Hepburn. Dark-haired, tiny, yet with that kind of huge-eyed, camera-loving presence. Everybody fell in love with Cynthia at one time or another, men and women alike.

One other thing about Cynthia, as noted in the diary: she shared the same secret. But her skills and abilities were far greater than anybody else's. Mom speculated in the diary that Cynthia might have the same powers as the women of legend.

Pages and pages about Cynthia and then nothing. Cynthia elected to stay behind in Europe that summer and wasn't mentioned in the diary for another fifteen years. Then she was mentioned in only one entry: "This woman must be an imposter. I drove over there and spied on her. How could this possibly by Cynthia? And that gross name she uses, Candy. Sounds like a stripper. And yet if anything serious ever happened, I'd have to contact her. Whatever has happened to her, she must still have her powers." Then the diary listed Cynthia's phone number.

Abby wrote the number down. Given everything that was going on, maybe it was time to contact this woman. Maybe she'd know if Abby was merely being suspicious or if the accidental deaths over the past five years hadn't actually been accidental.

She was curious about Cynthia now, too. Apparently, she'd had some kind of fall from grace. No longer a beauty. No longer traveled with aristocracy.

Life stories—virtually anybody's life story—had always fascinated Abby. Even the humblest of lives were filled with triumphs, setbacks, ironies, and juicy moments. Sometimes the illicit love affair a refrigerator salesman had was more interesting than the one a prince had. She'd learned this early on in her medical career. The most unlikely people had the most thrilling lives.

She was eager to hear Cynthia's story.

Now that she knew whom she should contact—and whom she could ask for help with Greer's situation—she could finally get to sleep.

Anthony and Cleopatra slept right next to her.

There was no rain, but the wind was cold and sharp. Streetlights swayed, branches cracked. Parked cars rocked, and lone, lonely dogs prowled long, empty alleys.

The town looked small and vulnerable under the onslaught, like a child cowering in the shadows.

The time was 2:00 A.M., and Greer was not only suddenly awake but dressing. Argyle socks, jeans, a sweatshirt, jacket, and finally her low-cut leather hiking boots.

In the pale glow of the streetlight insinuating itself upon the window, her eyes gleamed with frightening nonrecognition. No personality, no reality shone in her eyes. Psychiatric hospitals were filled with eyes and faces like hers. The results of being over-drugged.

As she started to leave her room—uncertain of where she was going—she tripped against the edge of her dresser and pushed it back against the wall.

Cam heard her.

Correction: heard something.

A noise.

And awoke.

For all his well-being when he went to bed, his dreams were filled with images of Greer sitting at her window waiting for somebody. Or listening for something.

Cam heard her bedroom door open now. Heard her steps on the hardwood floor of the hallway. Threw back the covers. Needed badly to piss. But no time for that. Hurried out of his own room. Saw her approach the stairs.

She was dressed. That was his first surprise. His second was the gleam of her empty eyes in the light filtering through the skylight above. The same emptiness he'd seen when she'd sat next to the window the other night.

"Where're you going, honey?"

Nothing; she said nothing. Just looked at him. And started toward the stairway.

He reached out and grabbed her arm. He sensed she would need to be shaken before she was able to recognize the situation and him.

"Honey, you're scaring me."

She twisted away from him. "Leave me alone, you fucker."

His third shock. She'd never spoken to him like that before. Once again he saw this body before him as an imposter. All those science fiction movies where an alien being inhabits a familiar human form. This had to be an example of that.

She started down the stairs.

He lunged for her. But missed.

He grabbed—in one long instant—for her and then for the banister. He missed both. And that was when he started his headlong tumble down the stairs.

He might have been able to stop himself if his head hadn't slammed against the edge of a step, knocking him out briefly. His body and the forces of gravity pitched him the rest of the way down the stairs.

Pain. Great pain. And from competing points on his body.

His arm pinned, twisted, beneath him. Broken?

Darkness. The smell of dust in the vestibule rug. Shadow shape of his daughter near the top of the stairs.

Slowly descending. Hand on banister. One careful step at a time.

"Honey, please, help me. Maybe something's broken." His head pounding. Dampness on the left side of his head. Blood?

Nothing; she said nothing.

Came down the stairs and stepped over him.

He tried to reach out and grab her, but she jerked away.

Went right to the door. Unlocked it.

"Honey, something's wrong with you. Let me help you. Please, honey."

Struggling to his feet. Pain inhibiting, crippling him.

Reaching out like a doddering old man for his daughter. "Please, honey." Sounding both hysterical and pathetic, his voice soon lost in the rainy wind as the screen door slammed shut.

Cam attempted to go after her. Hobbled to the door. Pushed it open. His arm felt better. But his leg didn't. He crumpled to one knee on the porch. He'd twisted the knee, maybe badly.

"Greer! Greer!" he called out into the night.

Clutched the banister of the front porch. Levered himself up. "Greer! Greer!"

But she was gone. Shadow shape again. Saw her faintly, three-quarters of the way down the street, in and out of a circle of streetlight.

Running; she was running now.

Running away.

3

JEFF almost wished nobody had ever told him how much he looked like the country singer Dwight Yoakam. Because as soon as people started telling him that—and that was about the time he'd turned fourteen—he got it into his mind to be a country-western singer. And he started dressing and acting like Dwight Yoakam, too. The white Stetson with the upswept side brims. The petulant, sort of eternal-punk scowl. And those faded Levis that were so hard to get into, even though Jeff, at seventeen years of age, was fifteen pounds underweight.

Jeff. Once had a 4.0 grade average. Once was considered an easy candidate for an Ivy League scholarship. Now he was a high school dropout and lounge singer at Holler Inn, a redneck joint out on the highway. At least he was a lounge singer there until the manager figured out he was underage, which could get said manager's liquor license lifted.

Two-thirty A.M. and headed home on this miserable night, just turning off the two-lane highway onto the asphalt stretch that led to the upscale housing development where his parents lived.

His parents. Every once in a while, he actually felt sorry for them.

The truth was, Jeff was probably going to give up the singing gig and go back to school next January. His sinuses couldn't handle all the smoke, and his ego couldn't handle all the indifference he met. You ever tried to sing above the din of a hundred drunks?

Besides, he was starting to put on weight and the resemblance to Mr. Dwight was starting to fade. You had to be real, real skinny to look like ol' Dwight.

He yawned. Rolled the window down. Out in the boonies like this, tired the way he was, it was easy to fall asleep. No oncoming cars to distract him. So, some cold fresh air. Damp air, misty air.

The ground fog was up to the hood of the old Mazda he drove. It turned in upon itself like cotton candy being made.

He couldn't be sure at first that the girl was even a girl. Maybe he was so horny—he was the only one of his friends who was still a virgin—that he'd started imagining girls coming up out of small gullies and standing at the edge of the road.

But no, she was real.

And she was probably drunk.

He based this impression on her staggering walk. She seemed to be on the verge of falling straight down on her face.

He realized who it was and couldn't believe it. Greer Morgan—what would she be doing out here in the middle of the night? He'd had crushes on her throughout his school years. He'd had crushes on many other girls, too, of course, being the sophisticated and worldly type of virgin he was. But Greer had been one of the prime ones for sure.

He was just starting to slow down when she lurched out into the roadway. His immediate impression: something wrong with her eyes. An inhuman, dead quality that not even the beam of his headlights could enliven. She didn't seem to understand that she was walking directly into the path of a moving car.

No comprehension showed in her eyes even when he hit the horn. She just kept walking in front of him, so intent on reaching the other side of the road that nothing was going to stop her.

He hit the brakes hard this time, brought the car to a halt, jerked on the emergency brake, grabbed a flashlight from the glove compartment, and jumped out of the Mazda.

She was just going down into the gully on the other side of the road. You couldn't see much, what with the fog and all, but he had the idea now that her destination was up on the hill looming in the distance. It was an isolated place, nobody on either side of it for at least half a mile.

The shape of a house swam like a secret on the bottom of a fog ocean: the Coopers' cabin, which was really a summerhouse.

But why would she be going there? Especially at this hour?

"Hey! Greer! It's me, Jeff!"

She just kept walking.

"Greer! Hey, Greer!"

He didn't think she was the kind of girl who took drugs but these days, you never knew. She certainly had to be stoned on something, man.

To his right, his car lights pierced the rolling fog.

Greer disappeared into the darkness below.

He went down after her.

"Yes, it is an emergency."

"Give me your name again and your phone number. I'll call the doctor and have her call you back."

Abby's answering service. Cam hadn't thought of checking Greer's phone list. She probably had Abby's private number there.

His first instinct had been to call the police. But what could he tell them? His daughter had called him a dirty name and walked out of the house? That she'd looked spooky?

There was something Abby wasn't telling him. He was sure of it. She'd be more help than the police, especially if she'd finally tell him everything that was going on with Greer.

He was up now, dressed. His knee hurt, his head hurt, and his shoulder hurt. But none of his injuries were as bad as he'd feared at first.

He went into the kitchen and started the Mr. Coffee going. The coffee smell was welcome.

He poured half a cup as soon as it was ready then put the pot back on to let it fill up.

He wished he knew more about posttraumatic stress. Was that what he was seeing in Greer? The death of her mother must have affected her much more deeply than he'd realized.

When the phone rang, it stunned him out of his thoughts. Left him standing disoriented for the moment, looking at the kitchen, stark now and not comforting as it usually was.

"What's going on there, Cam?" She didn't identify herself. Didn't need to.

"She—ran away. I don't know how else to say it."

"You couldn't stop her?"

"Maybe if I hadn't fallen down the fucking stairs, and maybe if she'd bothered to see if I was all right or not, and maybe if you'd tell me exactly what the fuck is really going on here—"

"Don't be your usual jerk self, Cam."

"Oh, yeah? You're the one who's keeping information about my daughter from me and I'm the jerk?"

"Cool down."

"Where the fuck did she go, Abby? And what the hell's going on here? Please tell me because I'm going crazy. I really am. I'm so worried about her, I can't think straight." Pause. "I'm sorry for yelling at you."

"I would've done the same thing."

"No, you wouldn't have."

"Sure, I would've, Cam. Poor Laura had to put up with both of our tempers."

"Just tell me the truth, Abby. That's all I'm asking."

"Not on the phone. I'm going to throw on some clothes and drive over there."

"Hurry."

"I will."

When he replaced the receiver on the wall phone, he noticed how badly his hand was shaking.

Where the hell did she go?

She'd gone down into the shallow gully and then vanished into the fog.

Jeff stood in the gully now, waving damp fog away as if it were a cloud of smoke at a poker game.

No sight of her.

She was moving faster now. That was the only explanation. Moving faster. Had somehow scrambled up the gully before he could reach her.

Phantasmagoric. There was a nice word he remembered from ninth grade when they'd read Poe. And that's what tonight was like, too. The headlight beams on the road above him—he had to be careful that old heap didn't die on him—pierced the fog like the cunning eyes of a monster. Raindrops dripped ponderously from the top of a culvert into a puddle. There was a sour smell on the chilly air, the kind of smell he associated with carcasses.

He heard her footsteps. Not too far away. Still moving in the direction of the Coopers' cabin. She'd apparently slowed down again.

He knew he should go back to his car, pull it even farther off the side of the road, kill the engine. But if he did that, he'd lose her. And finding her again had become vital for some reason—maybe that very first crush he'd had on her back in third grade.

He scrambled up the far side of the gully.

How could she explain it to him without sounding insane? Abby wondered. Or as if she were lying to him?

The fog slowed her drive to Cam's house, but it also gave her time to think. To rehearse the words she'd use when she was trying to explain the secret she shared with Greer.

Flashing overhead light lost in the silver shifting fog. A distant siren. A sense of isolation. No evidence whatsoever that she was anywhere near other human beings.

Fifteen miles an hour.

She still didn't have the words. No amount of doctor-patient training could prepare you for a moment like this.

She saw Cam's street and pulled on her left turn signal.

How do I say it, Cam? What Laura wanted to tell you all the time you were married. What Greer wants to tell you but can't find the words. What I want to tell you but don't know how. How do I say it, Cam?

The secrets the women shared, the ancient history of persecution, and the terrible ability to share the death of loved ones. She had experienced Laura's death—and the death of her own daughter. A seizure of a kind had overtaken her and she literally became a part of them as their souls fled their bodies and merged with the life beyond. Only heavy doses of tranquilizers had gotten her through the months following their deaths. She couldn't see a shrink; couldn't confide in her staff. Greer had gone through the same thing when Laura died, too, and Laura's death had bonded them together forever. Greer couldn't confide in her father. She virtually lived at Abby's house for a month. This wasn't uncommon with witches, the sharing of each other's death. Some of them were destroyed by the experience, sank into permanent depression.

Help me, Abby, help me.

But Abby hadn't been able to help her.

And then their minds merged—Abby was Laura for a time—all of Laura's memories, none of her own—she was Laura—and yet not Laura.

And screams and pleading.

And then *feeling* Greer in the mindmerge.

Mom! I love you! Mom! I don't know what to do!

Three people—far apart from each other physically but somehow sharing the same death: the panic . . . the terror . . . the desperation, and then one of them was dying and the mindmerge was less and less vivid and intense and then Greer was crying out for Laura to come to her.

Some of the witches even took their own lives after sharing a death experience. But how to explain all this to Cam?

It took two tries to find the driveway, but finally she could feel the tires on the stretch of concrete leading to the garage. She moved through the murk, in a circle of hellish night that would have given even Dante pause.

The fog was so thick here, Jeff could hear her breathing before he actually saw her.

And when he did see her, it was only because he'd stumbled into her.

Apparently, she was as lost as he was.

She stood absolutely still, like a large, lovely doll whose windup key needed to be turned again before life was returned. He reached out and touched her face. Her gaze seemed to be upon him, but she gave no response in the fading beam of his flashlight. Not even a blink.

The loneliness of the night overwhelmed him

momentarily, the fantasy element of this moment. Life sure was weird. Greer had always been several rungs above him on the social ladder. She wasn't a snob, but she didn't make herself accessible to boys like Jeff. But here he was in this lonely, foggy night in the middle of some lost farm field trying to help her out of a situation he couldn't fathom. What the hell was she doing here anyway?

Then he saw where she was staring. Dr. Cooper's cabin in the foggy distance.

Trucks rolled by unseen in the distance; a train.

"I want to help you, Greer. Do you understand me?"

A friend of his had done acid a while back and ended up in a state not unlike this. It had been like trying to talk to a Venusian.

"Greer, I'm going to take you home. And I don't want you to be scared. All right?"

The flashlight batteries were fading fast. He pulled the light away momentarily and gave the flashlight a good rattle. The batteries slammed against the tubular sides of the device.

When he raised the beam again, it seemed a bit stronger.

"I'm going to take your hand. I'll lead you back to the car. You ready?"

No response whatsoever.

He reached out. Slid his hand in hers. She jerked it away, snake quick.

"All right. Let's try it this way."

He twined his arm, light as he could, with hers.

"We'll have you back home in no time."

Her silence embarrassed him for the first time. Here

he was jibbering and jabbering and she wasn't saying anything at all. It was like when he had intense, prolonged, lonesome talks with his sweet golden Lab, Princess. Every once in a while, he'd become self-conscious about what he was doing and break into a big grin. *You've come a long way, Jeff. You've dropped out of school, you're stealing Dwight Yoakam's act, and you're having this really long, intense conversation with a four-legged creature who's spending most of her time trying to stay awake. Looks like you're sitting on top of the world, Jeff.*

She moved. Not far. Not fast. But she moved. A kind of half step. His arm urged her forward gently. And she took another half step.

It was going to be a very long walk back to the Mazda—if the cops hadn't towed it away by now.

So many feelings when she walked into his house. Amazing how many how many different things a human being could feel in the space of a moment.

She was here, and he was grateful. And yet she'd held the truth back from him and he was resentful. And she was so pretty, even 3:00 A.M. rumpled, and he almost resented—felt guilty because of Laura?—how appealing he found her. Age-old enemy, new-found friend?

He led her into the kitchen. The house felt barren, sterile. Fear replaced all his other primary emotions.

Coffee for her, coffee for him. The breakfast nook where almost all the meals were eaten. Fog sinuous, sinister, pressing against the window like a clever, waiting, hungry sentient monster.

He almost started with, "All right, what the hell's

going on here?" but caught himself in time. His worst, imperious self always seemed to come out in moments of stress.

Across from him: sleepy face, slightly mussed hair, no makeup, clean good features, the first pinched hints of middle age.

"I've been thinking," he started off reasonably enough. "And I think I should call the police."

"No, please don't, Cam."

"Why not?" Voice rising just a bit. A hint of his imperious self in the tone.

"She wouldn't want you to."

"I'm the parent here, Abby. And why wouldn't she want me to?"

"Because the police would ask questions."

His voice rising to the next level. "What the hell is she, Abby? Some bank robber on the lam? Some international terrorist? She's my fifteen-year-old daughter, why the hell would she be afraid to have the police question her?"

"Because—there are things she wants to keep private."

"Such as what?"

She had her slender hands folded on top of her coffee cup as if for warmth. "Laura was going to tell you someday—about us."

"Us?"

"Laura and me and Greer. And two other people in this town who unfortunately died over the past five years."

"What the hell are you talking about, Abby? You're a doctor. You're supposed to talk about the mechanics of the human body and the human mind. This other stuff sounds—insane."

"I don't know of any other way to say it. We need to find her. And fast. But I'm also saying we can't afford to involve the police."

"Oh, great. What, we watch a couple of private eye shows and then go look for her ourselves? Is that what you've got in mind?"

He was about to say more when he heard the unmistakable sound of a car engine in the drive. His front door was open. The motor and the muffler needed help.

He nearly tore the table from the wall when he stood up. She had to grab both their cups to keep them from spilling.

He ran to the door and Abby was right behind him.

The porch was damp from fog. By now, the fog had a radiance and scent and feel that gave it body, hinted at a sentience: the monster image again.

Headlight beams pierced the gloom for a few feet then were smothered as if beneath a blanket.

A young man's voice said: "Is this the Morgan house?"

"Yes. Are you here about my daughter?"

"She's in the car, sir."

"Oh, thank God."

And he was hurrying down the steps, giving no due to his injured knee nor the other aches and pains he'd suffered earlier.

The boy came through the fog bearing a weak-beamed flashlight. He went over to the shotgun door of the rusted-out Mazda and opened it. There, sitting very much as she had the night he'd seen her at her bedroom window, sat Greer.

Mud and leaves covered her shoes and jeans. She'd obviously fallen several times. Her face was smeared with dirt. She sat unmoving, staring straight ahead.

"I don't know what's wrong with her, sir."

Cam reached in and began the delicate process of extricating her from the car. He didn't want to bang her head against the doorframe. "Where'd you find her?"

"She was on the side of the road out on Post Road. Oh, hi, Doctor."

"Hi, Jeff. Thanks for doing this."

"Sure, I just hope she's all right."

Cam got Greer out of the car and into his arms. "If you'll catch the front door for me, Abby, I'll get her inside and onto the couch. Jeff, could you stick around a few minutes?"

"Sure, Mr. Morgan."

He watched her face all the way inside. He wanted to see any sign of life in the gleaming eyes—like doll's eyes, that curiously dead glittering—and to watch the tiny pulsing in her temple.

The couch was big enough to make a comfortable daybed. Abby asked where the blankets were. She brought two heavy ones from the closet upstairs. She asked Jeff to run out to her car and get her medical bag off the front seat.

Cam stayed around for the first five minutes as Abby set about her examination. Jeff stood close by, too.

There was no discernible response in Greer's eyes

as Abby examined her. Not even when the tiny flashlight beam shone directly in her eyes.

"You figure anything out yet?" Cam said.

"Not yet, Cam."

"I smell coffee," Jeff said. "Maybe we could go have a cup."

"Good idea, Jeff," Abby said.

Jeff had obviously got the message and Cam hadn't. Abby preferred to work without a terrified father hovering over her.

"You sure you wouldn't mind, Abby?" Cam said.

"I'll muddle through somehow," she said, listening to Greer's heart through a stethoscope.

"That coffee sure does smell good, sir," Jeff said.

They went out into the kitchen.

One of the problems with marijuana was that it sometimes made you wonder if you were dreaming something or actually experiencing it.

After Stuff had left, Candy climbed into bed, lit up a joint, and watched the end of a sci-fi flick until she fell asleep.

And that was when she saw the young, dark-haired woman in the car. Driving inexorably toward Hastings Corner. Karen, her name was. Yes, definitely Karen. There was no doubt about her reason for coming here. She was the enemy of all the women with the secret. And she was coming after a teenage girl, who lived in Hastings Corner. Candy had known her mother Laura and now she saw the girl's face and knew that the dark-haired woman was coming for the young girl.

A moment of total confusion as Candy sat up in

bed, confronting the dark pane of glass four feet away. She'd forgotten to draw the curtains tight.

Someday, she'd have to give up grass. There was probably an age limit. They should send you pamphlets about using grass along with your social security information.

She swung her legs out of bed—pretty damned good gams for a sixty-eight-year-old, if she did say so herself—and reached for her dentures and then for her cigarettes. She probably should give up her Marlboros, too, one of these days.

The final thing she reached for was the .45 she kept in the nightstand drawer. Nobody fucked with Candy Archer. And lived to tell about it. Let the little bitch—the girl in the dream couldn't have been more than seventeen, eighteen—let her come. Candy was ready.

She sneezed. Her nose felt itchy. And cold, as if mountain winds had just roared through her sinus passages.

She inched her way up toward the front of the trailer. She liked the feel of the gun in her hand. Made her feel young. She'd always thought that the B-movie chicks of the forties and fifties crime films—Gloria Grahame and Marie Windsor and Lizabeth Scott—always looked cool with guns in their hands. Cool and sexy. That's how she looked in her mind's eye now. Dressed in a lovely, long, goddess-style diaphanous gown, beautiful blonde hair touching her shoulders—the way the lights were situated you got a very good sense of her sumptuous young body. And then the big confrontation with the mysterious but handsome intruder and—

But there was no intruder, mysterious or otherwise.

The front door was locked tight.

The windows were sealed tight—who could fit through a trailer window, anyway?

She went to the small, rattling fridge—did they even make Kelvinators anymore?—and fished herself out a brewski. She had a choice between smoking brand-name cigarettes or drinking brand-name brew. She chose the former—Marlboros and generic beer.

What you had here was another marijuana situation. She often assumed that such incidents were the fancy of the hemp. People saw mighty strange things through the haze of pot.

She sneezed again. And smelled—felt—the scent of cold wind in her nostrils.

And realized at last—tonight's brewskis and marijuana leaving her a little thick-brained—just what was going on here.

Of course. It had been so many, many years she didn't realize the significance of the sneezing and the peculiar odor in her nostrils.

The girl was real. But not tonight. She was real sometime in the very near future.

This sort of thing had happened a lot in the life of young Cynthia Archer. But after age twenty-five or so, it had happened rarely.

Premonition was the word she wanted here.

Remember the time she knew in advance about the fire at the plastics factory? About the explosion at the boat dock gas storage tanks? About the disappearance of the little Pendleton girl? She'd sent each of the appropriate people notes in advance, giving them sufficient time to make sure that her premonition didn't come true.

But there had been the disbelievers, the people who'd ignored her anonymous warnings. That small plane did crash, killing two. That bleacher section did collapse, badly injuring three. That house did catch on fire, badly injuring four. And there had been several others, as well.

She sat there, thinking back to the years when all the powers she'd been born with were intact and functioning.

And then she started thinking about the long, slow, sad descent of her life, these past decades when she'd tried to pretend she had the same old powers.

She knew that she'd soon find out who "Karen" really was.

She hadn't been this excited since—hell, she hadn't been this excited since she got her new dentures a year or so ago. These didn't pinch like her old ones at all.

There were those who felt that Dr. Tom Cooper had been sent to Hastings Corner directly from the man upstairs. He was a good doctor, first of all. He'd delivered many of the people walking the town's streets. And second of all, he knew more secrets than a priest—and kept them secret.

Third and most important, he looked the part. Tall, gangly, with a kind face, white hair, a patient and almost whimsical manner, he made most people feel better just by being in the room.

So what the hell was he doing breaking into the hospital's blood lab at three-fifteen this morning?

Technically, he wasn't breaking in. He used a key, one he'd "borrowed" from the lab manager's office earlier in the day. And he held a part-time staff position here. He kept his own practice but had long ago agreed to oversee the hospital work of the town's other three doctors. The other doctors didn't mind. Dr. Tom, as most people called him, was as easy on them as he was on his patients. If he had a criticism, it was always offered inside a compliment, and was quickly followed with a positive suggestion on how to improve this or that in the future.

So what the hell was he doing breaking into the hospital's blood lab at three-fifteen in the morning?

The lab was dark, of course, this time of night. The processing machines were all covered—the primary tests done here would be for hemoglobin, white cell count, thyroid levels, iron, blood type, potassium—the lab tech's corner desk and filing cabinets outlined in the mauve light of the mercury vapor parking lot light just outside the window.

He needed to move quickly. There was a security guard somewhere on this floor. He probably wouldn't be suspicious of Dr. Tom—who would?—but he'd certainly remember the man being here in the middle of the night.

And there was the refrigerator.

Large, rectangular, gleaming white even in the gloom, the interior of the big Amana was usually filled with blood tests all marked with the individual patient's name, computer test number, date, purpose of the test, and the identity of the person who drew the blood. Many of the blood tests were done here in the hospital. The lab had one person who went out and picked up the others from doctors' offices.

Dr. Tom yawned.

Now that's a hell of a thing, he thought in his usual wry manner. *Here I am doing something highly illegal—something that would get my bony old ass thrown right out of the medical profession—and yet I am yawning.*

He wasn't used to staying up this late, that was the trouble.

Sure, he got phone calls at all hours, but he usually went right back to sleep after answering the question of the frantic caller. For this little number, he'd had to stay up drinking coffee. The middle of the night was the only time he could do it.

He yawned again and moved to the side of the refrigerator.

He couldn't open the door wide. If he did, the light would be seen by anybody passing by. He'd open it just a bit and start his search that way.

Something in the hall? He'd been about to open the Amana's door. He froze.

Something in the hall?

He listened, yawning as he did so.

He decided what he'd heard was the heat kicking on. Probably the blower acting on all the sheet metal ductwork.

He reached down, gripped the refrigerator handle, and eased open the door a quarter of an inch.

This time when he heard something, he knew exactly what it was. His heart. He was scared.

At best, if he got caught, they'd think he'd just snapped. Old age. The pressures of modern medicine—all the bureaucratic nightmares of semi-socialized medicine called HMOs—and the knowledge that he was no longer up-to-date in his thinking or his practice. A figure of pity?

At worst, they'd see him as a figure of malevolence. They wouldn't know why he'd broken into the lab. They'd just know that he'd done something unethical.

The word would get out. Some people would defend him, they'd trusted and loved him too long to do otherwise. But most would walk wide of him. Pitying glances, nervous smiles, empty affirmations of support. . . .

And he would shrivel up and die.

He'd seen people his age do exactly that.

The death of a spouse; a sudden downturn in business; the onset of a serious illness—and suddenly the will to live was gone. It was never a conscious decision, of course. But it was a decision made between mind, body, and soul. Now was the time to top it off.

He'd never had much luck in wooing such cases back to real life.

But what choice did he have?

He had the mark on him, didn't he? He knew the secret, didn't he? He ran the cell, didn't he? And he'd continue to run the cell until he was so old he had to give in to David Prescott and his damned computer and his damned hospital.

So what the hell choice did he have?

He looked inside the refrigerator and found that it was nearly empty. He'd hit the place on a very good night. Only half a dozen or so blood tests. They'd be stored here seven days and then tossed out.

He set to work.

"So I just brought her straight here, Mr. Morgan," Jeff said, sitting across from Cam in the breakfast nook. "Maybe I should've taken her to the hospital."

"You did fine." Cam sipped coffee. Pretty soon he was going to need a Tums. Anxiety and coffee had started to sour his stomach. "She didn't say anything at all, huh?"

"Nothing. And I asked her a lot of questions."

"Did you have any sense of where she was going?"

"I was just surprised to find her out there. You know, especially at this time of night."

"I'm glad you saw her."

"So am I. I—always kind of liked her."

Cam allowed himself a smile. Another one smitten by his daughter's charms. Somehow, all the boys who trailed after her hadn't affected her sense of self. If anything—except where it came to soccer—Greer always treated herself as if she wasn't popular or even quite acceptable. *Not unlike her mother,* he thought.

Then he went back through Abby's earlier words. Her enigmatic talk about dead people. And some vague connection to herself. And Laura. And now Greer. What the hell had she been talking about?

"I'll make sure she finds out who saved her," Cam said.

"I'm starting to fade," Jeff said.

"Don't blame you. It's late."

"I guess I should take off. My folks expect me to be late—what with my job and all. But not this late."

The boy flushed, looked nervous. "Uh, you think I could call and just see how she's doing?"

"Sure. Any time."

"Or maybe even swing by. Just to say hi."

"She'd probably like that. But call first to make sure she's up and around."

"I'll make sure to, Mr. Morgan."

They walked back to the living room.

Abby had pulled the blankets up to Greer's neck. Greer slept, snored lightly.

"Everything seems to be fine," Abby said. "Except that I suspect somebody has been drugging her. Maybe it happened again after she left my office."

"Drugged her?" Cam said.

"I'm not sure of it. But I'll know soon. I drew some of her blood to send to the hospital lab."

"But who'd drug her?"

"That's what we need to find out, Cam."

"So she's going to be all right?" Jeff asked.

"I think she's all right now. She just needs to sleep off whatever kind of drug somebody gave her."

Jeff went over to Greer and stared down at her. "She's starting to look pretty again."

And as a matter of fact, she was, Cam realized. Color touched her cheeks once again and the tortured expression she'd worn had started to diminish.

"Well," Jeff said, "I'd better go."

He said his good nights and left.

"Well," Cam said, "how about we have a cup of coffee and finish our talk in the kitchen."

"Cam, c'mon, have a little mercy. I've got rounds at the hospital starting in two hours. I need to lie down for a nap if nothing else."

"But you started to tell me—"

"I know what I started to tell you, Cam. But I can finish it tomorrow. It'll keep. I don't mean to tease you, but I really do have to think of my patients. They need me. And I've got to get at least a good hour's sleep before I go trundling off to the hospital. I'll call you during the day and we'll plan to get together, all right."

She did the unthinkable. She leaned into him and kissed him on the cheek. "I know how badly you want to know, but if we start talking now—" She began packing up her medical bag. "I need to go, Cam. I'm sorry."

"When he heard her car, lost in the fog outside, sputter into life, he wasn't sure which had been more shocking—her mysterious talk earlier in the evening, or the good-bye kiss she'd given him.

Two babies were born; men and women trudged off to factories, offices, car dealerships, schools; six flights took off from the airport despite the fog; and out on Wilhelm Road there was a bad accident because of the morning fog, an elderly man ending up in the hospital after his station wagon crossed the yellow line into the path of an oncoming dairy truck. Tykes in their high chairs got their baby food all over their faces and even in their hair; more than a few junior high girls checked in their bedroom mirrors to see that their Wonderbras were doing the trick; and in three hushed, sad houses, spouses were seeing to spouses in the rooms the hospice workers had fixed up. Dogs, cats, chickens, horses, bunnies—everybody and everything was coming alive.

Another morning in Hastings Corner.

As Greer came awake, she knew nothing of any of this. She had a fierce headache and felt real panic: what was she doing on the couch?

Dad's face leaned into her view. "Morning, honey."

"Morning."

"Anything you want?"

"How come I'm on the couch?"

"You don't remember?"

"Remember what?"

"Last night?"

"I guess I don't."

"You hungry?"

"Not right now. I do need to go to the bathroom, though."

"You all right to stand up?"

What a weird thing to say, she thought. *Why wouldn't she be all right to stand up? She was a star soccer player. How tough could it be for her to stand up?*

But he was right.

The moment she tried to sit up and move her legs, grogginess overcame her. All she could liken it to was the one and only time she'd had too much wine. The next morning she'd been dehydrated, twitchy, irritable, and flushed with body heat.

All these sensations were with her now.

"Did I get into some kind of accident?" She didn't try to move, just sat upright on the couch.

"We're not sure."

"Who's 'we?' " Irritation was strong in her voice. The irritation she often felt when it was That Time of the Month.

"Abby. And Jeff. The kid who looks like Dwight Yoakam."

"Jeff what's-his-name? That dweeb who dropped out of school?"

"One and the same. But I don't think you'll call him a dweeb after I tell you that he may have saved your life."

She put her head in her hands. Wanted to cry, pee, puke. Felt like total shit.

He told her what dweeb Jeff had done for her.

"But why would I just wander off like that?"

"Abby isn't sure, but she thinks somebody drugged you."

"God, I can't even think about this right now." Her body felt on fire. She needed a Pepsi. And she badly needed to pee.

She stood up. And nearly pitched forward on her face.

Dad grabbed her. Steadied her. Slid his arm through hers. Escorted her safely to the downstairs john off the den.

Once she was in there, she went about her business quickly. Then she ran ice-cold water in the sink and began daubing it on her face with her fingers.

There were memories—specific images—of last night but they seemed to be on the other side of a dark wall. She could hear them muttering, feel them pulsing, but she could not make sense of them. Drugged, Dad had said. But who would drug her and why? All she could think of—

Abby. What she'd been talking to Abby about lately. And what Abby had been talking to her about lately. Their secret. What else could this be about? Take away Greer's secret, and you had a nice, normal, small-town girl who was pretty much unremarkable in every way.

A nice, normal, small-town girl nobody would pay any attention to at all.

But somebody had not only paid attention to her, they'd drugged her.

And—my God!—Jeff the dweeb had found her wandering around out in the boonies somewhere. She didn't mean to be cruel to Jeff—she wasn't really a cruel person—but there were levels of society in school and Jeff was levels down, face it. It was just so odd.

A knock. "You all right in there?"

"Fine, Dad."

"Anything I can get you?"

"How about a Pepsi with some ice?"

"How about some bacon and eggs to go along with that?"

"Just the Pepsi for now, Dad. Thanks."

"You sure?"

"I'm sure. Thanks, Dad. And I shouldn't have called Jeff a dweeb. He's actually a nice kid. I was just being smart."

"I'm glad you said that. He really does seem like a nice kid. Just holler if you need anything."

He was so hyper. So cute. So sweet.

"I'll be fine, Dad. I'm just sort of groggy is all."

"I'll get the Pepsi and the ice."

Abby's early hours, after finishing her rounds at the hospital—five patients, each of them doing well—were spent in the clinic office going over various running battles she was having with HMOs. She could remember, in her early college days, when the established doctors considered the federal government the ultimate enemy what with all its forms and other paperwork.

But the federal government was a sweet and loving grandmother compared to the HMOs. These were the most ruthless people Abby had ever run up against. They treated doctors like idiots and patients like computer numbers. This morning's battle, which the office manager had laid out in spreadsheet fashion, was a series of letters questioning Abby's decision to order certain tests for her patients. Were they really necessary? Weren't there alternative routes? Hadn't one of these patients had the same test two years ago?

"Are they really necessary?" Abby said. "Say no, they're not necessary. But I do like to hear the noise those big machines make."

Angie Petrelli laughed. "How about alternative routes?"

"Tell them that of course there are alternative routes, d-e-a-t-h in three of these five cases."

Angie, a dark-haired mother of five, loved seeing the doctors get pissed, all their decorum gone. It was like hearing the Pope tell dirty jokes.

"Any comment about Mr. Vining having had the same test two years ago?"

"You know, even for these stupid fuckers that's a moronic question," Abby said. "Just because he didn't have the disease two years ago doesn't mean he might not have it now."

"Am I permitted to use the F word in any of my letters?"

"I want you to use it in all your letters. And use it liberally."

"God, wouldn't it be fun if I could?"

"I can't believe these people," Abby said.

Her morning: bad cold; mysterious headaches (she

ordered tests—take that HMOs); six month checkup for a forty-three-year-old, pregnant for the first time; checkup on a broken leg (looking good); and a nervous, little woman who'd had another "fall."

"This one I'm going to report, Nancy."

"You're going to report a fall?"

Abby sighed. "Please, Nancy. I don't know how you can even say that with a straight face anymore. Your husband's beating you again." Nancy was one of her most frustrating patients. Now matter how many times her husband beat her, she always took him back.

"He took those anger management classes."

"I know he did. And I was hopeful they'd work. You were lucky you didn't get a concussion falling down those stairs last night. Or worse. People break their necks in falls like that, you know."

Nancy started crying. Maybe ninety-five pounds max. Bleached, dry hair. She'd been pretty once. Tattoos on arms and neck. Four kids from three marriages. She was thirty-one. You shouldn't be able to reduce a human life to a few lines like that—lines didn't allow for the occasional joy and laughter and sweet melancholy—but with people like Nancy, frightened, cowering people who had no sense of worth nor any sense that they could do for themselves, with people like Nancy you could almost reduce them to a few lines on a page. The page of a police report on Nancy's death by homicide.

"Sean pushes me around, Dr. Stewart. I'll admit that. But at least he doesn't drink anymore."

"Is that the trade-off, Nancy? He doesn't drink, so it's all right if he beats you up?"

"He never hits me. He just pushes me."

Abby put all her frustration into her sigh. "Gee, that's nice of him."

"And the kids like him except when he's mad and throwing stuff."

"Nancy, listen to me. It's only a matter of time until you're seriously injured. I'm not doing my job as a physician if I don't report him."

"Then he'll really light into me. If you do, I mean."

"So we just let him continue?"

"I'll talk to him, I really will. I'll just put my foot down. I'll tell him if he ever hurts me again, I'll leave him."

"How about if he leaves? Aren't you making the house payments?"

"Only till he gets a job again."

"It's been a while."

"Jobs aren't easy to find."

What was the point of telling her that it was a boom economy? That employers of every kind were begging for workers? Somehow, Nancy's husband had convinced her that he sat around all day doing nothing because he just couldn't find a job anywhere.

"Please, Dr. Stewart. Please don't turn him in."

Nancy knew Abby would give in. Abby always worried she was being too arrogant with her patients—feeling superior to them, as if she'd handle similar problems much better than they did. But people like Nancy—consciously or unconsciously—they could twist and manipulate you far better than "educated" people did. They could break your heart and thus make you do things you'd never do otherwise.

"All right, Nancy. I won't call this time."

As Nancy left, a few minutes later, Abby started wondering when the lab would call her with the results of Greer's blood test.

This probably wasn't what she should be eating, the stuff in her shopping cart: generic brand caramel corn, a six-pack of Snickers, a box of Quackers, potato chips, four Totino frozen sausage pizzas, a can of Planters salted peanuts, a quart of chocolate milk, generic brand frozen waffles, Log Cabin syrup, Oscar Mayer bologna slices, Wonder Bread, French's mustard, Heinz hot ketchup, six Taco City frozen burritos, and a package of assorted Pepperidge Farm cookies.

But what the hell, she might get hit by a train this afternoon, too, so what good would eating good food have done her?

The supermarket was nearly empty. A man in a white uniform was spritzing the produce; a Coca-Cola woman (talk about butch) was filling up a huge display of her product; and a bratty little kid was stamping his feet and sobbing because his mother wouldn't let him buy the box of cereal he held in his pathetic little hand.

Nobody was watching her when it happened.

Pushing her cart toward the front of the store. Pushing past the magazine and paperback section.

And then the images—

A room—a basement, perhaps—a small group of people sitting like jurists as a tall man injects a girl in the arm with a hypodermic needle—the same girl she saw in her vision last night.

There is no sound. Silent movie. The images fragment now, shards of shattered glass. Needle. The girl screaming—no sound. Faces of the people in the chairs. Hard faces. Hateful faces—

"No! Stop!" Candy screamed, right in the middle aisle of the supermarket.

"Ma'am! Ma'am! Are you all right!"

Men in white uniforms standing over her.

Hospital? Was this a hospital?

A rack of books on one side; a wall of pots and pans on the other.

The supermarket—

She was pushing her cart down the supermarket aisle when—

The girl—she has to find a way to contact the girl. Warn her.

She wonders if the people in the room know what they are trifling with. What happened to her best friend when she was pushed too far by people who'd discovered her secret?

Helping her to her feet. Some of the customers looking worried. Some smirking. Candy wore her silver jumpsuit and the high high hooker heels. Probably never saw any old broad like her trying to look so hip—

She knew she looked ludicrous, pathetic. That's why she did it. It was her way of saying she didn't give a damn what people thought of her.

Go take a frigging hike—

"Are you all right, ma'am?" the store manager said, obviously sweating cannonballs over a possible lawsuit.

"I'm fine. Now kindly take your sweaty hand off me."

"Yes, ma'am."

I must have got so into the vision that I fell on the floor out of sympathy with her.

She brushed off her backside and pushed her cart—with great dignity—up to the checkout lane.

Jeff didn't get downstairs till 10:08 that morning.

The life of a vampire, he'd once joked, that's what I've got. Prowl all night, sleep all day.

Well, sorta.

Usually he was up by 9:30. Stuff to do around the house. His folks weren't about to let him sleep in all day. They wanted him back in school. They didn't want to make his vampire's life any more attractive than they had to.

Mom had already gone to work.

Dad sat at the kitchen table drinking coffee and reading his newspapers. Yancy Crawford, the town's bon vivant.

Dad looked up. "Morning." The black eye patch always made him look more severe than he sounded. "Your mother's off to the library already."

"I figured."

"She wanted me to ask you why you stayed out so late last night? I'm curious myself. If you're drinking and driving—"

They'd once been up one night watching some sixties movie when he'd come home pretty loaded from too many underage beers at the tavern.

They'd yelled at him so long and hard, he was sober by the time they were finished.

"You could've killed somebody. You could've killed yourself. Do you know how long they'd keep your license? Do you know what they'd do to our insurance rates? Once that's on your record, young man, it stays there for life. Maybe we should take your car away. Maybe we should make you quit your job there. Maybe we should send you to military school to finish your studies. How could you do this to us?"

"I wasn't drinking. Something happened."

"What happened?"

"You know Greer Morgan?"

And it was funny. There was just Dad sitting there of a morning, taking his time with his coffee and his paper—he only opened his used bookstore at noon because there wasn't enough business to justify a whole-day operation—and looking kinda cool for a guy his age, but when Jeff mentioned Greer it seemed Dad's whole body jerked, as if it had received an electrical jolt.

"Cam Morgan's daughter, you mean?"

The voice was different from the body language, though. Perfectly casual.

"Yeah. I'm in the same class she is."

"What about her?"

Jeff poured himself a cup of coffee and then came over and sat down at the old-fashioned Formica-topped table that was stuck in a corner of the remodeled kitchen. New oak cabinets, new countertops, new appliances, new tiled floor—and that old eyesore table because it'd been in sentimental Mom's family when she was a kid. They hadn't had Jeff until they were in their early forties—they'd been waiting for Dad to write that great novel and tour the world in triumph (who wanted a snot-nose along for a trip like that?)—and by then Mom was already entering her middle-aged sentimentality period. Hence the "Ozzie and Harriet" 1957 Formica-topped kitchen table.

"I nearly ran over her."

"What?"

"Coming home from work. It was real foggy. She was on the side of the road and just started walking out in front of me."

"When was this?"

"About two-thirty or so."

A sense of agitation in his father now. Very odd. As if Dad had some kind of personal interest in this thing.

The drinking thing. That was why the agitation. Next thing, Dad would accuse him of drinking.

"So what happened?" Casual Dad again. He had a lot of faces, Dad. Was one mercurial dude. Could slide in and out of different moods in moments. It was funny. Kids—even ones who said they hated their folks—had these intense relationships with them. But Jeff always felt he was dealing with them at one remove. He loved them, but he'd never felt close to them the way he imagined other kids felt close to their parents.

Sometimes, he wondered if he was adopted. He'd read that this was a normal feeling for a lot of kids. But it wasn't idle speculation on his part. He really and truly wondered if he had been adopted.

"She got away from me. Went down in this gully. She started walking toward the Coopers' place."

"Did she get away?"

"No, I went after her. And took her home."

"What did she say?"

"That was the thing. She didn't say anything. Noting at all. It was like she was—doped up or something."

"She doesn't seem the kind. I mean, just looking at her."

"You never know these days."

"I know you're not taking drugs."

"I'm stupid sometimes; but not that stupid."

"So how did you leave it?"

"Dr. Stewart was there and checked her out."

"In the middle of the night?"

"Yeah. I was surprised, too. They always tell you to go to the ER. But anyway, she didn't seem to think that was necessary and checked her out. She's all right, I guess."

"That's quite a story."

Jeff smiled. "I always had a crush on her. But this was a pretty weird way to meet."

"You going to call today and see how she is?"

"Yeah, I thought I would."

"You did a good thing, son."

"It was pretty spooky."

"Yeah, I imagine." Dad checked his wristwatch. "Well, time to go peddle trash to the masses."

Jeff liked it when his dad talked that way. Hip and cynical. Cool. How many kids had a dad who talked like that?

"Still selling those romances, huh, Dad?"

"Yes. And your mom's still reading them."

"I won't tell if you won't."

They smiled at each other.

"You done good, kiddo. Be proud of yourself."

"Thanks, Dad."

"Just think, if you were in school you might have a chance of dating her."

"You've always got to work the commercial in, don't you?"

"It's my nature," Dad said. "I'm a dad. It's in my contract."

Abby was simply overwhelmed by numbers. Two of her patients—a mother and daughter—had been involved in a house fire. They were going to be all right, but they'd be in the hospital for a while. And another patient of hers, a railroad man, had been injured falling off a boxcar. He, too, was all right but required her rushing from her office to the ER. Which backed up her patients, inconveniencing (and irritating) them. And put her even farther behind schedule.

Cam phoned his house several times to see how Greer was doing; Abby phoned the hospital lab twice to see if there was any word on the blood test, the answer to which was, "We'll do it as soon as possible."

Candy Archer spent several hours lying on the couch in her trailer, watching soap operas, drinking generic cola, smoking cigarettes. The spasm—it was the only way she could think to label it—in the supermarket was still very much on her mind. Long, long ago, when she was young and her gifts were plentiful, such spasms had taken slightly different tacks. She would be seized with an image of a person she despised—usually a person who had done something terrible to her or who suspected her secret and meant to use it against her—and in that moment of seizure, she would learn how to deal with that person.

Retribution. It was like opening a fortune cookie,

except the paper inside didn't predict your future, it gave you instructions on how to pay the person back. Her mother had warned her against acting on any of these instructions. "You want to be in grace, don't you?" her mother always said. "In grace" meant using your powers to do good rather than bad; using your powers the way the cosmic ruler of the universe—described by various religions in various ways—intended you to.

But today, this had been a premonition. The girl. Her terrible fate. Somehow, Candy had to warn her.

Dr. Stewart?"

"Yes," Abby said.

"This is Connie over at the hospital lab."

"You have the results?"

"That's just it. We can't find the blood sample."

"I dropped it off myself."

"I know you did. I found the form you signed. But—this is very embarrassing. Somehow, it got misplaced."

"Were any of the other samples misplaced?"

"Not that I know of."

So easy to explode. And Abby had been known to do it at the wrong time, in the wrong mood. Explode and rant and rave. But she was too tired for ail of that at the moment. Besides, something seemed wrong here. Or was she just being paranoid? Who would have a reason to steal Greer's blood sample?

How about a person who knew Greer's secret?

How about a person who meant Greer harm?

How about a person who didn't want it known that he/she had been drugging Greer?

"I'll have to have Greer come back, I guess."

"I'm really very sorry about this, Dr. Stewart."

"Mistakes happen. I've been known to make a few myself."

Abby could almost read the mind of the woman on the other end of the phone: *This is the hot-headed Dr. Stewart? This is the woman who makes hospital administrators cower and staff physicians quake? This self-effacing, soft-spoken woman on the other end of the line? Boy, people sure do like to exaggerate. Dr. Stewart probably had a bad day once and now there's this whole myth about her being a bitch on wheels.*

"I'll call Greer now, Connie."

"Sorry again, Dr. Stewart."

"Not a problem."

She sat in her office staring out the window at the overcast afternoon, convinced now that somebody was drugging Greer and did know her secret. But she still wasn't sure when and *how* they were drugging her.

Jeff stepped from the shower and started drying himself off. His mind was full of Greer Morgan.

God, he got crushes so easily. He'd never really had a girlfriend. His sexual exploits had been limited to getting his hands inside the bra of one girl and down the panties of another. Both at beer-heavy basement parties. He hadn't cared much for either girl and right-back-at-him they hadn't cared much for him. They'd been the Passed Over people at these particular parties and had to pair up with somebody, so they'd grabbed whomever was left.

The effects of the beer made them all much more desirable. He sure wasn't A-list and neither were the girls.

He wondered what it would be like to be in the basement darkness with Greer Morgan. And it wasn't just sex. He had a whole spectrum of feelings for her—he liked her, he lusted after her, he felt sorry for her that her mother had died, he felt protective of her now that he saw she was kind of messed up, and he enjoyed being in her presence. It was funny how a girl could make you feel better about yourself—stronger, older, wiser, even more acceptable to yourself. Other boys could never give you those feelings. But a girl like Greer . . .

He was just finishing up toweling his hair, when he looked out the bathroom window and saw the Coopers' cabin in the near distance.

From here, he could see where Greer had been standing last night.

He decided that his original feeling was right, given her position, she must have been walking toward the cabin, couldn't have been headed for any other place.

But why would she be interested in Doctor Cooper's cabin?

Maybe he'd ask her.

He figured what he'd do now was grab some lunch at McDonald's and swing by her place to see how she was doing.

He was scared of going over there—scared of her when you came right down to it—but he had to give it a try.

He just had to.

The call came just as Cam was wrapping up the monthly review of his billing. He supposed they weren't trying to make him—or any of the other nonpartners—feel like a child. But that was the ultimate effect.

Isn't this a fairly small bill for that kind of job?

Don't you usually bill him more than that every month?

I didn't realize your flu slowed you down that much; look at Thursday here. Only two hours?

And so on.

It was like being back in Mrs. Brumley's fifth grade class and having to answer for the twelve minutes you'd been late coming back from gym period. He remembered this because he'd gotten sick—thrown up in the bathroom. But she wouldn't believe him. He wanted to say: "Maybe I shoulda brung you back a handful of puke?" But of course he didn't. Not with Mrs. Brumley, he didn't.

She'd made him stay twenty minutes after school for three days running.

He wondered if the law firm was going to make him stay after work for not billing as many hours last week.

"Big prestigious law firm," his lawyer mentors had told him. "That's where you'll find the most action."

They hadn't told him that it was like doing hard time in Attica. (Hell, we all go for the slight exaggeration when we're mad. It probably wasn't quite as bad as doing hard time in Attica.)

And now the call: "Dr, Cooper on line one."

Fuzzy thinking. Dr. Cooper + Greer = Something Wrong.

He didn't stop to think that if anything was wrong, he'd be hearing from Abby, not Dr. Cooper. Abby was the physician in charge.

"Hi, Dr. Cooper."

"I'm sorry to bother you at work, Cam."

Dr. Cooper had delivered him. Dr. Cooper had seen him through a hernia when he was four, a tonsillectomy, mumps, measles, a couple of broken bones, a college physical, and then the pregnancy of Laura, the birth of Greer, and the well-being of Cam-Laura-Greer for many, many years.

"No problem, Doctor. Is everything all right with Greer? You haven't heard anything, have you?"

"No, I haven't. But I am calling about Greer."

Instant relief. Greer—so far as he knew—was all right.

"I—this is a little awkward for me, actually, Cam. I mean, patients change doctors all the time. Especially these days. But, well, I like to think I've been a family friend as well as your family physician."

"You know you have, Dr. Cooper."

"Well, if that's the case, I was just wondering if I'd done something to—you know, offend Greer in some way."

Cam smiled. Fondly. So that was it. Physician getting on in years. Trying to hold on to the patients he has. All of a sudden a lifelong patient, fifteen-year-old girl, suddenly goes to a different doctor.

"I should've called and explained, Dr. Cooper. I'm sorry I didn't."

"Oh?"

"It's just a friendship thing. Abby Stewart and Laura were best friends, as you know. And Abby's daughter and Greer were best friends. So they get together a lot. Greer is still having problems dealing with her mother's death, and Abby is still grieving over her daughter so—"

"I see. So they just decided to make their relationship professional as well as personal."

"Exactly. And that's a good way to put it, Dr. Cooper. Greer likes you just as much as she ever did. And you're still my doctor, don't forget."

"Well, that's a relief. I just hoped I hadn't upset her in some way. You get older, you know, and sometimes younger people have a difficult time relating to you."

"No problem at all, Doctor. I'm just sorry I didn't call you and let you know what was going on."

"Well, tell her to finish up the medicine I gave her. You should always finish taking antibiotics. And then Abby can take over. She's a very good doctor."

"Thanks, Dr. Cooper. I appreciate the chance to clear this up."

"Good-bye, Cam."

"Good-bye, Doctor."

Jeff was beginning to think nobody was home.

He'd rung the doorbell twice and knocked several times with no response.

He was just turning away to go back to his car when he heard footsteps inside. Coming in his direction.

The door was a slab of solid oak. He wasn't sure who'd be answering.

And then, abruptly, there she was.

She might have been the After picture for a drug clinic, last night being the Before shot. She was clean, her elegant red hair tied back in a ponytail, her clothes a blue long-sleeved, button-down shirt, jeans, no socks and a pair of ancient penny loafers. Pretty as ever.

"Wow," she said.

"What?"

"I was just going to dig out your number and call you."

"You were?"

"Sure. To thank you. For last night. Not that I remember much of it. But—c'mon in."

"Thanks."

The place looked different in the daylight. Last night there'd been a violated air to the place, like a crime scene where something terrible had happened, everything seemed grotesque. Today, even though nothing had changed physically, it was simply an ordinary, well-furnished middle class home. Comfortable, especially with the wide brick fireplace alive and crackling with burning wood. The smell was especially nice.

"I was just warming up some apple cider. Would you like some?"

"That sounds great."

"We usually eat in the kitchen. That all right?"

When he got himself situated, he looked out into their long, narrow backyard. "You've got a great view."

"Sometimes, I just sit there and watch all the traffic."

"Traffic in your backyard?"

She brought over their cups of cider. "Birds, dogs, squirrels, rabbits, cats, butterflies, groundhogs, and the occasional raccoons. Those're my favorites."

"My uncle always shoots them."

"Maybe somebody should shoot your uncle."

He grinned. "I'd be happy to volunteer. He's a jerk."

She grinned back. "I sort of got that impression. With the raccoons and all." The pain came without warning. She squeezed her eyes shut, touched long, graceful fingers to her temple.

"You all right?"

"It's like having a hangover."

"What is?"

"Being drugged."

"Wow, you really think somebody drugged you?"

"I don't know how else to explain it. I don't have any memory of anything—or not much, anyway—for about two hours. And Abby said it doesn't sound like sleepwalking, what I did. She took a blood test yesterday. We should have the results today."

"You don't have any idea where you were going?"

"No. That's what's so weird."

They sat there watching a garbage truck picking up cans. The two men who did it worked efficiently in the chilly day. You could see their breath when they talked.

"You mind if I ask you a question, Jeff?"

"What?"

"Why did you drop out of school?"

"Oh," he said, and felt his cheeks go feverish on him. "That."

"You don't have to talk about it if it makes you uncomfortable. I was just kind of curious. You're a bright student and—"

"Not bright enough to stay in school." He looked out into the backyard. Clothesline pole. Doghouse left though the dog was long gone. Barbecue grill. Redwood picnic table. Gazebo."I wasn't very cool."

"Oh?"

"I'm just one of those kids nobody ever pays much attention to. And I—wanted attention. I wanted to do something neat. And then when I turned fourteen, people started telling me how much I looked like Dwight Yoakam."

"The country singer."

"Yeah. Anyway, I thought maybe I could cash in on it. And I really got carried away. I started listening to his music constantly and reading everything I could about him and then walking and talking and dressing like him."

"You're not dressing like him this morning. He always has that cowboy hat on."

He laughed. "That was one of the troubles."

"What was?"

"I look pretty dorky in a cowboy hat."

She smiled. "That would be a problem."

And that wasn't the only problem."

"Really?"

"I don't like country music."

She grinned again. "That sounds like the biggest problem of all."

"All that pickup truck stuff. And everybody getting dumped all the time."

And always getting their husbands stolen by their cousins," she said.

"No kidding. So, anyway, I decided I could be a star. I'd work in a couple of local bars and then all of a sudden there'd be this big record contract and I'd be rich and famous."

"Sort of like in a movie, huh?"

"Exactly like in a movie."

"So now here I am with my parents really pissed and me feeling embarrassed. God, I can't believe I really thought this was going to turn into something. I sing some songs every night for a bunch of drunks and their girlfriends."

"You could always go back to school."

His cheeks colored again. "Yeah, and when I do I'll have the opposite problem."

"What's that?"

"You know how I said nobody noticed me before?"

"Uh-huh."

"Well, they'll notice me now, all right. They'll say there goes that dweeb who thought he was Dwight Yoakam."

Abby had some luck at day's end.

The waiting room was finally empty of people coughing, sneezing, rasping, gasping, hawking, honking germs. And being a Wednesday, most of the staff had wrapped up early. An unnatural calm, an even more unnatural silence, fell upon the long, narrow room of hopefully comfortable chairs, end tables cluttered with magazines, toys for children of various ages, and some of the most god-awful starving-artists' paintings that had ever affronted the human eye. They had been hung before she'd come here.

She swam in the calm and silence as if it were warm and nurturing South Seas water. She felt guilty for some of her thoughts—familiar thoughts on days as hectic as this one—when the patients became not people to be helped but The Enemy.

For this she'd gone to medical school? So she could see the people she'd been trained to help as whining, ungrateful, and frequently helpless idiots? So many infirmities and diseases (her black logic ran) could be avoided by simple common sense. Don't smoke. Stay as thin as possible. Don't drink alcohol to excess. Have regular mammograms. Have regular colon and prostate exams. Keep cancer's danger signals posted in a place where every family member can see it. This was her cold, schoolmarm side and, Lord God Almighty, she hated it. So pompous. So unforgiving. So arrogant.

But luckily, her black logic didn't last long.

Human nature being what it was, few people took care of themselves as they should. And that was understandable. With all the stresses of life, doting on your health wasn't something most people had time for. That's why they needed doctors. Not only so they could get that sore throat taken care of but so they could be nudged into getting the routine tests they needed, too.

Patience. That was a big part of being a good doctor. And on days like this one, she had to remind herself of that. Chastise herself for being less than tolerant, giving—patient.

She left the waiting room, went back to her office, and tried the number from her mother's diary. It was no longer Cynthia's.

No luck on her first two tries to find a new number.

"Do you list a Cynthia Archer, operator?"

"No, I'm sorry."

None in town here.

None in the adjacent towns.

None in the county.

The third operator said, "Why don't I try Ainsworth? See if I've got a Cynthia Archer there."

A patient, dutiful operator, Abby thought. *Extending herself. Really trying to do her best for her clients.*

"I have a Candy Archer in Ainsworth."

"Well, I suppose that could be it." She hesitated. "Oh, what the heck, why don't you let me have the number, I guess."

"Hold for your number, please."

She wrote it down and dialed the number.

Her first impression was that she'd dialed a honky-tonk tavern. Country music brayed in the background, followed by a hard, heavy smoker's coughing. "This is Candy Archer. The Futurist."

"Hello?"

"Didn't you hear me?" Cranky now. "I said this is Candy Archer. The Futurist." Followed by another cigarette hack.

"I'm trying to find a Cynthia Archer."

"Just a minute. I can't hear you. Fucking music's too loud."

The music was turned down. The coughing woman came back on the line. "Now what did you say?"

"I said I'm trying to locate a Cynthia Archer?"

"Who is this?"

"My name is Abby Stewart. I'm a doctor in Hastings Corner."

"Natalie Stewart's little girl?"

"Yes. But I'm not so little anymore."

"Well, I'll be damned. I always figured I might hear from you someday. Your mother and I—well, we shared a secret or two in our time."

The code word. Secret.

"Then this is Cynthia?"

Coughing. "Damn cigarettes. I should give 'em up. But I just can't seem to."

She was trying to imagine the photograph of the elegant young woman in her dance tights—the one in her mother's diary—with the coarse woman she was speaking to.

"I haven't been Cynthia in a long time, honey. Candy. That was the name I took when I went into stripping. This was long before XXX clubs, so we didn't show no tits or beaver. Strictly old-fashioned. But, anyway, I haven't been Cynthia in a long time. So, anyway, what can I do for you, Abby?"

"There's a girl here—"

"Damn."

"What?"

"Somebody's after her, aren't they?"

"Why, yes, I think so—"

"I had a premonition. Let me describe her to you."

She described Greer perfectly.

"That's Greer."

"You know her?" asked Candy.

"She's Laura's daughter."

"Laura Caine?"

"Yes. Laura Morgan," said Abby, "After she got married."

"Laura had a little secret, too."

"Yes, and so does Greer, I think. And I'm beginning to think that somebody knows about it. Listen, could I drive over and see you tonight?"

"Place is kind of a mess." The cough came as she

laughed. " 'Course, who'm I tryin' to shit. This place is always a mess."

"I'll be there," Abby said, "in two hours."

Around four they got hungry and ordered from Domino's.

Jeff got on the phone and put on this killer acting performance of a kid who'd just come down with everything short of the plague. "I'm afraid I can't come in and sing tonight. I'm running a pretty high fever and I keep throwing up."

"What, kid, you got some pussy lined up? Ha ha ha."

"No, I'm really sick."

"Yeah, sure you are, kid. See you tomorrow night."

They'd spent most of the afternoon on the couch watching TV. They were having a great time making fun of everything they saw—soap operas, commercials, old movies and especially MTV and all the veejays who thought they were so cool and all the girls with boob jobs and all the shirtless boys showing off their abs and pecs and all the gangsta rappers with their incomprehensible lyrics and practiced sneers—

God, wasn't it fun to feel superior?

A couple of times she trotted off to the john, leaving him there with an addled heart and an erection. Always before, he'd divided girls into two camps. Those he had crushes on and those he wanted to sleep with. This was the first time one girl evoked both feelings at the same time. Not that he wasn't leery of her. He knew as he watched her that she was going to break his heart someday. He was a virgin in that way, too, and that was far worse than being a physical virgin. Getting your heart broken lasted a lot longer than losing your virginity. He knew that for a fact because he'd seen his neighbor Rick try to deal with a broken heart and it hadn't been a pretty sight. Lost weight. Had to see a counselor. Got drunk all the time. Took him two years to put himself back together and even then he wasn't the old silly Rick, always with the jokes and the kid games. He never could figure out why they called women the weaker sex. Not only were they proving themselves in the military and on the sports field, but they had the ability to psychologically and utterly devastate men.

In the bathroom, Greer was wondering if she wasn't maturing more quickly than she'd realized.

She was having a good time this afternoon. A great time, actually. Laughing all the time. And with, face it, a dweeb. She knew it was cruel to apply that word to Jeff, but it was true. In the social scheme of things at good old Woodrow Wilson High, he didn't count.

But he made her feel good. He was somehow friend-brother-boyfriend rolled into one. She felt comfortable, safe, didn't have to worry about impressing him with her wiles and mystery the way she did with the popular boys. She just sort of hung out with him and was her goofy self and that was such a wonderful feeling.

So maybe she was maturing, finally.

Maybe she was seeing how artificial her relationships were.

While the murky events of last night still hovered just at the edges of her consciousness—and while she still felt dehydrated and depressed at odd moments—Jeff was definitely helping her get through the afternoon.

Just as he'd definitely helped her get through last night—by rescuing her.

Yancy was home to get the call.

He'd closed the store early. An endless series of romance purchases had reminded him of how far away from his true self he was; God, if he was going to sell books, they should be books of Baudelaire and James Joyce and F. Scott Fitzgerald. So he'd closed the store early and come home and gotten into that special bottle of sour mash he kept on hand for his worst moments.

Of all the calls in the universe, this was the one he'd least expected, and the one that did the most damage to his sense of well-being.

"Dad?"

"Hi. You go to work early, Jeff?"

"No, I told them I wouldn't be in today."

"Oh. So where are you?"

"I'm at Greer's."

The name stunned and paralyzed him. Greer. How easy it rested on his son's lips. Greer.

"How come you're there?" Collecting himself. Sounding properly Dad-like.

"Oh, just stopped in to see how she was doing."

"And she's doing fine, I hope?"

"Really great. Oh, and she told me to tell you she likes coming into your bookstore. She likes Sue Grafton."

"Well, good. And tell her I like seeing her in my bookstore. She's a nice young girl."

"Yeah, I was kind of thinking the same thing myself."

Yancy'd never heard his son so open about his feelings, particularly as they applied to girls. Greer really must be something.

"Anyway, what I called about, Dad, is Greer and I ordered a pizza. So I won't be home for dinner. I'll just eat here. Tell Mom for me, will you?"

"Sure. Any idea when you'll be home?"

"Well, I'm trying to talk Greer into going to the movies tonight. There're a couple of good ones on I've been wanting to see."

"Sounds like you're making progress."

"It's really weird—she's upstairs so I can talk a minute—it's like we've known each other all our lives. The way we get along and everything, I mean. Well, I hear her coming down the stairs. Tell Mom, okay?"

"Sure, Son. Have a good time."

Greer. Good old Greer. And her good old mother, Laura. Women with secrets. No: women with *the secret.*

So now it was sour mash time. And worry time.

There would have to be a meeting. He didn't want the burden on his shoulders alone. Greer had to be dealt with, but how did he go about that when his son might now be in the way?

For all his failings—and he was well aware of them, admitted them to himself if not to anybody else—he liked to think of himself as a basically righteous man. He considered his business with the women perfectly righteous. Doing what he'd been put on this Earth to do.

But he'd never had to consider a family member being in the way before.

Oh, yes, it was definitely sour mash time.

And worry time.

ONE WEEK AGO

FROM THE DESK OF
DR. DAVID PRESCOTT

Dr. Thomas Cooper
Hastings Corner, MA

Dear Tom,

I certainly appreciate hearing from you. I just wish our phone call had been a little more productive in terms of your coming to terms with the reality of the situation. Virtually all of the sects in the country have now complied with our recommended procedure. Identify the girl and let us take over. Unburden yourself of all risk. Enjoy life.

The situation is now in our hands. We will soon dispatch one of our own operatives to deal with Greer Morgan. We will also be monitoring you. I hope you don't act foolishly on your own.

This is the new world, Tom. The new millennium. You and your group served your area well for many years. But now it's time to let a new generation and a new method take over the service we are providing our species.

Please share this letter with your group and advise them to comply.

Sincerely,

David Prescott

TODAY

When he opened the door and walked inside, Cam Morgan wondered if he'd stepped into the wrong house. He hadn't heard his daughter laugh like this since the death of her mother. The only possible explanation would be Jeff Crawford, whose recognizable heap was parked in the curving driveway.

He followed the sound of the laughter as if summoned by a sea siren.

They were sitting in the all-purpose nook, across from each other with a Domino's pizza box between them.

"Hi, Dad."

"Hi, honey."

"You remember Jeff."

"Not likely to forget the boy who rescued my daughter."

"He rescued me today, too. Came over and kept me company all afternoon."

"That's another one I owe you, Jeff."

"My pleasure, Mr. Morgan."

" 'Cam' is fine. Except for my daughter."

"I have to call him Your Highness," she giggled.

"Have some pizza. There're three pieces left, Mr. Morgan. Er, Cam. Say—is it all right if I call you Mr. Morgan? I just can't get the word out, Cam, I mean. It just doesn't sound right."

"Mr. Morgan or—as my giggly daughter said—Your Highness. Either one."

Jeff grinned. "I think I'll make it Mr. Morgan."

"Good choice," Cam said. "I appreciate the offer of the pizza, but I think I'll go up, change clothes, and take a little nap. I didn't get much sleep last night and I'm pretty worn out. Abby didn't call, did she, hon?"

"Nope. Were you expecting to hear from her?"

"Sure. The results of your blood test."

"That's right. I forgot all about it."

"Well, enjoy your pizza. I'm headed upstairs."

As he was leaving the room, he heard her whisper, "See, I told you he wouldn't care if you were here. He likes you."

"If he does," Jeff said, "he's the first dad who ever has."

"I'll bet that's not true," Greer said.

There was fog and mist again on the early evening highway leading to Candy Archer's trailer. And loneliness. Fog had always had the effect of whispering ghosts on Abby—and never happy ghosts. They whispered of old fears and old regrets and old losses. The puppy lost to disease; the friend who'd spurned her through a misunderstanding; the boy who inexplicably snubbed her; even her battles with Laura. Close as they'd been, there had been certain battles, too. Several times over boys; more often over their secret and which of them was using it recklessly.

In those days, at the peak of their powers, the two girls were good at two things—the healing of animals (though she'd been too young when her little puppy got sick to be of any use) and the occasional premonition.

It had been Laura's idea to sneak into old Doc Baines' office and heal up all the animals they could in the middle of the night. Abby had always been against this. She was afraid they'd get caught and their secret would be exposed and then what? They'd be freaks the rest of their lives. This, anyway, was the wisdom of their mothers. And Abby stuck to it, wouldn't break into the vet's office, wouldn't help with the healing. Healing that one puppy and Laura's arm was all Abby was willing to do.

But one day Laura tricked her, rode up to Abby's place with a tiny gray kitten in the bicycle basket of her ten-speed.

Abby, of course, fell in love with the kitten just as Laura had known she would. And then Laura told her the truth—that she'd taken it from the vet's office last night. This little one was dying of a tumor behind the ear. But Laura couldn't heal it. She wasn't sure why. You never were. Some animals you could heal—or the Lord, however you defined such an entity, could heal through you, as the girls knew—but healing didn't always work.

It hadn't worked with this kitten.

Laura demonstrated by putting the little tyke on the grass. The kitten started to romp but then fell over suddenly. And began to cry in great pain.

What choice did Abby have?

She understood only one thing about the process of healing: you had to merge your goodness with the animal's. Your innocence with its innocence. And in that melding of purity and need, a healing could oftentimes be achieved.

Physically, the healing involved you touching the animal, closing your eyes, and making a contact you could feel but not explain with the spirit of the other being. This was when the wholeness and purity of your shared existence met and became one momentarily.

When she opened her eyes again, Abby saw the kitten still lying on the grass. Crying?

So it hadn't worked. This was one of the animals that neither of them could help, apparently. And Abby was devastated. Such a sweet, good, tender little creature. And as always, she took her failure personally. She was not good enough in her own soul. And it had been this lack of goodness that had resulted in the kitten remaining sick.

But then suddenly, the kitten wasn't sick. It was up on its tiny legs, romping about, its cute little rear bouncing up and down, tail switching, running after butterfly and bird and family dog, anything that crossed its path.

And Abby was rewarded with an elation, a singular joy, she had never known before. This was what she received from healing—a sense of having some purpose in the unknowable cosmos, a sense of bringing joy to other people and beings.

The next time Laura visited Doc Baines' animal hospital, Abby was with her. And every time after that, too.

She wanted to discuss all these things tonight with Cynthia—Candy—the once-elegant young woman who'd somehow become a cigarette-hacking ex-stripper and now (God only knew what it meant) The Futurist.

For her part, Candy was excited about seeing Abby.

She did the dishes in the sink, something she hadn't done for over a week.

She picked up all the beer bottles, whiskey bottles, crushed cigarette packs, Trojan packs (she'd gotten lucky a couple of times), socks, earrings, pantyhose, blouses, CDs, true detective magazines, and other personal debris strewn throughout the length of the Airstream.

Then—she wished she had one of those moon suits they wore when they went into a toxic spill—she even attacked the bathroom. And nearly lost her cookies in the process.

This having guests stuff was no job for the fainthearted.

"We'll need to call a meeting for tonight," Yancy said, taking the groceries from Sara.

"Will you at least let me get in the door first?"

"This is serious."

"I didn't say it wasn't."

"He's been at her place all afternoon."

"Mind telling me who we're talking about? And have you been drinking?"

"I'm talking about our son," Yancy said, putting the two grocery bags on the table. "He's been at Greer Morgan's house all afternoon. And they've ordered a pizza for dinner. And whether I'm drinking or not is none of your fucking business."

"Oh, it's so nice to come home to a drunken, abusive husband. Not hiding any blondes in the closet, are you?"

She carried her coat into the hallway closet and returned. Yancy sat at the table, drinking, while she put the groceries away.

"I'm sorry I asked you about drinking."

"I don't blame you. I've been doing too much of it lately."

The conciliatory tone of his words obviously surprised her. "This is a fix, isn't it?"

"It sure is," he said. "We certainly never thought about our son getting involved with one of them."

"Well, we can't say he's 'involved.' He only met her last night."

"You should've heard him. He was giddy, he was so happy."

The freezer was too small for all the odd-sized boxes that needed to go in there. "Are you ever going to eat this frozen squash you bought? Or this frozen okra?"

He smiled. "Remnants of my last health kick."

"Well, if you're not, let me throw it out and make room for some new things."

He waved a dismissive hand. "Throw it out."

"It's such a waste."

"Can we keep to the subject, please? What the hell are we going to do about Jeff?"

"Well," she said, dropping the frost-covered boxes of okra and squash in the wastebasket, "I think you're right. About calling a meeting, I mean. We need to let everybody know what's going on. See if they have any ideas."

"I hope they do," he snapped. "Because I sure as hell don't."

Greer felt alert for the first time that day.

She was showered, fed, entertained, back to being the old Greer. And that included being curious.

Exactly why had she gone off wandering last night? And what had compelled her to look in that particular area? Where had she been headed when Jeff, thankfully, found her?

This was the reason why they were putting on their jackets when Cam came downstairs.

"You two off to somewhere?"

"Just going for a ride," she said. "I just need to get some air for a while."

She'd already asked Jeff not to say anything about where they were really going. Dad would get worried. And Dad got worried enough as it was.

"You take good care of her, Jeff."

Jeff blushed. "I'll do my best, Mr. Morgan."

Greer gave Cam a kiss on the cheek. "We'll be back in a couple of hours."

"Just be careful."

Greer smiled. "You could always come along and ride in the back seat."

"Am I that bad?"

"Worse."

"My girl, the smart-ass."

On the way to the car, she said, "I hate lying to him."

"Yeah. I know what you mean. I always feel guilty

when I lie to my folks. They're such nice people. They deserve better."

"But he'd just say no. And I really do want to drive around out by your place. See if anything registers. I just can't figure out why I went there last night."

In a way I'm glad you did, Jeff thought. *Otherwise, there wouldn't be any way a dork like me could've met you and wormed his way into your life.* He had the feeling that this was a dream and was going to evaporate at any moment. Jeff Crawford and Greer Morgan. Hanging out together. Even touching each other's hand from time to time. Yeah, right. Had to be a dream. Had to be. And, oh, the loneliness and dread and depression when the dream finally evaporated. It was going to be a bitch, and he wasn't sure he could handle the pain. In just this short time, he'd fallen completely—dangerously—in love with her. Nothing had ever been so exhilarating or so frightening.

Gusty winds blew the little car around. The snow spun furiously, dervishlike. The ancient heater made enormous tinny noise without dispersing much warmth. The stars were clear along the upper fourth of his cracked windshield. They looked winter lonely. He kept the music low in case she wanted to talk. Soft rock instead of hard rock. It seemed more appropriate somehow.

"Maybe I wasn't looking for anything in particular. Maybe I was just walking."

"Maybe."

"Somnambulism."

"Now there's a nice word."

"Sleepwalking."

"Oh."

"But then again, why would I choose out here to walk? Why not someplace else?"

"That's a good point, too." He had no idea what to say. He had the love jabbers. He just jabbered, idiot-happy, not responsible for anything that fell from his mouth. Just being with her. That was all that mattered. "You were sort of headed in the direction of the Coopers' cabin."

"I was?"

"Yeah. I'll drive past there."

"You're probably tired of this, Jeff. I'm sorry I'm making you do all this."

"My pleasure."

"You're so nice."

Was that a good sign or a bad sign, that she thought of him as "so nice." Wasn't "nice" often a way of saying I think of you as a friend but not as a lover? Wasn't "nice" ultimately dismissive? Most of the girls he'd had crushes on were always telling him what jerks their former boyfriends were—and how much they loved them. In a world that made no sense, that made no sense at all. Why would you love a jerk? What was wrong with being nice? Life was so much simpler when he'd stayed in his room and read his science fiction paperbacks and dreamed his dreams of impossibly popular girls crawling in his midnight window to bring him the wine and fruit and the gentle touch of true love and endless sex. Actually being in the presence of such a girl was a whole 'nother matter entirely. It most surely was.

The city limits gave way to the farm fields surrounding the town, shadowy now in the cold moonlight, fields brown and winter dead even though snow wasn't sticking on the ground and probably wouldn't for at least a few more weeks.

When they reached his house, he saw that the lights were out and the left garage stall was open. His folks had gone somewhere, something they rarely did on a weeknight.

"That's where you live, right?"

He was surprised she knew.

"I saw you out mowing the lawn last summer. I always go to Myers' stable to ride horses. I honked, but the mower was making so much noise, you didn't hear me. You looked very earnest—and cute."

"I did?"

"Sure. You're a good-looking guy."

"I am?"

No narcotic in the world is as strong as a compliment from the girl you love.

"Except," she said.

"Except?" he echoed, terrified of what she was about to say.

"Except when you wear that Dwight Yoakam cowboy hat." She reached over and touched his arm and he was positively head-swimmingly joyous. "That doesn't look so good on you. Like you said."

"You saw me in it?"

"One day at the mall."

"Oh."

She'd withdrawn her hand. He wished she would've left it there.

As soon as he got home tonight, he was going to burn that cowboy hat of his.

He drove on.

Greer said, "I should give you some gas money."

"Why?"

"Why? Jeeze, because I'm asking you to drive around so much."

If she only knew how thrilled he was to be doing this. He should be paying her. And that was no exaggeration. But it would end in a few hours—and then what? That was an even scarier thought than driverless cars that attacked people in mall parking lots.

The heater was actually kicking out some heat now. It felt good. Only added to the sense of comfortable enclosure he was enjoying—they were in a space bubble of some kind, drifting through the universe, wonderfully alone.

That sense ended when a pickup truck came wailing down the hill a good two feet across the center line. Jeff hit the horn. The truck swerved back across the line. This time, Jeff could see the human driver. The all too human driver. The redneck-type flipped him the bird, apparently irritated that Jeff had reminded him of what a shitty driver he was.

"What an asshole," she said. It was the first time she'd used a dirty word, and for a moment it shocked him. Did princesses use words like asshole?

He grinned.

"What's funny?" she said.

"Nothing. Really."

"That I said asshole?"

"Well, sort of."

"I say stuff like that all the time. That one just kind of slipped out. I have a dirty mouth, a really dirty mouth. I was trying to fool you. You know, keep it clean. But that slipped out."

"I'm deeply offended."

"Yeah, I'll bet you never say words like that. And don't say it's different for a guy, or I'll slug you."

Which is exactly what he had been thinking: *It's different for a guy. Guys are supposed to have dirty mouths. It says so in the Bible, in fact. Somewhere in the back, as Homer Simpson always says.*

They reached the top of the hill and the roadside shelf that looked down over the valley and the town below. This was the best view of Hastings Corner. The town not only looked pretty from up here, it also looked much bigger than it was. Almost like a real city.

He pulled in, yanked on the emergency brake. There wasn't much to see from here. The weave of the snow was too thick. He cut the lights because the illumination just bounced back. It didn't help.

"You want to try outside?" he said.

"Yeah. Sure can't see anything here."

The snow cut at their faces like mutant mites with some damned good dentures. They stood near the edge of the natural shelf guarded on both sides by giant shaggy pines. And looked out and down.

"Heights scare me," she said. And took his hand. "You mind?"

"Yeah," he said, "it really makes me mad."

"Really?" she said, taking him literally.

"God, no," he said, sorry at once for his dry sarcasm. He held her hand tighter.

In the whipping wind, the lights of the town looked brave and timeless. The land had been settled, and nature, no matter how violent, could never reclaim it. That's what the lights said to Jeff, anyway. Above, he saw the lights of an airliner headed for Boston. He loved flying—he'd only done it twice—but he wondered if it wasn't a bit alarming to fly in weather like this.

"There're people down there," she said.

He lowered his gaze to the back of the Coopers' cabin. The lights were on inside.

"I wonder what they're doing."

"You got me," he said.

And then he saw his father's car. His father always said how much he hated the Coopers' cabin. Having Tom Cooper order people around. He wasn't sure why, but seeing the car down there now gave him a feeling that something was going on. He thought again of how tense his father had become when he'd mentioned Greer.

"You recognize any of the cars?" Greer said.

"Not from here," he lied. Then: "Why don't we go?" he said abruptly.

"Don't you want to find out what they're doing?"

"Nah; I'm getting pretty cold, actually."

"You sound funny all of a sudden."

"I'm all right. Let's just go, okay?"

"Sure. Fine, Jeff. Just relax, all right?"

But her hand fell away from his, and he felt her withdrawing from him emotionally. It was a physical sensation.

He didn't waste any time. Got in the car. Put the transmission in reverse. Got out of there before— He didn't know what was going on, but it felt bad for some reason. Real bad.

4

THEY called them mobile homes now and some of them deserved that august designation. They had all the modern amenities and lay on land that had been properly tended. Trees, grass, even certain subtle landscaping redeemed the mobile homes from being mere trailers.

The swirling snow didn't make Candy Archer's grim little Airstream any more glamorous. Sitting next to a tiny and long abandoned gas station, the trailer had the look of a tin can rusted by years of the elements. Small, crude, its silver sides rusted out in places, Abby could just imagine the life lived inside. A life on the cusp.

But maybe that's my snobbery, the way Dr. Gallagher said that day in the hospital, Abby thought.

Richard Gallagher had been her favorite instructor. He was chief of staff at the Boston hospital where she'd interned. He spent a private hour with each intern before turning them loose on a floor.

She'd come into his office nervous and afraid. Dr. Gallagher was known as the medical equivalent of a boot camp instructor. That he looked not unlike Santa

Claus—white hair, apple cheeks, small but obvious belly—was her first shock. The second was that he conducted his interview with her by standing next to his open window so he could chain smoke cigarettes. He offered no explanation or apology for the smoking. She put his age at roughly sixty.

The first thing he said was, "I spent some time with your file last night, Stewart, and I suspect that you're going to have the same problem I had when I interned here."

"What would that be?" She smiled, trying to lend some humor to the moment. He didn't return her smile.

"You come from money. It's going to be impossible for you to see your patients here as actual human beings."

"I'm not prejudiced, Dr. Gallagher."

"Of course you are. We all are. And you especially. You were taught—as I was—that most people are our inferiors. Our parents never said that to us explicitly—in fact, they probably went out of their way to tell us the opposite, to prove what kind, compassionate people they were—but that's what we learned, wasn't it? That we're superior, somehow. And not just to black people but to everybody who doesn't bask in the glow of our social position."

"So you're saying I'm a bigot?"

This time, he laughed. "Of course you're a bigot, Stewart. So am I. We're raised to be bigots. But a very wise man—a former president of Notre Dame—said something once that cut through all the liberal bullshit about bigotry. It wasn't anything that whites or blacks wanted to hear. He said that we're all raised to be bigots and that the measure of us as individuals is how we deal with it."

"So," she said, "speaking as one bigot to another, Dr. Gallagher, how have you dealt with it?"

"The last twenty years? Pretty damned well, if I have to say so myself. The first ten years—well, I used to tell black jokes to some of my colleagues. That's how I dealt with it at first. I was an insufferable, cynical, closed minded guy who considered his patients—white and black alike, I must say—uneducated dullards whose lives didn't have much point."

"And then something changed you, I take it?"

"You don't like me much, do you, Stewart?"

"Not so far, no."

"Good. Because if I was the buddy-buddy type, you'd forget what I told you as soon as you walked out the door." He inhaled deeply on his cigarette, exhaled the smoke out the open window. "I had a six-month-old black child die in my arms. That's what changed me, Stewart. I'm not a religious man at all, so I'm not going to say that it was any kind of divine force teaching me a lesson. As far as I'm concerned, the universe is a Chinese puzzle box of interlocking coincidences. No divine forces, I'm afraid, though there are times when I wish there were such things. But, random or not, it humbled me, that tiny body in my arms. I saw how all my arrogance and pride and superiority was diminished in the face of this little girl's death. I didn't cry—I didn't blame myself for her dying, there really hadn't been any way of saving her—I didn't think of giving up medicine. I just realized that we're all the same. You cut through all the bullshit—the cultural differences, the physical differences—we're the same. Just lonely, scared people running around on this fucking nowhere planet. Maybe you'll be lucky enough to have an infant die in your arms, Stewart. Because it's going to take something like that to cut through everything you've learned in the upper classes about humanity."

He seemed so smug. She wanted to tell him of her curative abilities. Of her secret nature. But even if she did tell him, he wouldn't believe her. She'd find herself on a psych ward—poor dear, just couldn't take the stress—or simply out of the medical profession permanently.

The thing was, he was right.

In the ensuing nights, days, weeks, months she found herself having a difficult time seeing many of her patients as human beings—or human beings, anyway, as she defined the term.

The junkies. The drunks. The wife beaters. The sexual predators. And not even many of the victims—excepting the children—were people she relished, either. *What's wrong with you? Why don't you take your life in your hands and get away from this shit-hole life of yours? You owe it to your kids and to yourself. Don't you have any pride? Any gumption? Any dreams? You must want to be a victim, that's all I can figure out. Because you won't do anything about it.*

She was ashamed of these feelings, of course. As a daughter of privilege, it was so easy for her to judge others. As a good-looking, bright, proud woman it was so easy for her to see herself as superior. And as a woman with her very special secret, it was so easy for her to see herself as superior. And as a woman with her very special secret, it was so easy for her to regard herself as being in a vanguard that might well herald a new direction for humankind.

But no matter how she berated herself, no matter how self-conscious she became, she still felt a certain cold condescension toward her patients.

Until the night the little girl burst into the operating room where her brother—a fourteen-year-old who'd been walking down the street and got in the way of a drive-by shooting—lay dying on the operating table.

The simple, pure goodness—and the simple, pure grief—of the eight-year-old girl allowed her to mind-meld the way she'd done with animals. The beauty of this small child—the beauty of her love for her brother—allowed Abby to see the ghetto world through the eyes of somebody forced to live there. She saw in that instant of empathy and mind fusion just how arrogant and harsh she'd been toward her patients; how most of them struggled every day for the simple necessities she'd always taken for granted; how they pushed against immutable forces to find shelter and a modicum of safety and hope; and how they grieved helplessly when they saw their children swallowed up by the dark forces of the streets.

Her whole attitude changed. And Gallagher sensed it almost right away. The little girl's brother had died, but on her Saturdays off, Abby began taking the little girl to a mall or the movies or the amusement park. They became good friends. And the little girl, Celice, taught her how to love other people. Not all people—there was nothing silly or sentimental about Celice's type of love—but how to find the good where it resided.

But it was something Abby had to work at because

every once in a while—as now, when she was pulling up next to Candy Archer's trailer—she felt some of her old arrogance. Her mood wasn't helped by the fact that she'd had to ask directions here not once but twice.

Who'd live in a place like this?

She huddled into herself as she pounded on the door of the trailer, the wind and snow lashing her as the twang of country music wailed on the barren night.

The door was flung open, and an obscene parody of a little old lady stood in the doorway.

Abby's first inclination was to laugh.

She couldn't have been five feet tall. She couldn't have weighed ninety pounds and half of that belonged to the rings she wore not only on her fingers but on her ears, her nose, her tongue. She had the spiky pink hair of a dance club denizen, the shadowy makeup of a Goth chick, the microminiskirt of a hooker and the steely eyes of an assassin.

She also had a piercing, eerie laugh.

"You seen that picture of me back when I was still a sweet, little rich girl and you thought I might still be the same!" A witchy cackle. "Well, darlin', I ain't the same at all, I'm sad to say."

And with that, she stepped back and allowed Abby the dubious pleasure of coming inside.

The Coopers' cabin had a stone fireplace and Danish furniture that was stylish and elegant. Colorful area rugs brightened the low-ceilinged room. A ski lodge atmosphere.

Hot toddies were quick in coming, and the fireplace was soon putting out enough heat to make sweaters unnecessary.

Small talk lasted through the first round of drinks, and then—after being served a second time—Yancy and the others settled in for a serious discussion.

"It's pretty simple," Yancy said. "You know what needs to happen with Greer Morgan. My son was coming home late when he saw her on the road not far from our place. He took her home to her father. And now he's spent the day with her. From what I can tell, he's more than a little bit smitten. I know we need to move now and get this thing resolved. But I don't want my son to find out what's going on."

Dr. Cooper seemed surprised. "Seems to me now would be a good time to invite him into the circle."

Russ Dryer nodded. "Our boy was about the same age when we told him."

"You told him everything?" Yancy said.

"Everything," Dorothy Dryer said.

"How did he react?"

Russ laughed. "He thought we were putting him on. Remember, Dorothy? He thought it was all a big joke. But fortunately we had some footage. Film footage. Your father shot it, in fact, Yancy. That was back in 1956, I believe. The Amis girl. We made her move a book. You know, with just her mind. Took a long time. Your dad kept turning the camera on and off. Was afraid he was going to run out of film. But then she finally did it. I mean, that's the rule. They have to reveal themselves. It was that way back in the original trials. Something the history books never recorded; they wanted good guys and bad guys. They didn't want the truth then, and they don't want it now. But when our son saw the footage—well, he knew we weren't crazy. We spent an entire night explaining things to him and why what we were doing was so important. He got so hyped up, he took care of the girl himself. I believe she slipped off a slope and died in the fall." He frowned. "Six years later he died in Vietnam. Marines. Two little ones back here at home. He would've been your age now, Yancy. Or thereabouts."

His loss was palpable. There wasn't a time when Russ talked about his son that his friends weren't hushed into stunned silence. You were back there with him—the phone call from his daughter-in-law telling Russ that his son was dead; Russ telling the boy's mother, then trying to console her at the funeral; and then two years of lonely nights, Dorothy alone in her bedroom, wanting to sleep alone because of her late-night crying fits; and him with his bourbon and useless dead cock and stinging memories of his little boy. Life after death, that was how he thought about it. Somehow, three years later, they were Russ and Dorothy Dryer again. There was sunlight and laughter and Japanese lanterns on the nights of country club dances. And Russ's cock was alive again, and Dorothy found herself excited by sex in a way she never had been before. Life after death. You have doubts that miracles happen? Just take a gander at the Dryers today and compare them to what they were during those years immediately following the death of their boy.

Only when, as now, one of them mentioned it directly to other people did the boy's death overpower them. And it never lasted long. Just an uncomfortable moment or two.

"The last six or seven, Yancy, we've got footage. Videotape." Russ wiped a stray tear from his cheek. Snuffled up some tears in his nose. "You show him that, and he'll know just what you're talking about. And he'll want to help."

"What if he's in love with her?"

"You really think he'll be in love with her after you talk to him, Yancy?"

"There's always that possibility."

"Why don't we table that whole thing with Jeff for now?" Tom Cooper said. "What we need to concentrate on is the girl. It's past time we dealt with her. She's the only one we know of who has to be addressed. Yancy can talk to Jeff a little farther down the line. When he's more comfortable with it."

Yancy listened carefully for any hint of disparagement in Cooper's voice, but there was none. For now, apparently, Cooper had put their past differences aside.

Russ Dryer said, "Anybody ready?" Hoisting his stein to show that he was. He alone was ready. On his way to the corner bar—as he cutely liked to call it—he said, "I guess what we need to know is whether Tom here can woo her out one more time."

"That shouldn't be any problem if she's still taking her medicine," Tom Cooper said.

"That's what we need to do," Yancy said, "and the sooner the better."

"What if somebody sees you take her?" Dorothy said.

Cooper sighed dramatically. "Dorothy, I've been in on the secret for more than fifty years now. And I haven't been caught yet, have I?"

"I was just asking, Tom. For God's sake, I wasn't accusing you of anything."

"Of course, she wasn't," her husband Russ said. "And this all sounds very sensible."

"When's it going to happen?" Yancy asked.

"The sooner the better," Pam Cooper said. "I think we've waited long enough."

"How about two nights from now?" Tom suggested.

"That sounds great," Russ said. "Everybody go along with that?"

"There's one more thing," Cooper said. "Dr. Prescott is not going to be happy."

"The hell with Dr. Prescott," Russ said. "I'm not going to let some damned yuppie climber push me around."

At which point, they all raised their steins again—and toasted Dr. Prescott—may he fall down the stairs and break his damned yuppie neck.

Nice friendly upscale group of older suburban people enjoying a cozy night by a large fireplace, their hands filled with hot toddies, their minds filled with good thoughts about folks in general and their friends in particular.

That was the impression you'd get from looking at a snapshot taken at this very moment.

But aside from the smaller tensions of conflicting personalities, there was now the larger tension that was always in the air when they decided to move on a particular target.

Because despite the tradition they were honoring—their sacred tradition, as most of them thought of it—what they were advocating—no, planning—here was what the law would call First Degree Homicide, i.e., planned in advance and with malice aforethought if you went in for legalese.

We the jury find the defendants guilty of . . .

Because that was always the risk with this particular endeavor.

You take a homicide detective aside and try to explain to him what you were doing. And he'd just laugh. And then lock you up to prevent you from carrying out your loony toony plan. If you were lucky, you'd wind up in a psych hospital, heavily medicated, where you'd stay until they'd broken your spirit and your will. And then you'd emerge months later very different from the person who was first elevatored down to the second basement level where the electroshock treatments were administered.

If you were lucky.

If you were unlucky, you would be charged with conspiracy to commit murder in the first degree. And the bail would be stiff. And this one charge would lead the coppers to start mucking about in your past looking for other charges to inflict on you. And, by God, they'd eventually put it all together. Generations of the same few families—some of the most respectable families in Hastings Corner—branded as cold blooded murderers.

Talk about the proverbial shit hitting the proverbial fan.

So they had to be very, very careful. And it was judicious of Dorothy Dryer to ask Dr. Tom Cooper (who did not like to be questioned in any way, especially by womenfolk) if it was taking too much of a chance picking up Greer just after she left her house.

"How about a toast to our good luck?" Russ Dryer said, playing the host.

"Good idea," Pam Cooper said.

Everybody held up his glass.

"May the Lord be with us," Russ said. "And protect us."

And just then Yancy held an image of her before his eyes—lovely young erotic Greer Morgan. And he thought: *May the Lord be with us. And protect us—from ourselves.*

Oh, it was quite a tale the little old lady with the spiky punk hair, the miniskirt, the cigarette, and the tattoos told. Some of which Abby had heard before. But so what? It was well worth hearing many times over, this particular tale.

Long before the witch trials in Europe, long before the similar trials in Salem, Massachusetts, long before the reign of Hammurabi in Babylon, long before the farming villages along the Nile in 4000 BC, it became clear to a few people that there were two human species.

Though they looked identical, spoke the same languages, had the same need for food and shelter and joy and love, had the same fear of fire and flood and pestilence and death, the secret species possessed talents that the first did not. There were circumstances in which the second species could heal the dying, predict the future, start fire through simple willpower, move objects with simple willpower, and even link minds with other people and read their thoughts.

The first species knew that if this small group were ever permitted to grow in number, the first species would become a subjugated race. Slaves, perhaps.

There were those among the first species who wanted to accommodate the second. True, there were a few bad ones among the second group, but not many, these people reasoned. And the second group swiftly punished their own by death if they inflicted any harm on the first. Why couldn't the two groups live side by side? Perhaps the second could teach the first how to develop similar powers of their own. And even if that didn't happen, what right did the first species have to destroy the second?

This was the truth for a very small number of the first species.

The majority weren't as tolerant. And they quickly began seeking out and murdering the second species wherever they found it. The hunted were given many obscene names but the word "witch" or some semblance thereof—always meaning Dark One—was the most popular and carried from land to land because within a few centuries that hunt had extended to empires as far flung as the Shang dynasty in China and the developing Mycenaean culture on mainland Greece. A number of particularly clever prisoners were taken and studied to see if the first group could somehow steal their powers. The answer to that was no, they could not. But in this process they learned several truths: that females had the dominant talents, and girls between the ages of eleven and nineteen had the strongest talents. The talents begin to fade by age twenty or so and in every group of witches, one is dominant and this is the one who tries to destroy her kind's persecutors. Upon occasion, the talents reappeared in middle-aged witches.

The first great witch war wasn't even recorded. Virtually all of them were wiped out except among the oral tales of the witches themselves. By the time Julius

Caesar reformed the Roman calendar, witches accounted for less than half a percent of the worldwide population. And by the time of the Second Punic War, witches were little less than legend, mythic night creatures to amuse adults and frighten children.

Christian prelates revived the myth and found it useful as a way of punishing those who disagreed with their religious precepts. Witches, in this version, were not simply a human species on a parallel genetic track but something far more sinister—the workers of the Dark One, Satan, himself. He was the ultimate enemy of the kind and gentle man, and perhaps divine emissary, whose simple philosophy these prelates distorted for their own purposes.

And thus began the scourge of the European witches, though of course very few of the people stabbed, drowned, set afire, hanged, and beheaded were actually gifted with the secret. They were mostly political enemies of the various prevailing establishments—religious, political, social, economic.

The witch trials in Salem were a different matter. Six families of true witches had settled in the Salem area. Three of their girls had healed people who'd fallen to a brief plague in the area. They had not only healed the sick, they'd stopped the plague from spreading. But their largesse had been witnessed. And so, crazed rumors started about the girls. And the entire Salem episode was set in motion.

As usual, though, the people who were executed and imprisoned weren't actual witches. They were simply the odd, the insane, the aggrieved whose presence upset the community.

The six families vanished overnight, resettling in the

area of Hastings Corner. Not until a chance meeting years later did the jurists of Salem know where the families had gone. And then the jurists—who by now believed all the lies they'd spread and felt they were actually doing the work of their God—dispatched three young families of their own to Hastings Corner. It would become the business of these three families to purge each generation of young female witches. They would die what appeared to be accidental deaths after the leaders of the three families had decided there was enough evidence to make their executions necessary.

Gathering evidence was important. Not all young females from these six families (or their descendants) were witches. Few were, in fact. So they observed the females, looking for signs and deeds of witchery, and if they saw any, they called a meeting and decided how to dispatch the young witch. This became easier as the years pressed on. Drugs and hypnosis could be used eventually to make the girls confess to their true nature—and to demonstrate it. There weren't that many witches, good or bad, left in the world.

Cynthia and Abby's mother had been good friends. If Cynthia had returned from Europe with Abby's mother instead of remaining there for fifteen years, her life might have been very different. But after her count abandoned her, she got so used to living on the streets that she lost all the poise and polish on display in that old photograph Abby found in her mother's diary.

"These days, I'm as crude as a beer fart," Candy laughed. There was no remorse in her words. She seemed to find herself amusing.

"Those jurists killed my mother?"

"Oh, yes. And they were going to kill me, too—God knows why. I didn't have any gifts left. I couldn't've moved a paper napkin across a table with my mind. But they'd been watching me and knew that I had the powers once. So they came after me just to make sure. So I went into hiding."

"How did you find out about them?"

Candy smiled with her wrinkled face and clicking dentures. "Kidnapped one of them one time. Put him under a spell—this was when I had a few powers left—picked his brain clean. He was nice looking, too. So I made him have sex with me."

The Madonna of witches, Abby thought, amused but vaguely shocked by some of the things Candy had revealed about herself. But then she decided the prig side of her was coming out. The woman had had a tough life. And had survived. Give her the respect she deserved. Abby's secret had been kept with little trouble.

"The other thing you have to understand is that this goes on all around the world," Candy said. "These little purges from time to time."

"There are more of us?"

"Hell, yes, kiddo. All over the place. Black, yellow, red—all colors, all types. There are even a few cells of us that have plans for taking over the world. It's not gonna happen, but they talk like it will. French, mostly. And real Nazi assholes, believe me. I wouldn't mind seeing the first race bump them off, believe me."

"Why didn't you ever contact me or Laura?"

"Simple enough. By the time I got back here, my talents were so shot, there wasn't much sense in even thinking I had the secret anymore. Because I didn't. I was just this broken-down so-called mind reader. Astrology—now there's a crock of shit for you—and reading palms. Crap like that. Didn't figure two refined gals like yourself and your friend, Laura, would even believe I'd had the talents at one time. So I just stayed in my little Airstream here and did my own thing."

"They're coming after Greer Morgan now."

"I know. I still have premonitions every once in a while."

"You know who they are?"

"Not really. Wish I did."

"So how do we protect Greer?"

"Lock and key's about the only way I know."

"You're serious?"

"Sure, I'm serious. How else you going to keep them away? At least for the time being, anyway."

"I have to tell Cam."

"I'd be glad to help you if I could." She splayed her hands in a gesture of helplessness. "But I'm too old to fight, and all my mental tricks're gone. When I had my talents, I saw 'em as a curse. They set me apart from everybody, and I resented that. But the last few years, I wish I had 'em back. Lot of little ways I could help people I see. I get premonitions now—like with Greer—but that's about it."

"I'm not any better off, believe me," said Abby. "I lost my talents about the time I started med school. They'd sure come in handy now. With Greer's situation."

"I wish could help you, kiddo. I really do. Care for a joint? I got some really wild Colombian shit this hairdresser I know got from his cousin. You don't know what stoned is till you try it."

It was funny, listening to the older woman speak, and then picking up stray telepathic thoughts. In her mind, Candy often reverted to type—to the sweet, elegant, sheltered girl she'd been in the house of her rich father. But she had perfected her street girl exterior. You couldn't tell that it had been consciously layered on over the years.

"I'm afraid I'll have to pass," Abby said, managing to keep from smiling. "I've got a lot of things to do."

"And one of them is to get out of my little trailer as soon as possible, right?" She giggled and her dentures clicked. "Straight people always want to run and hide after about a half hour with me." She winked. "I wonder why that is?"

Wayfaring Hospital had once been a psychiatric clinic where rich Boston people came to dry out. Dr. David Prescott had been a resident at a nearby general hospital. As both neurosurgeon and psychiatrist, he was fascinated by the process people went through when they were withdrawing from the addictions of alcohol and drugs.

This was his stated reason for spending so much time at Wayfaring, anyway.

The real reason was one he obviously couldn't share with the other doctors. He'd been raised in a family that not only believed in, but had witnessed firsthand, the existence of witches. He had seen the awkward, clumsy way in which they tried to purge the land of these devils. No wonder witches had thrived down through the centuries. Nobody had ever used sound scientific methods for exterminating them. He married a lovely girl from the local cell of witch-hunters and then between them they evolved the idea of bringing the techniques of modern science to witch-hunting and witch-finding and witch extermination.

And then the dark witches had killed his wife. And his daughters. Prescott no longer made a distinction between the dark witches and the others. Witches were witches and meant to be destroyed. Like most fanatics, he saw his beliefs as perfectly reasonable. And whenever anybody in his hospital even suggested that maybe not all witches were the same, they were reprimanded by a stern memo within a single working day. And the memo went on their computer file.

Twenty-three years after he first began evolving his idea—twenty-three years in which he battled not only witches but all the small pockets of witch-hunters throughout the country who wanted to cling to their autonomy and their old ways—he was now taking over as the chief witch-finder not only in America but throughout the world. He had computerized everything. He had the name, age, and location of every suspected witch on the planet. Knowledge was power. He had killed more than two hundred witches in his time. Now when they learned of new witches, they fed all the data into his computers and let him dispatch one of his own young women to exterminate the witch—a young woman he'd trained right here in his hospital. If that meant flying her to London, Moscow, or Missoula, so be it. All the tiny groups of witch-finders had started to send him major contributions. He wanted the witch-finders out of the way. They were the old way. He was the new way. Wayfaring

Hospital—he'd bought out the doctors who'd originally built it—now contained the computers and the experiment rooms that made Prescott a genuine folk hero to the thousands of people who'd been battling witches in secret.

His secret—if looked at in its simplest terms—was one he loved to quote to skeptics: send a witch to find a witch. Because he was both a neurosurgeon and a psychiatrist, he understood how thought reform and psychological reform could work very well.

He captured young women and brought them here and installed them in the locked ward on the third floor of the hospital. His object was to destroy them and then rebuild them.

As he told his staff (most of whom had grown up in his cell of witch-finders) there were simple rules for breaking down and then rebuilding a person:

Control the person's time and physical environment.

Create a sense of powerlessness, covert fear, and dependency.

Suppress all of the person's old behavior and attitudes.

Instill new behavior and attitudes.

Put forth a closed system of logic.

Punish any serious doubts or criticism.

And the system was working very well, thank you.

A knock. He knew who it would be. The embodiment of his system—Karen. Except for her problems with precognitive abilities—he'd always known that this would be the most difficult of all their skills to achieve and sustain—she was his most successful student thus far. And she was about to embark on her first real hunt.

Though she'd been scheduled to leave a few days

ago, he'd held her back, wanting to go over and over who she was looking for and what Karen was to do when she found her. He'd keep Karen here for a few more days.

He'd also decided to have her check in on a special phone with a scrambled line so it couldn't be monitored unless you knew the exact frequency. It looked like a perfectly harmless cell phone.

She hadn't seen it yet. But she was about to. And soon she'd be on her way.

"Come in," said Dr. David Prescott.

The hope was she'd ask him in.

Ask him in. And then find that Dad was sound asleep upstairs. And then ask him if he wanted to watch a little TV in the den. You know, the den with the time lock on the door and the Dobermans standing guard in the hall and the nuclear warhead that would explode should anybody try to get in? And then kind of get snuggly-wuggly on the couch. And then—My God, is this a dream?—find out that both of them were down to their underwear. And then she'd whisper, "You know, I've been waiting for the right person and right time to make love for the first time. And this is it, Jeff. I know it in my heart. Just remember I don't have your experience. I mean, I'm not sophisticated the way you are. So just please be kind with me, Jeff. Please be kind."

It wasn't quite like that.

Dad—glimpsed in the living room from the porch where they stood—was in his recliner watching the local news. And not looking as if he were going to go upstairs any time soon.

And then Greer herself was saying, "I'm really tired, Jeff, or I'd ask you in."

"I'm a little tired myself." Awkward pause. "You like a ride to school in the morning?"

"But you don't go to school."

"I know. But I thought I'd stop in and talk to them about coming back."

She took his hand, squeezed it. "That's great. And sure, if you're going there anyway, I'd be glad to get a ride."

"Around seven-thirty. Maybe stop off at McDonald's first or something."

"Great."

There in the porch darkness—the immemorial good-night-kiss porch darkness so inextricably a part of spooning and mooning and juneing—she leaned forward and kissed him, a simple kiss on the cheek, but it curled every hair on his body, it was so sweet and meaningful to him.

He fought against saying I love you.

He really wanted to say it because: a) he'd never said it to anybody but his dog before and he knew that as scary as it was, it would make him feel great, and b) he really did love her. But he'd barely known her twenty-four hours. You probably should wait a minimum of thirty-six or even forty-eight hours before you told a girl you loved her. There was probably a rule about that somewhere. Maybe in the *MTV Book of Dating* or someplace like that.

"Well, I'll see you in the morning."

"Thanks again, Jeff. It's really fun hanging out with you."

"It sure has been. With you, I mean."

"Night."

Going in.

"Night."

Gone.

He didn't notice the snow or wind on his walk back to his car. He just touched his finger to the spot where she'd kissed him on the cheek. He was sure that spot was glowing.

At Jeff's house, his parents and Dr. Tom Cooper sat in the living room. Yancy had turned the FM on to a jazz station. Miles Davis contemplated suicide through the tones and notes of his trumpet—at least that's what the good doctor thought. Jazz was profoundly depressing to him. He assumed Yancy played it just to piss him off.

Dr. Cooper sat in the armchair, Yancy and Sara on the couch. They sat apart, like strangers. Cooper wondered how often they had sex. Thanks to Viagra, he was having lots of sex these days.

"This drug won't hurt Jeff?" Sara asked anxiously.

"Absolutely not."

"I want your word on it, Tom."

"God, Sara," Yancy said, "he said it won't hurt him. Just because your parents—"

So there it was. The other reason that Sara and Yancy had lost their affection for each other in the last ten tepid years of their marriage. She'd bloomed, going back to school, becoming an important figure not only in the library but the town in general. And she had resisted all of Yancy's attempts to indoctrinate Jeff in the ways of witch-stalking.

Late in their lives, her parents had left the group

they'd spent forty years with finding and then destroying witches. They'd come to see their work as evil. Most of the women they'd destroyed had done nothing wrong except to be born with certain powers that could be used for sinful ends—if they elected not to control them. Her parents had recanted in front of Tom Cooper and his friends. And they had virtually been shunned ever after. Four people had attended their double funeral following a bus accident.

Sara believed as her parents had. Early in their love affair—you know how it is early in love affairs, you believe what you want to believe—Yancy had assured her that they would raise any child they had according to her wishes. But by the time Jeff had come along, disenchantment had set in. He spent too much time with the witch-finders. He was too lustful and bloody a hunter. She shielded Jeff from all that, forbade Yancy to say anything about the heritage they shared. And now Yancy was trying to draw their son into becoming an active participant.

"It's just a drug that'll make him more susceptible to posthypnotic suggestion is all, Sara. I'll be here with you. We'll give him something—you said he likes chocolate milk before he goes to bed, so we put it in his chocolate milk—and then I'll go upstairs after the medicine has started working on him and I'll hypnotize him. We'll do it right before we bring Greer in."

"Can I be there with him?

Tom smiled at Yancy. "A very trusting lady you've got there, Yancy."

"Sara, do you really need to—" Yancy started to say.

"He's my son. And I just want to make sure he's all right."

"No problem, Sara. You can be right in the room when I'm hypnotizing him."

"Thank you, Tom. I appreciate it."

And then there was the sound of a car in the drive.

"It's him," she said, and went anxiously to the window. She'd always thought this moment would somehow be put off—the moment when her son would be involved in all this; the moment his life would be changed forever by being a part of it—but it was here. Now. And there was, she knew, no way to stop it.

Headlights pierced the snow, washing the front of the house as he backed up now. He always turned around in the drive and then parked out front at the curb. Their cars took up both stalls in the garage.

"It's him," she said, and sounded as if she were going to cry.

Cam was waiting for Greer to get out of the shower. He wanted to talk to her. See how she was doing. She must be feeling better. Long showers were something she enjoyed. When she was depressed, she was in and out of the bathroom as quickly as he was.

He was sitting up in his bed reading the latest Grisham, warm in his robe, pajamas, and slippers. He could hear her when she came out of the bathroom. He'd call to her. He knew he was probably being overly concerned. She liked to joke about how he'd take her temperature every ten minutes when she was running even a low-grade fever, but what the hell. Better too much than too little.

The phone rang. Client. That was his first thought. The important ones felt they had the right to call whenever they chose. Wanted you to know just how important they were.

He was surprised to hear Abby's voice.

"Did I wake you?" she said.

Car phone. Not a great connection.

"Just reading a little before the sandman comes."

"I—" Hesitation. "I wondered if you could stop in and see me tomorrow?"

"At your office?"

"I know it's inconvenient but—"

"I could stop before I go into the city."

"I'd really appreciate it."

He put his book facedown on his lap, swung his legs off the bed. "You don't sound so good."

"We just need to talk, Cam. I'd do it tonight, but I'm just worn out from the day. Tough one today. And I need to be a little fresh."

And then the worst thought of all. "Isn't that what you said last night? Why do you keep putting me off? You didn't find out something about Greer's health, did you?"

"No. Not the way you mean. Greer's health is fine."

"Not the way I mean? You're starting to scare me, Abby."

"I know I am. And I don't mean to." Pause. "Oh, hell. Why don't I just drive to your place now. Is Greer home?"

"Yes. But she's headed to bed. She said she was exhausted."

"Good. Maybe we could have a couple of drinks and talk in your study."

"That'd be fine. I wouldn't have been able to wait till tomorrow anyway."

"I'm sorry I scared you. I—it's just something we need to discuss."

"Mind if I'm in my robe?"

"Oh, yes. I'll be shocked and scandalized. Being the proper woman I am and all."

"I'll pop for some twenty-year-old Scotch."

"Sounds fine to me."

Candy opened herself a beer and a fresh pack of smokes and logged on to the Internet. This was going to take a while.

A long, long time ago in a place that now felt like a fantasy land—the wealthy home she'd been brought up in—her mother kept certain dusty and secret books locked in the attic so that inquisitive servants couldn't get at them. The cobwebbed attic with its steamer trunks and human torso sewing forms and skittering mice was the perfect place to lift the huge, leather-bound books (or tomes, as her mother liked to call them) up onto the table and look through them.

They'd been centuries old, her mother had said, and a lot of the pages were in the original Latin. They contained not only a history of the secret people but things the secret people needed to survive.

Her mother took great comfort in her tomes, the way other people took great comfort in their Bibles.

There was a rocking chair up there, and her mother would sit in it for hours, rocking back and forth. Forth and back, looking through her tomes.

Candy's favorite reading material—much to her mother's dismay—had always been "Wonder Woman" comic books and true crime magazines. So the tomes were pretty slow going for her when she'd sit in the rocker and read. In those blissful days, she didn't even know why she was reading. She just thought it was neat to imitate her mother. Made her feel older.

But Mom and her tomes were long gone. And there was no way Candy would've lugged them around Europe anyway.

Her conversation with Abby about Greer had started reminding her of her own youthful days—the fear of exposure, the feeling that she would never live a normal life, the dread that her powers would prove too much or too little. When she expressed these things to her mother, Mom always said the same thing: "You go up in the attic, honey, and look in those books. I'm up there three and four times a week. And I've been doing it since I was ten years old."

Candy's life had been filled with boys, boys, boys, and then fast cars, sloe gin, Viceroy cigarettes, and boys, boys, boys. Who had time for some dusty old attic and some musty old books?

But she felt obliged to help young Greer. Candy knew her precognition had kicked in again. That girl was in bad trouble. Candy had to help her if she could.

Maybe she didn't have the tomes. But she had the Internet. And she knew the code words to use when seeking out others with the secret.

"You kidding?"

"Nope."

"You're offering me a beer? How come?"

"It's just the right time for it."

Jeff just kept staring at his father. Yancy was acting strange enough tonight. He had a business size envelope in one hand and was tapping it nervously against his other hand. Standing in the kitchen.

"Where's Mom?"

"In bed."

"And you waited up for me?"

"Looks like it, doesn't it?"

"You've always told me you don't want me to drink."

"There are exceptions to every rule."

"And this is one of them?"

"This is one of them?"

"How come?"

"Why don't I get you a beer and while I'm doing that, you read this letter."

"I was wondering what that was."

Totally weird. His dad had virtually stopped him from leaving the kitchen. Had even taken his coat from him and hung it on a hook just inside the back door. And had then steered him to the small table that sat across from the cooking island. And now was offering him a beer.

"Who wrote the letter, Dad?"

"I did."

"You did."

"Yep. I wish I had time to take one more shot at it. I've been polishing it for over five years now."

"You realize you're scaring the shit out of me."

"I do. But it scared the shit out of me when my dad told me, too."

They stared at each other.

"Maybe I'm gonna need something stronger than a beer." He grinned.

His dad grinned back. "Three-point-two percent alcohol. A beer. One beer. No hard stuff. You read this while I get you a beer."

He leaned over and handed his son the envelope.

"I already know the facts of life, Dad." He grinned again.

"Not these facts of life, you don't, Jeff." Dad didn't grin back.

"Wow. This is getting very, very heavy."

"Read. I'll even pour it out in a pilsner glass for you. Just like a fancy Boston restaurant."

"You really are scaring the shit out of me, Dad."

Dad looked at him a long moment. "Maybe that's the way to handle this, after all. Scaring the shit out of you."

He went and got Jeff his beer.

Abby told it in a rush and gush, and when she got through, Cam sat there—this was in the living room after he'd made sure that Greer was sound asleep in her bedroom—Cam sat there and said, "I don't know what to say."

"I know it sounds crazy."

"Let me understand this. You're telling me my daughter is a witch?"

"Yes."

"And my wife was a witch?"

"Yes."

"And you're a witch?"

"I shouldn't have used the word witch. I hate it. It makes you think of '*Bewitched*' or something. Elizabeth Montgomery wriggling her nose."

"Do you know what a shared psychotic disorder is?"

"You're playing lawyer."

"Damned right I am."

She sighed. "I guess I don't blame you. I thought you might be—accepting. I guess when I stand back a little—"

"A shared psychotic disorder—and there was a trial that hinged on this just two years ago in upstate New York—is where several people share the same psychotic misperception of reality. You see it in satanic cults. A bunch of impressionable teenagers work themselves into a frenzy and begin to believe they're actually devils with all these supernatural powers. They believe it so strongly that they pass lie detector tests. There was a serial killer in LA once who'd convinced himself he was both a vampire and Satan. No amount of dissuading by the shrinks could change his mind."

"So you think that's what we're dealing with here?"

"I'd say that's at least a possibility."

"What about the fact that it's been going on for centuries."

"Well, first—if you'll allow me to continue playing lawyer—you have only your mother's word that it's been going on for centuries."

"Hers and Candy's."

"The fake psychic in the trailer?"

She laughed uncomfortably. "That's why I admire lawyers so much, Cam. You don't even know the woman, yet you're destroying her reputation."

"Is she or is she not a fake psychic?"

"Well, I suppose you could put it that way."

"And does she or does she not live in a trailer?"

"Yes, sir, your honor, she does."

"Thus my reference to her as the fake psychic who lives in a trailer is just, is it not?"

"You get off on showing off, don't you?"

He smiled. "It's my only pleasure in my old age." He put his hand over his eyes, shook his head. "This is just all so weird."

"You never thought there was anything a little odd about Laura or me?"

He looked up at her. "Sure, I did. I thought you were lesbians, remember?"

"Oh, yes, I remember."

"I didn't, really, and I was shit for writing that on the car. One of the partners in the firm is gay and so is my niece Lucy. It was just I didn't know what word to put to it. For the 'strangeness' I sensed in you two, you know? So I called you lesbians. But, sure, hell, yes, I sensed it in Laura. Some secret. And now that you mention it—I've never exactly thought of it till now—I guess I sense the same thing in Greer. But witches—"

"Please try and forget that word, all right. We're just normal human beings whose ancestors developed slightly differently from the rest of humanity."

"But that the Salem witch trials are still going on today—"

"And have been going on, in one form or another, since probably about the time our two species started walking upright."

He hesitated. "You ever talk to a shrink about this?"

"Are we back to shared psychotic disorder?"

"It's a possibility."

"No, it isn't, Cam. I'm sane and Laura was sane and Greer is sane."

He laughed. "How about Candy?"

"I know you find her hilarious, but she's actually a sweet little woman in her way. Had an incredibly tough life. And she's quite sane. So please lay off her."

"All right. I probably am being a shit." And: "So what're you saying?"

"I'm saying that we need to protect Greer. That there's a good chance they'll try and harm her in some way."

"How do we protect her? The police?"

"We can't go to the police. You know better than that."

"There's a security service, a bodyguard—"

"That's what she needs. A bodyguard. Follow her everywhere she goes. School, shopping, jogging. That's why I have to make you believe me."

"What if we split the difference?"

"And how do we do that?"

"What if I keep my reservations about what you told me, but I go ahead and hire a bodyguard, anyway?"

The darkened living room always reminded Jeff of when he was a little kid and creeping down early on Christmas morning for a sneak peek at his gifts. No matter how quietly he crept down the stairs, Mom and Dad always seemed to hear him. And joined him early. One of their great abiding pleasures was watching the expressions on his face as he opened one gift after another—a different expression of joy for each new gift.

Very different occasion tonight. Shape of furniture

in TV glow. Texture of carpet. Crabbed fingers of leafless limbs against frosted window. Alien somehow.

Dad was putting a videotape into the VHS machine. Jeff sat on the edge of the couch. He still had half his beer left. He kept waiting for Dad to turn around and say, "April Fool!" or something. He wished Dad had shown a practical joker side before because then Jeff could be assured that that's what this was, some weird gag that Dad—who could be quite weird—was pulling on him.

"I mean, this fucking letter, Dad. You really expect me to believe in witches? And that we're descendants of the shitheads who ran the Salem witch trials? And that we've been holding our own witch trials in secret ever since then, right here in our little city? And that—this is where you really lose me, Dad—that Greer is a witch?

"C'mon, Dad, tell me it's a joke. I mean, otherwise, I'll have to have Mom call good old Dr. Cooper and we'll have to get you some heavy duty medication. You know, Prozac to the highest power or something."

"I know all this sounds crazy, Jeff. But you just watch the tape and you'll see that I'm telling you the truth."

"What're we going to see?"

"You remember Greer's mother, Laura?"

"Sure."

"Well, we had a trial for her."

"Dad, you're shitting me. You had a trial for her."

"I know it sounds crazy—"

"No, Dad. Not just crazy. Barbaric. How the hell did you have a trial for her?"

He came back and sat down, the remote in his hand.

He sat next to Jeff on the couch and started advancing the tape. "We kidnapped her."

"Now I know this is a joke."

"It isn't a joke."

"You kidnapped her, and she didn't go to the police?"

"First of all, she was drugged. So she didn't know she was being kidnapped and didn't have any memory of it. And second of all, she couldn't go to the police. None of them can."

"Why not?"

"Because they'd expose themselves."

"As witches?"

"Yes, as witches. And I don't appreciate you sitting there and fucking smirking at me."

"I've got to give you one thing."

"What?"

"That you can keep a straight face through all this bullshit."

"Yeah, well, you won't be smirking when you see the tape, smart ass. Believe me."

"A darkened room. A small table lit from some kind of spotlight placed above. The table is oak, scratched and worn from use and time.

The woman sits alone at the table. Even in a hair-tousled, druggy-eyed state there is no hiding the elegance of her face and slender body in her white blouse and designer jeans. Greer's mom, Laura.

In front of her on the table sit three small gift boxes such as a wristwatch might come in.

Laura stares at the boxes.

Very bad home video, by the way. Handheld and shaky. And extremely grainy because of the lighting situation.

An off camera voice. Male, familiar, but one Jeff doesn't recognize at first.

"Laura, do you remember what I asked you to do a few minutes ago?"

No response.

"Laura. Did you hear me?"

"Yes."

"Do you remember what I asked you to do a few minutes ago?"

"Yes."

"Will you do it?"

"Then you'll know. If I do, I mean." Her voice sounds weary. As if speaking each word was a chore. The drugs.

"What will I know, Laura?"

"About me."

"What about you, Laura?"

"What I am."

"And what are you, Laura?"

No response.

"What are you, Laura?"

"I think you know. I think you've always known."

"I need you to show me, Laura."

"I'm afraid."

"Don't you trust me?"

"I'm not sure."

"Are you hungry?"

"Yes."

"Well, as soon as you do it, I plan to give you a nice big sandwich and a nice big piece of cake and a nice big cup of coffee. Doesn't that sound good?"

"Yes."

"Then will you do it?"

No response.

"Will you do it, Laura?"

No response.

"I'm hungry."

"Then do it, Laura. You know it won't take long."

"I'm afraid."

This time, it is the male voice that hesitates. "Aren't you being a little bit silly, Laura? You've felt safe with me all your life. Why not now?"

And then it happens.

No warning other than the fact that she shifts slightly in her chair.

The first gift box explodes into flame.

"Very good, Laura. Now the next one."

All Laura does is stare at the box in the middle.

And it ignites.

That male voice—so damned familiar to Jeff—yet who is speaking?

"Now the last one, Laura."

Laura hangs her head.

The final box just sits there.

"Are you all right, Laura?"

"Now you know about me."

"The last one, Laura. You know you can do it."

"You're going to kill me, aren't you?"

"Laura, you know you're being ridiculous. Think about the sandwich and the piece of cake and the cup of coffee."

"I guess it doesn't matter anyway, does it? I've already done two of them."

"Go ahead. Do the last one." Pause. "Please, Laura, then we can be done with this nonsense."

"I'm cold."

"The coffee will make you warm. Just go ahead and get it over with."

And so she does.

And then the lights come up and there they are, suddenly revealed: his parents, Dr. Cooper and his wife, and the Dryers.

No wonder the voice talking to Laura sounded familiar. It was Dr. Cooper, who had been Jeff's doctor since he delivered him.

And then an ugly realization: *this isn't any bullshit. Any joke. This tape was for real.*

"So you see I'm telling you the truth about them, Jeff," Yancy said. "They really do have powers. They lose their main ones in their twenties, but they hold on to a few of them the rest of their lives."

"That isn't what I'm thinking about, Dad?"

"You've just seen a woman start a fire only by willing it and you're not amazed?"

"No, Dad, I'm not. What amazes me is that my own parents would persecute these poor people. I'm ashamed you're my father."

It was sort of like sitting in a shrink's outer office. You speculated on what the other people were doing here. The well-dressed woman with the mink coat reading *Time*. The workingman in the khaki shirt and trousers and heavy boots staring forlornly out the window at the gray wintry sky. The black man in the new blue suede jacket and white shirt and tie with the fancy collar buttons. Reading a James Patterson novel he'd apparently brought himself.

The reception area of Metro Security. With the comfortable but bland furnishings—only the Chagall prints showed a little decorative courage—and the tailored-suited, slightly remote receptionist, Metro tried hard to be anything but what it was. If you were a company, you brought them your somewhat impersonal security problems. There's a spot near the loading dock that you need to rig some new lights. Internal theft is still rising in the warehouse. Here are some potential new employees; we need background checks. Business as usual.

But if you came here as an individual, you brought some very personal terrors. A stalker. Your home broken into for the second time. Your spouse suddenly staying out late at night. Very personal.

Metro had been recommended by two lawyer friends of Cam's. Professional and discreet, and they won't jack you around on prices. If they work for ten hours, they won't pad it out to reflect sixteen hours. Ex-homicide cops is what they are, Cam. You'll like them.

"Mr. Morgan?"

He'd been reading the morning paper. "Yes?"

"Mr. Steiner will see you now."

She led him, in her svelte long-legged way, down a long, narrow hallway with more Chagall prints on the wall and the smell of fresh paint on the air. "We're doing some remodeling. That's the smell."

"Good clean smell."

"Reminds me of when I was a girl."

Somehow, he couldn't imagine her ever being a girl. She was born five-ten with a model's long-waisted body and an ice-queen face you prayed would bless you with at least one fleeting smile. Oh, yes, and born with your standard great ass, too.

She knocked on a door, heard, "Yes?" and opened it.

She stood back while Cam went inside, closed the door softly behind him.

John Steiner was a tall, slender man with a serious face, thinning brown hair, and kind blue eyes. His blue two-piece suit, white shirt, and rep tie were tasteful but not expensive. His office was much the same—gray being the color scheme, contrasting grays of carpet, walls, desk. He went over to a Mr. Coffee on a small table neatly stacked with file folders. "Get a cup for you, Mr. Morgan?"

"Please. And it's Cam."

"Good. I'm John."

The chair was an imitation Eames, which turned out to be much more comfortable than a real Eames. Gray leather, in keeping with the rest of the decor.

Steiner's desk was clear. He opened the middle drawer, took out a white legal pad and ballpoint pen, and said, "So how can I help you, Cam?"

"My daughter."

"Her name and age, please?"

Cam told him, and he wrote it on his pad.

"And she's having what kind of trouble?"

Careful, Cam. You agreed not to go into any detail at all about the real story. Abby, in fact, had suggested a kidnap scenario.

"I'm afraid somebody is trying to kidnap her."

Steiner wrote something down briefly and said, "Any idea who this might be?"

"Lawyers make enemies."

"So you think it's a former client?"

"I'm not sure. And it doesn't really matter."

Steiner seemed surprised. "Why doesn't it matter, Cam?"

He realized how foolish he'd sounded. "I just meant that no matter who it is, the threat is the same."

"Not really. If this is somebody who's not too bright and just plans to sort of lunge out of the woodwork, that's one thing. But if this is a bright, organized, clever person—"

"I see what you mean."

"So, do you have any idea who we might be dealing with here?"

Yes. See, there're these descendants of the Salem witch trials, see. And my daughter's a witch, see. Not a witch like Elizabeth Montgomery on "Bewitched." *But a human being who developed on a kind of parallel track from other human beings and kind of—*

Oh, yeah, even if he hadn't agreed with Abby not to mention any of the real story—even then he couldn't imagine himself telling the truth here. It was just too crazy. And he still wasn't quite sure he believed it himself. There were moments when he was accepting of the story. And moments when it made him want to laugh out loud.

"No," he said, sitting there in the office of the sensible, practical ex-homicide cop named John Steiner—the same sensible, practical homicide cop whose most drugged-up, craziest criminal had never laid a witch story on him—"No, I really don't have any idea who might be after her."

That afternoon, Jeff quit his job. The boss said, "Figured you would. I don't think you're cut out for this kinda life, kid. Sorry."

He spent most of the afternoon lying on his bed, smoking an occasional cigarette, trying to read one of his science fiction paperbacks. And of course thinking about last night.

He'd wanted to take Greer to school this morning, but after the long hours with his father last night, he hadn't been up to it. He wasn't sure what to think about anything. He'd called Greer and told her his car wouldn't start.

Now, he heard his mom pull into the drive around three o'clock. He hadn't seen her since his session with his father last night.

He heard her coming in the back door. Hanging up her coat in the closet. Microwaving herself a cup of coffee. Coming up the stairs. Knocking gently on his door. "May I come in?"

"Yeah."

She had her Shakespeare coffee mug. Shaped like the head of the bard. Hot coffee steam writhing upward.

"How're you doing?" She went over and sat in the straight-backed chair next to his bureau.

"Dad talked to me last night."

"That's what he said."

"I keep going back and forth. I sorta believe it, then I sorta don't believe it."

She sighed. Touched her head as if it hurt. "My parents were part of the group once—the people who hunted the witches—" He started to object, but she stopped him. "But they quit. They said murder was murder. When your father and I married, he promised he'd quit, too. But he never did."

"And you've stayed married all these years?"

"Sometimes," she said, starting to cry, "I wonder if I should have."

Then he came to her and held her tenderly. He tried to think of what her marriage had been like for her . . . Dad being unfaithful . . . and hunting witches.

Sometimes, Karen went up to the ward and peeked in the window. She didn't sneak up exactly—no tiptoeing or lurking around corners—but she definitely had the sense that Dr. Prescott wouldn't be happy with her being here.

She stared into the gloom of the place. She'd heard of sensory deprivation chambers and this was sort of like them. No light. No sound. No clocks. And the girls drugged most of the time.

She'd been here herself.

In the ward.

One of those girls.

She didn't know when or how or why. Just that she'd been here.

Every so often she'd get a memory leak from her other self, her other life—the false memories as Dr. Prescott and Maria called them—this Karen, the one standing here now, being the real one.

A portentous melancholy came over her as she stared through the small window in the ward's metal door. It was as if she'd lost something vital inside her, as if those memory leaks were somehow calling her back to a better time.

And every once in a while, she'd get the urge to warn the girls in there what she'd gone through—even though she couldn't remember exactly what she had gone through.

Warn them.

Help them flee.

"Oh, honey, I'm not sure the doctor would like this."

The sweet, chirpy voice of sad Beverly.

"We'd better get you back downstairs now, hon."

Talking like a nurse. All that "we" business.

A final long glance into the darkened room.

The girls lying in their beds like infants in incubators.

Being reborn. Transformed.

"C'mon, now, hon. C'mon, now."

Beverly treating her as if she were very, very fragile.

As, perhaps, she was.

The man's name was Frank Bailey. He hated his name. Take the name Cam Morgan. Now there was a sexy name. Cam. Masculine. Memorable. Who the hell remembered Frank Bailey? Task was a name he'd heard on one of those nighttime soap operas his old lady was always watching. Task Bailey. Not bad.

Cam Morgan was the name of the client former detective Frank Bailey was working for. He'd been in the Metro offices this morning, and now Bailey was following Greer Morgan around.

Or would be soon enough.

He'd gotten a photo of her, her license number, and the make and model of the car she'd just gotten. Bailey didn't have any trouble finding it in the high school parking lot.

Now he sat six cars away in the facing row, waiting for her.

Not that he knew why, exactly.

One thing Metro usually did was type an advance profile of the case they assigned you. If, for instance, your nemesis was a husband who was stalking the woman, you got a bio of the guy—where he worked, drank, played, names of girlfriends, buddies, etc. and etc., including any priors.

Not this case.

Bare as a baby's butt.

Somebody was after her. She needed escorting to and from every place she went. Three eight-hour shifts a day. Three different operatives. Frank (Call me Task) Bailey taking the day shift. Seniority. He'd been the third employee hired by the two cops who'd started the place.

His stomach gurgled, even though he'd already cheated today and had two Danish and a Snickers.

That's what happened when you were on a strict diet like he was, except, of course, for the daily cheating, it was strict anyway. At least by his lights. The old lady worried about all the heart attacks in his family. His brother dead at thirty-eight, poor kid. Tried to tell her it was the booze and the cigarettes, but she wouldn't listen. Bought him a treadmill (nobody who wanted to be called Task should ever have to put up with the pussy indignity of a treadmill) and then got him this diet tape. At least it wasn't Richard Simmons. Task didn't hate fags the way most cops did. Live and let live, he figured. (He'd even spared a few of the poor bastards from getting messed up by other cops.) But Richard Simmons drove him up the wall. He hated ranting, Task did, no matter what kinda guy was doing it.

He scratched his butt and then remembered how the old lady had glowered at him when he said he got plenty of exercise on stakeouts—scratching his butt, his balls, and picking his nose. The old days, she woulda laughed. But she got all these health magazines now and he was up shit's creek.

The bell rang inside the school.

He sat up, scanning the door he supposed she'd come out of.

Task Bailey, Private Eye. At Your Service.

School felt funny today. Greer couldn't explain it exactly. Just—as if she no longer belonged here. Had a new life somewhere else.

The women with the secret had agreed down the ages that it was best to assimilate. Have a normal, productive life.

But somehow Greer felt apart from her classmates today. Exposed. Vulnerable. She wanted to be home on the couch with Jeff. Laughing at stupid things. Eating pizza. Making out a little. It felt as if she'd known him a long time; a long, warm, good time and it was barely— As the bell rang and she picked up her books to carry them to the next class, she was tempted to find a quiet spot to use her cell phone. She'd call Jeff and see how he was doing—

But no, for a shy girl like Greer, that was pushing too hard, too fast.

She'd call him when she got home from school.

And she felt better now that Abby and Dad had had "The Talk." And that Dad knew about "It" now. About Mom and herself. And the history of the secret.

She wondered if she could spot the "operative" (as Dad had called him) who'd be following her. Protecting her.

At 3:00 P.M., the bell rang. The usual rush and gush

to the doors. The usual glee at school day's end. But Greer took her time. Strolled to her locker. Shrugged into her tweed sports jacket, the nice one from last Christmas. Took home the two books she'd need for homework.

Amazing how fast the school corridors emptied.

One moment they were a gladiator pit of shouts and laughter and slamming metal locker doors and feet slapping the concrete floor. And then they were empty, echoing silence the only sound, shadowy and deserted, almost forlorn now that all the life had been drained from them.

She went outside. Overcast sky; the faint scent of snow on the air. Early winter for sure this year. Probably only a matter of a day or two.

She walked to her car. She glanced at the few remaining vehicles. They all looked empty. So where was this great, grand operative?

Ever since Abby had told her this morning on the phone not to see Dr. Cooper under any circumstances—saying she'd explain later but certainly implying that Cooper was the enemy and had been drugging her—Greer had been frightened for the first time. She was supposed to go to Abby's office right now and learn the whole story. But where was the operative?

Oh, well.

She was sure she'd be fine. She'd keep to main streets. The doors would be locked. She'd be sure and be home before dusk.

She was two blocks from school when she realized that the dusty blue Ford sedan was the operative's.

She smiled. Once she became aware of him, she felt self-conscious. It was like being in a movie. You know, where somebody is following you. Sometimes a good guy; sometimes a bad guy. Sometimes, she liked to imagine she was in a movie. It was fun. Chic young princess driving her sports car in the hills above the Monaco coastline. Her mother had been a big fan of Grace Kelly movies and daughter Greer now shared that fondness.

But this was different.

This was unglamorous Hastings Corner. Roadwork badly needed on the streets. A few homeless scuttling here and there. Couple of chubby badass bikers venting their Harleys at a stoplight. Decidedly unglamorous.

And yet she was part of a real-life movie.

She was being followed by an operative.

She was thinking it was cool until muzzy memories of sneaking out of the house came back to her with gauzy terror. Something with Dr. Cooper, those nights. But now she couldn't tell if this was just the power of suggestion because Abby had mentioned the doctor or because he'd really played a role in those nights. In luring her out of the house. Or meeting her somewhere. Of—a memory of a needle, then. Or was it just a fancy from a movie she remembered? A needle. Dr. Cooper and a needle. And the dark interior of a— Her first impulse was to say car but it wasn't a car. A vehicle of some kind. Truck or—van. Yes, van. That was the most likely kind of vehicle.

All this while she waited next to the two leering bikers at the stoplight.

Then she smiled. Sometimes, bikers scared her. She'd heard all the stories girls do. How they drag you into the woods and gang rape you and then threaten to kill one of your parents or your little brother if you tell anybody. She had no idea if these were true stories or just more urban legends, but they were spooky whatever they were.

But it was so cool to have your very own private operative sitting one car back from you. He surely had a gun. And a temper. And a penchant for rescuing young damsels in distress.

So just let these two furballs try anything, and her very own operative would kick their butts clear across the county.

Yes, she decided. Every girl should have her very own operative. It was the American way. Or damned well should be.

Pam Cooper drove out to the cabin to get things ready for tomorrow night. She had pleasant memories of the Tudor-style structure build of wood and native stone. She'd lost her virginity here back in 1949, just before her husband was flown off to Germany where he would be an Army physician for two years. He'd convinced her that it was a dangerous assignment—Krauts were, after all, Krauts—and wondered aloud (not without some drama) how she'd feel if she never gave herself to the man she loved. She was eighteen at the time but even then could see through his manly tale. The reason she gave herself to him—and she was a prize, too, coltishly attractive, especially those giant Audrey Hepburn eyes of hers and that surprisingly curvy body—was she was sick of being a virgin. All the girls she'd made friends with at college that fall made a point of losing their virginity within the very first month. Why should she be any different? They made love that first time in front of the vast stone fireplace, a gorgeous soft-focus moment spoiled only slightly by his terrible head cold. He kept sneezing.

Now, it all seemed so remote. As if it hadn't happened to her at all but to a relative, a shirttail cousin perhaps, a story she'd heard long ago. She'd been true to him all these decades. Only once had she seriously been tempted, a flirty tennis pro at the country club who was later driven out of the state when he gave a rich man's wife the clap.

The first thing she did was get the furnace going. The four rooms and the basement took hours to get warm.

The second thing she did was pour herself a cup of coffee from the Thermos she'd brought along. She needed to arrange everything in the basement and that, of course, was the coldest spot in the place.

She hated leaving the pleasant living room with the fireplace, the wall of books, the comfortably plump armchairs. The kitchen was nice, too, oak cabinets, an older but very efficient gas range, and a fair supply of canned goods. The refrigerator was bare.

There was a time when Pam and Tom Cooper came up here many times a year, summer and winter. The fishing was good and the kids loved to sled down the steep hills in back.

But that changed when Mike Dodge died. Dodge had been one of the jurists and had held the trials in his attic for years.

Tom volunteered this cabin. After a few women had been tried, the place was no longer the same. Hard to just sit around and pretend it was a plain old cabin where you came to have fun—hard to pretend when the fate of other beings was decided here.

They kept it up—rather the people they hired kept it up—but they rarely came out here except when there was a trial.

And now, as she stood here, her ears filled with echoing screams, her eyes lacerated with images of the girls driven to the very edge of insanity—it was impossible to think of anything as trivial as losing one's virginity.

God forbid, it was a place for serious business now.

She went to the basement and started preparing for the night ahead.

"I could go for a cigarette and a bottle of beer right now," Candy said.

Abby laughed. "You'll probably survive another half hour or so."

"This place must've set you back one hell of a lot of money."

Candy had arrived twenty minutes earlier than their scheduled meeting. She was clearly taken with the clinic and anybody who owned a piece of it. Perhaps it reminded her of her girlhood, when she'd grown up in the warm arms of money and society.

"There are four of us. We each took on a quarter of the debt."

"Well, nice digs."

"Thanks."

They were sitting in the darkened lounge now, waiting for Greer, who was coming here straight from school. She should be on her way here now.

"You know what I've always wanted to ask a doctor?"

"What?"

"How come you never get colds when you see sick people all the time?"

"Oh, we get colds. But we also build up some immunity to everyday health problems."

"I thought maybe you folks knew a secret or something."

"About how to avoid getting colds?"

"Yeah."

"Well, if we did, we'd put it on the market right away and then retire to Florida. We'd all be gazillionaires."

"Now let me ask you something." Abby said. She had duly noted—and been duly touched by the fact—that Candy was wearing her civilian clothes today. An honest-to-gosh wine-red dress, dark stockings, black flats. She had washed the pink rinse out of her hair and combed the spikes down so that it looked just like a fashionably short cut. No nose rings. In this attire, you could see the faint traces of the graceful, fetching girl she'd once been. The young beauty in that long-ago photograph.

"Ask away, kiddo."

"Do you think there are more of us around here? Girls and women who just haven't told us about themselves?"

"Oh, sure. We're all over the world. Some of us announce ourselves to each other and some of us don't."

"So, there could be more of us in this area?"

"Oh, yeah, absolutely."

The phone rang. Answering service. Abby was on call tonight. "Excuse me."

As soon as she got up to answer it, she watched Candy slip out the front door and light a cigarette. The woman was so tiny, she looked lonely standing there in the shadows beneath the entrance arch, the wind whipping her dress around her skinny legs, and her short hair into the near-spikes of the other night.

Child with flu. Fever climbing. Mother scared. Abby gave her instructions to get her through the night—didn't sound all that serious—and said bring Tommy in first thing in the morning. Tommy's regular doctor was one of Abby's partners, Susan Briney.

She went outside and stood with Candy. It was gray winter. First of the year, winter would be sparkling blue skies and gorgeous red-streaked sunsets. But this was bleak winter, the wind the voice of all the dead who'd ever lived, and the moon a spectral eye over the bleak land below.

"You going to give me a speech about not smoking?"

"Not me."

"I figure if I didn't get lung cancer by now, I'm probably all right."

"I won't give you a speech about not smoking. And I won't tell you how wrong your logic is about lung cancer."

"You know something?"

"What?"

"I like you."

Abby laughed. "Well, I like you, too."

"You say what you think."

"Well, if I said what I think, Candy, I'd tell you to

put that damned cigarette out and never light up another one. But thanks for the compliment. I do try to be honest most of the time."

"You got a thing for Cam Morgan?"

"Now where did that come from?"

"Oh, just your tone of voice when you were talking about him earlier."

"C'mon, let's go back inside. I'm freezing."

Candy laughed this time. "I guess you're not as honest as you thought. Here I ask you a question about Cam Morgan, and you just say let's go back inside."

Abby was glad to be out of the wind and wrapping her hand around her cup of coffee. "You asked me about Cam."

"Yeah."

"It's strange. If you had asked me forty-eight hours ago, I would've said you were being ridiculous. But now all of a sudden I feel close to him. And I think he feels the same way about me. I used to think that Laura kept us apart—she'd always be a point of contention between us—but now I think Laura and Greer bring us together."

"You lost your best friend and your own daughter to them. And now you don't want to lose Greer. And that's brought you together with Cam."

Abby smiled. "You could go on "Oprah." That's exactly what I think's happening here. Both Cam and I have a stake in protecting Greer. And that's made us look at each other for the first time."

"You think Greer could handle that?"

"Oh, she wants it. She plays matchmaker, in fact. Always hinting we should be together." Headlights beamed through the front window. "And speaking of Greer, I'll bet this is her now."

"I wouldn't happen to have a daughter there, would I?"

"What's her name?"

"Let's see now. What's her name? Gosh. I seem to've forgotten."

"Very funny, Dad," Greer said into her cell phone.

Abby, Candy, and Greer were in the employee lounge and had been for nearly an hour. They'd pretty much discussed everything, from how they'd first become aware of the secret, to how they'd used their powers. They'd all stinted on using them. As their mothers had told them to. They had to think of all the other girls and women who had the secret. If one was exposed, they would ultimately all be exposed.

Greer hadn't been crazy about Candy, at first. Greer was a nice middle-class girl. She wasn't used to world-coarsened older women. For one thing, Candy sometimes swore like a biker in a fistfight. For another, she didn't seem all that interested in Greer. Always brought the subject back to herself, usually some memory of her days on "The Continent" as she called it. And usually about who she had happened to be sleeping with at any particular time. She even included references to the venereal disease she'd suffered from for several years. Information Greer—and Greer knew that she was sort of a prig sometimes, just as her father was—didn't really want to have.

But then Candy had abruptly started crying. Talking about living in London one spring and becoming aware that her powers were waning. "I didn't have no money, I didn't have no man, I had this VD I told you about, and I was putting out just to keep myself in a sleeping room and booze."

Greer found herself sitting next to the old woman. And then mindmerging with her for a few seconds. That was all the merge lasted. But it was enough to make her see the deep grief and genuine decency of this woman who had once been the Hastings Corner version of a princess.

"You melded me, din't ya?" Candy had asked.

"Yes. I'm sorry. I didn't mean to. It just—happened."

"I could feel you in my brain. It's like a tickle."

"I'm glad I did. I—really like you."

Candy smiled, and not without some mischief. "And you didn't before, huh?"

"Well, I—"

"It's all right, sweetie. I'm what you call an acquired taste." She'd winked at Abby. "I'm not sure Dr. Abby here has acquired it yet herself."

"Of course I have, Candy. You bet I have," she'd said.

"So when can I expect you home?"

"Oh, forty-five minutes or so. Oh, by the way, I saw my guardian angel. He followed me here."

"Guardian angel?"

"The man you hired to follow me. Except now he's a she. They swapped a while back. She must be on the night shift."

"I feel better since we hired the security folks."

"So do I, actually. Well, love you."

"Love you, too, honey."

After she hung up, she looked at the two women and said, "What's the wildest thing either of you ever did with your powers?"

They both looked stunned—and then started laughing.

Jeff's room. His father had been in there twenty minutes now. Trying to make his case. It was like arguing in favor of concentration camps. At least for Jeff.

"In other words, you kill people."

"They aren't people. And that's the point."

"Dad, I was with her for a real long time, and she sure seemed like people to me." Jeff had wanted to escape out the window the way his mother urged him, but his father had been too quick for him.

"I'm not sure I want to hear about your sex life."

"Well, I've sure the hell had to hear a lot about yours. That girl giving you blow jobs in the back of the store."

"Cheap shot, and changing the subject. Greer Morgan's the subject. Not you or me."

"So we just kill her."

"If she fails the tests Tom Cooper gives her, yes. Because then we'll know she's a witch and has to be done away with."

"And no regrets."

"If she were human—if she weren't trying to wipe out our species—then maybe I'd have some regrets. I'm not exactly a monster, you know."

"Oh, no. You just kill people and don't have any regrets. But you're not a monster."

"You won't be going anywhere tonight, Jeff."

"What the hell are you talking about? You can't stop me from leaving."

"I already have. That hot chocolate I brought up had a heavy sedative in it that Tom Cooper gave me a while back. I'd hoped that he would be here to help us through this, but something unexpected came up. Still, you won't be going anywhere, believe me."

"You sonofabitch."

"I fought it just the way you are. I hated my parents until long after they were dead. But eventually I came to see that I had to do my duty. It sounds corny and all that other bullshit, but I really do owe it to my own kind."

"What if they're harmless? Have you ever thought of that? Mom said there are good ones and bad ones—this doesn't mean that I'm buying into this craziness—but she said—"

"Your mother just doesn't want to face reality. They're not harmless when you consider their potential. If enough of them got together— See, you're yawning. I'll bet you can barely stay awake."

"You—you bastard."

"You get some sleep, Son, and we'll talk in the morning."

Her name was Heather Malloy, and she didn't take no shit from nobody.

Having been a B+ student at St. Regina's Catholic School, Heather knew of course that taking no shit from nobody was ungrammatical. (Not to mention impossible. Everybody, including the Pope, took shit from somebody.) But ever since she'd been turned down by the Boston police force because she didn't meet the height requirements—one inch too short—she'd made it a point to sound as tough as anybody on Death Row.

How she came to work for Metro Security was a sad comedy. Her fallback position was to work for a security company. But then she actually worked for a security company, and there went all her hope. Her Jewish boyfriend Keith Fleckstein had a word for such people: schmucks. The security people she worked with—all of them in faux-cop blue uniforms, some of them with guns—were dumb, lazy, and many were at least as dishonest as many of the people they arrested. Talk about your shoplifting. Nobody lifted stuff like security cops.

Discouraged, she quit and started making the rounds of employment agencies. She had two years of junior college was all. (She'd met Keith there, but Keith had gone on to get his BA.) Not a lot of employers clamoring for her, and the ones who did clamor were: a) men and b) horny men who had obvious idle fantasies about getting to know the slight Irish girl much, much better. If you know what I'm saying here.

Then Keith called his Uncle Bud who was a former Boston homicide detective now working for Metro Security. Bud said it was the best and most sophisticated such outfit in the state. And that its employees were strictly monitored. Everybody, from the president of the place on down, was given lie detector and urine tests monthly.

The one problem, Bud said, was that Metro really

preferred hiring ex-cops. There were exceptions, however, he added, and suggested she stop in and talk to the guy who hired everybody, Sam Flaherty.

After ten minutes of talking to her, Flaherty said, "Why're you talking that way?"

"What way?"

"You know. Like a tough guy in a bad movie."

"It's just the way I talk."

"No, it isn't."

"Yes, it is."

"If it was the way you talked, you wouldn't have blushed when you said motherfucker."

"I blushed?"

"You blushed."

"I usually only blush when I say cocksucker."

"Well, you blushed when you said motherfucker."

"God, I've really got to be more careful, don't I?"

"Huh-uh. What you really have to do is quit talking that way altogether. I had a daughter talk like that, I'd kick her ass around the block. No matter how old she was. Capeesh?"

"Capeesh." And she grinned. Relieved she didn't have to talk that way anymore.

So, sans dirty mouth, she was hired. And Metro was able to use her in a lot of different ways. She had one of those perky little faces that lent themselves easily to disguise. She did everything from tempt married men in bars while carrying a concealed tape recorder (Metro hired by the men's wives to do so) to infiltrate shoplifting rings to stakeouts.

She was on a stakeout tonight.

Sitting on the far edge of a medical clinic parking lot. Waiting for young Greer Morgan to appear.

She was thinking about the one thing that she'd been thinking about for the past week. The first hint—"We're getting serious here, aren't we?" Keith had said—that Keith might just have marriage in mind. Which presented problems, not the least of which was their respective religions. While neither set of parents could be called bigots (not exactly), neither set of parents was all that keen on seeing their child convert to another belief system. The truth was, neither Heather nor Keith felt any strong ties to their respective religions. To the cultures those religions spawned, yes. But not to the set of beliefs and rules the hierarchies had set down thousands of years earlier.

She loved Keith very much. But she knew that the road to the altar was heavily mined. Very heavily mined.

"I know what it's like to really love somebody."

"Oh, shit, Sara, do we really have to go through this tonight? I'm tired and I've got a lot of things on my mind."

"I don't think you've ever loved anybody or anything in your life, Yancy. And I don't say that as a criticism. Just an observation."

She was a little bit stoned on the wine. Sitting on the divan in front of the fireplace. Flames warming the entire living room. Shadows making everything elegant. Mozart on the stereo. Yancy in the rocking chair across from her. Yancy reading Yeats. Her reading *Passion's Pawn*. Or trying to. Thinking really of Jeff. Poor Jeff.

"He loves her, Yancy."

"Oh, God, spare me. He's known her, what, forty-eight hours? And haven't we already had this conversation about Greer?"

"My point is, you and I had to accept being part of the trials. Our heritage and all that. But we didn't have to stand by and watch the person we love being killed."

He finally put his book down. "So what do you recommend, Sara? That we don't take care of her? That we don't do our duty?"

"You're sure that sedative is safe?"

"You've asked me that ten times already."

"Well, is it?"

"It's perfectly safe. Just as I've told you ten times."

Then, without any warning, she was crying. "What are we going to do, Yancy? He's our son."

And with equal suddenness and helplessness—all the malice gone from his voice, fear replacing it now—Yancy answered, "I don't know, Sara. I really don't know."

Dr. Tom Cooper always drove past the clinic on his way home. In its early days, the mere sight of the place irritated and upset him. It symbolized that there was a new era in etiquette and folkways of medicine.

In the days of his youth—and well into the eighties—young doctors wanting to settle in a town had first to seek out the informal—but substantive—permission of the older docs already there. And it was no forgone conclusion that you'd be accepted, either. You had to be careful with Jews and blacks because you were dealing with civil rights. But then Jews and blacks weren't a problem because few young docs from those communities wanted to come here in the first place.

Still, if one applied, you had to be careful of how you dissuaded them from coming here. And that meant staying aloof, even cold, so that they got the message without you saying anything that could later be used against you. Foreigners, in general, were no problem. Americans were suspicious of anybody whose degree came from abroad. Nobody was likely to protest if you turned down foreigners. Same with women, until Affirmative Action became a problem.

Now, it was different. Jews, blacks, foreigners, and women didn't even bother to introduce themselves before settling in or around Hastings Corner. They just set up shop and proceeded to chip away at your business.

The Medical Clinic (creative with names, they weren't) was owned and run by four women—one Jew, one black, one Catholic married to a Jew, and a truly combative French woman (she was the unpopular star of all county medical association meetings). That's why Cooper saw red when he looked at the clinic.

But he'd be retiring soon, anyway. Medicare had been bad enough. The federales on your case constantly, costs endlessly rising because you had to put more and more gals on to handle the paperwork. Bad enough, the federales. But then came the HMOs, and docs of every age found themselves longing for the days when the government had been their chief adversary. At least government had seldom meddled in the daily practice of dealing with patients. But HMOs—my Lord. They got richer, and the patients got worse and worse medical care. And the docs got ever more paperwork.

As he passed the clinic now, he noticed the nondescript black car sitting near the clinic exit. Some older foreign economy car. He wouldn't have paid any attention to it, but he saw a GORE bumper sticker on it and that made him feel a pang for casting his first-ever vote for a Democratic presidential candidate. The Republicans—his party of choice since he'd been in med school—were owned by the HMOs. And so he'd voted for Gore. And what had happened? Gore gets the presidency stolen from him down in Florida. Maybe God had punished Cooper for voting for a Democrat, a party he actually loathed.

So, anyway, he noticed the bumper sticker on the car. Noticed the young woman in the car. Wondered why she was sitting out here instead of being inside.

And then noticed Greer Morgan's car. Lord knew she'd been thrilled to show it to him when she first drove it to his office.

He had no idea why, but he sensed that something wasn't right here. The way he felt when a patient was inarticulate in describing a symptom—but just articulate enough to make some warning device go off in the doctor's brain.

A perfectly harmless scene, the parking lot of the clinic, Greer Morgan's car sitting next the front door, the older foreign make sitting next to the exit.

Something was wrong here. Something he should indeed be alarmed about.

And not too many hours later, he would learn exactly what it was.

5

MORNING broke fine and clear. It was going to be a pretty day, an anomaly for most Novembers.

All the blue sky and the sunshine inspired people to be happier than they would normally be. Sanders, the Pepsi delivery man, who didn't usually smile till at least 10:00 A.M., was beaming as he made his first stop of the day at Thrifty-Mart. Helen Sloane at Best In Beauty was not only cutting hair but humming as she did so, an old Luther Vandross ballad called "Take Time to Love Me." And Artie Moore down at the Allstate office was thinking about playing golf today, even though it would be in the thirties. Why the hell not? If nothing else, he'd get some exercise.

Plans were afoot everywhere in Hastings Corner. Plans for making money, buying houses, selling houses, committing adultery, catching people committing adultery, driving an SUV full of wiseass kids to school, sleeping in late, baking some homemade bread, getting the car winterized, calling the party giver and apologizing for last night's boorish and drunken behavior, seeing the doc about that strange discolored wart you'd discovered on your shoulder last week, thinking you maybe needed to start taking a laxative after all, finally figuring out a way you could sneak some ketchup into Jimmy Colgan's chocolate milk during lunch period without his ever figuring it out—and so on and on and on.

At three houses in the venerable old town, however, a single plan was being made. That being for tonight's trial. Most of the trials—despite the lurid history of the Salem years—were actually pretty perfunctory and low-key affairs. The sodium Amytal Dr. Tom used was quite effective in breaking the girls down quickly. He used a few other drugs, too, but he always said that that was the principal one.

Once the girls were tested and revealed their true nature—the tests were simple but conclusive—then it was decided how their deaths would be staged. Dr. Tom was already thinking aloud about injecting her with heroin. As the county medical examiner, he'd be doing the autopsy anyway. He'd been autopsying their victims for the past thirty-seven years. Finding heroin in her system would shock a lot of people—maybe even make them wonder just how reliable his autopsy was—but then they'd settle down and realize what kind of drug-infested era they were living in. Didn't drug addiction span the entire social spectrum? Wasn't Greer known to be something of a high-strung, secretive girl? Did she really have a lot of people who knew her intimately? Wouldn't her father lie to spare her reputation and say that the idea of Greer taking drugs was preposterous? And couldn't Dr. Tom himself say that over the past year or so, when he saw her as the family physician, he sensed that something bad was going on in her life?

Oh, sure. The heroin route was definitely the way to go.

Dr. Tom was up early and on the treadmill, while his wife Pam was in the family room working out to the aerobics show on the PBS station.

The Dryers were having sex. Dorothy had dropped some Viagra in Russ's orange juice this morning. Suddenly, just as he was about to rise up from the table, he noticed that something else was also rising. "I don't suppose you'd consider going back to bed, would you, hon?"

"I'll meet you there in two minutes."

Yancy and Sara Crawford sat at their usual silent, sullen breakfast. Especially silent, especially sullen today. After all, they'd had to drug their son. Jeff was still asleep upstairs.

"Have you figured anything out yet?" she said.

"No, have you? Why the fuck is it all on me? You could come up with an idea for once in your life."

"I was just asking."

"You weren't asking. You were accusing. The way you're always accusing."

"Well some of my accusations are true, dearie. Or have you forgotten the blow job?"

"You know what's funny? She didn't even know how to do it. She nibbled. The way a rabbit nibbles at lettuce. Left little bite marks on my cock."

"You poor thing."

"So that's what you're holding against me. A few blow jobs that were so bad, they shouldn't even count."

"You also slept with her."

"Once. One single fucking time. And she was even worse at that than she was at blow jobs."

"You're almost making me feel sorry for her. Don't you think you owe her a little loyalty? Her dignity, if nothing else?"

He scowled. Looked out the window. "Well, at least it's a nice day."

"Oh, yes, just ducky."

"I hate that word."

"It's Wodehouse. And Noel Coward."

"There's a pair of great writers for you," he said.

At least they finished their material and got published, she wanted to say, knowing how he hated writers he saw as "entertainers."

But no, she couldn't.

"How long before Jeff wakes up?" she asked.

"Cooper said twelve hours. So he should be up any time."

"Maybe he'll be calmer about this today."

The scowl again. "You and your little fantasy world. Think it through, Sara. When he wakes up, he'll remember that we drugged him. And then he'll be even angrier than he was last night."

"I just don't know what we're going to do."

"Believe it or not," he said, "neither do I."

"I'm feeling kind of sick to my stomach, Maria."

"You're just scared."

"I don't want him to be mad at me."

Maria Gomez gave Kylie her one hundred and thirty-ninth hug this morning. Even though the girl had been drugged—wildly over drugged considering the double dose of Corazin—she was still afraid of disappointing Dr. Prescott.

The largest of the experiment rooms was in use. They were in Room C. A small rectangle with a bare table, a videotape unit and a refrigerator. There were four hardwood chairs. Two with cushions. A window opened on the west side of the grounds, which, for the moment anyway, were sun-soaked.

The door opened. Prescott came in without any amenities. He carried a small, square cage. Inside was the squirrel.

He set the cage on the table. Glanced at his watch. It was clear he was in a hurry, wanting to get back to Room A where more interesting activities were taking place. It was clear he was simply walking through this one. He had no expectations that she'd wound, let alone damage, the squirrel. There were some white witches whose resistance to killing could not be altered even with triple dosages of Corazin or other drugs.

"I'm in a bit of a hurry," he said, going over and flipping on the various buttons and switches that set the video camera and recorder to work.

"Really," Maria said, "I hadn't noticed."

As he walked back to the cage, he said, "You should work on your sarcasm, Maria. It's much too obvious." Then: "How're you feeling this morning, Kylie?"

"Kind of tired."

Maria noticed that the girl avoided looking at the squirrel that had spread itself against the wire cage on its hind legs. Usually, she smiled at it, even spoke to it.

"When this is over, I'll have Maria take you outside. It's a very nice day. The fresh air will pick you up."

"Thank you, Dr. Prescott."

Maria always felt betrayed when Kylie was so grateful to Prescott. The girl, much as she feared him, always sought his approval. And much as Maria disapproved of what was being done to the child, she'd continued to participate rather than see Tom Fletcher take over her own role, hoping she could in some way protect Kylie by her presence.

Prescott checked his watch again.

He said, to the camera, "Audio slate. Prescott. Room C." Then gave the date and time. "Ready, Kylie?"

"Ready."

Maria looked anxiously at Kylie. She would feel even worse when this was over—she would have failed once again and her self-hatred would cripple her. She really did want to please Prescott. It seemed everybody in the clinic did—except Maria. She didn't care about pleasing anybody who'd use children this way.

Kylie closed her eyes. Maria had never seen her do this before. Closed her eyes. And set her fingertips to her temples. Even Prescott looked surprised. He glanced at Maria as if she could explain—had perhaps inspired-this new approach. But Maria just shook her head.

For the following two minutes there was no sound in Room C except for the faint mechanical passing of the videotape recording; and the squirrel.

The squirrel sounded afraid. This, too, was something new. In previous experiments, Kylie had not affected the squirrel's behavior in any way. The animal had gone on its happy way being a squirrel.

But now the squirrel definitely showed fear. It was

crouching in the corner of its cage. Making a strange, small shrieking noise in its chest.

Kylie had made telepathic contact with the animal. The shriek grew louder.

Prescott put a nervous hand to his face.

The shriek grew louder. The squirrel began to run frantically, insanely, back and forth in the cage. And then it collapsed in the cage and seemed to cover its head with its paws protectively.

And then the plump belly blew apart, spraying blood and innards far enough to spatter Maria's face and Prescott's white coat.

And then the little animal began bleeding from its eye sockets and mouth. And what was left intact of the body began to jerk and spasm in some kind of death throes.

Prescott was almost as much of a child in that moment as Kylie herself. He strode over to her and lifted her up from her chair and hugged her. "Oh, Kylie, you've made me so happy. So very, very happy."

Maria felt like crying. Kylie was lost to her now. Prescott had defiled her forever.

At this same time, in an Airstream trailer thirty miles away, Candy Archer sees the dead girl again. The killer. Very dark, shoulder-length hair. Black turtleneck sweater. Expensive jade-colored jacket. Black leather gloves. Black jeans. Black boots.

Standing at the stove, just breaking an egg over the frying pan, the vision comes blindingly, brilliantly to scorch her mind's eye:

Greer is sitting in a room. Where? And why is it empty except for straightback chairs and a sofa?

The killer opens a door. Looks down a flight of shadowy stairs.

A basement. Greer is in a basement.

And the killer is on the main floor. About to go down the basement stairs.

Run, Greer! Run! Hide! Candy tries to scream but—helpless—cannot get her voice to cooperate.

The killer begins to descend the stairs.

One slow step at a time.

Greer looks up.

Candy can now see that Greer has been lashed to the chair. Can't run or hide even if she wants to.

And something else—something about the killer.

Something familiar.

Something intimate.

Some kinship.

For the first time (watching the killer descend the stairs), Candy begins to wonder about the nature of the killer. Hadn't wondered before. Just accepted her as a Bad Person.

But who is she? What is she? Where does she come from? Who sent her?

So many questions all of a sudden.

Questions she should have asked herself before . . .

The killer has reached the floor of the basement now.

Stands staring at Greer.

And for the first time, Greer opens her mouth and speaks.

Only then does Candy realize that this entire tableau is silent. Like watching one of those old movies. Greer speaks. And the killer speaks. But Candy can't hear either of them. And she knows that the clue she is searching for—the nature of the killer—has just been revealed.

But why can't she hear them?

And then the vision ends. No logic of course to how or when it began or why it ended.

Shit.

Then the reality of the splattered egg in an overheated frying pan. The margarine she used to cook in already burned off and evaporated into rancid smoke. The yellow yolk burst, the egg burned on the bottom.

What the hell had Greer said to the killer? And what had the killer said in response?

And why the hell did the egg (her last one) have to be burned up already?

Shit shit shit.

Every time Greer looked out the school window, she saw the car of her protector. He was reading a paperback this morning. She wondered what sort of books he liked. Somehow, she didn't associate private operatives with reading, but why not? Then she smiled to herself. Maybe he was reading porno. A girl at school had stolen an "erotic" novel from her mother's closet and brought it to school. Everybody at the lunch table had taken turns reading it out loud. It had been grand hilarious fun, especially the way the purple prose had described the various positions, most of which sounded kinda painful to Greer.

So maybe that's what the operative was reading.

She'd dreamed about the killer again last night. The top page of her notebook was covered with sketches of the young woman. Fiercely beautiful—sculpted features—but more fierce than beautiful. And probably not much older than Greer was.

"Maybe Greer can help us with that," Ms. Grundy said. Ms. Grundy was the girlfriend of one of the math teachers here. The bets were she could kick the crap out of him. Ms. Grundy was also the soccer coach and worked out two hours a day. You could be forgiven if you mistook her for a man from the back. Not that there was anything wrong with this. It was just that Ms. Grundy was mean. And she liked to demonstrate to the non-soccer players in her classes that just because a girl was an athletic star didn't mean she got cut any slack. Not by Ms. Grundy. In fact, Ms. Grundy went out of her way to pick on jocks and (as she called them) jockettes.

Greer, hearing her name, jerked to attention.

"We're discussing the Civil War, Greer," Ms. Grundy said, putting her butt on the edge of her desk, her new white running shoes sparkling in the sunlight through the window. She wore, as usual, a dark cable sweater and loose dark slacks. She was actually pretty in a big-boned way. Especially on those days when makeup was allowed to work a little magic. And she was certainly endowed with lust. On any number of occasions she and Norm Olson, the math teacher, had been found making out like tenth graders in various closets, storage rooms, and empty classrooms. Maybe you didn't have to look like Brad Pitt and Jennifer Aniston to enjoy sex after all.

"Yes," Greer said, "the Civil War."

"To whom did the average Southerner look for

leadership following the first months of the Civil War?"

"Uh," Greer said, embarrassed that she'd been caught with her mind drifting, "Jefferson Davis."

"Why would they look to Davis?"

"Because he was President of the Confederate States."

"Anybody else take this question? Yes, Marcy?"

"General Robert E. Lee was who they looked to."

"Very good, Marcy. Why?"

"Because Davis was never a very strong leader to begin with. And his own generals lost most of the battles they got into. Lee had the best fighting units. And so most of the good news came from him. You know, to keep morale high among the citizens. In fact, Lee himself considered Davis to be pretty incompetent and didn't pay much attention to anything he said."

"Thanks, Marcy. Excellent answer."

She was jolted so violently in her seat, she was nearly flung to the floor. Most of the class heard her, including Ms. Grundy, who came rushing down the aisle at full speed.

"My God, Greer! Are you all right?"

But she clearly wasn't all right.

Her entire body danced in a cartoonish parody of somebody being electrocuted. Arms flinging wildly. Eyes rolling back in her head, only the whites visible. The desk itself jerking and jumping about.

"Epileptic seizure!" one girl shouted.

And so it would seem.

She's here. In town. She's here to kill me.

The image of her: the dark hair, the brilliant features, the dead black eyes that seemed to suck in all color and emotion and kill it.

Here. To kill me.

Her very first intimation of her own mortality and her body was dong many crazy things. All she could do was try to bring it under control. But she couldn't escape the knowledge that the killer was in town now.

"Somebody run and get Nurse Temple!" Ms. Grundy was saying.

"Look," a boy said, "she's stopped shaking."

"You can see her eyes again!" a girl said.

And it was true. Her seizure or whatever it had been was now abating. She became aware of being in homeroom. She became aware of all her classmates gathered around her, peering down at her with concern and terror. Even the snottiest kids seemed worried about her.

And then this great sense of shame and embarrassment came over her.

This was what she'd forever be remembered for. Not for being a nice girl who cared about others. Not for being a good soccer player. Not for being a good student.

But for having this fit and nearly flinging herself out of her desk.

"How're you feeling?" Ms. Grundy said, sounding just as she did whenever a player injured herself. Like a mom.

"Better. Gosh, I'm so sorry—"

"Sorry?" Ms. Grundy said. "You don't have anything to be sorry for, Greer. Nothing at all."

And several of her classmates seconded that feeling.

Ms. Grundy helped her sit up straight at her desk.

A boy brought her a glass of water.

Mrs. Temple, the school nurse—tall, looming, imposing—came in. "Hi, Greer."

"Hi, Mrs. Temple."

"Hear we had a little problem."

"I'm all right now."

"Why don't you come down to the office with me and we'll have a look at you?"

Ms. Grundy smiled. "I promise never to call on you again, Greer. One harmless little question and look what happened."

Greer laughed. Or tried to. "That's right. If you just hadn't asked me that question." But her voice was weak, vague.

And when she got to her feet, she found that her knees were shaking so badly, she had to walk slowly and carefully.

The silence in the room remained.

The kids just didn't know what to say.

There was a McDonald's two blocks from Abby's office, so they ate there. Both of them, though gravely concerned about Greer, had the stray thought that this was how love affairs started. In movies—the old-fashioned kind, anyway—the meeting place was usually fab-fab-fabulous with snooty waiters and Continental decor.

In reality, most folks had their first lunch dates in crowded, noisy, and sometimes greasy places. And who cared? The point was that they were together and they could have been eating alligator burgers and a robbery could be in progress and the roof could be collapsing. And they wouldn't notice. She'd just be looking into his brown eyes and he'd just be looking into her blue eyes and—

He thought of this as he watched her rush in, a few minutes late. And not grand entrance late. Medical late. Permissible when you were a doc, with all the unexpected twists and turns their normal workdays took.

She looked endearingly and enduringly pretty at this moment—not glamorous, not beautiful, not gorgeous—earnest and pretty. And earnest and pretty had always been his favorite in women. Serious, bright, fetching in a low-key way.

The chill day gave her cheeks a soft red glow, her smart berry-colored beret added a smidgen of great low-budget style, and her brisk, slender-girl walk reflected the kind of serious woman she'd grown up to be. She carried a small tray with a paper-wrapped fish sandwich and a cup of steaming coffee she'd got in line.

"Sorry," she said, out of breath as she sat down.

And then all the noise he'd been so aware of—conversations, babies crying, shouts of food orders from the kitchen, cash registers, ice cream machines, deep fat fryers, cars in the drive—all the humdrum noise of the daily hassle fell away and there were just the two of them. And it felt so good for this one tiny moment to sense the possibility of someone else moving into his life. He felt seventeen and loved it.

And then—remembering—he felt his age as he worried about Greer.

"I had another dream last night," she said.

"The killer?"

She nodded, starting to eat her sandwich. He picked at his fries. Not hungry. Too damned worried.

"And then about twenty minutes ago—"

"What?"

"I'm not sure how to explain it."

"You've got a little tartar sauce above your lip."

"I'll bet it's attractive."

"Not nearly as attractive as the tartar sauce on your nose."

She smiled. "I've never really outgrown the bib stage. Laura used to say I ate like a truck driver."

"And swore like one, too, as I remember."

"Look who's talking." She took another bite of her sandwich. Daubed at the corner of her mouth with a napkin. "She's in town now."

"Who is?"

"The killer."

"How do you know that?"

"I just sensed it. I was talking to one of our nurses and I broke into this cold sweat. I had to put on my winter coat, I was freezing all of a sudden. And I saw her. Right here in town. She was checking out the clinic. Or she will check out the clinic. I couldn't tell if I was just seeing her or if I was having a premonition. Anyway, she's in town."

"No more sense of who she is?"

"No. Just that she wants to kill Greer. And probably me, too, while she's at it. Are our friends at Metro still following Greer?"

"From the time she leaves the house."

"Good. I hope they have very big guns. And lots of them."

"Don't worry. They do."

"I was thinking maybe I'd spend the night at your house. She'll be at my office around five anyway. The way she usually is. I'll just come home with her.'

The way she said it, so casually, surprised him.

Seeing this, she smiled. "I'm not offering you my body. Not in the way you think, anyway. I just thought that maybe it'd be better if I could be there with Greer. I'm sure she's having premonitions of her own. And they're very difficult for her to handle."

"Sure. There's the spare room right down the hall."

"That'd be great. Sorry about inviting myself."

Just then, his cell phone buzzed.

"Hello."

He listened. His secretary, a very efficient middle-aged woman, laid it out simply, coherently, and dispassionately.

While he listened, Abby watched his face. His emotions were big, violent as they played silently across his face. By the time the call ended, he was pale.

"My secretary said that the school called her. Greer was down in the nurse's office. She had some kind of seizure or something in class. But she insisted on going home herself rather than waiting for me."

"Seizure or premonition. Sounds like she realized that the killer is in town."

"That's what I was thinking."

"Poor Greer."

"She should be there any time now." But he didn't sound sure of that at all.

"I'll get there as soon as I can. Probably around suppertime."

He reached across and took her hand. "Thanks in

advance for coming over tonight. It's nice of you to offer."

She smiled, but it was a melancholy expression that lent a sadness to her pretty eyes. "Who would ever believe that Abby Stewart and Cam Morgan would ever spend the night under the same roof together?"

Pam Cooper seldom suffered from depression. Just wouldn't allow herself to feel sorry for herself. Why should she? She had damned near everything a reasonable woman could want out of life.

But there was something about tonight.

She called her husband's office. Elaine, the receptionist, who was one of those women who disliked the boss's wife on principle, said that the doctor was busy (implying that any fool should know that) and that, yes, she would have him call back as soon as it was possible (implying that that might be a very long time indeed). If Elaine were more attractive, Pam might have started to wonder if she and old Tom weren't occasionally having sex down there among all the throat cultures and bloody gauze. But Elaine was a wall-eyed, flat-chested, ill-mannered, pushy woman who actually seemed to intimidate Tom. He seemed afraid to fire her, in fact. Pam called the office only when she absolutely needed to. The truth was, Elaine intimidated her a little bit, too. She was always kissing Elaine's ass and the sound of her voice doing it was truly sickening to her.

"Hi, sweetheart, I don't have long," Tom said when he called.

"Elaine was in one of her better moods today."

"I take it you're being sarcastic."

"God, I wish you'd get rid of her."

"What's up, sweetie? I really am swamped down here."

She couldn't say it. He was so busy. And he sounded so sweet. And here she was about to lay all this anxiety on him. *I just don't feel right about tonight. Something's going to go wrong. In all the years, Tom, I've never had this feeling before. I really haven't. And don't ask me why I'm feeling it. I just am, is all. And I have been since I woke up this morning.*

Instead, she said: "I just wondered if you'd bring me home something for this cold I'm coming down with."

"I didn't know you were coming down with a cold."

"Yes. In my chest, it feels like."

"Well, I've got some good stuff—some new samples—right here in the office. I'll bring those along with me. Oh—and I'll be a little late. I have to drop a petition off at The Medical Clinic for those gals to sign. I was supposed to get it in the mail by yesterday and then I forgot. You know, with everything going on."

"Won't you be a little uncomfortable seeing Abby Stewart?"

"I'll just push it through the mail slot at the front of the place. Won't have to go inside or anything."

"Those wild women would tear you apart."

"Oh, they're not so bad. Just a different generation. They see me as an old fogey, and I probably am."

"You are not and you know it. Didn't the *Hastings Corner Courier* call you the most handsome bachelor in the county?"

"Let me remind you, sweetheart, it's a very small county. And anyway, that was back in 1946 or something like that. So I'll bring you that medicine and see you about six or so. You'll recognize me. I'll be the most handsome old fart in the driveway."

He'd got very drunk on Scotch one night. Aside from vomiting several times, falling down a flight of stairs, and wetting himself, he'd had a pretty good time. Oh, yes: one more thing. For the first ten minutes upon waking the next morning, he'd been totally disoriented. Totally being the operative word. Literally could not identify where he was, who he was, or where he'd been. An ominous streak of blood was on his left hand. He had a terrible lump on the back of his head. He wondered—quite seriously—*is this hell?* But why the hell would he have Metallica and Jimi Hendrix posters on the wall? And why would he have a CD player? And what appeared to be schoolbooks? And a closet crammed with clothes?

Only gradually was he able to form the thoughts:

I am jeff
crawford
I am
in
my
home
last night i

(but what? What about last night? had something terrible happened? what was the blood on his hand? was it his own? how had he gotten the bump on his head?)

no memory
shit fuck
what happened to me last night?

He came awake at three in the afternoon. He knew it was three o'clock because he heard the grandfather clock chiming in the hallway. And he knew it was afternoon because of the sunlight in the window.

What happened to me last night?

He remembered the time he'd gotten so loaded on Scotch.

God Almighty.

This was like that except he didn't have the same volatile headache. Or dehydration.

But he was damned disoriented. No doubt about that.

He moved. Groggy. But no pain. With that hangover that time, even moving his arm had shot pain up and down the left side of his body.

What happened to me last night?

Easing his legs off the bed. Sitting up.

And then it was there, unbidden.

What his mother had told him. About the days of Salem. About the women with the secret. And what his father had told him. About Greer. About the trial. About how she would be killed.

A joke. A fucking joke.

Had to be. Had to be.

But it wasn't.

And the rest of it came back. The urgent need to warn Greer. To protect Greer. To run away with Greer, if necessary.

The phone. Get to the phone.

But the phone wasn't there. Usually sat on the corner of his desk. But it was gone. One of those phones you could unplug and move about the house. Gone.

He went to the door. Turned the knob.

As he suspected. Locked.

Incredible.

His own house.

In-fucking-credible.

Witches and ghoulies and things that go bump in the night. His own father.

"Yes, I kill them, Jeff. But you have to understand. It's what God wants me to do.

"They're evil, Jeff. That's what you have to understand.

"They'll take over our species. Our planet.

"And that's what they want. And nothing less.

"God is on our side, Jeff. He's assured me of that.

"I talked to Him on the phone last night and that's what he said. Keep on truckin', folks. Jes' keep right on truckin'."

A fucking nightmare was what this was.

But one Jeff couldn't wake up from.

What Candy really wanted to do was take a nap. But she was afraid the killer would visit her again. And the killer—in the words of the kids—was really creeping her out.

What she did instead was sit at the table and clean and load the .38 Smith & Wesson Chief's Special Model 37 a cop had given her long ago. This was when she'd still had her looks. He'd been sweet on her, the cop had, and worried about the risks of her chosen calling. Much as she claimed she'd never had any trouble with her johns, the cop had wanted to know that she had at least a modest amount of protection. And since the town, at that time, was upgrading the quality of its arms for its police officers, he didn't have any special use for the gun, anyway. It was a fine weapon, double action, five rounds, a thumb piece, and special rosewood grips.

Sometimes, she went for target practice.

And she kept it clean.

She slept with it under her bed, where she could get at it easily, appended to the bottom of her box spring in a shelf she'd had specially made.

She had the sense she'd need it soon. She'd never fired it at anybody, but given the way this whole thing with Greer was going, she knew she'd be using it sometime in the next twenty-four hours or so.

The phone rang.

She carefully set the weapon down. Carefully set aside her cleaning articles. And picked up the phone.

A silence that was not a silence. A wordlessness and yet very much a presence at the same time.

She knew who was on the other end of the phone. No doubt about it.

"You leave that little gal alone, sweetie. Or I'm going to blow your fucking head off. You understand me?"

That roaring intense wordlessness.

"I said do you understand me?"

The click on the other end was anticlimactic. The killer just cut the connection.

Candy sat there, gun in her hand now, picturing the killer. The cold, enigmatic loveliness of that face. Especially the dark dead eyes that glistened no matter whether it was night or day.

Candy started feeding bullets into the chambers.

You leave that little gal alone, bitch. Or Candy's gonna kill you. And don't think I won't do it. I'm ready as hell. Ready as hell.

Then she made a sign of the cross to seal her resolve.

6

DALE Williams was the man's name. Hauled milk from farm to dairy five days a week. Had a big eighteen-wheeler, stainless steel tank for the milk, and a shiny fine red cab with his name written on both doors.

His days were pretty much the same. Up at 4:30 A.M., started his route about 7:00. Pumped out the holding tanks on the farms he visited every day, then drove the milk to the dairy. He liked his independence, no boss standing over him; yet not as risky as farming itself. And he liked the fact that he spent most of his time in the cab looking out at the countryside, which he loved. And he could smoke. In peace. About the only place left for that particular pleasure. If he smoked at home, his two high school-age daughters climbed all over his ass. And his wife made him stand out on the back porch—even in subzero temperatures—soon as he put one of the devil weeds to his mouth. He couldn't go to taverns much anymore because his prostate was acting up again, and Doc Cooper said that alcohol only aggravated the situation.

That left the truck.

Driving the country roads on a pretty day, listening to The Dixie Chicks on the radio and trying to figure out which one of them he'd pork if he was given his choice (now there was a realistic daydream for ya) and smoking his Pall Malls. He loved it. Plain damn loved it.

But that was all to change. Forever.

A few more minutes and Dale Williams, who was a decent man, a loving husband, and a dutiful father, would never be able to look at the countryside the same way again.

But he didn't know that just yet.

He was listening to the Chicks (my God, were they pretty) and smoking away and heading home after a particularly tiring day.

The time was 4:20.

The time was 4:23.

When he was younger, Jeff had prided himself on his ability to do it.

And he hadn't been scared.

Now, the jump didn't look so easy. They said that as you get older you took fewer risks. But seventeen?

Here's how it worked: Jeff would climb out his bedroom window, hang from the sill while he steadied himself, and then sort of fling his body to the right, at which point he'd meet the roof of the back porch, which was approximately three feet away.

As a kid, he used to do this at least once a week.

None of his friends would even try it. It was one of the few cool things he'd ever been able to do. Otherwise he was strictly nerd material.

Today, the jump, or body-fling, or whatever you

wanted to call it, looked a lot farther away. Six feet? Ten feet? Twelve feet?

Whatever, he had to do it. Had to get to a phone and warn Greer and her father. And he'd talk to the police, too. As much as he loved his parents—and he did still love them—he had to stop them. For Greer's sake. And for their own. They were deeply disturbed people. Even if these girls and women really were—

That was the funny thing. Part of him was still denying what he'd seen on that videotape.

They definitely had powers. You couldn't fake what he'd seen without an awful lot of money and special effects, neither of which the lousy camera work indicated.

No, what he'd seen was real. And true. They did have some kinds of abilities not known to the normal human being. But did that really make them not human beings? Couldn't they simply be human beings who were able to capitalize on certain potential skills most humans had?

And anyway, whatever the explanation, their nature didn't have anything to do with Satan or any of that medieval nonsense.

The fact that these trials had been going on since Salem—and long before Salem—was both stunning and in a perverse way fascinating. Times changed, but people didn't. Some of them kept the same beliefs and superstitions their ancestors had brought with them from the days of the caves.

And acted on those beliefs and superstitions to this day.

He eased up the window. Thumbed the latches in the screen and eased the screen off as quietly as possible.

Any other time his parents would have the TV on. But not now.

He brought the screen inside, laid it against the wall. Put his head out the window. Gosh, how had he ever flung himself all the way to the back porch roof? And without any problem. Had not missed once.

He thought of Greer. That would give him the courage and skill he needed. The picture of Greer in his mind.

He'd get on the back porch and drop to the ground. Get on the ground and run around the garage to get to his car. And then shoot down the road into town.

The only iffy spot would be between the back porch and the garage. Plenty of opportunity for his folks to look out the kitchen window and see him. There was a ten-foot gap between porch and detached two-stall garage.

He pushed the window all the way up. Turned around and began the process of feeding himself to the air, clinging only by his fingers to the sill.

An arthriticlike cramp seized his hands. He thought he would fall. He redoubled his grip. He knew better than to look down. It was a considerable two-story fall. He wasn't worried about dying. But he was worried about breaking a leg. Then how could he get away and warn Greer?

He felt almost giddy as he prepared himself for the circuslike sideways leap he was about to make. One, two, three. Ladies and gentlemen, the death-defying Jeff Crawford will now—Those were the cornball words he used to whisper to himself as he made the death-defying leap—

But he was a little old for such melodrama. And

the stakes were a lot higher than simply acting out a fantasy.

He took several deep breaths. He eyed the porch as clinically and objectively as he could.

Just then a United 747 from Boston was arcing wide for a landing and distracted him, silhouetted as it was against the utterly blue sky.

And then, another deep breath, words vaguely resembling a prayer in his head, he took one more look at the porch roof.

And made ready for the death-defying sideways body-fling that only Jeff Crawford had ever successfully achieved.

Good ole death-defying Jeff Crawford.

The time was 4:25.

"I don't know what's going to happen." Sighing, exhausted. Looking older than she ever had to him, his sweet bride of so long ago: Sara Jean Needham Crawford.

They'd been arguing. She didn't want Jeff brought into the group. She wanted him apart, the way she had always been.

Something bumped against the house.

"What was that?" she said.

"Wind, maybe."

"I don't think so."

Something bumped against the house again.

Yancy tried to picture various explanations. The wind snapping off a piece of tree limb and smashing it against the house. A piece of their new vinyl siding tearing off. Maybe their dish antenna falling over.

Another bump.

They both had the same thought at the same time. But it was Sara who expressed it first: "Jeff."

"Sneaking out that damned window."

A mental picture formed perfectly in Yancy's mind. Jeff hanging from the sill by his fingers. The toes of his boots striking the house as he prepared to do that crazy sideways fling of his. He used to get away with it about half the time, sneaking off like this. The other half they always caught him. And usually for the same reason. The noise he made trying to escape.

Sara grabbed him. She wanted Jeff to escape. He yanked himself from her clutches.

Yancy went through the back porch. It smelled of the apple cider and fireplace wood stored there. He pushed open the screen door and went down the steps just in time to see the death-defying leap.

Jeff damn near fell short of the porch. The kid was rusty.

In order to stop himself from pitching to the ground, Jeff had to grab on to the edge of the roof where he hung by the tips of his fingers.

"You all right, Jeff?" Yancy said, coming around to the west side of the porch so he could stand beneath his son.

"Just get away from me, Dad. I don't want to talk to you anymore. Or even see you."

"We need to talk."

"We've already talked."

Hanging on to the edge of the roof—the back porch was a long, screened-in rectangle with lawn furniture covered with a tarp until spring—he redoubled his grip every thirty seconds or so.

"This time your Mom's going to join us."

"She isn't any different from you. You're both insane, and you're both killers."

"You haven't had time to think it through. You're still in shock. The same as I was when my folks told me—and your mom was that way, too. Now drop down here and we'll go inside. Please, Jeff. This is difficult enough for all of us. Please don't make it any worse. All right?"

Instinctively, the way he did when Jeff was a little boy, Yancy put his arms up as if he was going to catch his son.

Jeff had other ideas.

Yes, he dropped to the ground. But as he was dropping, he swung his body in a small arc so that he slammed into his father, knocking him to the ground.

He needed half a minute for a clean getaway. This was the only way he could get it.

Yancy tried to stay upright when Jeff collided with him. But only a few seconds later, Yancy was over on his back, cursing, watching Jeff scramble to his feet and run to the far corner of the house.

His car. That's where Jeff would be going.

Get in his car and get out of here. Warn Greer. Warn Cam Morgan. Warn the police.

Yancy knew the rules. The sect held parents strictly responsible for the behavior of their children, up until age eighteen or until such time as the children left home. If a parent suspected that a child was going to inform on the sect, it became the terrible duty of the parent to destroy the child. That was the language used in the book. "Destroy the child."

All this flashed through Yancy's mind as he forced himself to his feet and automatically started yelling for Jeff to stop and listen to reason.

Yancy recovered faster than Jeff might have expected. In less than sixty seconds, he was not only on his feet but closing the gap between himself and Jeff.

Jeff, seeing this over his shoulder, apparently realized that he would have a difficult time getting in the car, starting the car, and backing out without having a major physical confrontation with his father. Maybe he didn't think he could win such a confrontation. Maybe he didn't think there'd be time to escape even if he won such a confrontation.

For whatever reason, he veered to the right abruptly, running faster than Yancy had ever seen him move before.

Jeff had several options now. When he reached the highway that ran past their place, he could go east to a heavy area of timber and lose himself or west along the highway. Not far ahead was a busy intersection where he could easily thumb a ride into town.

Very little time to stop him, Yancy realized, as his middle-aged legs tried to make some teenage time.

The time was 4:29.

The time was 4:30.

It was funny, Dale Williams noted, how caught up the average man could get in the lives of celebrities. Some of the people you worried about were probably assholes, anyway, and would back over your mother for fifty cents.

Just as long as Johnny Cash wasn't one of them.

Johnny had had a lot of health problems these past

five years or so and Dale Williams had kept up on that news pretty damned good. First one thing then another. Dale even included Johnny in his prayers some nights when the TV news of the country star wasn't so good.

"Folsom Prison Blues" was what had done it for Dale. Any man who could write the line "I shot a man in Reno just to watch him die," was all right in Dale's judgment. Because most folks had thoughts like that sometimes. Got so down or so mad or just plain damn summer-heat crazy that you felt these terrible impulses about other human beings, human beings who, at any other time, you'd feel a bit of compassion for. Or maybe even like.

Took a smart man to recognize that impulse as far as Dale was concerned, and an even smarter man to write it down.

What had brought Johnny Cash to mind was that the "Golden Oldie" this hour on the radio was "A Boy Named Sue," which was the one and only Johnny Cash song Dale couldn't abide. Once you heard it, you knew the punch line. It was like being told the same joke over and over again.

So Dale did the unthinkable.

He punched off the Johnny Cash tune and found another country station.

One of The Hats, as he called them. All these twenty-somethings with those stupid cowboy hats.

But even though he hadn't liked the Johnny Cash song didn't mean he stopped thinking about Johnny Cash the man.

Oh, no. He barely heard what The Hat was singing at all.

He was just flying down the highway, window cracked some, end of his Pall Mall burning like a small hot berry, when he saw him.

Some kid. Appearing out of nowhere. Obviously being chased by somebody because he kept looking back over his shoulder as he ran.

And then the other person appeared. Man. Maybe Dale's own age or thereabouts. The man was chasing the boy down the edge of the highway.

Dale started hitting his horn. Stupid bastards didn't even seem aware of him rushing toward them. And they were only a couple of inches from being on the roadway itself.

The boy ran out in the path of Dale's truck. No warning. Not the slightest hint that this was what he'd be doing.

Panic seized Dale. Did he have enough room to stop?

He hit the brakes, slammed the heel of his hand on his horn, cursed and prayed at the same time.

But the insanity wasn't over.

The older man followed the boy right onto the roadway and jumped on him. Were these two clowns deaf and dumb? You have all this machinery bearing down on you and don't hear it? Or the horn fer gosh sakes?

As the big rig came sliding, screaming, jerking to a too-late halt, Dale leaned on the horn again. By this time, his face was a mask of sweat and horror and he anticipated—his stomach clenching and unclenching, his entire body shaking—what it would feel like to have two bodies splatter against the front of the truck. He was the kind of guy who felt bad for hours after accidentally running over a squirrel. Hell, he felt bad when he hit a damned skunk.

God, why wouldn't they look up and see him?

But they were still wrestling with each other, the boy trying to get away from the man. If there'd been time, Dale would've wondered what was going on here. In this milli-instant, so packed with thoughts, impressions, dreads, he recognized the resemblance between the two. Father and son, no doubt.

One more time—the horn—as the rig came sliding into them now.

And now—finally—they did look up and see him bearing down on them. And then their faces went all cartoonish, expressions of horror, confusion, and panic so big they looked like Saturday morning faces.

Hands over their faces, as if they could deflect the truck. Mouths wide in screams he couldn't hear. Starting to run. Stumbling. Stumbling, for God's sake, in their realization that Death was this shiny new eighteen-wheeler, not something dark and sinister and reeking of the grave. Hauling good-for-you milk, in fact, Death was, for all the good little boys and girls in the county.

He felt an instant of hope for them as they wisely looked to their right rather than their left. They'd never have time to get back to the side of the road they'd come from. Too far.

But they could easily step into the oncoming lane—

Then Dale Williams realized that he'd been so engrossed in trying to get them off the road that he hadn't seen what was in the oncoming road—

A rig much bigger than his own.

And father and son didn't see it either, not until they stepped right into its path.

It was like the feel and sound of a car wash when the first wave of water hits you, Dale Williams thought.

Just as the oncoming truck smashed into them, Dale's rig came abreast of them. And they sprayed his windshield and his door with blood, flesh, bone. That hard splattering car wash sound.

And Dale—all fucking crazy now, just losing it completely—Dale was crying and laughing and vomiting all over himself as he saw a piece of scalp slide down the windshield and saw a glimpse of white that just had to be a piece of bone.

This was the stuff they didn't show you in those trashy horror movies where the chicks were always taking showers just as the slasher showed up. Oh, they showed you the blood all right but they didn't show you what the sight of that blood did to the person who found the body.

Acrid stink of vomit. Somehow wrestling the rig off to the side of the road. And still laughing. What the fuck was the laughing all about? What was so damned funny, anyway? And then crying again.

He just sat there for a long moment. The vomit smell was getting to him. But for this moment, he didn't care. What a petty concern—the stinging odor of vomit trapped in your olfactory senses—after what he'd just seen.

He pushed open the door. And swung his legs out. And looked back down the highway.

The other rig had stopped, too. Still sitting in its lane.

A woman was running out to the rig now. Probably the mother. He could feel her grief even from here. Waving her arms and head about so wildly, they looked as if they'd fly off her body.

Oh, shit, I'll have to go down there. The sheriff'll come and he'll want me to tell him what I saw and I'll have to see what's left of those bodies. And I've got this puke all over my shirt.

Then he remembered the old football jersey his son Kenny had left in the back.

Kenny.

God, he loved that kid. Loved both his kids. And his wife. And his dog. And his house. And his life. And it all just hung by a thread. You thought you were so nice and safe. All smug and snug, aren't you?

And in just a second or two, it can all be taken from you.

All of it.

He changed shirts and walked back down the highway to where the other rig sat.

7

HE was looking for blood. He'd been driving up and down roads looking for her car. Now that he found it, he was looking for—

He didn't want to admit that to himself, but that's what he was doing.

Searching through his daughter's car, looking for blood. When he was done looking, Cam walked away from the stranded car and started looking around the underbrush.

Night fog. Dampness. Dropping temperature. His nose running. An ache of fear seizing his entire body and mind and soul.

Where the hell was she? And where was her bodyguard?

She had a cell phone, didn't she? The rational answer to a car stranded like this was that she'd had car trouble. But equally as rational—she had a cell phone and would've called him. Before she called anybody else with the exception maybe of Abby. But she hadn't called him. Or Abby.

A car hurrying by.

Maybe not even seeing him. Maybe not wanting to

see him. His own car pulled off the road and facing Greer's. Headlights on.

He was just starting to walk into the surrounding woods when he saw the swirling blue emergency lights stain the fog.

A squad car pulled off the road, parked behind Greer's.

The seemingly interminable wait before the cop got out of his car and walked over, heavy shoes crunching small stones and frozen earth.

"Evening, Mr. Morgan."

"Evening."

"Looks like you've got some car trouble."

And then—for the very first time—he felt the same caution that those with the secret had felt for centuries. You had to be careful of what you said. You couldn't in any way intimate the truth. Because if you told them the truth they would either think you were crazy—or, worse, believe you and begin to investigate. And if they began to investigate—

"Yes. This is my daughter's car."

"Oh." The cop looked around. He was a good-sized black man with an easygoing manner. "You need me to call a tow truck?"

"I think it's all right now. I started the engine a couple of times. I think she just flooded it and then gave up on it."

The cop looked around. "She go on ahead?"

"Yes. She called a friend of hers, and the friend picked her up."

For the first time, the cop's easygoing manner seemed to fade. His eyes narrowed and started taking in the scene more carefully. And something shifted in his voice, too. It was tighter; an air of puzzlement. "So she went home, huh?"

"Right. Home."

"How're you going to get two cars home?"

"I guess I'll just have to have her come back."

This time the cop looked at him more carefully, too. He smiled. But it was a fake smile. One intended to put you at false ease. "Seems it would've been easier if she'd just stuck around and offered to help you."

"Well, you know how teenagers are. There's a party tonight. That's her chief concern."

"I'll be back."

He unholstered a flashlight and began to examine Greer's car the way Cam had a few minutes earlier.

Cars sped by. He could see pink faces gawking and squinting at him through the haze. Headlights like dirty yellow eyes. A sad, bony dog sniffing along the edge of the tree line.

The cop finished up with the trunk—he'd already looked through the rest of the car—and then walked back to Cam.

"You sure everything's all right, Mr. Morgan?"

"Yes, sure, why?" Cam said much too quickly.

"Just want to make sure." Not taking his gaze from Cam's. "It's my job."

"Everything's fine, Officer. It really is. I appreciate your concern. I really do."

"Well, if you do need anything, you be sure to call us." The smile on his face again. But the hint of skepticism in his voice and eyes just the same.

"I will, Officer."

Kidnapped. That's what he thinks. Kidnapped or

abducted. And I'm afraid to tell him. And that's the hell of it—I am afraid to tell him. I can't tell him.

"Thanks again, Officer," Cam called to the man's retreating back. "Thanks again."

Eleven minutes later, Cam pulled into his driveway. He went quickly inside. He was about to ask if Greer had called, but Abby just shook her head solemnly. "But the police called."

"The police? For what?"

"They didn't say. They just said to have you call right away and ask for a Detective Ridge. I was about to call you on your cell phone."

He lurched to the phone. Dialed.

"Detective Ridge, please."

"Hold, please."

Ridge spoke in deep, careful tones. "Ridge here. Help you?"

"This is Cam Morgan."

"Oh, yes. Thanks for calling. I need you to verify something for me."

"Is this about my daughter?"

"Yes, it is. It looks like there's been a mix-up. About an hour ago an officer found a Mr. Frank Bailey sitting in front of The Medical Clinic. The officer arrested him and brought him to the station."

So she wasn't protected. She was completely vulnerable. And now her car was sitting deserted on a road—

"We checked with Metro Security, and they've verified his employment there. Will you verify that you hired them to work for you and your daughter?"

"Yes. They're working for me."

"I'm sorry about this mix-up. You were assuming somebody was taking care of your daughter—and we pulled him off. Did she get home all right?"

You incompetent bastards. You pulled off her body-guard and now somebody's taken her. You're the ones responsible! But I can't say that. Because if I don't lie and say everything's fine, then you'll start asking questions. And if you start asking questions—

Once again he shared the sense of the hunted—from the Christians in the Roman Empire to the Jews during the Third Reich to the many, many innocents slaughtered trying to escape Pol Pot—the sense of the hunted and the despised throughout history.

"She's fine."

"Well, then things are all right, after all."

"Yes, things're fine."

"Sorry to bother you with this, Mr. Morgan."

"Not at all. I appreciate you checking."

When he hung up, he turned and faced Abby and Candy.

"We're going to check out Tom Cooper," Abby said.

"Check him out?"

"See what he's doing. So far, he's the only lead we've got."

"Because of the medication he was giving Greer?"

"Exactly. It's very strange the way that chemical analysis just vanished. The analysis would've been done at the hospital. Cooper could've gotten in there very easily."

"And I just sit here?"

She touched his arm. "Somebody has to be here in case Greer calls. It's easier for us to move around."

"And don't forget his cabin," Candy said.

"Oh, right. Candy has a friend who's a cleaning woman. Every spring she cleans that house the Coopers have out of town. They call it a cabin, but it's a house. If we can't find Cooper anywhere else, we can check the cabin out there."

"I couldn't stop you even if I tried, could I?" he said.

Abby smiled and kissed him on the cheek. "No, you couldn't."

In times past, the trials had a heavily religious tone. A good number of prayers were said before the trials began.

But over the decades of this century, the sect found itself with agnostics in its midst, people who believed that yes, this other race—more talented and gifted than the human species—had to be done away with. But not because it was inherently evil and certainly not because it had anything to do with a being as unlikely as Satan. These people felt they were just protecting the human race.

While everybody present tonight was a believer in a deity—including, ironically, Greer herself—prayers and invocations were sparing. These were modern people. They watched "Saturday Night Live" and HBO sex comedies, and it was hard to make yourself sound like somebody out of a bad horror movie without laughing out loud. So the prayers were rather rote and the one and only invocation was made so quickly that several key words were skipped.

Just as well.

Dr. Tom put more of the drug into the IV he'd set up for her—sodium Amytal and two other drugs of his choosing—and then waited the mandatory ten minutes before asking her to levitate the small green rubber ball in front of her.

She resisted, of course. They always did. The drugs had yet to take full control of her. Her resistance to him was still very strong. With her under the influence of lesser drugs, he'd been able to call her house, say a few key words that he'd hypnotically planted in her head, and get her to leave the house. This was a form of thought control leading up to tonight. He wanted to get her used to his powers as a hypnotist.

In just a few minutes, when the drugs held sway, he would hypnotize her once again and then the evening would move quickly.

As he waited for the drugs to take control of her, Cooper wondered if her car had been found by now, and whether Abby and Cam were searching for her yet. Cooper had already decided how she would die. She would be depressed over young Jeff's death and would commit suicide. No trouble at all in pitching her into the cold waters of the river. No trouble at all—since he would be performing the autopsy—in overlooking the various drugs in her body.

Two stages with this particular mixture of drugs.

The first thing she would do—and was doing now—was slip into a deep sleep. She was already snoring.

Not long after, her eyes would open. A fine sheen of sweat would glaze her face. A certain sequence of involuntary muscle spasms would take place. During none of this would she be receptive to his commands. She would still be, in most respects, asleep.

But then, if his past experiences held true, she

would respond to his key words and begin to do as he told her.

He wished the others were more interested.

It was funny how just about all experiences could become dull after a time. He could remember the first trials they'd all shared in. Years ago. These people here tonight looked like imposters. They'd all been so young and vital back then. And completely consumed by what they were doing. The trials were exciting. Fulfilling. To see one of the witches reveal herself by performing some impossible task—my God, you were rocked in your seat.

But tonight there were dulled eyes and yawns and talk—unbelievable—of a certain sitcom that would be on later tonight. And wouldn't it be nice if they wrapped this up here in time to get home and see it. And then, inevitably, the discussion turned back to Yancy and Jeff. And Sara. What would Sara do now? Tom had talked to her briefly and knew that she felt resentful toward all of them, toward the sect itself. If her husband and son hadn't been arguing about the sect, Jeff would never have run out onto the highway. And Yancy would not have had to follow him and—

Could be a problem. A big one.

"Can you hear me, Greer?"

"Yes." Slow, fuzzy voice.

"I need the word to your soul."

That was his entry phrase.

A long pause. "Sunset."

"Very good, Greer. Now I need for you to sit up straight and concentrate very hard on what I'm saying."

Some of their interest returned. Eyes focused on

Greer now. There was a sense of anticipation in the shadowy basement.

Greer did as she was told.

"Let's start with the ball. Do you see it?"

"Yes." The voice still robotic; the body movements jerky, robotic, too.

"Pick it up, please."

No response. Greer just sitting there. This always happened. It was like a loose connection. Not all commands seemed to get through the first time.

"Pick up the ball, please."

She picked up the ball.

"Now, throw it up in the air and make it stay there."

"I can't. I don't know how."

"Listen to me very carefully, Greer. Throw the ball up in the air and make it stay there. Do you understand me?"

"Yes."

"Then please do it."

She hesitated but finally complied. Threw the small ball up into the air. It came right back down, hard, on the table in front of her.

"You didn't do what I asked."

"I can't."

He knew that it would take a little more time to overcome her defenses. She had been taught from an early age never to reveal her powers to anybody, that doing so could lead to her death. So she had great resistance to using her powers under any circumstances.

"Please pick up the ball."

Cooper smiled over at his friends. They always

needed reassurance. At this point, or one like it a bit later on, a few of them would be thinking, *Maybe she's not a witch. Maybe we've got the wrong person here. Tom keeps working on her but it doesn't seem to be doing any good. Maybe Tom should give her a drug so she doesn't remember any of this. And then maybe we should let her go. Maybe we just made a real bad mistake here.*

He repeated, "Please pick up the ball."

She picked up the ball.

"Throw it up in the air."

She threw it up in the air.

"Now keep it up there! Keep it up there!"

The ball dropped back to the table.

"I can't."

He said nothing. Just used the IV drip to put more drugs into her body.

"You need to trust me."

She said nothing.

"I'm trying to help you, Greer. You've been carrying a secret around all your life. It's almost more than you can handle sometimes. It's so bad you think you might lose your mind over it sometimes. I want you to share that secret with me. Because I understand. I'm your friend, and I can help. Do you understand?"

A long, long pause. "I'm afraid."

"I know you're afraid. You're afraid of yourself. And you've been afraid for a very long time. Won't it be nice to share your secret with somebody else? Somebody who knows the word to your soul?"

"I–I–guess so."

When the tears came, soft tears, nothing dramatic,

he knew she was his. He felt like a boxer who'd just knocked down a supposedly unbeatable opponent.

"Are you ready, Greer?"

"Yes."

"Then throw the ball up in the air and make it stay there."

Another hesitation. But not much of one. She took the ball from his slight, white hand and tossed it gently in the air.

Where it stayed.

"Make it spin, Greer."

Where it spun.

"Make it spin in a wide circle."

Where it spun in a wide circle.

"Make it bounce off the furnace over there."

Where it raced across the basement and bounced off the furnace.

"Now bring it back and make it sit down gently on the table."

No bored onlookers now. The stage show had begun, and it was a stage show the human mind would never tire of. Because all these tricks, however simple, were something that the human species had dreamed of since dreams had poem-formed in the mind.

The ability to move objects just by willing them to do so. And to control them when you moved them.

"And now set the paper bag on fire, Greer." A lot of witches down the years had made objects move. But few of them had ever been able to start a fire. No matter how long they'd been threatened, there had been no fire.

"I'm not sure I can do that."

"Yes, you can. You made the ball move."

"But fire is different."

"I know the word to your soul, Greer."

"I'm afraid."

"Say the word, Greer. That will make you feel better."

"Sunset."

Except for the furnace kicking out warm air, the basement was silent.

"Say it again, Greer."

"Sunset."

"Very good. Now I want you to focus your attention—all your attention, Greer—onto the paper bag. And I want you to set it on fire."

Within seconds, the paper bag—one large, unremarkable paper bag—bloomed in blue-red-yellow flame.

"My Lord!" Dorothy Dryer exclaimed.

"All right if I roll down the window and smoke a cigarette?"

"I guess."

"You worried about my health? That's sweet, Abby. Thanks."

"Actually, I was worried about my car. The smell of smoke."

"Oh."

Seeing she'd hurt Candy's feelings, Abby added quickly, "And your health, too. I'd like you to stick around for a long time."

Candy believed her. "Thanks. I guess I don't need to smoke."

"You could always throw the whole pack out and go cold turkey." She did want Candy around for a long time. All the things the old woman had endured. She deserved some happy years. And healthy ones.

They were on their way to Tom Cooper's outsized native stone house that an eccentric Boston architect had built after the big war. Abby had always figured it was her lack of sophistication that kept her from appreciating the then futuristic-looking angles and curves of glass and jutting stone that made up the house. If Captain Kirk ever settled down on Earth, this was the house where he'd live. And that was the trouble. Way too cold a place for her, and way too proud of itself.

No lights.

"Nobody's home," Candy said.

"Doesn't look like it," Abby said. "Think I'll knock, anyway."

She was about to pull into the driveway when an older woman in a heavy winter jacket appeared in the headlights. She was walking a friendly-looking sheep dog. She was angling toward the large Colonial-style house next door.

She pulled into the drive, rolled down her window and said to the woman, "Excuse me, ma'am."

The woman turned back. Her body language was tentative, leery. "Yes?"

"Do you live in that house?"

"No. But I'm a friend of the people who do."

"I'm looking for Dr. Cooper but I don't see any lights. I thought you being a neighbor and all—"

"Aren't you Dr. Stewart?"

"Yes, I am."

"Sally Lord, Dr. Stewart. The Junior League last year?"

"Oh, right. I spoke at a luncheon there."

"Women's health issues. You were very good." The woman turned her dog around now. They walked back to the car. "Just giving Dirk here his evening exercise."

"Dirk?"

"My husband loves Clive Cussler books. So we named him Dirk after Cussler's hero, Dirk Pitt." She laughed. "Crazy, huh?" She leaned in the window. She was very Junior League. Perfect hair, perfect makeup, perfect suburbanite. Even walking the dog. She seemed puzzled by Candy. Why would a woman who looked like that be sitting in Dr. Stewart's car? Dr. Stewart had decided against joining the League despite two or three invitations. But did that have to mean she hung around with downscale people like this one? Maybe the old woman was a patient. There. That made Sally feel much better. The world was an orderly and knowable place, after all. Doctors didn't hang around with lower-class women like this one, after all.

"I was wondering if you'd talked to Tom Cooper tonight?"

"Not tonight," Sally Lord said. Dirk chose just then to let out a bark so deep it seemed to jostle trees. "Be quiet, Dirk. Some bark, huh?"

Despite herself, Abby sort of liked this woman. She remembered that she was a tart observer of her own failings—and the failings of other League members. An arrogant snob, true, but she seemed aware of it. And that lent her at least a semblance of humility.

"I haven't seen Tom. But I know Pam's spent the last few days out at their cabin. Cleaning up. They like to have winter bashes. They might be there. You might catch them out there. You know where it is?"

Abby's family had property near there. She'd trekked through the surrounding woods many times as a youngster.

"I think I can find it."

Dirk bellowed again. Was that the ground shaking?

"We tried to mate him once, but all the girl dogs were afraid of him," Sally Lord laughed.

Gee, I wonder why, Abby thought.

When they were driving again, Candy said, "You see the way she looked at me?"

"I guess not."

"Like I was the scum of the Earth."

"Sure you're not overreacting?"

"My father could've bought hers three times over at one point in his life."

She heard the hurt in Candy's voice and felt sorry for her. She still had some of her pride, and that was all to the good. She was a bright, decent, caring woman and expected to be treated as such. Abby was glad she got to see this side of her. She'd been afraid that Candy was nothing but a collection of bad habits.

"I'm sure glad we met, Candy."

"You don't have to bullshit me."

"I'm not bullshitting. I am glad we met."

"Why?"

"You must've been a lot of fun when you were going through menopause."

Candy laughed so loud her dentures clacked. "You don't want to know. I took it out on everybody I came across."

"I believe it. I give you a compliment, and you jump all over me."

"That's just what I was like, too." Laughing again. Cigarettes and whiskey in the sound of it.

"I'm glad we met because now I have somebody to talk to about the secret."

"You have Greer."

"I love Greer. She's like my own daughter. But you're an adult, and there's a difference."

"That's funny."

"What is?" Abby said.

"Old lady like me, I still don't think of myself as an old lady. When I'm breathing my last, I'll still think of myself as eighteen."

We all will, Candy; we all will. That was one of the sad truths Abby had learned working every day with the dying. Very few people of any age were ready to die. And even the hundred-year-olds, deep in their souls, had yet to turn twenty.

Karen parked a long distance away from Cam Morgan's place. She didn't mind the walk. Walking calmed her. The anxiety was upon her again and she felt like weeping but could not weep; and felt like screaming but could not scream.

She wondered where she was going and why she was going there. Shattered pieces of nightmare: faces contorted in horror, faces that seemed to be looking at her. But why would they be afraid of her? That's what made no sense in these nightmares. As if she had some kind of power. As if she hurt these people in some way.

Awareness: night. Overawareness, actually, to the point of increased anxiety and the beginnings of a headache. Sounds overloading her hearing: squirrel in a tree, dog in a yard, 747 in the sky, water gurgling in the sewer, TV set, car a block away, her feet on the gravel in the alley—crunching noise momentarily overwhelming.

Temperature dropping. Mist turning to fog. Garbage cans. Ground-sniffing dog.

She would knock and stand at the door and when they came, maybe they would recognize her and explain everything.

Why was she here? What meaning did this house have for her?

But she was compelled forward. Had no idea why. Or by what forces. Just—compelled.

The backyard was well-kept. Good-sized flower garden now littered with leaves after the perennials had been cut back to the ground. Outdoor grill. Clotheslines. Long, deep screened-in back porch. Gazebo. The moonlight made everything seem somewhat sinister and forbidding but also lovely and elegant—perfect as a painting.

Her footsteps in the wet grass. Her breathing, faster and faster. A shudder traveling through most of her body, a violent shudder as if in anticipation of—what?

Image of the terrified woman again. Pleading. *But why would she be afraid of me?*

She raised her hand to knock. Perfectly respectable social call. Even if it was at the back door. Even if it was night. Even if it might be disconcerting to the person inside.

Then stopped herself. *No, don't knock. Just go on inside. Nothing to worry about. Just go on inside.*

Apples. Grease on a bicycle axle. Cat droppings.

Bird nest. Tarp over summer back porch furniture. Wood. Just a few of the scents on the back porch.

Now go inside. Up to the door. The lock won't be difficult to pick. The tools are in your pocket. Easy enough to do. Show a little confidence, Karen.

But why am I doing this?

You're helping people. That's all little Karen Dupree has ever wanted to do. Help people. Now open the lock and go inside.

8

CAM was in the living room. On the cell phone. He kept the regular phone line open in case Greer tried to call.

He was using her phone book, dialing all the numbers she had written in the lines on the inside back of the cover. Having no luck.

When he heard something.

The sound wasn't disturbing or alarming. It was just a sound he couldn't interpret. In the back. Kitchen, probably.

"Well, thank you, Kelly. And if you hear from Greer, please have her call me right away."

Listening now. And curious now. And starting to get up from the couch. And starting to cock his head so he can listen better out of his right ear.

And there she was. In the doorway.

Age, face, body about those of Greer's. Dark raincoat, collar up, long dark hair touching her shoulders. Sparkling with fog-mist from outdoors.

"Who are you?" he asked. "And where's Greer?"

He knew then that she was here to kill him. He watched the violent reconfiguring of her blue pupils.

They held him. All the dorky stage hypnotists he'd seen on TV. How he'd always laughed.

He couldn't look away from her, hard as he tried. He couldn't even close his eyes to her.

He lurched over to the couch. Grabbed an amber-colored throw pillow. Clamped it over his eyes.

A momentary respite. Her eyes radiated an almost palpable heat. No other way to describe the sensation of being in her line of vision.

He deluded himself that he was free of her now. He began to back up slowly, slowly, across the living room to the front door. He was going to lunge outside, run. Hide. And wait for her outside. And then he'd jump on her when she came out. Jump on her and make her tell him where Greer was. Because she knew—she had to know.

The throw pillow caught fire.

No warning heat; no warning smoke.

Just—no warning—he was holding the throw pillow, and then it was a throw pillow no longer. Just flames burning his hands, making him cry out. He flung it in the fireplace.

No escaping her eyes now. Quietly, purposefully, she moved closer to him. And then a sensation that made him almost giddy with fear.

A sick feeling of being cold. Shivering.

She was sharing his mind with him. As silent mentally as she was physically. But she was there. Inside his consciousness. With him.

And then he was watching himself fall under her sway entirely. A part of his mind was functioning perfectly.

I am Cam Morgan. I am walking down the hall to the study.

—but I don't want to be walking down the hall to the study.

I am Cam Morgan. I am sitting down at my desk.

—but I don't want to be sitting down at my desk.

—I need to get away from her before it's too late.

I am picking up the phone. As she tells me. I am dialing the Brents, Cassie Brent. A girl who plays on Greer's soccer team.

"Hello, Cassie This is Cam Morgan."

"Hi, Mr. Morgan."

"I'm trying to find Greer, Cassie."

"Is everything all right, Mr. Morgan?"

"I'm pretty sure it is. But I just wondered if you'd seen her or heard from her?"

"No; no, I really haven't."

And then he knew what was going to happen.

Why she'd had him make the phone call. Perfectly staged.

The chest pain started as a pinprick but soon became an evolving, paralyzing force that doubled him over as a new pain—a burning lance straight up his left arm—started to blind him.

He dropped the receiver on the desk and cried out in his final moment of awareness.

Cassie shouted on the other end. "Are you all right, Mr. Morgan! Are you all right?"

Perfectly staged. This whole thing. A man half-crazed with concern for his daughter. Who could ask for a better heart attack candidate than that?

And a teenage girl hearing it on the other end of the phone conversation. The perfect witness.

(Cassie to the police afterward: "Gosh, he sounded like he was losing his mind. I mean, he tried not to sound that way. But I could hear how worried he was. The poor guy. And then I heard him drop the receiver and— Such a nice guy, too. My folks liked him a lot.")

Perfect witness.

Perfect victim.

"She's one of them," Tom Cooper said. "Not much doubt about that now."

Greer sat fully upright in the chair. Eyes glazed, staring straight ahead. If she was aware of what the others were saying, this was not reflected in her expression. She had no expression.

"At least we know for sure now," Russ Dryer said.

Cooper went over and put his hand under her chin and raised her head up. Still no response. Eyes empty. "Poor damned kid. It's always the nice ones."

"You know what Sara would say at this point, don't you?" Dorothy Dryer asked.

Cooper nodded. "That we should pray for her soul. So that he'll take her to Him when—when she isn't with us anymore."

"I suppose you're right," Dorothy said.

"Still can't say it, can you, Dorothy?" Cooper prodded.

"Don't pick on her, Tom," his wife said.

"I'm not picking on her. I've always worried that we'd lose our own souls in this process. Nice to know that one of us still can't even say the k word."

"The k word?" Russ Dryer said.

"Kill."

"Oh. Right. Nope, she still can't say it." Russ sounded proud.

"But there's still a lot of business to sort through

before we get to that point," Tom said. "We need her to write the note, first of all. Her bereavement over Jeff Crawford."

They all heard the noise upstairs at the same time. Somebody had come in. Somebody who didn't care much if they were heard, either. The door was slammed shut. The footsteps, while not heavy or loud—indeed, the weight of the steps suggested somebody with a very light body—were not tiptoeing or stealthy in any way.

Russ started to say something, but Cooper put a finger to his lips.

The steps continued. Through the living room. Into the kitchen. Right up to the basement door.

By now, wild looks of apprehension could be seen on all but two faces—Cooper's and Greer's.

Cooper made another shushing signal with his finger and then moved on the tips of his feet to the bottom of the basement stairs. He was making a good show of being in control and being more curious than afraid. But his armpits were already boggy with sweat, and the bottoms of his feet were cold with sweat.

He stood there, staring up the eight steps to the basement door, knowing that at any moment it would be opened. There might be a cop there. Or a reporter. Or an enraged parent of one of the young women they'd killed over the years. Could be anybody. On any sort of mission.

Russ started to stir off the sofa, but Cooper waved him back. Hard enough to control himself, let alone control others.

He stared at the door again.

And then Greer made a mysterious sound.

Somewhere between a grunt and a moan. He knew instantly what it was—a sign of recognition. The kind of sound cows make upon seeing each other, or squirrels, or sheep—or humans. Species recognizing like species.

A glance told him that she was awake now. That she knew who or what was beyond the door at the top of the stairs. Her eyes moved about quickly, assessing the room and the people in it. And the dark door. That same sound of recognition was repeated, not so loudly this time, seeming trapped halfway up her throat.

"What the hell's going on here?" Russ Dryer shouted. Sprang to his feet. Lurched toward Cooper at the bottom of the stairs.

"Go back and sit down, Russ."

"I want to know what the hell's going on."

"So do I. But panic isn't going to help anything."

"So the big, brave doctor isn't scared, huh?"

"Hell, yes, I am. But I'm trying to stay as calm as possible."

Russ wheeled and pointed an accusing finger at Greer. "She knows what's up there."

"Yeah, I think she does. But that doesn't mean she's going to tell us."

"Oh, she'll tell us, all right," Russ said. And lunged toward Greer. He grabbed her hair and yanked it hard enough to pull out roots.

"Russ!" his wife cried.

But before anybody could stop him, Russ brought a chopping openhanded blow down across Greer's face. Hard enough to draw instant blood heavy and red in one nostril.

Cooper grabbed him, flung him back down on the couch. "Now you just stay the hell there."

"We'll finish this up when this is over," Russ Dryer said. Cooper was fifty pounds lighter and the most exercise he got was changing the channels on his TV surfer. Dryer was the outdoorsman, the quiet but decidedly macho man of the two, and his self-image had been demolished. Cooper should never have been able to throw him around like that.

"Just be quiet, Russ," Dorothy said, angry with both men.

Cooper went over to Greer, took out a bright white clean handkerchief from his back pocket and daubed at her nose.

"Are you all right?"

"Yes." Her voice was still sluggish from the drugs, but she was coherent at least.

"Who's up there, Greer?"

"My friend."

The basement door creaked open. No more than an inch. But open.

Cooper's eyes scanned the stairs. They seemed to go on forever. And the door itself seemed to loom as never before. "Greer, tell me about your friend."

Russ Dryer was on his feet and charging at Greer before Cooper could stop him. "Quit being so damned easy on her!" He seized Greer by the hair and wrenched her head back. "Now I want you to tell us who the hell is up there!"

But by now, Cooper had grabbed Russ Dryer's arm and was yanking him away from Greer. "Get back there and sit down."

Dryer still obviously remembered being pushed around just a few minutes ago. He put his fists up like an old-fashioned boxer. "You want to try me now, Cooper? You got lucky before. But not this time."

"My God, Russ," Cooper said, "I wish you could see how stupid you look. Now get back over there and sit down."

Dryer made even tighter fists and ducked into a fighter's crouch. "C'mon, Tom. This's been coming for a long, long time."

"Has it? I guess I was under the impression that we were friends," He nodded to Dorothy. "Would you please tell your gladiator here to go over there and sit his butt down."

"Don't be so damned smug," she said, not playing along. "That's what irritates him so much, Tom. You treat us all like little children."

"I'm afraid that's something you learn in med school," Cooper said.

"C'mon, Tom, hit me, c'mon."

It was as if the Dryers had suddenly started smoking some very bad dope. There was some kind of threat at the top of the stairs waiting to descend upon them—they couldn't explain the dread they felt, but it was real nonetheless. And the Dryers were picking a fight with him.

"C'mon, Tom. Hit me. And then I'll knock you on your ass."

"We're nearly seventy years old."

"I don't care. C'mon, Cooper. You think you're such hot stuff. C'mon and hit me."

So Tom hit him. The last time he could remember hitting anybody was when he was in eleventh grade and a kid named Bolan had falsely accused him of stealing something from his locker. Bolan had followed him all the way down the hall, shoving him, calling him names. So, finally, Cooper—who'd never been in a fight in his life, except when he got into it with his older sister who always won by getting him in a hammerlock—finally, Cooper just turned to Bolan and decked him. What nobody had ever told Tom was how hard on the knuckles hitting somebody was.

His knuckles were stinging now as he looked down at Russ Dryer on the floor.

"You bastard. You sucker punched me."

"I don't even know what that means, Russ. Now will you please go over and sit down and keep your mouth shut?"

The door at the top of the stairs opened two or three inches this time.

Greer angled her head—she was not quite in line with the stairs—for a better look.

Cooper, sucking on his bruised knuckles, also angled his head to see better.

The door creaked open a few more inches. And she stood there. Because she was backlit, Cooper didn't have any detailed impression of her.

Young, probably. A few years older than Greer, probably. Eighteen, nineteen. On the thin side. Dark-haired.

And now coming down the stairs, one very slow step at a time.

A couple of mysterious things were going on here as far as Abby and Candy were concerned.

There were two cars—one of them was Tom Cooper's—parked in the driveway of the cabin. But when they crept up to the window for a peek inside, they didn't see anybody. TV was on—the MUTE button had been hit—flames were blazing away in the fireplace. But they didn't see anybody.

This was like a situation in the Nancy Drew books Abby had read as a girl.

When they walked around back, they saw the young woman opening the basement door and putting her foot on the first step.

Abby whispered, "That's her? The one in your dreams. Karen?"

"Yeah."

"I thought you said she was a monster."

"She is."

"She sure doesn't look like a monster."

"Not all monsters look like monsters, Doctor. Look at George W. Bush."

Abby smiled. Candy's supply of sarcasm never ran out. Not even when they were skulking around in a creepy fog, cold, confused, scared.

"That's where everybody is," Abby said. "The basement."

"Let's see if we can look in the windows."

"Good idea."

It took several minutes to learn that there was only one basement window, and it had been completely painted over with black. But the black was streaked in places.

"Can you see anything?"

"Yes," Abby said.

"What?"

"Some kind of storage bin. That's what this window opens on."

"Fuck."

Abby still hadn't figured out if she found Candy's foul mouth to be endearing or annoying. Maybe a little of both.

"Now what?" Candy asked.

Abby, who'd been crouched on her haunches, stood up, knees cracking. "I'd say we try to sneak inside and find out what's going on."

"What about Karen?"

"Well," Abby said, "I guess we're about to find out if she's a monster or not."

Cam is aware but not aware.

There is a zone that is neither life nor death and yet not exactly between them either. Cam sees no glowing tunnels with vague figures summoning him—much as he wants to—(please let there be an afterlife, how many people having cried out that plea just as the final darkness smashes all awareness?)—out-of-body experience is probably the closest term.

Cam is watching it all take place below him. His perch seems to be on or near the ceiling of the ER where a fervid pack of medical-uniformed people are working on him.

Out-of-body experience, yes. That is the best way to describe this. Relaxed, calmly witnessing what may well be his own death, he no longer feels the cleaving pain that seemed about to rip his chest apart in two pieces.

He is simply a tourist. Watching.

The sequence of frantic work below him is not without fascination. They find a vein in his arm and insert an IV so they can administer fluids and medications.

Then a series of quick questions: What type of chest pain have you had? Any heart attacks previously? History of heart disease in you and your family? Then oxygen is rubber-capped over his mouth. Then a urinary catheter inserted. Then an ECG to test levels of pertinent chemicals in his blood (the EKG having been started immediately). Then a quick blood test to search for any indicators of heart muscle damage.

From what he can tell, the indicators are tilting in his favor. Some of the desperation is gone from the voices of the medical people working on him, the sweat sheening their faces starting to dry and their movements not so frantic and angular.

She did it. The girl who walked into his house.

He has the sense that he was able to block some of her power by holding that stupid throw pillow in front of his face. As if she had a rifle and didn't get a clear shot at him. Meant to kill but only wounded. Gave him a heart attack but not a fatal one.

And what does all this mean for Greer?

There's no doubt that's who the girl is after. But why? And where did she come from? Is she part of the secret sect that has been killing young witches over the past three hundred years?

But the sect uses crude methods, deaths faked by contriving accidents. With a power like hers, none of that would be necessary.

And, as in his case, she wouldn't have to fake anything. Even the most scrupulous medical examination would reveal that he'd had a natural heart attack and who could prove otherwise?

Greer.

Rising anxiety for the first time in this odd out-of-body state. An urgent need to find and protect Greer. Anger, now. Dread, too. Fear.

The heart monitor reflects this.

The medicos all glance at it as the unwelcome beeps begin to sound.

What the hell's going on? they must be wondering. Bastard was coming along just fine and—

The female doctor snaps an order. Some kind of medication. A black nurse sends something into the IV system. The beeping holds steady, strong for a time as all eyes watch him. In increments, the beeps slow. Are less loud. Less fatal sounding somehow. Whatever the medication was, it worked.

A strange sensation: even though he is out of his body, the most recent medication seems to be affecting him, too. His fear over Greer is blunted somehow. His will to get off this table, to find his car, to find Greer is fading as the new drug begins to overwhelm him, pull him into the center of a comfortingly gray womb.

"Much better," the female doctor says.

No picture now. Only sound.

And he knows he is no longer out of his body. But deep inside it.

Karen said, "They told you to stop this five years ago."

"Who the hell are you?" Russ Dryer said.

Karen frowned at him and turnd to Tom Cooper. "They've warned you many times. And you wouldn't listen. The way you do things has become too dangerous. There are better ways."

"And you, I take it, are that better way?" Cooper said.

"Yes." Tonelessly.

"So now what?"

"Now I take her with me."

"Greer?"

She just looked at Greer.

Cooper said, "You're one of them, aren't you?"

Karen just looked at him.

"That sonofabitch Prescott converted you somehow, didn't he? Turned your powers to work for them. Focused your powers. I've always said that. That these young girls aren't so dangerous in their natural state. But if they ever find a way to really use their powers— And that's just what that crazy bastard is doing. He's just making everything worse, and he doesn't even understand that." He looked at her. He seemed both disgusted and fascinated with what he saw. "And that's just what they've done."

"What the hell are you talking about, Tom?" Dorothy Dryer said impatiently.

"Can't you follow anything?" her husband replied. "What he means is they took a young witch and turned her into an assassin for our side. She goes everywhere and kills other young witches."

Karen said, "Untie her."

"You're giving orders now, eh?" Cooper said, some of his wry small-town mannerisms in his words.

"Yes," she said, "I am."

And so she was.

"I have to find my daughter."

"What you have to do," Dr. Emily DeWitt said, "is lie here and rest."

"She's in trouble. Very serious trouble."

"Then let me call the police for you, Mr. Morgan."

"No—you can't."

Dr. DeWitt had a pert, sweet face, silken dark hair styled short. She looked confused. "Why can't I call the police if your daughter's in trouble?"

"You just—can't. Is all."

"I see."

Delusional, he thought. *She thinks I'm delusional.*

A small, boxy white room. A window looking out on the tops of several mercury vapor parking lot lights. Three different kinds of monitors wheeled up next to the back of his bed on carts. A nurse checking an IV.

"The last thing you need right now is to be agitated, Mr. Morgan."

"I appreciate what you're saying, Dr. DeWitt. I really do. But—"

"Sedating you heavily may be the right thing to do for now."

"No, no, please. I—don't want that. I'll relax. I promise."

"What about your daughter?"

"It's just—" A quick lie. "She and her boyfriend are breaking up. He doesn't want to. He's got a bad temper. He might—"

"I'm sure she's all right, Mr. Morgan."

"I am, too. I just got overwrought, I guess."

She smiled. Touched his shoulder. "Things always seem worse when we think we're helpless."

"You keep trying my house?"

"Every ten minutes. But there's still no answer. But that doesn't mean anything. I had a boyfriend in medical school. It used to take us an entire long night to break up."

He knew he needed to convince her that he would be fine. That he'd been sedated enough already. He returned her smile. "Yeah, I guess I had a couple of relationships like that myself back in school."

"You promise to lie here and try and sleep?"

"I promise."

"I'm going to have the nurse checking on you constantly. If you're not asleep in twenty minutes, I'm going to put some more Valium into that drip."

"I'll be fine. Really."

"Anything you need, you can just press that button there. One of the nice things about ICU is that nurses are only a few seconds away."

"I know. And I appreciate it."

She touched his shoulder again. He liked that. He liked her. "Good night, Mr. Morgan."

"Good night, Doctor."

Even before she was quite out the door, he was planning on how he was going to get out of here. All he could hope was that they'd brought his clothes up here and that his wallet was in his trousers. Otherwise he'd be leaving the hospital without cash. He had to get to a phone and call Abby. He wondered if she'd found Greer yet. There was a telephone on the table next to his bed, but he was sure if a nurse heard him talking, she'd come in and put some more Valium into the drip.

Now—just how the hell was he going to get out of here?

Karen let Greer precede her up the basement stairs.

The Coopers and the Dryers sat on the sofa watching. Saying nothing. Doing nothing.

"I'm taking her with me now. And this'll be the last time you hold any kind of trial here. Do you understand?"

Russ Dryer started to say something, but Dorothy put a halting hand on his arm.

"Where are you taking Greer?" Tom Cooper asked.

"Just remember what I told you," Karen said. "No more trials."

None of them had any doubt that she would destroy them if they tried to stop her.

Then she turned and climbed up the stairs after Greer.

By the time she reached the kitchen, the image had formed perfectly in her mind. When the gas valve of a furnace stays open too long following the end of a heating cycle, too much gas is pumped into the burner so that when the sparker ignition is fired up again at the start of the next cycle, a catastrophic explosion can occur even in the most modern of furnaces.

"Hurry," Karen said to Greer.

Her mind had already opened the gas valve. The burner was flooding badly.

"Who are you?" Greer said.

"I'll explain everything later. But right now we have to get out of this house fast."

The explosion flung Abby and Candy to the ground. Neither had ever experienced an earthquake before. The sensation of the ground literally shifting beneath them was horrifically aline. Ground didn't move.

They'd been watching Greer and Karen hurrying from the house, and then they were hugging the ground, trying to understand the phenomenon at work here—huge explosions, fireballs, choking oily smoke, cracking wood, crumbling stone edifice.

Abby recovered in time to see Karen backing her car away. The explosion hadn't deterred her from her purpose—she was getting away from here fast, no matter what else was going on.

Cries, screams from the fiery interior of the house. Abby knew there was nothing she could do. But even though she hated the people in the house for what they'd done to her kind down through the years, she wanted to help them. Nobody should die this way. But what could she do?

The screams had distracted her.

She needed to be in her car. Following Karen.

Candy was already at the car, calling for her over the popping flames and collapsing wood and dying cries.

Then Abby was behind the wheel, backing up, shooting down the driveway to the highway.

"She went right," Candy said.

And right it was.

"Damn fog," Candy complained.

Even this early in the evening, the fog was getting heavier—almost cottony—and visibility was fading fast. Abby was familiar with all the curves of this stretch of asphalt but even so she couldn't drive any faster than forty. Not safely, anyway.

Blood-red taillights appearing-vanishing, appearing-vanishing in the murk ahead.

"I hope that's her," Abby said.

"It is."

"How do you know?"

Candy grinned. "I have special powers, remember?"

9

HIS clothes were there. His wallet wasn't. He'd unplugged the monitors, but he'd have to move fast.

He went to the door of his room and peeked out. Several doors to the left was a corner. Around it was the Intensive Care nurses' station. To the right was a door with a sign: KEEP CLOSED AT ALL TIMES. This would lead to the general hall and the elevators.

He was just about to try his luck when his nurse came around the corner from the station. He recognized her as the one who'd been with Dr. DeWitt.

What if she were coming here? What if she came looking for him in his room?

He started to rush back to his bed. He'd throw covers over himself, pretend to be sleeping.

The pain started in the center of his chest—just as it had in the house earlier tonight—and jumped up to his shoulder. Oh, my God, not another heart attack. Not now.

The pain slowed him considerably. He was freezing with sweat and shaking with fatigue by the time he reached the bed. He crawled up in it and pulled the covers over him.

She went on by. Squeaking shoes.

He heard the door to the unit open and close.

So how the hell was he going to get out of here when he couldn't even get to the door and back without nearly collapsing?

They were out of familiar territory and the fog was getting thicker, ghostly snakes of it coiling and uncoiling around Abby's car, undulating, slithering damply across the windshield.

A miasma; wraith-shapes. Poe words from high school English. A hell.

The taillights in front of them shone more often now. Karen had to slow down, too.

Faintly in the distance, through occasional tatters of fog, they could glimpse lights. A truck stop? A small town? Some kind of optical illusion?

"The 'Twilight Zone'," Abby said.

"No kidding."

Another slow smile. Distant lights no longer so distant. One readable red neon sign behind wisps of roiling gray: GAS.

"I used to go out with this guy," Candy said, "this county sheriff. Every single time we'd go by a sign that said GAS, he'd put his hand on his stomach and say, 'I sure do.' Every single time. Talk about runnin' a joke into the ground. That's why I broke up with him."

"That's a good reason."

"Well, that and the fact that he was the cheapest

bastard west of the Mississippi River. And he didn't change his underwear more than once a week. And that he was married."

"Say, he sounds like the kind of guy I'm looking for. You wouldn't still have his phone number, would you?"

"You won't need no phone number. You and Cam Morgan'll be gettin' together."

"If you say so."

But somehow that didn't sound nearly as ridiculous—unthinkable—as it would have forty-eight hours ago.

The town, lost to coiling, wet gloom, appeared gradually. There was the GAS truck stop, a bowling alley, a lumberyard, a post office, two taverns, a tiny white church. This was the first of two blocks that had been zoned commercial.

No sign of Karen's car.

Oh, and there were no people. Not outside. Nor—from what they could see—inside any of the buildings. A resolute and unnatural silence was upon the place, and only the sound of a lonely lost dog—or perhaps of a wolf—could be heard. The baying sound like that of the people trapped inside the fire at the Coopers' cabin.

And there was no sign of the car they'd been following.

Abby pulled over into the parking lot of a darkened gas station. The whitewashed walls of the small building glowed in the gloom; you felt phantoms at the windows, peering out at you.

"We've lost them," Candy said. "I never have any of my powers when I need them. I wonder if Wonder Woman ever has times like this?"

They sat silently at the bottom of a swirling sea of fog. Oncoming cars passed; little more than headlights and the suggested shapes of grilles and hoods; and pierced deeper into the gloom and vanished, ghost-shapes that might have monsters for drivers, or no drivers at all.

"It's getting worse," Abby said.

"Maybe they had to pull off, too."

"That's what I was thinking."

"I hate to just sit here."

"Then let's go."

This was one of those nights when the radio stations would be warning drivers to stay off the roads unless absolutely necessary. So here they were.

Driving.

She started out at about fifteen miles an hour. Increased it to twenty and just stayed there, creeping through the silver wraiths that encircled her car.

A few oncoming cars, moving about the same rate of speed as hers. Suggested shapes of houses on the right. The left was lost to them. They seemed to be out of the tiny business district. The windshield wipers made enormous noise in the quiet car. They were in hell.

The fog began to thin enough so they could see the moon and the outline of gnarled, mist-blackened leafless tree limbs. The car began to labor slightly. They were going up a hill. She hadn't realized till now that the town had been in a deep abrupt valley. Her attention had been so fixed on the road that she hadn't appreciated the feeling of descending. But now they were ascending and the fog was being pulled apart, like sticky kid fingers on cotton candy. She could actually see now, place herself in a context. They were right on the edge of town and—

"There!" Candy practically yelled.

She'd seen the motel before Abby did. One of those shabby, one-story, six-room jobs. Karen's car was pulled up in front of one of the doors.

"I see it," Abby said.

She was already pulling in.

He found the EXIT sign.

Stairway. Stairwell. Cold. Empty. Echoing.

Hurrying down.

Find a door on the ground floor leading outside.

Call Abby and—

This time, the pain started in his arm rather than his chest. He slumped against the wall, holding tight to the metal railing. The rough concrete wall was cold when he pressed his face against it.

Sweat. Hot and cold at the same time, it seemed. How was that possible?

A swift feeling of unreality. He was pain, he was chills, he was panic.

And yet unreal. This was a dream somehow.

The pain—the terrible pain—was in his chest now.

He reached out. He cried out.

He collapsed.

There was no warning. There was no drama. They were there to take Greer, forcibly if necessary.

One moment Abby and Candy were standing outside the door of Room 6 of the Traveler's Friend Motel when it happened. It happened to both of them and at the same time.

Abby had just been about to raise her hand to knock when Karen entered her mind. And Candy's mind.

Abby became aware of her surroundings. Damp cold. Warped and faded wooden door. Cracked smudgy window to right of door. Cracked sidewalk beneath her feet. Rumble of distant truck. Country music a few doors down. A lone and lonely light in the parking lot. A dumpster with its lid open.

Karen didn't speak in words exactly. But she did express a thought, a command: *Leave here and don't come back.*

There were no words between Abby and Candy, either. Abby's head gave a little jerk, as if it had just experienced an unpleasant sensation. Candy's left eyelid went into a brief tic.

They looked at each other. But not with any particular meaning or import. Candy sneezed. Abby walked back to the car, got in, keyed the ignition.

Abby said, "You hungry?"

"Yeah; I kind of am."

"Why don't we head back to Hastings Corner and get a pizza or something?"

"That sounds great, actually."

"Sausage."

"Veggie," Abby said.

"Veggie? Who eats veggie pizza?"

"I do."

"God made pizza to put sausage on."

"I'm glad to know He spends His time weighing in on such lofty matters."

"And He wants us to drink Pepsi with it. Real Pepsi. Not that Diet crap."

"I learn so much when I'm with you. Anything else I should know about God?"

"He thinks I'm pretty cool for an old broad."

"Well, there, God and I are in perfect agreement," Abby laughed. "Because I think you're pretty cool for an old broad, too."

They went on this way for some time.

They traveled down in the valley where the fog was worse. But when they came up out of the valley on the far side, the visibility got at least marginally better.

Abby felt a queer peace. A kind of Valium peace. *Sure there are wars going on all over the planet. Sure disease is running rampant. Sure our political system is corrupt and in shambles. Sure I'm falling in love with that damned Cam Morgan. But I'm so happy. I'm so blissed out. . . .*

She smiled at the thought of the seventies phrase, "blissed out." At least, she thought it was a seventies phrase. Maybe it was sixties. Sometimes, it was hard to tell. There was an overlap between the time of acid rock and disco music. She'd participated in both eras without quite being a part of either. Laura had been the same way. They'd both regarded themselves as somehow outside of fashion and time. Probably because their secret was ageless and their secret was both freedom and prison for them.

Abby said, "What the hell happened back there?"

"Back where?"

"That motel. I'm just starting to remember—"

"We followed the car there."

"Yes. And then what?"

"Then we went up to the door and—"

"And what?" Abby asked. And Abby was starting to remember even more details—

"And then—"

"And then we turned around and went back to the car and drove away."

"God, that's right, isn't it? Now I remember it."

Abby saw it all clearly. Going up to the door. Wanting to raise her hand and knock. And then the message in her head. *Go away. Don't come back.*

And they'd done it. Hadn't resisted in any way. Had simply done it.

"We're going back," Abby said.

"Damn right we are," Candy agreed.

Dr. Emily DeWitt was drinking coffee and joking with some of the ER people when a code blue summoned her back to work. This had been quite the night. Two bad car accidents due to the fog. And Mr. Morgan with his heart attack. But it was one of those nights when her training made her feel useful. The people in the accidents, while pretty badly injured, were going to survive handily. And Mr. Morgan was asleep up in Intensive Care.

She jogged down the long corridor to the ER, steeling herself for what lay ahead. Just as long as it wasn't a kid. She'd had a spate of kids in the past three weeks. And had lost two of them. Both car wrecks. Both sitting free, no child safety seats. On one of them—a woman who'd lost it and shrieked and blamed her child's death on the incompetence of the ambulance crew—Emily almost lost it. Almost told the woman that if she had been a good mother and had properly secured her child—and hadn't impaired her driving abilities by having whatever number of alcoholic drinks she'd obviously had—maybe her little boy would still be alive. But, thank God, she hadn't. The woman would suffer enough for the rest of her life. She didn't need some smug, thirty-two-year-old snot of a doc making things worse.

The gurney was just bursting through the doors—just like on all those TV medical shows except she wasn't beautiful and none of the staff males here were hunks—the doors burst open and then she saw him and couldn't believe the information her eyes were feeding her brain.

There lay Mr. Morgan—or his clone—on the gurney. Wearing the same clothes he'd worn when she'd worked on him earlier tonight. And the male nurse was saying, "Heart attack, Doc."

"Heart attack? Heart attack?" Emily said. "I must be losing my mind. This guy was down here a couple of hours ago, and we got him all set up and shipped him up to Intensive. Why the hell does he have his clothes on?"

"One of the janitors found him in the stairwell."

Oh, this was going to look good in the papers. Heart attack victim found wandering around—fully clothed—in the bowels of the hospital. The hospital director had just warned them that because of a few minor screwups—and they were minor and every hospital made them—one of the local TV stations (sweeps week being on the horizon) was angling for a scare story on hospital incompetence.

And here they'd just handed them a beaut. Morgan had obviously gotten himself dressed and sneaked away from Intensive. But still and all, hadn't anybody seen him? The monitors should have signaled the nurses' station that something had gone terribly wrong—

"He's in bad shape," the nurse said.

"He's not the only one," Emily DeWitt said.

And got to work.

Thank God there were still a few competent people left around here, anyway.

Abby and Candy got out of the car and walked back to the door of Room 6. Everything seemed the same except that the country music had been turned off in one of the nearby rooms. Fog. Spectral neons—blue, red, pus-yellow—faint in the mist.

As before, Abby raised her hand and . . .

Karen: *You can't help her now. I want you to go away and leave us alone.*

"Bitch," Candy said.

What before had simply been a command—*leave*—was now articulated language inside the heads of Abby and Candy.

Instinctively, Abby reached for the doorknob.

The jolt—she could only think of it as a ragged arc of electricity—paralyzed her entire right side and forced her to slump against the door.

But even with the physical grief, she knew what she had to do—somehow push Karen's thoughts from her mind. She didn't have enough power to battle Karen. But she had to learn how to keep her at bay.

Candy tried the door now.

Instantly, blood boiled from her nostrils, as if someone had crushed her nose. Candy clamped her hands over her face, trying to staunch the blood. She stumbled forward toward the hood of Abby's car, blood sieving through her fingers.

The partial paralysis still kept her from moving with any power or force, but as she slumped against the door, she once again tried the knob.

Karen: *I have no reason to hurt you now. Just leave, the way you did before.*

Abby: *I don't know who or what you are. But you're not going to take Greer.*

The answer was swift. A second ragged arc of electricity traveled up Abby's spine and she went into a grotesque, momentary dance that would be comic to anybody observing it.

Karen made her pay this time. Object lesson, no doubt. Show Abby and Candy once and for all who was in charge of this moment in front of this fogbound motel in this nowhere little burg.

But, for all the agony, rage was now developing in Abby. Before there had just been pain and helplessness. Yet now she found herself furious that, for all Greer had suffered, this young woman—whoever, whatever she was—was going to make her suffer even more.

As Abby's own daughter had suffered. As Laura had suffered. As Abby's sisters down the ages had suffered.

Abby: *I'm coming in.*

Karen: *You can't. I won't let you.*

"Abby, don't," Candy said, grabbing her arm. "Next time, she'll kill you."

"I'm getting Greer. And she's not going to stop me."

Karen: *Don't make me hurt you any more, Abby.*

Candy noticed it even before Abby did. Karen was in both their heads.

"She's not as strong," Candy said.

And she was right. Like a radio signal fading, Karen's mental voice had ebbed considerably.

And then Abby looked down to see Candy's hand in hers—she hadn't been aware of it till now—and a memory came rushing back. The day with Cam. Laura's broken arm. Abby trying to heal it. Unable to until they joined minds and concentrated as one to effect the healing.

That's what was happening now.

Their hands were joined. And their minds were joined.

And together they had strength enough to push Karen out of their consciousness.

"Do you see what's happening here?" Abby said, still hunched over with pain.

"I sure do," Candy said, "we're gonna kick her ass around the block."

All Abby could compare it to were those long ago hokey Coca Cola commercials where teenagers from various countries standing on a hill held hands and sang to the heavens. Which was pretty much what you had here. Except they weren't singing. Except that they weren't teenagers. Except that they weren't on a hill. Well, the motel was sort of on an incline, anyway.

The two previous times they'd touched minds with Karen, she'd initiated it. And they'd been startled. This time, they initiated it, and it was Karen who was startled.

Karen: *They said you couldn't do this.*

Abby/Candy: *Who said we couldn't do what?*

Karen: *Couldn't mindmerge.*

Abby/Candy: *Well, obviously they were wrong. We want in.*

Karen: *I have to take her back.*

Abby/Candy: *Back to where?*

Karen: *I—I can't say.*

Abby/Candy: *You're one of us, aren't you?*

Karen: *No!*

Abby/Candy: *A witch.*

Karen: *No. I am against witches. That's why I'm taking her back.*

Abby/Candy: *And that's why you killed all those people back at the cabin? And they were your own kind.*

Karen: *They wouldn't do what the sect leader had told them to.*

Abby/Candy: *So you'll take Greer back, and you'll destroy her, too.*

Karen: *No, they won't destroy her. They don't destroy the ones I bring back.*

Abby/Candy: *Then what do they do?*

Karen: *I'm not sure.*

Abby/Candy: *We're breaking the merge for now.*

Karen: *What? Why?*

But Abby/Candy withdrew.

Abby said, "I guess they assumed that we didn't have any powers left. That we were too old."

"Well, they were wrong, those shitheads."

Abby grinned. "Did your mother ever wash your mouth out with soap?"

"No, but the maid did a couple of times."

Abby nodded to the doorknob. "Think we can open that?"

"Together? No problem."

"I hope you're right. It's the only way we're going to get in there."

Candy held out her hand. Abby took it. This time, the merge was even purer than it had been when they'd conversed with Karen. They left their damp, foggy world behind and existed now on a plain that was without sensory data impeding them in any way. Darkness—and yet beyond darkness, a richer, deeper, truer absence of color than simple darkness could ever be. And they were as one, without individual identities at this moment, a single soul.

In the face of such power—and this only hinted at the potential for power their merge represented—the lock was suddenly sprung open and hung limply from the door.

They could feel Karen trying to enter their merge, trying to take over their consciousness as she'd done earlier. But this time, she had no control over them whatsoever. It was as if she were flinging her frail body against a wall of steel.

Abby/Candy pushed the door inward with their minds.

And then—the merge broken again—Abby and Candy walked inside the motel room.

Greer sat hunched in the far corner of the small room. Apprehension played on her face. She started to say something, but an angry glance from Karen silenced her.

The place reeked of stale cigarette smoke and cheap

carpeting soaked with everything from beer to vomit. It was one of those grubby places that hadn't been cleaned, or touched by sunlight, in long grim years.

Candy turned on a massive table lamp. They got their first real look at Karen. To Abby she resembled one of those heavily drugged patients you saw on the nonviolent wards of psychiatric hospitals.

"You let Greer go, you bitch, or—" Candy started toward Karen, making fists of her small hands.

Abby put a hand on Candy's shoulder. "It's all right, Candy. Let me talk to her."

Abby was trying to understand what had happened here. Karen, whomever and whatever she was, had just lapsed into a stupor. She'd lost her bearings when they'd defeated her in the mindmerge. She had obviously been programmed to take Greer. But now she seemed lost. Attacking her verbally was no way to deal with her.

Abby went up to the young woman. "There's no reason to be afraid."

And then Greer was on her feet. "Oh, Abby! I was so scared!"

And running around the side of the bed and throwing her arms around Abby.

Greer was trembling. Abby could smell the drugs Dr. Cooper had used on her.

Candy said, "This calls for a smoke." And promptly sat down and lit it up.

Greer went over and sat down on the bed. And nodded to Karen. "Something happened to her just a few minutes ago. She kind of—shut down. Just stopped completely. She's been like that ever since."

Abby took Karen by the hand and led her over to

a straight-backed chair. Over her shoulder, to Greer, she said, "You'd better call your dad, honey. He's very worried about you."

Greer got an outside line and called her house. She got the answering machine. "He's out somewhere. I'll try his cell phone." She dialed the number and was surprised to hear a female voice say, "This is Cam Morgan's phone."

"Who's this?"

"This is Katy Bannion. I'm a nurse in Intensive Care."

"Intensive Care," Greer said. And when she said it both Abby and Candy snapped their heads around, looking at her. "Is my father there?"

"May I have your name, please?"

"I'm Greer Morgan. His daughter." Her eyes wild with fear, Greer cupped the phone and said, "Dad's in Intensive Care, Abby. I don't know what's going on." The kidnapping and the drugs had left Greer in a precarious mental state.

Abby gently took the phone. Candy helped Greer to the bed, where she sat down. Candy had a cigarette burning in the corner of her mouth, and blinked every few seconds from the smoke scorching her eyes.

"This is Dr. Stewart."

"Oh, hello, Doctor. This is Katy Bannion."

"Tell me about Cam Morgan."

Bannion gave her all the pertinent facts with professional dispatch. Abby felt terrible for Cam when she heard he'd tried to escape from the hospital. A lion searching crazily for his cub, even at the cost of his own life. She wasn't sure if she loved him in the romantic sense—though she certainly was edging right up to that—but she felt a kinship with him she'd never known before.

Abby said, "I'm sending Greer and a friend of ours named Candy there right now. It'll take them a couple of hours, because of the fog and all. If it's at all possible, I'd like Greer to see her father. Right away."

"Is Mr. Morgan your patient?"

"He is now. He and Greer have both become my patients." She smiled at Greer as she said it.

"What's going on?" Candy said, as soon as Abby had hung up. "Where are you going?"

"For now, nowhere," Abby said. She nodded to Karen. "I want to spend some time with Karen. Find out where she came from and what's going on."

Candy looked Karen up and down and shuddered. "She gives me the creeps."

"She's one of us," Abby said. Then she explained to Greer why Cam was in Intensive Care.

"Could we go?" Greer said. "I want to see Dad as soon as possible."

Greer gave Abby another hug and then went to the door. The long night was beginning to show in her posture. She managed to look anxious but exhausted at the same time, stoop-shouldered in a way that didn't fit anybody her age.

"Just drive carefully," Abby told Candy, "with the fog and all."

"We'll be fine," Candy said. Then smiled. "But thanks for the tip, Mommy."

Abby sat in one of the spindly wooden chairs listening to Candy back out of the parking spot in front of the door. Plumbing sounds. A large commercial airliner somewhere in the murky night above. And Karen sitting perfectly still, perfectly silent in the stained and tattered armchair with the soiled doilies on both arms. Still passive, still staring out at something not in this room.

"Karen, I'm a doctor, an M.D., but I've had extensive training in psychology. I want to help you. Can you understand what I'm saying?"

Karen didn't respond in any fashion.

"A few minutes ago, we merged minds. You're one of us. That's what I want to explore with you. Your background and who sent you to Hastings Corner. Whoever they are, Karen, they're not your friends. They've manipulated your mind to make you think they are. But they're not. They're using you to destroy your own kind. Tonight, they even used you to destroy their own kind. I'm still not sure why you killed all those people at Dr. Cooper's cabin."

Disappointment again. If Karen was taking any of this in, she didn't let on. Sitting perfectly straight. Staring at something well beyond Abby's ken.

"I know the mindmerge frightened you," Abby went on patiently. "It sort of frightened me, too. I couldn't accomplish it on my own. It took two of us working together. But you're having some kind of breakdown now. Your mind has sort of shut down here. I need to talk to you, Karen. But I need your help to do it. I want to mindmerge again. But you have to be my partner, the way Candy was. You have to help me mindmerge."

A faint sound in Karen's throat. It could have been a simple accidental sound. Abby hoped it was a signal of recognition. Karen understanding what was about to happen.

Abby: *Karen. You can trust me. That's the first thing you have to understand.*

(nothing)

Abby: *Karen. You have to open your mind. But before you can do that, you have to trust me.*

(nothing)

Abby: *Karen.*

Karen: *My parents.*

Loud and clear; so loud and clear, the two words startled her there inside her mind.

Abby: *What about your parents, Karen?*

Karen: *Dr. Prescott wouldn't let me call them.*

Abby: *Who is Dr. Prescott?*

And then Karen slowly began to explain it all.

They had a son in college at Harvard and a daughter who lived in LA and worked for CBS News there, the Prescotts did. In this day and age, anything could go wrong. Middle-of-the-night phone calls tended to do appalling things to one's heart rate.

The phone was on David Prescott's side of the queen-sized bed he shared with his wife Diane. "Oh, God," he heard her say just before he picked up.

"It's Bev," the voice said. "I'm really sorry about calling at this hour, Dr. Prescott." Prescott cupped the receiver and said, "It's the clinic, honey. You go back to sleep."

She groped across the darkness and found his hand. Touched it momentarily. Then rolled back over on her side facing away from him and went almost instantly back to sleep. She was one of the lucky ones who could do that.

"What's going on?"

"We've lost all contact with Karen, Doctor. Doesn't answer her cell phone. Hasn't made contact the last three call-periods."

Tonight was supposed to be the night. By now, the entire circle of sect members should be dead and Karen headed back to Wayfaring. With Greer Morgan in tow.

"Anything on the news?"

"The explosion at the cabin has been reported."

"Did they account for all the bodies yet?"

"No. The news is just saying 'several.' "

"So she got at least that far."

"But something must've happened. For her not to check in with us, I mean."

He knew why Bev had called. What if Karen had been detained by the police for some reason? What if Greer Morgan had hurt her in some way? Or what if the drugs—always risky—had started acting negatively on her? Any number of early trials with other witches had resulted in complete mental breakdowns, the way the CIA LSD experiments of the fifties and sixties had led to suicide and murder. No reason it couldn't happen to Karen.

There would be three of them down there working and waiting for Greer's call. Now that it hadn't come, they wanted Daddy to come in and hold their collective hand, Daddy being Prescott, of course. He was the boss—and more importantly, he was the one who'd sent her on this mission. Let him be the one who handled it now that it seemed to be in difficulty of an unknown nature.

He had laid in several urgent commands for her to make her designated calls. Let him figure out what the hell was going on—and deal with it.

"I'm coming down."

"We really appreciate this."

"I need half an hour."

"Fine."

After he hung up, he rolled over and lay for a time no more than an inch from the sleeping form of his wife. The heat of her body had always been erotic to him. She was a warm woman in every respect—images of her in the delivery room, the flush of motherhood; of her in sex, the blush of lust; of her in prayer, the rosy glow of reverence—and he was caught up in a need to hold her now. But he couldn't be that selfish. If he did hold her, she'd wake up. And if she woke up, she'd ask questions. And if she asked questions, and he answered them honestly, she'd probably never get back to sleep.

She spent three days a week working at a local orphanage. She hadn't known about his obsession when she married him. As a member of the sect, she knew of course that some witches needed to be hunted down and destroyed, but—but her husband's zealotry was something that overwhelmed her sometimes. For this reason, he rarely discussed his work with her anymore. She had her orphans— "You're about death, David; I need to be around life, the little kids I see, or I'm not sure I could handle this marriage at all." And it was all the more angry for the simple and unemotional way she'd said it. Twice a day, every day of his life, he replayed those words.

He eased himself out of bed.

And then he started worrying about Karen.

The drive to Wayfaring took forty-six minutes. They stopped twice, once for Karen to go to the bathroom, once to get something to eat. Abby had coffee, a waffle, and scrambled eggs; Karen had an English muffin and coffee. Karen went to the john and returned quickly.

Abby was still having a difficult time judging if Karen's mind had cleared of Dr. Prescott's influence. Though she'd told Abby everything she could remember, there was still anger in her response when Abby said anything negative about Prescott.

"He's just doing what he thinks is right, Dr. Stewart."

"I wish you'd call me Abby. And what he's trying to do is destroy us. You, me, everybody like us. We're not a threat to anybody. At least, most of us aren't. We could be a great boon to the rest of humanity if they didn't try and eradicate us first."

"He's a sincere man, Dr. Stewart. And a nice one."

Some variation of the Stockholm syndrome, Abby supposed. The victim identifying with her captor. Or maybe this was simply the residual effects of the drugs he had pumped into her during his brainwashing sessions. Karen didn't seem to understand that was what had happened to her—that her entire identity had been altered by drugs, psychotherapy and autohypnotic suggestion, i.e., brainwashing.

Karen used her napkin to wipe away some butter from her lips. "I need to go to the bathroom again."

Abby didn't want to give Karen the impression she was Abby's prisoner. She said, "Want me to order you some more coffee while you're gone?"

"Thanks. That sounds nice." She still sounded confused, as if she weren't quite sure how to respond to Abby. Friend or foe? Karen had come here to do some things for Dr. Prescott. She'd killed the remaining members of the sect but Greer had escaped.

"Karen."

Karen was on her feet. "Yes?"

"I'm trying to be your friend."

"I know."

"I'm sorry if the—if when Candy and I merged with you—if that made things even more confusing. But I need to confront Prescott and tell him to let you go. To purge your mind entirely. And to stop what he's doing in general. I can always go to the police."

"But that—"

"That would expose us, yes. But it would also put all these people in prison for murder. Including Prescott."

Karen said coolly, "I'll be back in a little bit."

Abby watched her go.

So hard to know what was going on in Karen's mind.

On her way back to the john, Karen noticed a cove-like section in the wall in back of the coatrack. A pay phone. She was pretty sure Abby wouldn't be able to see her if she ducked in there. She went into the bathroom.

While she was washing up at the sink, Karen watched her reflection in the mirror. And was frightened. Dr. Prescott would be very unhappy if he ever found out that she'd told Abby everything. The clinic. How Dr. Prescott converted witches into hunters, hunting down and sometimes destroying their own kind. She had to tell Dr. Prescott what she'd done and maybe because she was so honest, he would forgive her. Something had happened to her back in that motel room when the mindmerge had taken place. Candy and Abby ganging up on her that way. Confusion. Conflicting loyalties. Memories.

She had to act quickly.

She left the bathroom and went right to the pay phone that was in a small knotty pine cove. She dialed the number to reverse charges, then gave number and name to the operator.

"I have a collect call here for a Maria from Karen. Will you accept the charges?"

"Yes, of course." Maria—excited. "Karen. Where are you? We've been worried sick."

She told her everything, quickly. Then: "She's coming back with me. She's going to turn Dr. Prescott over to the police if he doesn't go along with her. She scares me."

"Don't you worry about her, Karen. You just bring her back here and then she'll be our problem. You need a good long rest."

"You're my friends. I want us to be together. I love all of you."

"And we love you, too, Karen. Dr. Prescott's on the way here now. He's going to be very happy you called. See you in a little while."

"Sorry I took so long," Karen said when she came back from the john.

"No problem."

"Could we go? I guess I don't need any more coffee. I'd just have to slow us down with pee breaks, anyway."

Abby nodded. She was eager to get going again, too.

Abby paid the bill, and they were soon on the road.

David Prescott listened as Maria recounted the conversation for the third time. Prescott worried that there might be some kind of code buried in the message. Maybe somebody had literally been holding a gun to Karen's head; or maybe the police had arrested her and were using her to get them inside Wayfaring peacefully. Or maybe it was simply lack of sleep—maybe he was getting paranoid the way he always did when dawn was near. Something about the transition from night to day had always spooked him. He'd never known why.

They were in Prescott's office, drinking coffee. The sky was a blanched white color except for a few heavy dark storm clouds. There was an unreality to this time of day. A netherworld feeling.

"She didn't sound scared?"

"No," Maria said. "In a hurry. But not scared."

"She didn't say where she was?"

Maria sighed. "I don't think we're going to learn anything by going over this again. No offense."

Prescott shrugged. "No, I guess you're right. I guess all we can do is let them come in here and see what happens."

"I just wish you'd leave Kylie alone. Being a young woman is one thing—but being a little girl—"

He didn't respond to her complaint. "Think I'll run upstairs and see how Kylie and the others are doing." Then: "I've got to give you one thing, Maria. You're certainly relentless."

"She's not a killer. She's an innocent little girl. You're perverting her whole nature."

"Don't forget you're a part of our sect, too, Maria. We have to destroy witches where we find them. And use whatever tool God gives us."

"I don't think God would approve of using children this way."

He smiled coldly. "Guess I'll just have to talk with God about that, won't I?"

He took the elevator. Halfway to the third floor, he wished he'd walked. The exercise would help him focus on the situation better.

The floor was dark except for the red PRIVATE sign burning over the entrance door. He took out his master key and let himself in.

Thunder growled as he stepped inside the small, shadowy room. And then a sudden slashing rain. No warning whatsoever. It ticked against the barred windows with the force of small hailstones. If any of the girls heard it, they didn't let on. Three beds. Three female forms beneath matching sun-yellow blankets. Damp snoring from one of the girls; a moaning from another, a nightmare perhaps, or a sexual fantasy—or a melding of both. The third girl was the only one sleeping on her back. Her hands were folded primly on her stomach, the way she'd look in her coffin.

The room was warmer than he'd like. But this was the temperature they seemed to prefer. He liked to keep them as comfortable and happy as possible.

What he was doing to their minds was so invasive they at least deserved to enjoy their surroundings.

He went to each of them, touched their foreheads in the manner of a minister anointing someone. And in a way, that's what he was doing. As much as he was a medical and scientific man, he was also a spiritual man. He was redeeming their souls. They were now walking in the light instead of the darkness, making this Earth safer for those who knew the true ways of God. This was an ancient battle, the one with the witches, but thanks to modern science, it would someday—and not too far in the future, either—be won.

They were, in a way, his daughters. And he loved them very much.

He walked to the next door and looked in on Kylie. Maria was right. She *was* an innocent. And that's exactly what would make her such a deadly weapon. Who wouldn't invite this young girl in? Who wouldn't trust her?

He went back downstairs to prepare for Karen's return.

"Rain scares me."

The first time Karen had spoken in half an hour.

"Scares me sometimes, too."

It was a cutting rain. Gutters filling. Front yards soggy. Intersections starting to flood. They were passing through a handsome little town still in slumber at 5:43 A.M. Everybody would want to sleep in. Nice and warm under the covers. Have a late breakfast. Read the paper. Watch TV. Read a novel. Or just raise rainy-day hell if you were a tyke. Those were the thoughts that would be dancing in their heads now. But they were whimsy and nothing more. Today was a workday. Duties. Deadlines. Bosses. Warm beds exchanged for the cold, cold world.

"Are you scared about going back to Wayfaring?"

"You're the one who should be scared."

A threat, a definite threat in Karen's voice. Defiance. Hard to figure her out. Sometimes she'd be almost friendly. And then a harshness would fill her eyes and voice and— It was almost as if she were phasing in and out of the mind control techniques Prescott had used on her.

"Why should I be scared?"

"He's not going to like you."

"I don't care if he likes me, Karen. I just want him to stop what he's doing. Neither one of us can afford exposure, so we have to work out some kind of solution to this. It's way past time. They've been destroying us for centuries. In a way, they're our prisoners just as much as we're their prisoners. They should want to end this as much as we do."

"They don't, though." Her voice was suddenly neutral again. No hostility at all.

"You realize that at some point, he'll have to kill you, too. He'll have you recruit others, and he'll brainwash them. They'll be younger and stronger and fresher, and his techniques will keep on evolving so that they're smarter, too. More cunning. More adaptable. More useful to him. And so he'll kill you and all the others of your group. You'll be too dangerous to him, everything you've done and know, I mean."

Karen stared out the window. They were in the

country again. The rain battered everything. Abby felt weary, somewhat disoriented. Needed sleep. Needed to see how Cam was.

Karen again said, to herself really, "Rain scares me."

The nurses finally let Greer in just after the shift finished changing. She'd been in the waiting room for two hours. Candy had been good company right up to the point where she'd fallen asleep with a copy of *The National Enquirer* over her face. Greer had to admit the headline was interesting, anyway. "Barbara Bush's love child!" Who woulda thunk it?

Then finally she was standing next to her father's very white bed in this very white room. They had enough monitors going to outfit a spaceship. Each one had a different face and made a different sound. They were impressive and spooky. She knew that if any one of them suddenly stopped, her father's life would be in great peril.

She didn't wake him, at first. He looked too frail, too pale, too waxen to wake. She reached out, hand trembling, and touched his face. Her hand almost jerked away, as if she'd just touched a hot stove. But this sensation was the opposite. He was cold. She thought of frogs in bio class. He was like that. Dead cold.

His left eyelid lifted. It was one of those sudden acts that was so graceless it was amusing to see. As if he was playing hide and seek with her the way he used to when she was little. He'd pretend to be asleep, and she'd run and hide, but sometimes she'd catch him with that left eyelid lifting.

She almost smiled. But stopped herself. Because she realized that there was no recognition in the odd blue gaze of the eye. Some kind of autonomic impulse had opened it. He wasn't seeing her. Her impression was that he was seeing—nothing.

One of the monitors gave a tiny bleep, and she wheeled on it, as if to confront it, accuse it of something heinous. Death was everywhere now—her mother's death—Jeff's death—and now the possible death of her father. The monitors should all be going berserk. All over the world monitors should be going berserk. People should be teeming in the streets and looking up at the sky and screaming hysterically, the way they did in those rotten *Godzilla* movies her folks used to watch on TV and giggle over. Death was everywhere, but people pretended otherwise. They went about their daily lives, their daily chores as if everything were just fine and dandy. As if death weren't waiting in their car with the brake linings worn or hovering near a grade school playground just itching to get a tiny one in the front seat or just pulling into a convenience store parking lot with a semiautomatic pistol ready to shoot the shit out of everybody and everything in the store.

But now Greer was aware. The awareness consumed her, overwhelmed her, made her see that there was really no place to hide.

And then she was leaning down and hugging her father. . . .

And her hot tears were glistening on her father's face.

And then there were two very white nurses in the very white room by the very white bed and they were gently leading her away as she sobbed, "Oh, please don't die, Daddy! Please don't die!"

10

THE town of Bannister was everything a sentimental landscape painter could want. Towering church steeples; a large octagonal-shaped bandstand in the center of a town square that dated back to the early 1800s; street after street of small, well-kept houses and yards in an explosion of New England styles; and a college campus that had been kept in a time capsule since the 1930s, when coeds were jitterbugging to Benny Goodman, all vine-snaked buildings with mullioned windows and enough dormers and cornices to please even an Oxford graduate.

The clinic was two blocks east of campus. In the rain, the black iron fence surrounding it looked even more forbidding, and the building itself, a faux Italianate two-story of red brick, looked both domestic and institutional at the same time. A front-gabled central section was flanked by two wings. Lights burned through the louvered windows on the ground floor. Smoke smudged the sky with a sooty color. The place had the air of a century-old mansion just now beginning to feel its age.

Abby pulled right up to the gate. There was a small gatehouse but no guard in sight.

"Four quick honks."

"What?" Abby said.

"That's the signal."

"I see." Abby wasn't sure why, but it seemed odd that Karen would have retained this information. Even though she'd need it upon her return from a successful mission, given all her confusion—escaping from then sliding back into her brainwashing—how would she ever remember such a detail?

But it was the morning, and all the stress was probably making her paranoid. There was likely a simple and believable explanation for how Karen had come to know the signal.

Abby gave her horn four light taps.

Nothing happened.

"Maybe they changed the code."

"Wait," Karen said.

The black wings of the iron gates began to open slowly. Abby had a clear look at the asphalt road that made a U up and around the house. A three-car garage near a wooded backyard was shut tight.

Abby slowly moved the car inside.

"I told them we were coming."

"What?"

"At the restaurant where we had breakfast. There was a pay phone near the women's bathroom. I called them and told them we'd be coming."

Literal chills. Goose bumps up and down her arms. "Why would you do that, Karen?"

The two women looked at each other intently. "I

haven't told you this till now, Abby. I wanted to get you here so you'd give Dr. Prescott a chance."

Abby's eyes were back on the road. "A chance for what?"

"The technology isn't all there yet. You're right about that. You're also right that it'll take several more groups of women like me to help him perfect it. But I don't mind being a part of it all. A small part."

"A small part of what, Karen? Vigilantes who hunt down their own kind and kill them? That's how you want to spend your life?"

"He'll convert us, Abby. He'll use us for good instead of evil."

"But we're not evil. Not inherently. We have free will just like everybody else."

Karen was just saying, "He can explain it much better than I can—" when the two men in black rain gear and black helmets came zooming up behind Abby's car on black Honda racing motorcycles.

And two men who appeared to be putting on an L. L. Bean fashion show came out of the front door and began running toward them. One carried a shotgun, the other a pistol.

No escape.

"Well, looks like your tip-off did the trick, Karen."

"I want to be friends with you, Abby. I want you to understand why Dr. Prescott is really trying to help us."

So fucking irrational, Abby thought. *She betrays me and then says she wants to be friends.*

The older man, gray-blond crewcut, bulky but not fat, was opening the car door and saying, "We'll take the car from here, Dr. Stewart." He smiled. "Don't worry, we'll take good care of it. No hot-rodding around."

"Hi, aren't you glad I came back," Karen said. She sounded like a child seeking attention.

"Oh, hello there, Karen. We were very worried about you."

The guard beamed at Karen. The paternalism in the smile was hard to miss. In some fashion—part of the entire process of psychological coercion, no doubt—Prescott and the others at the clinic had turned her into their daughter.

"We've got coffee and Danish waiting for you inside," the younger guard said. "And a nice, warm fire."

And they did.

Twenty-three minutes later, Abby was on the second floor of the clinic, in a large den complete with open brick fireplace, half the floor finished in parquet, genuine Persian rugs, two walls of built-in bookcases, and a dark massive desk such as the robber barons of the late 1800s had always favored. The only thing that spoiled the otherwise elegant country scene was the barred window to her right.

To keep werewolves in and vampires out, presumably.

And—witches . . .

She was too thirsty to resist the tea. Fire and tea and general weariness consorted to push her into sleep. Her head kept bobbing; sleep kept rushing through her body like a drug. Eels of rain on the window, so melancholy; warmth of the fireplace, so womblike. She needed to be awake and strong for the signal appearance of the signal Dr. Prescott.

And when it came, it was not the dramatic moment she had expected.

The long mahogany doors behind her opened—they'd been locked, no doubt to confine her—and a tall, somewhat stooped man in a knee-length medical smock came charging in. She couldn't see his face at first. It was covered with a handkerchief and he was bassooning his nose into it. His quite patrician nose, she saw, when the handkerchief was taken away.

He rushed to his desk, sat down. She half-expected him to quickly open up a manila folder and say, "So how're we doing with that sore throat these days, Abby? Still giving you trouble?"

Instead he said, "If you're worried about Karen, she's fine. Resting down at the end of the hall."

"She's one of the things I'm worried about."

"She told me you haven't had much sleep."

"No, I guess I haven't."

"We have a very nice room for sleeping."

"I have a feeling I'm not going to have much choice."

He leaned back in his leather desk chair. She'd expected—wanted—him to look ghoulish. The Witchfinder of all the Salem tales, of all the child-burning stories of witch-obsessed Europe. But then she realized, as she'd realized so many times in her professional life, the truth of Hannah Arendts' statement about Adolf Eichmann: the banality of evil. Into her office had come wife beaters, dope pushers, child molesters, even, on one occasion, a murderer. And they all had one thing in common—their commonness.

These were people who mowed their lawns, paid their taxes, shopped at Wal-Mart, got all misty-eyed (and probably genuinely so) hearing a TV entertainer milk a patriotic moment.

The good Dr. Prescott was no different.

Tall, balding, a mouth on good terms with smiling and laughing, blue eyes so grandad-gentle your average pediatrician would pay millions to have them, and a masculine but compassionate voice that was perfect for calming a patient's nerves.

And yet this man was responsible for killing so many of her kind. She sensed—feared—that he would soon add her to that number, whatever it was.

"Karen told me about your idea," he said.

"My idea?" Abby said.

"Of how we're both prisoners of each other."

"Oh," Abby said.

"Very interesting. You must have studied philosophy somewhere along the line. Philosophers love ironies like that."

"I suppose they do."

"But there's a problem."

His face changed. He didn't become hideous. He didn't become dramatic. But there was harshness now in the eyes, a tightening of the mouth, the drawing of lines from his high cheekbones to his jawline.

"A problem?" she said.

"Good and evil. Unfashionable as it is these days, I'm afraid that's what guides me—guides all of us here at the clinic."

"You're good and we're evil?"

"There was a tiny smirk in your voice when you said that."

"I was being ironic. Like a philosopher."

He smiled. "You're not afraid of me, are you?"

She shrugged. "I'm afraid to die. But not of you, personally, no."

"The younger ones—Karen's age—we can convert. We can change them from evil to good. But I'm afraid at your age—"

"We're not useful to you. We don't have their powers. Ours are diminished. If we still had powers, you'd convert us, too."

"You're being cynical."

"Practical. From your point of view, it makes sense. Send a witch to catch a witch. But the witch you send has to be more powerful than her prey. Yet I have to question how well you're succeeding. You've developed Karen's powers, but her loyalty seems to fade in and out. Brainwashing's always been controversial. There're a lot of psychiatrists who swear that it doesn't work at all."

"And they're right. At least the way brainwashing used to be defined. But we're using experimental drugs that are changing these girls very quickly. That's not to say there aren't problems. But we're making a lot of progress. A lot of it." Then he took out his handkerchief and tooted another bassoon note. "Sorry. Darned head cold coming on."

"So you keep on working with Karen until you get her running all nice and fine and smooth like a car engine?"

"Something like that."

"This tea is drugged."

"I'm afraid it is."

"People know where I am," she bluffed. "There'll be a lot of questions. My death'll be hard to cover up."

The smile. "There, I'm afraid I'm as cynical as you are. It's a very corrupt world, Dr. Stewart. Murders are much easier to cover up than you might imagine."

The drug, whatever it was, was a tricky one. It had acted slowly, stealthily. But now it was taking its toll quickly—

In the afternoon, Cam Morgan was moved out of Intensive Care to a private room in the east wing of the small hospital. Sunlight dazzled his eyes and warmed him. He had walked through the valley of death and come out the other side. He was well aware that he was very lucky to be alive. He'd never felt such a desire to stay alive, either. An insatiable almost frantic need to smell flowers, feel breezes, see the innocent rapt faces of infants, hear beautiful music, sate himself with love both as giver and receiver, know the joy of rivers and forests and mountains. How little—if at all—material things mattered amidst such bliss. Didn't matter if he was ever promoted or ever drove a fancy car or even ever had enough money saved up for his old age. All that mattered was life itself. Bad memories were but wraiths far back on the horizon of his consciousness—the joy of Valium.

For three days he remained like this. Nothing had ever stoned him—and that was the only thing this time could be compared to, a chemical high—nothing had ever stoned him like this simple appreciation of his existence. Greer was there for much of it, but she seemed to know that he wasn't up for talking much or reading much or watching TV much. Sometimes, he'd cry silently. But he'd smile as he did so, and she knew it was all right. He was going through some kind of reaction to his two heart attacks. He asked about Abby, of course. She told him that Abby's aunt had fallen critically ill and Abby'd had to fly to Rochester to be with her. She'd be back soon, Greer said.

For those three days of reverie, Cam just accepted what Greer had told him about Abby. He was too lost in himself to puzzle through the odd coincidence of Abby being called away so abruptly. There were questions he would have asked immediately under other circumstances. Who was taking care of her patients? Why hadn't she at least called to say hello? And hadn't the sick aunt in Rochester actually died a couple of years ago?

Doctors came and went. Nurses came and went. Monitors monitored. He found himself actually looking forward to hospital food, one sure way of knowing that he was experiencing a kind of deep satisfaction unknown to most folk who trod upon this Earth. He developed fleeting crushes with each shift change—in the morning he loved the redhead; in the afternoon the blonde; and at night the dark-haired one with the saucy smile. He hadn't thought of the word "saucy" since his days of reading skin magazines back in his college years.

He might have remained in this state of grace for a day or two longer if events hadn't caused him to learn that truth that had been kept from him for so long. And if Candy hadn't said exactly the wrong thing and shaken Cam from his perch high on the bliss tree.

* * *

Dr. Prescott kept Abby unconscious for three days. She lay in the shadowy ward with the other three witches, sleeping in the bed Karen had once used.

Prescott had a number of matters that needed overseeing, the most important of which were the deaths in Hastings Corner. He needed to make certain that all of them would be judged accidental. No doubt about the freak accident taking the lives of Yancy and Jeff Crawford. But how about Sara Crawford? Would the coroner report that she'd been too depressed to go on with life after the death of her husband and son? That was the way Karen had been trained to make it appear. And even more problematic, the explosion at the Coopers' cabin. Would that, too, appear accidental, a malfunction of the gas furnace? The one disappointment was that Cam Morgan, Greer's father, hadn't died from the heart attack that Karen no doubt induced. He was a wild card right now. Prescott didn't like wild cards.

Prescott was busy inside and outside the clinic. He had to help file a grant petition. A New York philanthropic organization required about six pounds of paper before they'd let loose so much as a dollar. There were parts of the grant petition that only Prescott himself could write. He despised writing. But they needed the money to continue with their experiments here. The true nature of the experiments was disguised, of course. Philanthropic organizations didn't take kindly to medical clinics that specialized in the psychological coercion of witches. They were very narrow-minded folk, those philanthropists.

Not that he didn't check on Abby. He looked in on her several times a day. She was quite a lovely woman and easy to gaze upon. There were certain expressions of hers in repose that made him ache for his lost youth. Oh, Lord, to be twenty again and walking across a college campus on a sunny May morn. He'd never been a part of the hippie movement, but the braless girls and their open way with sex— He'd lost his nineteen-year-old virginity to a very stoned antiwar protestor who kept calling him "Sam" all the way through their three-minute relationship on a thin grubby mattress on a thin grubby floor beneath a poster of Che Guevara. "Wow," the girl said, afterward, "I never got it on with a guy who wore a crew cut before. You aren't a narc, are you, man?" A few days later he'd learned that he had some new friends. Crabs.

Abby wouldn't have given him crabs. Or lived in such a sty. Or had a Che poster on her wall.

He'd learned all he could from her—questioning her under the sway of his drugs—and now was the time to kill her.

Candy was just leaving when it popped out. It wasn't malicious. It was just one of those automatic reassurances made to people who are in some kind of distress. "I'm sure your car will be fine, honey. The windshield and two of the doors and the motor stolen doesn't mean it's a total loss. Oh, yeah, and all the tires, too, I guess." Bland, empty and almost comic reassurances that nobody ever takes seriously.

Except all three people in the hospital room took what Candy said very seriously: "I'm sure they'll find her, Mr. Morgan. Only a matter of time."

And then Candy froze, realizing the import of what she'd just so foolishly said.

Cam looked confused. He looked at his daughter. "Fine who? Who's she talking about, honey?"

"Oh, this, uh, nurse. Remember the heavyset one you had when you first came in here? Nancy, I think her name was." Nimble, frantic lies tumbled from her lips. The doctors had made a big thing of keeping anything stressful from Cam. And now Candy had said this.

"I don't think I remember her."

"You were pretty out of it, Mr. Morgan," Candy said, coming back to his bedside. "When Nancy was here and all, I mean."

He looked first at Candy and then at Greer. "You sure you're telling me the truth?"

"Sure we are, Dad. Why would we lie about something like that?"

"So how long's she been missing?"

"Two days, Dad."

"She just vanished?"

"Found her car in a ditch, Mr. Morgan. They think maybe she was carjacked or something."

"Wow. A carjacking out here. That's really something. She have a family?"

"Husband but no kids," Candy said.

"I just wish I could remember her."

"You liked her a lot, this Nancy I mean," Candy said.

Cam seemed confused again. "Wish I could remember her."

He was going home this afternoon, Greer thought.

How was she ever going to keep the truth about Abby away from him then? She couldn't. But he should enjoy a few more hours of innocence, anyway.

"You just rest now, Mr. Morgan," Candy said.

"I sure wish you'd call me Cam. That Mr. Morgan stuff makes me nervous."

"I'll try to remember that, Cam," Candy smiled, oozing urchin charm. She wore earrings the size of saucers and enough makeup to paint the Painted Desert. Oh, yes, and a nose ring. Just your typical grandma.

"See" he laughed, "I knew you could do it."

Greer sighed deeply, luxuriously. Dad hadn't caught on after all.

Candy said, "Well, I need to get going."

"Thanks for coming up to see me."

"My pleasure. And next time I see you, you'll be at home."

"Quite a lady," Cam said after she'd gone.

"Yes, she is," Greer smiled, not adding that just a few minutes ago she'd wanted to grab Candy by the throat and strangle her for six or seven hours.

But Dad hadn't caught on to Candy's reference to Abby, after all. He'd know soon enough that the woman he'd managed—against great odds—to fall in love with, hadn't been seen for three, going on four days now. And there wasn't a clue as to where she might be.

Somebody was talking to her.

Or not talking.

But communicating thoughts at any rate.

Sensory data: darkness. Need to pee. Slight headache. Stiff back. Electric blanket. Sides on—the bed.

A single bed with sides on it. The metal sides chill to the touch, Hospital?

Girl: *You're in a ward, Dr. Stewart.*

Abby: *You're in my mind.*

Mindmerge. The motel. Candy and herself. Merging to break into Karen's room.

Kim: *I'm Kim. The other two are Joyce and Mika. This is Dr. Prescott's ward.*

Abby: *Dr. Prescott?*

Kim: *You came here with Karen. You wanted to try and reason with him. I guess it didn't work.*

Abby: *What did he do to me?*

Kim: *Drugged you. Probably learned as much as he could with injections and hypnosis. Now you're on the ward. This is where he keeps the witches when he's not working on us in the basement.*

Abby: *What does he do there?*

Kim: *He calls it psychological engineering. It's really brainwashing. Using drugs and hypnosis and things like that so that he can use us to hunt down other witches.*

A fog of memories: distinct words, images here and there. Her conversation with Karen. Not being able to decide if Karen was friend or foe, her seeming to shift back and forth.

Kim: *Foe, I'm afraid, Dr. Stewart. The conversion seems to have worked pretty well on her. It won't last forever, but in the meantime, she's a very dangerous girl.*

It was so odd—disturbing in many respects—thinking something and having somebody answer it telepathically.

Kim: *You'll get used to it. But it takes a while. And just remember that we're all on the same side.*

Abby decided to sit up, look around. In the shadowy room, they looked like wraiths, the three slender, white-gowned witches in the other beds. Pale faces, pale hair.

Kim: *This room is bugged. Video and audio. That's why we're communicating this way. You arrived just in time to break out with us.*

Abby: *Are you serious?*

Kim: *Yes; of course. You don't think we want to stay here, do you?*

Abby: *I guess not.*

Kim: *Tonight, we're going. We've been practicing our mindmerge. You'll give us even more power when we merge.*

Abby: *Most of my power went a long time ago.*

Kim: *You'll be surprised, Doctor. Wait and see.*

Abby: *He doesn't suspect anything?*

Kim: (Laughter) *He can't read minds.*

Prescott couldn't read minds, true. But Karen could. Or that was the hope, anyway.

Prescott and Karen sat in the security room looking at the two monitors that covered the ward where the witches were generally kept. It was clear they were communicating. They were sitting up in the beds and looking eager and active. It was a bit like watching a silent movie. Their body language was fluid, animated. They made gestures, formed expressions, cocked their heads, narrowed their eyes. They were obviously carrying on a conversation telepathically.

"Can you hear anything yet?"

"I'm trying, Doctor," Karen said. "But you're making me nervous."

The security room was a former large storage closet on the west end of the second floor. There was a monitor for each room banked against the north wall. A control console sat before it. Karen and Dr. Prescott sat side by side. Few—if any—of the witch powers were always reliable. Sometimes Karen could read minds, sometimes not. There seemed to be a number of variables involved, and Prescott would be the first to admit that he didn't understand most of them yet. Paranormal science, so long scoffed at, had a long, long way to go.

"Anything yet?"

"No."

"Water?"

"What?"

"I asked if you'd like a drink of water." He'd bitten off his words so she wouldn't hear the frustration and anger in them. He wanted to slap her for letting him down this way.

"No water. But you know what I'd like?"

"What?"

"For you to go somewhere else."

"What're you talking about? I run this clinic, or hadn't you noticed?"

"Yes, I noticed that, Dr. Prescott. But I also noticed that you're a gigantic pain in the ass. And if I have any chance of concentrating here, you have to leave."

He startled her by smiling. "I'm that much of a pain in the ass?"

She smiled back. "Even more than I let on."

"Wow."

"Wow is right. So will you get the hell out of here and let me try and work?"

He gave a mock salute. "Yes, sir, commander."

"That's better."

Still smiling, amazed and pleased with her sudden authority, he left.

Abby: *He feels you up?*

Kim: *Sure, Abby, just because he's a man of science doesn't mean he hasn't got a dick.*

Abby: *I just can't believe he'd do that.*

Kim: *Oh, it's nothing obvious. It's like he can't even admit to himself what he's doing. Like it would shatter his self-image or something. Tell her Mika.*

Mika: *He pretends like he's just using the old stethoscope to check your heart. But, boy, does his wrist keep bumping your boobs.*

Kim: (Laughter) *He'd probably use his stethoscope on your vagina if he could think of a reason to do it.*

Joyce: *Plus he always seems to be here when we take showers. One day I flashed him.*

Kim: (Giggles) *I remember that. Mika and I laughed all morning. Joyce just opened her towel and gave him a good peek, and he jerked back like somebody had used a cattle prod on him. It was really funny.*

For this, Karen thought, *I'm going to sit here all day monitoring what they're talking about in their little ward?*

Ninety-three miles away, Cam Morgan was settling into his home life. Or trying to. The key word was relax. The doctors had warned him that he would be very self-conscious about the rhythms of his heart. He'd get scared that the beat was irregular or that an angina-like attack was striking. Or that his breathing was suddenly too fast. Or too slow. Or that there was a strange, darting pain in his left arm.

All very normal, they had assured him.

He could no longer enjoy the notion that death was an abstraction. He'd nearly died. Now and forever, death was as real as sneezing or sweating or blinking. Another bodily function. The final one.

Greer and Candy were doing their best to distract him. The living room bloomed with flowers, funny-face balloons, and a large sign reading WELCOME HOME!

Candy, in addition to a deep-cut pink blouse, her aqua miniskirt, her black hooker hose and her three-inch heels, wore a white apron and served him his Diet Pepsi in a glass with ice, along with a fresh fruit salad. No cake or whiskey for Cam Morgan. Not for a long time.

Then they sat around and pretended that everything was just okey-dokey. You know that kind of conversation you have where you keep smiling to indicate that everything's just fine because otherwise you have no idea what to say? Cam says, "Gosh, the house sure looks nice." And Greer says, "Well, that's because Candy pitched in and helped me clean it up." And Candy says, "Oh, no, Mr. Morgan, she did ninety-five percent of the work and don't let her kid you." And so on and so forth until Cam finally says the obvious—the thing he's been wanting to say since he got here and the thing they've been dreading he'd say all along—he says: "So where is she?"

Greer sat on the couch with him, Candy perched on the ottoman across from them.

"She?" Greer asked innocently, glancing desperately at Candy.

"You know. Abby."

"Still with her sick—"

"Cut the bullshit, Candy. And you, too, Greer. I went along with your story about her sick aunt when I was in the hospital because I was too sick to think it through. But I'm better now. And I don't buy your story at all."

Nice crackling fire. Some nice videos to play a little later when the snow started. Popcorn. Maybe a blanket across the legs if you got a little chilly. Nice pleasant afternoon at home.

And then he had to go and spoil it.

"The doctors said you were supposed to have zero stress, Dad."

"Where is she, Greer?" He sounded angry.

"You don't even like her, Dad. You told me that yourself, remember?"

"Greer—"

"The thing is, Mr. Morgan, nobody knows where she is."

"Dammit, Candy—"

"Let her talk, Greer. I want the truth."

Candy looked guiltily at Greer. "He'll have to learn sometime."

"Learn what?"

And Candy told him most of it. And then Greer reluctantly told him the rest of it. The kidnapping. The motel room. And then Abby staying behind with Karen.

"She didn't tell you where she was going?"

"No," Candy said.

"And you weren't interested enough to ask?"

"She wanted us back here. Dad. At the moment, you were our biggest concern."

"Oh."

"Everything was such a mess—I mean, emotionally, you know—that when we heard about your heart attack, Mr. Morgan, all we could think of was getting to you."

"I appreciate that, Candy. And will you please start calling me Cam?"

She smiled. "I'll try."

"We kept the papers and the TV news from you, Dad," Greer said.

"We were afraid if you heard it—"

"So the whole state is looking for her?"

"Right."

"And they haven't turned up a clue?"

"Right."

"And you can't tell them about Abby and Karen because that'll expose the whole witch thing?"

"Right."

"And Karen didn't give you any idea of where this Dr. Prescott has his clinic?"

"No."

"We went over and over it, Dad. Trying to think of anything she said that might give us a hint but—nothing." Then she looked sad. "Jeff could've figured this out. He had a quick mind."

He patted her hand.

"Anybody know which car they took?" Cam asked.

"Which car?"

"When they left the motel?"

"Oh," Greer said."They must have taken Karen's." Cindy and I used Abby's car to come to the hospital."

"So what happened to Karen's car?" Cam said.

"Karen's car?"

Candy and Greer glanced at each other. "I guess we never thought of that, Dad."

"What's the name of that motel? Her car—"

After a moment's pure, intoxicating excitement, Greer started to say, "But, Dad, you're not supposed to—"

"There's a lot of things I'm not supposed to do, honey. But there's only one thing you're not supposed to do?"

"What's that?"

"Remind me of all those things I'm not supposed to do."

He got the name of the motel and picked up the phone immediately.

At about this same time, all of Karen's waiting finally became worth it. She'd been monitoring the ward for nearly three hours before any of the girls mentioned the plan for tonight. She needed to make up for her failure with Cam Morgan. She knew how unhappy Dr. Prescott was—all his patient training—and she'd pulled back from killing Morgan there at the last.

Karen went down the hall to Dr. Prescott's private office and knocked on the door.

"Yes."

"It's Karen."

"Come in."

With his white medical smock and sitting behind his big, pompous desk, he looked like a TV pitchman playing a doctor.

"What they're up to is a mindmerge. They think they can break their way out of here."

"Shoot," he said.

"What?"

"Oh, my wife thinks we're going to a dinner party tonight. But I'll need to be here, won't I?"

Karen smiled. "Sure looks that way."

11

"GOD, Dad, calm down."

Not easy to talk on the phone with Greer and Candy standing over him and telling him to, variously, "calm down," "cool off," and "chill out."

He cupped the phone. "Will you two please sit down?"

But it was weird. They were closing in on him now and extending their hands, Candy to touch him on the back of the neck, Greer to touch him on the shoulders. And then he realized what they were doing. He'd seen con-job faith healers do the very same thing on TV.

But this was different in one important respect. He could feel an almost electrical charge surging through his body, top to bottom.

They pretended that nothing was going on at all.

"You're getting excited, Mr. Morgan, that's all we're saying."

"I thought you were going to call me Cam."

"Cam, then."

"And I'm not getting excited. I'm just getting emphatic. I want this guy to understand the urgency of this." It would be so much easier to just call the police. They could make all the connections here.

I'd like to report a missing witch. Which would be worse? That they would believe him or they wouldn't?

"Your face is getting red, Dad."

"I'll take deep breaths, how's that?"

"You shouldn't be doing this, Dad."

"You don't want to find Abby?"

"Of course I do, Dad, but—"

"Then please let me talk to this gentleman."

"You're really not supposed to be doing this, Dad."

"Please, honey. Just sit down on the couch. That's why God invented them. To sit down on." Then: "You two did something to me, didn't you? I feel a whole lot better all of a sudden."

Candy smiled. "We just sorta recharged your battery. If Abby was here, we could've used her and done a whole lot better."

"Witches," he said, but fondly.

"Very funny."

They finally went over and sat down.

Cam took his hand from the receiver. "Sorry for the interruption."

"Maybe you should be talking to the police."

"Mr. Peterson, will you just listen to me? Please? You said that there was a sedan there that belonged to the young woman named Karen, is that correct?"

"That's right. Right out in front of her room."

"And that car is no longer there?"

"Right."

"And then you said that you wrote her license number on the registration card, right?"

"I said we usually do. But sometimes at night it gets so busy that the desk person forgets."

"All I'm asking is for you to check for me."

"I wish I knew why you won't just go to the police."

"It's a family matter, Mr. Peterson. There's a cousin of mine who has some mental problems and— Well, I really don't want to go into it. Nobody broke any laws. Nobody was hurt or anything like that. But I just need to check on a few things. And to do that, I need the license number."

Peterson, the motel owner, said, "I'll go look. Hope I don't keep you as long as you kept me."

Seeing that her father was waiting for Peterson, Greer said, "If you don't stop this, Dad, I'm going to call the hospital and have them come get you."

"I don't think that's legal."

"I saw them do it on TV."

"Just relax, honey."

"You're telling me to relax?"

"Honey, I'm not upset. I'm not feeling any stress. I'm just trying to get a little information is all. What's wrong with that?"

Peterson came back. "Easier than I thought."

"You've got the license number?"

"Yes, right here."

"Honey, hand me that pad and pencil, will you?"

Greer got up and got him the pad and pencil. When she handed them to him, she said, "You really shouldn't be doing this, Dad."

Dr. Prescott also spent time on the phone that late afternoon. He called a pharmacologist he knew. He wanted to check on the ability of certain drugs to curtail dreams and to put a patient into a virtual coma.

Forty-five minutes later, with Greer and Candy trailing behind him, Cam hurried out to his car.

"I'm going to call the police and have you arrested," Greer said.

"Arrested for what?"

"You know."

He turned around and faced her. She'd been moving so fast, she nearly ran into him. "Honey, I have the name of the clinic the car belongs to. It's the only information we have. We can't go to the police. And the private detectives won't be any help, either, because we'd have to tell them what's going on. That leaves me. Now, I want you and Candy to go back in that house and wait until you hear from me."

"No way."

"I'm the dad here. Remember? And you gave me some extra juice, remember? You did that witch thing."

"That just boosted your energy level a little, Dad. It doesn't mean you have the strength for a long drive."

"Take her inside, Candy."

"I'm coming with you."

"No way, right back at you. You're not going with me."

"You don't seem to understand, Dad. You're sick. At any minute you could—" And then she stopped herself. Unable to say it. And kind of folded in on herself. And started crying. Just a moment ago, she'd been a mouthy teenager. Now, she was a scared little girl.

He took her into his arms. Held her. "I don't have any choice, sweetheart. I have to find Abby. And this clinic is the only lead we have. It won't take that long to drive there. The weather's good." He'd called a friend in the police department. They'd checked out the registration number the motel owner had supplied for him. The name of the clinic had shown up on the computer.

"I can just sit here, Dad," she said."I love you too much for that."

"She's right," Candy agreed. "That's a lot to ask of her. To just sit here and wait. Maybe we could help you, anyway. You don't know what you're going to run into."

"Now, you want to go, too?"

"I sure as hell don't want to sit here and do my nails the rest of the night."

Maybe they were right, he thought. In his condition—God, he hated thinking of himself as a weak, vulnerable man; he wasn't used to it and didn't want to get used to it—maybe he needed somebody along for the ride.

"I'm driving," he said.

"Fine," Greer said.

"And I don't want you to keep telling me how sick I am."

"Fine."

"And I don't want you and Candy exchanging meaningful glances every time I cough or catch my breath. You two could give me a heart attack the way you hover over me."

"Fine."

He smiled. Held her tight. "I sure do love you. And I sure do appreciate how much you love me."

"Aw," Candy said, sticking a cigarette between her lips. "This is the kind of shit you see on TV all the time. That's really sweet, Mr. Morgan."

"Thank you for pointing that out, Candy. You two go get your jackets. Then we'll leave."

"How about Greer goes and gets our jackets and I wait here in case you try and sneak off alone?"

"Trusting soul, isn't she?" Cam said to Greer.

Greer laughed. "Just cautious."

Then she went and got their jackets.

When she returned, she saw how her father had sort of slid down in the seat. "You'll have a lot more energy for when we get there if you let me drive."

He looked relieved—tired and relieved. "You make a pretty good case."

"Move over, Dad." she said. "I'm driving."

And she did.

Kylie said, "Hearts."

"You're getting good at this."

"It's fun."

They were in Kylie's room. Beverly had created a monster. A few weeks ago, she'd shown Kylie how to play hearts and Maria had yet to win a game.

Maria heard the elevator doors slide open down the hall. Prescott. He checked on his burgeoning assassins several time a day. He obviously took pleasure in how they were responding to the drugs and the psychotherapy and the brainwashing. Perfect puppets.

"I like it when it's just you and me," Kylie said, hearing Prescott's footsteps.

"So do I."

Kylie's face was pinched now. Something troubled her. "Can I tell you something?"

"What?"

"I feel bad about that squirrel."

So he had not changed her after all, Maria thought. Even though she was a member of the sect—even though she knew there were evil witches who had to be destroyed—she wanted this one little girl spared from all the bloodshed and lunacy that had been a part of this aeons-old war.

Kylie said, "Gosh, Maria. You're crying. I didn't mean to make you sad."

Maria hugged her. "Sometimes, people cry because they're happy."

"They do? Boy, that's weird."

The ward was quiet. The three young women slept. They had been drugged so long and so much that every few hours, not unlike cats and dogs, they drifted into a light sleep.

Abby lay awake, wondering if escape was really going to be this easy. A mindmerge and then freedom. She wanted to discuss another plan with the women when they woke up. If they had enough power to overwhelm the staff, then perhaps they had enough power to destroy Prescott's computer database and all its linked computers. Once all his information on the locations and identities of various witches was destroyed, the various Children of Salem groups around the country could no longer function. They would have to resort to the old ways and even that would take some time before they were up and running again.

A noise. Rubber soles. Coming this way.

She closed her eyes.

Prescott. His cologne was identifiable as soon as he opened the door.

She played an old child's game she used to enjoy with her younger sister. Abby would pretend to be dead and Sally would have to bring her back. She told jokes, blew on her face, stuck her fingers in her ears. All this Abby could endure. But then Sally always resorted to the same last-hope trick. She tickled her. Abby could resist even this for a while. But then her whole body would start shaking as she'd try and hold her laughter in. But it was no good. She'd suddenly explode with guffaws and her wily little sister would've won the game.

Now she was playing the game again. Only much more seriously.

A tiny sound. One that was somehow familiar but—

He spent time with the three young women first. Probably two or three minutes at each bedside. She couldn't see exactly what he was doing to them. She was afraid that if she started to rise up, he'd know that she was just faking sleep.

Her body was rigid. She alternated hot and cold flashes. She needed to pee very badly. She also needed to see what he was doing.

For the second time, she heard the tiny popping noise.

She listened as his shoe soles squeaked from bed to bed. When he reached the one before hers, she heard a tiny pop. The sound was still familiar. For a moment, she didn't recognize it. Then it came clearly to her. The protective cap on a hypodermic needle.

He was giving them injections.

No; no way.

She didn't know what sort of drug he was giving them. She only knew that she didn't want any of it. Even if the other young women couldn't escape, she was going to escape. And then come back and help free them.

He was using a fresh hypodermic on each of them. He'd been trained well. No sense risking infection even when the test subjects were completely in your control.

Shoes squeaking. Cologne harsher.

God, was she going to sneeze?

Then he was there. Right side of the bed. His white-smocked body pressing against the safety bars. Cold fingers lifting her wrist. Checking her pulse. Then the stethoscope routine. A dirty old man indeed. Copped several very cheap feels while practicing medicine on her breasts.

And then the pause. Rustling in one of the pockets of his smock.

The injection.

Her next move was wholly instinctive. If she'd thought it through, she probably wouldn't have done it. Would've calculated the risks and decided she couldn't pull it off—

—but instinct took over.

She rose Lazarus-like from the dead, her hands seizing the hand that held the hypodermic. Her teeth tearing into his wrist and slashing open a two-inch streak of blood.

She bounded up on her feet, grabbing the man by his ears and then slamming her knee into his face. His nose cracked into several pieces. Blood sprayed. He screamed.

But then he grabbed her. That he'd gathered himself, focused himself, so quickly startled her. He clawed at her body, yanking her off the bed with him. Slamming her against the buffed concrete floor.

She was stunned. Her left hip abruptly started sending out SOS signals of deep pain, but she stayed angry enough to bring her fist up between his legs and connect with his crotch.

He cried out and bounced against the bed. But then, in his own anger, he managed to overcome his pain and find one of the used hypodermic needles in his smock pocket.

She was just struggling to her feet when he leaned over and started to stab downward with the needle. She saw it just in time to turn away.

She stood in a half-crouch, desperately looking for a way to escape, while she watched as he took a small bottle of amber-colored liquid from his other pocket. "You're quite a fighter, Dr. Stewart. But you won't be after this. And there won't be any mindmerge, either. Those girls will be asleep for two days."

He filled the hypodermic, dropped the bottle back into his pocket. "This is twice what they got. It's enough to kill you. You're just not worth the trouble, I'm afraid." He smiled. "Nothing personal, of course."

He lunged for her.

Got her hair. Twisted.

Now it was her turn to cry out.

Kept twisting and twisting. She tried to kick, claw, punch, scratch. But there was just the pain as he continued to spin her slowly around by her hair. Tears, spittle, sweat. She was a monolith of pure pain. He kept turning her, turning her.

She screamed.

Neither Maria nor Kylie had any trouble hearing the scream. A closed door couldn't keep out that kind of noise.

"Wait here a minute," Maria said, rushing from the bed to the doorway. "I'll be right back."

Maria closed the door behind her. She knew how violent Prescott could get with the witches.

As much as Maria disliked Abby Stewart and what she represented, she felt uncomfortable seeing how Prescott had flung her up against the wall and was about to stab her with the needle.

He heard Maria coming and glanced at her. "Get Kylie."

The response was instant. "No."

"No? What the hell are you talking about? This is a perfect test for her."

She knew what he had in mind. Try to see if Kylie could graduate from squirrel to human.

"You go get her and right now, Maria."

His attention was dragged back to the squirming, flailing, angry form of Abby Stewart.

She kneed him expertly in the groin and then managed to get one of her hands near his right eye.

He shouted, "Kylie! Get out here, Kylie!"

Kylie appeared.

"Go back to your room, Kylie." Maria started toward the child.

"Don't listen to her, Kylie," Prescott said. "She doesn't want you to have your powers. She's jealous." He looked at the wild face of Abby. "You can will her dead, Kylie. Just close your eyes and picture her and will her dead. The same way you did with the squirrel. Just the same way, Kylie."

"Come here, Kylie." Maria held her hands out to the girl.

But she knew that Kylie was feeling an almost tidal surge of loyalty to Prescott. To free her from the grip of his drugs and his brainwashing would take a break of faith on his part, not hers. He'd have to do something basic and brutal to repel her.

"Come here, Kylie."

"Don't listen to her, Kylie. You know who your true friend is." And then he began to speak in code words that had been embedded in her subconscious. Nonsense syllables to the untutored ear. But meaningful exchanges between Prescott and Kylie.

She walked to him. She looked sweeter than usual in her blue pajamas and bunny slippers.

Prescott decided the only way to control the struggle with Abby was to knock her out for a time. He punched her with breathtaking accuracy and force. She slid down to the floor.

He took Kylie's hand. "Do you remember what I told you about witches?"

She nodded.

"This woman is a witch. A very bad witch. If I don't stop her, she'll kill both you and me. That wouldn't be very good, would it?"

Kylie shook her head.

"I think you know what to do, don't you?"

"Yes, sir." A whisper.

"What would that be, Kylie?"

"What you told me before, Dr. Prescott."

"All right, sweetheart. But I need you to say it out loud for me. Can you do that, honey?"

She looked back at Maria, who was inching toward them. "Don't say it, honey. Don't say what he wants you to. And don't *do* what he wants you to."

"Dr. Gomez, I order you to go down to my office and wait for me there."

"Then I'll take Kylie with me."

He gently turned Kylie back toward him. "Do you remember the special words we went over?"

"Yes, sir."

"And the special thoughts you have to have to kill someone bad."

"Yes, sir."

"Then it's up to you now, Kylie. Do just what you did with the squirrel. All right?"

Another glance at Maria.

Maria was close enough to grab for the girl. Which she did, snatching her up and tucking her into her arms before Prescott could even get close to Kylie.

Maria turned, started running down the hall to the EXIT door.

Kylie was crying, scared.

Prescott cursed, shouted, ran after her.

And then he leaped for her, leaped skillfully enough to grab the back of her medical jacket collar.

He yanked her back toward him. She clung to the sobbing Kylie.

He spun her around so hard that when her body

cracked against the wall, Kylie dropped from her arms.

By this time, Prescott was in a paroxysm of fury. From his pocket, he took the hypodermic needle he'd been going to stab Abby Stewart with. He grabbed the barely conscious Maria by her hair and started to plunge the needle into her jugular. It would do the job well as a knife.

"No! No! She's my friend!"

He'd managed, in his rage, to forget all about Kylie. She was behind him somewhere.

He stabbed the needle deep, deep into Maria's neck, breaking it off, using the silver stub of the remaining metal to claw and shred the prominent vein.

Only then did he become aware of the small fists pounding him. Of the pleading. Wailing. Shrieking. Not even Prescott had understood how much Kylie loved Maria.

Her screaming and pummeling finally drained him of rage. He turned to face her, stepping over the pile of death that had once been Maria Gomez. He instinctively bent down and offered his hand, in the eternal pose of the adult being kind to a child.

And then he felt it.

A kind of suffocation. He'd always wondered about the exact sensations the victims went through. It was funny that a part of him could remain so objective at a moment like this. It was also funny that after all the trouble he'd had with Kylie, now she was willing him dead with ease and acumen.

Kylie: *I loved her, Dr. Prescott. She was the best friend I ever had. And she loved me, too. And you killed her.*

His autonomic system was shutting down. And then blood began spraying from his eyes.

He noted each new development until the frenzy of death made it impossible. Memories-pleas-terror-confusion. The entire universe of which he was lord and master collapsing in upon itself.

Candy sat in the back seat. Every five minutes or so, she'd put her elbows on the back of Greer's seat and start talking. Working her way out of her anxiety. "I just have this sense she's all right."

"Good."

"I don't mean a premonition or anything."

"I know," Greer said.

"Just this sense."

"I know."

"Am I driving you nuts?"

"A little bit, Candy."

"Then I'll shut up."

And she would. For at least another five minutes. It was kind of sweet and kind of annoying. The older Greer got, the more she found that there were a number of things like that in life. Kind of sweet and yet kind of annoying at the same time. God, it was all so hard to figure out sometimes. Everything.

Cam half-dozed and then woke to think things through. What was the right way to handle this? He watched the passing towns he would've doted on at other times. He loved New England, especially the rural parts, where you could see two, sometimes three centuries of history in just a few fleeting moments. Now, all he could think of was Abby. So many feelings. Still some guilt, of course. How would Laura feel knowing that he'd somehow managed to fall in love with Abby? And what if Abby didn't love him, what if their new involvement was only of the moment, and would fade? Or what if, worst of all possible outcomes, she was killed at this hospital?

His impulse was still to go to the law. Boston law. Not the locals. Tell them everything. Tell them that these girls and these women weren't freaks, simply human beings whose paranormal powers were more fully developed than the average human being's. In this era of the human genetic code being mapped and explored, that shouldn't be so difficult to understand, should it?

But then the more rational part of his mind would take over. Of course, he couldn't divulge the nature of his daughter's and Abby's abilities. Not only would word leak to the press, they would be beset by every kind of would-be empire-builder, from the predictable folks at the Pentagon, to all sorts of entrepreneurs who would find a hundred insidious ways to use their paranormal powers.

No, the only way to handle this was the way they were doing it. Go to Prescott's clinic. Find Abby. Pray she was still alive. And save her. Somehow—save her.

They sped on.

Dr. Prescott lay sprawled on the floor, his body rigid and somehow comic in death. His pose was studied—stuffy somehow—like the man himself had been.

Close by a young girl wept over the body of the doctor known as Maria. It was clear what happened. The doctor killed Maria. And then the little girl killed the doctor.

The girl needed help. Abby found jeans, a sweatshirt and some running shoes in a closet. She slid into them quickly and then trotted down the hall to the girl.

"C'mon, honey."

The girl offered no resistance. She was grateful to have an adult in charge of her fate once again.

Abby heard one of the Security men—in their uniforms and matching helmets, they looked very military—pounding up the steps. Shouting orders to men below him.

She frantically tried two doors. Locked. But the third door opened and she hurried inside. A storage room. Bed frames, cardboard cartons, new brooms, a large leather desk chair still wrapped in plastic, many, many other items. And a large walk-in closet. Her only hope, the closet.

She got inside, pulled Kylie in after her, slid the door shut as quietly as possible.

Abby forced herself to calm down. Deep breaths. Twenty of them. Had to be as rational about this as possible. There was no way she could get out of this room. Which meant that she had to make do right here and right now. Had to find someplace to hide.

The closet offered her nothing. Once somebody swept the sliding door back, there'd be Abby and the girl, cowering in the corner, just waiting to be found.

There had to be someplace in this room to hide. She eased out of the closet.

She made a sweep of the place as quickly as possible. She even eased open the window to see if there was a ledge she could hide on outside. But—nothing.

Then, as footsteps pounded up the steps again, she

raised her eyes and saw the small rectangle of door in the ceiling. Some version of an attic, most likely. The door was painted the same institutional pea green as the ceiling.

The security people would be in this room in the next few minutes.

She had to move quickly. She whispered to Kylie what she was going to do. Kylie, who had managed to collect herself by now, nodded that she understood. She also helped out.

Abby dragged three of the largest cardboard cartons to the floor directly beneath the attic door. She scrambled up them deftly. She pulled Kylie up after her. Then she stood on tiptoe—out of breath now, her entire body soaked with cold clammy sweat—and pushed up against the small door.

Her first impression was that the door had been permanently closed in some way. It wouldn't budge no matter how hard she pushed upward with the palms of her hands.

Voices in the hall. Male. Security.

"You take that end of the hall, I'll take this one."

"Right."

Footfalls. Heavy. Powerful. Angry.

Doors opening and closing. Key rings dragged out. Jangling keys inserted. More doors pulled open.

Then the rectangle against which she was pushing popped open.

She boosted Kylie up through the opening, then caught her hands on the edge of the open rectangle like a trapeze artist on her bar and pulled herself upward. She felt every single coffee break donut, every Big Mac, every extra slice of pizza she'd had for the past fifteen years. The muscles strained; the hands started to slip. But somehow—by the grace of God—she was able to pull herself up just in time. She quietly set the door back in place just as the Security men entered the room.

Gloom. And dust.

She clamped her hand over her nose and mouth to muffle a sneeze.

A dozen tiny red eyes peered at her through the cobwebs and cold darkness. Rats. She could feel their droppings on the floor. They lived up here in the freezing, empty, long unused tomb of an attic.

She had the same problem here she had in the closet below. No place to hide. The Security men would soon figure out that they were up here and they'd come for them.

And once again, she'd be cowering in the corner. Passively waiting for them to seize her. To seize both of them.

The hell she would; the hell she would.

And so it was, with Greer and Candy suddenly silent, that Cam drove past the gates of the small hospital. He had talked Greer into letting him drive a while back. It was full night now, silken sky and lustrous stars, and Cam felt a sense of inevitability he'd never known before. It was a very dramatic feeling and since he was anything but dramatic himself, he was uncomfortable with it. And yet he couldn't deny it. Though he'd never seen the hospital before, everything about it—its shape, its grounds, even the strangely turreted tops of the black iron gates . . . He had a sense that all his life had led up to this very moment. He half smiled. The feeling was as ditzy as some of his old college marijuana bong fantasies.

But this was real.

Lights shone in the windows on all three floors. Somewhere, Abby was inside. About that, he was positive. About her exact state—dead or alive—he wasn't so sure.

Cam drove slowly, looking around. No guard was apparent. A small black mailbox-like apparatus was likely a communication device between the gate and the hospital. The hazy streetlight made the night much softer and prettier than it deserved to be.

He headed off down the lonely, narrow road fronting the hospital. The nearest houses were a block away. The hospital comprised its own block.

"Where're we going, Dad?" Greer asked.

"Well, there's no way we can get in through the gates."

"Then what?"

"I'm going to run over Candy."

"What?"

"I run over you near the gate and then run up to the gate and tell them you've been hurt. And that we need their help. I'm assuming they have some kind of medical staff on hand. It's a hospital."

"A psych hospital," Candy said.

"It's worth a try," he insisted. He looked first at Greer and then at Candy. "Unless either of you has a better idea."

Candy said, "Just be careful when you're running me over."

There was a narrow, elongated dormer window and Abby damned near made her way through it before the two Security men reached the attic and stopped her. They also stopped Kylie, who was waiting to follow her.

She was just pulling her way through to the ledge from which she planned to jump to a jut of roof one floor below, when one of the guards grabbed her and began the process of dragging her back inside.

He didn't waste time trying to be nice about it. He got the ankle and the shoulder of her sweatshirt and proceeded to get enough of her inside to fling to the floor.

There wasn't enough room for both guards to work on her, so the second uniformed man stood to the side with a flashlight the size of a small baseball bat. He kept the light trained on Abby. She was like a trapped giant bird—every inch of her body seemed to be flailing, fighting the Security man. But he was bigger, stronger, and trained to secure people.

She tried to summon her mental powers—she thought of how they'd come to her outside Karen's motel room that night—but he obviously sensed her trying to penetrate his mind so, while he held her by the hair with one hand, he took out a small spray can attached to his large belt and simply blasted her in the face with a sticky mist. He sprayed Kylie, too.

There was no more resisting.

She slumped forward.

He took her out quickly.

The Security man watched it all on the monitor that swept the front gates of the hospital.

Things had calmed down since he'd caught Abby Stewart and young Kylie. Not exactly difficult to find them in that attic-like room above the storeroom used for cleaning supplies. Now they would have to see who took over the clinic. Probably young Dr. Redmond. He was in Chicago. But the head of Security had already called him and explained what had happened here tonight.

He was just starting to eat a cupcake when the old woman bought it right there on the monitor.

A car came sweeping past and its right fender knocked her flying to the ground. Damn.

He was up out of his chair immediately, packing the cupcake into his mouth as he rose. Was the driver drunk or what? Didn't he see her? She pitched into the iron bars on the side of the gate and then fell to the ground.

The second Security man was just now drifting back from checking on Abby Stewart and Kylie.

"Some old lady just got creamed," the first Security man said.

"Where?"

The first Security man swallowed hard and said, "Check out monitor two."

And there she was. Sprawled facedown.

"You sure she's an old lady? Look at the clothes she's wearing."

"I saw her face. She's an old lady, all right."

"Ninety going on fifteen." Then: "Who hit her?"

"Don't know. Maybe we can run the tape back and get the license number for the cops."

Cam's car appeared in the frame suddenly. The Security men couldn't quite see his face beneath the wide brim of his racing cap as he jumped out of his car and rushed to the woman.

"That's the car," the first Security man said.

"At least he came back."

The unidentified man bent over the fallen woman. He didn't try to move her in any way. You could see him saying something to her. But his voice was so faint, his words were unintelligible. They still couldn't get a good look at his face.

Then the man was up and walking toward the intercom. "My name is Sam Breslin. I accidentally hit a woman out here with my car. She isn't responding to anything I say. I'm from out of town. And I see this is a hospital. Could somebody come out here and help me?"

"You wait here," the first Security man said. "I'll go help him."

The second man nodded.

While he waited for the Security man to show up, Cam flattened, crouching behind the far side of the car. The tire iron was gripped hard in his right hand.

Greer had been totally against this, of course. Too much stress. Too much physical activity. But he'd finally convinced her that unless they followed his plan, they'd never get inside to find Abby. She relented, agreeing to stand over Candy's body and wait for the Security man to appear.

The man was big, his dark uniform impressive. He'd obviously jogged down the winding interior road leading from the hospital itself. He carried a silver tube of a flashlight. He sounded faintly out of breath when he spoke. "Where's the man who called us?"

"He needed to go to the bathroom. He's pretty

shaken up. He just went down the road. He'll be right back."

"He your father?"

"Yes, sir. God, he didn't mean to hit her. He—we didn't even see her until it was too late."

"All that'll be for the police to decide, miss. All I can do is call an ambulance."

"Could you please look at her?"

Candy still lay facedown, unmoving.

"I've had some medical training but not enough to really be a help."

"If you could just look at her, please. See if she's still alive. I'm afraid to—touch her."

He looked at Greer and then put a paternal hand on her shoulder. Then he went over to Candy, sat down on his haunches, and began to survey her with his flashlight. He was at an angle to the car.

Cam moved fast. Up from his crouch. Covering the distance between himself and the Security man in just a few seconds.

The man had well-trained ears. Even though Cam made little noise, the man heard him coming. He was just starting to look up when Cam brought the tire iron down. He'd never struck another person like this. He felt his stomach twist when the tire iron made a bone-crunching sound as it reached the back of the man's head. The man seemed to freeze for a moment—Cam hoped he wouldn't have to hit him again—rocking back and forth on his heels, as if he couldn't make up his mind which way he wanted to fall, forward or backward.

Finally, he pitched backward, his back hitting the

bumper of Cam's car. Then he slid sideways, unconscious.

"We have to hurry," Cam said.

Candy jumped to her feet, brushing road dust and leaves from the front of her jacket and dress.

"They'll be watching us on the Security monitors," Cam said. "We need to get inside, and fast."

They spent five minutes behind the hospital looking for a way in. Apparently Security didn't want to involve the police. No alarms sounded. The Security people must be combing the grounds.

The shadowy back of the hospital offered two different garages, a double-sized door for off-loading materials, a Security site that was lit up inside but empty, and a small screened-in porch that would be nice in summer.

They were just making their way to the porch to try the interior door when they heard the dogs. Fierce. Angry. Eager to please their masters. The dogs were working their way around from the front of the hospital. Only within the last ninety seconds had the full Security staff been notified of the intrusion.

Just as Cam, Greer, and Candy opened the screen door and stepped in, two things happened simultaneously: Greer made her first telepathic contact with Abby and the timbre of the dogs' barking became deeper, even more feral. They were getting their first sniff of nearby prey.

The dogs hurried.

The door was locked.

"You'll have to help me here," Greer whispered to Candy.

Candy knew just what she was talking about.

They joined hands and then put their hands on the locked interior door. The mindmerge was instantaneous.

Greer felt the knob turn beneath her hand.

The three of them got inside and closed the door just as the dogs reached the rear of the hospital.

The hospital was even larger than it looked from the outside.

Cam, Greer, and Candy walked on tiptoes down a shadowy corridor on the first floor. Tramping footsteps sounded somewhere nearby. Security men. They needed someplace to hide. Fast.

They found the basement stairs. Then, just as they started down, somebody opened a door below and started up the steps. They had to back up the stairs and hide in the nearby closet. Then they peeped and crept out again, getting all the way downstairs.

Long, narrow corridor. A couple of empty gurneys. Several doors on each side. Metallic pop of metal as the furnace kicked on. A voice, muffled by the furnace. Was this the door they wanted?

They hurried down the hall. Hurried as fast as tiptoes could carry them, anyway. Listened at each door for the voice they'd heard only faintly, briefly. Nothing.

A shout from upstairs. Anything to do with them? Probably.

Cam searched for any place to hide. None.

No choice but to keep trying doors for the voice.

Another shout from upstairs. Female voice.

Damn. Only moments before they'd be down here.

And then Greer—her ear pressed to a door farther down the hall—waved them forward. Had she found the door?

Cam, breathless, put his head next to hers at the door.

Tried the door. Locked.

Pointed to it, Greer and Candy both nodding at each other. Joining hands as they'd done before and then bringing those hands to the doorknob. Willing the lock to open, the knob to turn, the door to push open.

Greer helped the door along by shoving it all the way open with her shoulder.

And that was when they found the bound-and-gagged bodies of Abby and a young girl.

The alarm was silent. It was heard only as a beeping on the various cell phones of the Security men. Four of the Security men gathered quickly in the first floor hallway near the bodies of Maria Gomez and Prescott.

"The prisoners," one of them said.

And they hurried toward the room where Abby and Kylie had been imprisoned.

Cam untied Abby and the girl.

Abby tried to stand up but couldn't do it. She'd been bound too long.

"Prescott's dead," she said. "We need to destroy the computer in this place and get all the witches into a van. And then head back home."

Cam took her in his arms. Her faced was bruised, scratched, filthy. She looked drained.

A Security man began pounding on the door.

"How much of a Security staff does he have?"

Abby shook her head. "Six, seven at night, I guess."

"We won't hurt you if you open this door and come out with your hands above your head," the Security man said.

Kylie started to cry. Her eyes shone with fear. The misery was unending. Life wasn't supposed to be like this. Especially not for a young girl.

Greer slid her arm around Kylie's shoulders. "It'll be all right."

But it wasn't. One of the guards opened fire, a burst of automatic weapons fire filling the door with holes and the air with the hot sour smell of gunplay.

"The next time, we'll shoot the lock off," the guard said after the echoes of the gunfire had started to fade in the hallway.

"There's only one thing we can do," Abby said.

Greer and Candy understood instinctively what she was talking about. Greer left Kylie's side and joined hands with the two women.

"Are you going to kill them?" Cam asked.

"No," Candy said, "but we're going to give them headaches that will make them wish they'd never been born."

Cam realized that the three had worked out the plan telepathically before they'd joined hands. He stared at Greer—proud of her, and just a little afraid of her. Most teenagers become strangers to their parents at one time or another. Part of the process of growing up. But her powers made her even stranger, almost alien. He still wasn't sure how he felt about that.

The guards opened fire again.

Kylie screamed, threw herself to the floor, covered her ears with her hands. She was at her limit. No more terror. She just couldn't handle it.

The women made no noise. Their expressions didn't even change. They did close their eyes briefly but that was the only way Cam could tell that they were focusing their powers on the guards.

The firing stopped.

The guards began screaming.

"Hurry!" Abby said.

Greer grabbed Kylie.

Abby rushed to the door and flung it open.

The guards were bent over on the floor like supplicants. They clutched their heads as they moaned and cried out every few moments. There was nothing to see. Their blinding, tumor-like headaches were invisible. One man began to weep.

Abby dropped to the floor. Grabbed the man by the hair. "Where's the computer room?" she said.

He stared at her with uncomprehending eyes. She slapped him.

One of the other men said, "He can't think straight because of the pain. The computer room is down at the far end of the hall and to the left. But you gotta help us with these headaches." His whole body jerked with fresh cranial pain.

"Oh, God!" he sobbed, and then, like his compatriot, began weeping.

Candy was in the rear. She kept glancing over her shoulder, making certain that nobody came sneaking up behind them.

"Will this be a big room, Dad?" Greer wanted to know as they hurried down the hall.

"Probably not. Probably just be a small mainframe. With all the compression and data storage techniques they have today, the computer won't be much bigger than a stereo console or something like that."

Outside the computer room, they found a Security guard. He started to aim his Uzi.

"I'd better warn you," Cam said, stepping toward the man. "Every one of these females is a witch. And right now they're operating at max capacity. If even one of them gets to you, your life is going to be hell."

"I have the gun," the guard said.

"Not anymore, you don't," Greer answered.

They all watched as the Uzi sprang from his hand, spun in the air, then dropped into Cam's hands.

"Now get out of the way," Candy said, "or my man here'll shoot you right on the spot. Won't you, Cam?"

Uh, sure, Cam thought. "Damned right I will," Cam said. He just wished he sounded a little more convincing.

Cam had been correct about the size of space required. A small office. The computer itself was built into the wall. Before it sat a simple metal desk with a monitor and a keyboard.

"I'm assuming this can't be accessed anywhere but here," he said to the guard whom they'd dragged along.

The super secret computers could never be accessed by anyone except the person sitting right in front of it. No Internet connection of any kind.

He put the gun to the guard's temple.

"That's right," the man said.

"Then everything's right here and no place else?" Greer questioned.

"Right here and no place else," Abby said. "If all of Prescott's bragging was true, he's got data on virtually every witch on this planet except for those in the most remote areas. Let's download that before we go any further."

Abby and Cam went to work. The downloading went quickly.

Cam smiled, pointing his gun at the gray console that sat on a shelf in the wall, a snakepit of red-green-white-coated wires leading from it to the computer terminal itself.

"Would you ladies care to have the honor?"

And with that, Greer, Abby, and Candy joined hands and set to work, erasing from the machine forever every single piece of information it contained.

EPILOGUE

DAD was still in his pajamas and robe when Greer came down to breakfast the following Sunday morning. The scents of coffee, bacon, and eggs filled the kitchen with memories of past mornings when Mom was still alive and they had all enjoyed a leisurely breakfast together, commenting on things they saw in the bulky morning paper.

They'd always divided the paper up, each getting the sections he or she wanted. Dad and Mom had alternated making the breakfast. When she'd turned twelve, Greer had started taking her turn, too, with making the bacon, eggs, and toast.

Dad was engrossed in whatever he was reading. Greer went to the refrigerator and poured herself a glass of orange juice, drawing her robe tighter around her on the way back to the table. The morning was definitely chilly.

She sat down across from him and saw the headline on a story about halfway down the front page: EVENTS AT HOSPITAL STILL A MYSTERY.

Dad said, "We lucked out, honey."

"Lucked out?" she inquired, sipping her orange juice.

"The paper says that the guards now think they were gassed with something that caused memory loss," he said, still consulting the interior of the newspaper. The story had obviously been continued inside from the front page. "So they won't be telling anybody what went on there. They've got the kind of amnesia where your memory is spotty—some things you can remember, some you can't. I'd feel sorry for them but they took money to inflict pain on people."

Greer asked, "Can I borrow a piece of your toast?"

Cam laughed. "That's a new one."

She leaned across the table and swiped a half piece of buttered toast.

"And," Dad continued, "with the hospital hard drives and the security tapes all erased, the authorities can't figure out exactly what kind of business the good doctor and his staff were up to."

"Wow," Greer said, "we're safe."

Dad put the paper down. "Sure seems like it." He sipped his coffee. "How's Kylie?"

"Still sleeping. She's really excited about going back home. She got everything packed up last night."

"Her parents should be here sometime around three this afternoon to get her. Their plane gets in around two."

Greer bit down on her toast. "The other three should be home by now, too. Abby said they shouldn't have any trouble working all the drugs out of their system and getting back to normal. She said she talked to their parents and told them what to expect at first. God, just think of all the time they spent in that little room in the hospital while he fed them all those drugs. Of course Karen is a different story. But Abby's found a good place to work with her. And hopefully over time she'll be able to undo the damage Prescott inflicted on her."

"He was some piece of work, all right," Dad said. "And I'm happy to report that he got what he deserved." Sipped more coffee. And said, with studied casualness, "Oh, by the way, Abby and I thought we'd get a pizza tonight. Care to join us?"

Greer smiled. "No, I think I'll let you two kids just have some fun on your own."

"Smart-ass."

"Look who's talking," Greer responded.

And just then Kylie, yawning and rubbing her eyes, came into the kitchen wearing a rumpled pair of pajamas Greer had outgrown, and a pair of house slippers so big on her they made flapping noises as she walked. "You think I could have some breakfast?" she asked. She sounded intimidated and uncertain.

"No, I'm afraid there's not enough to go around," Cam said. And then laughed. "Get up here and sit down, young lady. I'm going to fix you a breakfast you'll be telling your grandkids about."

And she did sit down at the table.

And he did fix her a breakfast every bit as good as he'd boasted.